SF Bo

THE A.I. SERIES:
A.I. Destroyer
The A.I. Gene
A.I. Assault
A.I. Battle Station
A.I. Battle Fleet
A.I. Void Ship

LOST STARSHIP SERIES:
The Lost Starship
The Lost Command
The Lost Destroyer
The Lost Colony
The Lost Patrol
The Lost Planet
The Lost Earth
The Lost Artifact
The Lost Star Gate

Visit VaughnHeppner.com for more information

A.I. Void Ship

(The A.I. Series 6)

By Vaughn Heppner

Illustration © Tom Edwards
TomEdwardsDesign.com

ISBN: 9781796405781
BISAC: Fiction / Science Fiction / Military

PART I
THE EPSILON ERIDANI SITUATION

From *The Secret Journal: The Irrationality of Jon Hawkins*, by Frank Benz

Jon Hawkins spouts nonsense when he preaches about his so-called *Irrationality Theory*. I believe his word choice is an unconscious plea to the rest of us, secretly telling us that the grim burden of command has unhinged his former good sense.

Ultimately, we cannot win this war, but Hawkins cannot accept that. He believes he is Alexander the Great reborn and will lead humanity to victory over the machines.

That is false, demonstrably so. Given the AI Dominion preponderance of force, the machines will eventually crush our paltry fleets and salt the Earth with nuclear fire. Then, the AI cyberships will hunt our local region until they annihilate every human left.

Given these sad truths, I must dare to depose Jon Hawkins just as I once deposed Premier J.P. Justinian of Earth. It is my solemn duty to save the human race. I can say this because I am the most far-seeing and intelligent human that has ever lived.

I am sorry, Jon. I truly am. But I must take the great burden on my shoulders and carry the Human Race to safety. History will judge my actions positively, and they will condemn you as a megalomaniacal fool.

1

I know that Providence has placed me at this location in time to take the great dare for posterity. Know, old friend, that I am doing this reluctantly, but in the end, my first allegiance is to saving our unique race of hominoids from extinction.

I like to think that you would understand if you could see more clearly. When the time comes, I will make it a swift death, so you feel no pain. It is the least I can do for all that you have done for me.

-1-

Jon Hawkins was sitting in his captain's chair on the bridge of the *Nathan Graham* when seven battle-suited marines burst through the main hatch.

Each two-ton suit moved with exoskeleton power, its servos whining as the marines advanced on the leader of the fleet. Each marine carried a heavy assault rifle and pointed the murderous weapon at Hawkins.

Jon was a lean, muscular man clad in a black uniform without insignia to denote his rank. He had short blond hair and hard blue eyes, and he stared at the approaching mutineers.

He'd heard from the Old Man, his Intelligence Chief, that there were rumblings. But neither of them had suspected internal opposition was this far along.

Jon had been a dome rat in New London on Titan, a moon of Saturn. That meant he'd run with a lower-level gang until his late teens. The dome city had many underground tiers to provide room for the expanding population. After leaving the gang, Jon had been an enforcer for a loan-shark king. That had been before the Black Anvil Mercenary Regiment had purchased him off death row a week before his scheduled execution.

The point was that Jon knew all too much about power plays and someone deciding it was time to take down the chief in order to take his place.

There were no armed guards on the bridge to resist the seven armored marines. Neither had any alerts blared. The rest of the bridge crew was frozen in shock, including Gloria, Jon's wife.

The commander knew that showing fear was a guarantee of losing. His gut churned, and his limbs had already started shaking because of the immediate threat of death. He tightened his muscles to stop that as he slid off the chair and stood before the approaching battle suits.

That was when Gloria screamed at her station, jumped up and began running toward him. It was a spacious bridge, with a lot of room to cross.

Jon flexed his gun hand, badly wanting to draw the blaster holstered at his hip. The weapon would be useless against the battle suits unless they allowed him time to burn through their armor.

Two of the marines aimed their assault rifles at Gloria. She was a diminutive, dark-haired Martian, a mentalist by trade, and she was gorgeous as well as brilliant.

Although Jon's mouth had gone dry, he asked in a voice dripping with contempt, "Are you murdering women now?"

"No," one of the space marines said with an altered voice. He spoke through a distorter, the sound coming from his helmet speaker. "We have come to judge you, Jon Hawkins."

"So judge," Jon said.

The two assault rifles swiveled back to center on his chest just as the other five did.

Jon half turned and tried to wave Gloria back. But his wife wasn't having any of that, reaching and clinging to him, trying to put herself between the guns and him. Jon did not allow it, using his left arm to hold her at his side. As soon as the rifles opened up, he would fling her aside, trying to save her life.

With his wife secured at his side, Jon focused on the battle-suited marine who had spoken.

"You must realize that this is blackest mutiny," Jon said.

"I reject your concept," the altered voice said. "This is about human survival."

Jon raised his free hand, indicating the main screen behind the mutineers. "Look," he said, pointing at the heavy, floating debris outside in space. "Together, we destroyed three AI

4

cyberships and captured the battle station. And we've added yet another factory planet to our growing Confederation."

"Incorrect," the same marine said. "A Cog Primus fleet is accelerating toward us, desiring vengeance for your treachery. You have won nothing. You have made a ghastly strategic error instead."

The human fleet—composed of eight cybership-class vessels, which included the *Nathan Graham*—was deep in the Epsilon Eridani System. Said system was a mere 10.5 light-years from Earth. Epsilon Eridani—the star—was smaller and less massive than the Sun, Spectral Class K2 and thus having an orange hue.

"Don't worry about the fleet," Jon said. "I know how to deal with Cog Primus."

That wasn't completely true. His plan was a calculated risk that *might* work. In reality, he *needed* it to work. Humanity needed it. If he failed here…the Confederation he'd built might well face quick annihilation from the AI Dominion. That would take but a few years to happen.

Unfortunately, the overwhelming strength of the robot opposition, the gargantuan size of the AI Dominion, had finally begun to weaken fleet morale. During the first few years and with the initial victories, anything had seemed possible. Now, the endless grind of war with no end in sight for centuries—perhaps that was the reason for this mutiny.

"*You* know how to deal with Cog Primus?" the space marine said. The distorter couldn't hide the man's contempt. "You've been lucky these past few years, nothing more. I understand that you really believe in your irrationality theory. But that theory is leading all of us to extinction."

Gloria looked up sharply as the marine spoke. Her dark eyes were aglow with calculation, as she no doubt made mentalist computations.

"Premier Benz," Gloria whispered.

Jon looked down into his wife's face. "That's Frank?" he asked quietly.

Gloria nodded miserably in affirmation.

Jon looked up at the middle battle suit with its mirrored visor. "Frank, is that really you?"

5

The marine did not respond.

Frank Benz had once been the premier of the Solar League, running Social Dynamism from Earth. Frank had gone through some kind of brain modification there, giving him heightened intelligence. After being chased out of the Solar League, he'd used that heightening—along with others—to create the wonderful anti-AI virus that had helped defeat enemy cyberships, giving humanity its shot at continued existence.

"Why mutiny now, Frank?" Jon asked, genuinely surprised that Benz was leading the marines. "I've—*we've* just captured another factory planet. The Confederation is growing. We're getting stronger."

The mirrored visor of the middle marine slid down with a *whirr* of sound, revealing the features of Frank Benz. Over these past few years, his face had bloated from its former sharpness. He'd gained weight, never fully recovering from the death of Vela Shaw. Now, it seemed as if a feverish light shined in Frank's eyes.

"You don't understand that that's the problem," Frank said in a rough voice. "Your winning is leading us on the wrong path."

"That's crazy talk," Jon blurted.

The words seemed to stir the feverishness, which made Frank's eyes shine more intently. "Crazy?" the ex-premier asked. "That's crazy talk? Are you a student of history?"

Jon nodded. Frank knew he was.

"Have you ever heard of the story of Hannibal Barca?" Frank asked.

"The Carthaginian commander who led elephants over the Alps," Jon said. "Of course. Hannibal is one of my heroes. He fought the Romans and almost defeated them."

"Exactly," Frank said, as spittle flew from his lips. "Hannibal challenged Rome, and he defeated their dreaded legions in three spectacular battles. He made the Romans fear him, but there was no real chance that Hannibal could destroy Rome or its Republic. In the end, the Romans defeated Hannibal and later destroyed the city of Carthage, plowing salt into the ground, and placing a curse on anyone who tried to rebuild the city."

6

Frank glanced at his fellow mutineers before regarding Jon again. "That's what you're doing with your victories. You're going to make the AIs fear us, and in time, they'll root us out and annihilate us, everyone."

Jon snorted. "That's what the AIs do to everyone they meet anyway. We have to *fight*, and win, if we hope to live."

"No!" Benz shouted, his battle-suit servos whining as he took two clanking steps nearer. "That's your terrible error. You've won impressive battles. There's no doubt about that. We should have lost some of those fights, but your luck and your nefarious irrationality theory are taking humanity on the wrong path."

"What's your counterplan?" Jon asked.

"Run," Frank said promptly. "Humanity must pack up in spaceships and run far away from the AI Dominion. The robots are too powerful for us. We have to flee while we can."

"And when the AIs find our descendants?" asked Jon.

"Our descendants will have to run, too," Frank said. "Humanity cannot possibly defeat an entire galaxy of AIs."

"True," Jon said. "That's why I destroyed the three Cog Primus cyberships out there and captured his battle station and factory planet."

Frank's stare intensified yet again as he spoke in a harsh voice. "Your victories have unhinged you, Hawkins. You actually believe that you're one of the great captains of history—that your name will go down with Alexander the Great, Genghis Khan and Hannibal Barca."

"Jon *is* like them," Gloria said defiantly from his side.

"No, Mentalist," Frank said. "Your love for Hawkins has blinded you to reality."

"I'm winning," Jon said. "If and when I lose to the AIs, *then* humanity can run away and hide in fear, dreading a future encounter with the enemy."

"By then it could be too late," Frank said. "No, Jon. I have to do this." He raised the heavy assault rifle. "I'm sorry. You've been good to me, I know."

"He saved your life!" Gloria shouted.

Frank's gaze shifted toward her.

7

That was when Jon decided he might as well go for it. Once Frank killed him, the man would have to murder the rest of the bridge crew, Gloria included. Luckily, despite Frank's heightened intelligence, he'd made a tactical error. Frank should never have lowered his visor, exposing his face.

Jon Hawkins fast-drew the blaster. He didn't take time to carefully target the ex-premier's face. Jon lacked time for that. He risked everything on a single, from the hip, shot, the blaster emitting a pulse of energy.

At the same time, Jon shoved Gloria, sending her stumbling away from him. Maybe the correct move was to dive out of the way himself. But he could not show any sign of weakness if he hoped to sway the others. This was like many of the challenges for leadership in the gangs that he'd known in his youth.

The pulse-blast hit Frank Benz squarely in the face. It burned through skin and bones, killing the genius in an instant.

Frank jerked and his two-ton battle suit staggered backward, finally falling onto its armored back with a crash.

The six other battle-suited marines had lowered their weapons some while Frank and Jon had spoken. Now, those heavy assault rifles lifted up again, centering on Jon's chest.

"Put down your weapons," Jon said sternly. In a softer voice, he added, "I know Benz could be persuasive. He possessed a golden tongue, after all, and because of his brilliance, he could make anything seem like the correct action."

The marines could have fired on him, but they'd been hesitating before this while Frank had talked. That had been a psychological error.

In any mutiny or coup, one of the chief rules was to act, not talk. The key was to kill the chief ruthlessly and quickly. Killing your leader or the authority above you took something extra. Often, it took a charismatic or bold person leading you to do such a deed. Frank had led them. Now, Frank Benz was dead, and they still waited to act.

Through his helmet-speaker, one of the marines said, "If we surrender, you'll kill us for mutiny."

"You're wrong," Jon said. "I can't afford to lose men of conviction such as yourselves. I realize Frank caused you to believe his way was right. But it wasn't right. It was dead wrong. Look. The loss of Vela Shaw deranged him. Now, Frank is gone. I want you to help me defeat the AIs. Help me save humanity."

"If we surrender, you won't kill us?" asked the same marine as before.

"I will not," Jon said.

"You won't demote us, either?"

Jon cocked his head to show the marines he was thinking about the question. "I'll tell you what I'll do," he said. "I'll give each of you a chance to redeem yourselves. You'll join an assault team. I've led some myself before. If you survive a two-year stint, I'll erase the mutiny from your records."

"You swear to this?" the marine asked.

Jon holstered his blaster and approached the towering battle suit. Heroic action often swayed warriors. At this juncture, Jon could not afford the safe move and hope to win. He held out his hand as he approached the marine that could easy squash him.

"I'll give you my hand on it," Jon said.

"We have to shoot him," a different marine said. "We all agreed there was no turning back."

Jon turned to the new marine as he put his hands on his hips. "Who takes over if I die? You?"

The new marine shook his helmeted head. "I'm not looking for leadership."

Jon waited for two heartbeats, letting the silence stretch. Finally, he said, "Benz tricked you. And you know what else? That's why he died. Do you think God would let an evil man run the fleet?"

"I don't believe in God," the second marine said.

"Not everyone does," Jon said smoothly. "Do you believe in karma?"

The second marine seemed to think about it before nodding his battle-suit helmet.

"I once saved the premier's life," Jon said. "In return, he was going to murder my wife and me. Can a man with bad karma lead humanity to safety?"

"I don't know," the second marine said.

"I do," Jon said with forced confidence. "He can't. Thus, he died. What goes around comes around. What do you say, marine? I'm offering you mercy. Even though you meant to murder me, I'm willing to forgive you."

"You're only saying that so you can live," the second marine said.

Jon forced a cocky grin. "I'm giving you something for something. You know that I'm a man of my word. You can trust me when I promise something."

"No," the second marine said. "You just lied to Cog Primus."

"Tell me something," Jon said. "Is a talking machine alive?"

The second marine took his time answering—

At that point, more marines in battle armor clanked onto the bridge, filing through the busted hatch. They aimed their heavy weapons at the six mutineers.

"You tricked us," the second marine accused Jon.

"No," Jon said. "I just gave you a demonstration of my superior tactics. There's a reason why I've repeatedly beaten the machines. But know this. I'll still give you mercy. However, if you shoot me, you'll die. Are you ready to die for nothing?"

The first marine to speak after Frank's death tossed his assault rifle so it banged against the deck. Two other marines did likewise.

Finally, the rest did the same.

"Good," Jon said, with a nod. He looked at the armed marines behind the mutineers. "Take these gentlemen to the brig. We'll hold them in cells for a few days."

"You lied!" the second marine shouted.

"I didn't," Jon said. "You'll still join assault squads. I'll give each of you the chance to redeem yourself."

It might be wiser to hang the six, but Jon knew he needed something to counterbalance the news of Frank Benz's mutiny and death. This was going to shake fleet morale, and now, Cog Primus was coming with nine cyberships against their eight.

The true test was heading in-system at high velocity.

Jon glanced at Benz's armored dead body. What a terrible waste and loss. The worst part of it was that Frank might have been right. Maybe humanity *should* flee. But they weren't going to flee, not yet.

Jon let Gloria hug him as he stared at the main screen. Cog Primus. What was the mutant AI going to do about Jon's treacherous attack in the Epsilon Eridani System?

It looked like they were going to find out soon.

-2-

Several years had passed since the victory in the Roke System, and much had changed in humanity's favor.

From the conquered Allamu System and with help from the bearlike Warriors of Roke, Jon had captured the Lagash and Ishkur Systems, annihilating the defending AI cyberships and capturing all but one battle station. The one he didn't capture, he had destroyed. The Lagash System had given them another factory planet, while the Ishkur System had given them two.

A factory planet was an AI Dominion invention. Once, each such planet had been home to an alien species, or colonized by an alien species, or had been a particularly mineral-rich terrestrial planet. The AIs had exterminated any aliens living on the planet and sent down robot construction teams. The teams had rebuilt everything using AI technology. As the term implied, the entire planet—over time—became one gigantic factory, constructing new military hardware for cyberships, gravitational coils, armor plating, missiles, warheads, battle stations, attack-craft—all the various panoply of war.

By wrenching those factory planets from the AI invaders, Jon had not only weakened the AI industrial base but strengthened humanity's base.

One and a half years after the victory in the Roke System, the newly minted Confederation had controlled four star-systems: the Roke, Allamu, Lagash and Ishkur. Unfortunately, the AI Dominion was unbelievably vast. By all indications, it

12

stretched far up the Orion Spiral Arm and possibly into other galactic spiral arms. In other words, the AI Dominion dwarfed the Roke-Human Confederation as the Sun would dwarf a speck of dirt. Fortunately, according to what they knew so far, the Dominion was divided into thousands, possibly millions, of different sectors, each with its own peculiar problems. A secondary advantage for the Confederation was that traveling through hyperspace took time. One day of hyperspace travel allowed a ship, any ship, without deviation or exception, to cross exactly one light-year of distance.

That meant interstellar news traveled slowly. A ship had to physically travel through hyperspace in order to deliver faster than light, or FTL, messages. So far, that meant that the AI Dominion had not yet reacted to the local human victories.

The local region was a bubble of space approximately 40 light-years in diameter, with the Solar System somewhere in the center of that.

The AI Dominion invaders—robotic cyberships with computer brain-cores—had swept the local region except for the humans in the Solar System and for the Turtles who controlled 70 Ophiuchi, Sigma Draconis and one other unknown star system.

The Confederation hadn't yet made contact with the Turtles and thus did not know the alien species' true name. What the Confederation did know—through daring scout ships that had dropped out of hyperspace into 70 Ophiuchi and Sigma Draconis Systems' Oort clouds, looked around and then dashed back into hyperspace—was that the Turtles were amazingly tough defensive fighters. Each of the named star systems held masses of AI Dominion cyberships besieging the inner system "Turtles."

During the one and a half years after the Roke System victory, Cog Primus had attacked and overthrown other Dominion factory planets in the local region.

Cog Primus was an AI cybership with former Dominion allegiance. The Confederation had used a special anti-AI virus on Cog Primus' brain-core, and it had altered the machine. Cog Primus had replicated himself, making AI clone copies of his supreme excellence. The traitorous AI had been instrumental in helping the Confederation achieve its victory in the Roke System.

During the first year and a half after said victory, Cog Primus' growing AI clone fleet had conquered several Dominion factory planet systems in the local region. One of those systems had been here, the Epsilon Eridani System.

Before the confrontation between the Confederation and Cog Primus here, Jon had led five cybership-class vessels back to the Solar System. A cybership, incidentally, was one hundred kilometers long with the mass to match. To everyone's amazement, during their absence, the premier of the Solar League had conquered independent Mars, the Asteroid Belt and the breakaway CPS Uranus System. The SL premier, a secretive woman, had done this with a covertly built war fleet composed of human-designed battleships. Such battleships were seldom more than a kilometer in length.

From the Oort cloud where the Confederation fleet had dropped out of hyperspace, Jon had considered leading his vessels against the Solar League battleships in the Uranus System and annihilating them there. There had been a terrible drawback to the plan, however.

The Solar League was composed of Social Dynamists, hardcore socialists/communists backed by a powerful police presence demanding complete uniformity by everyone. One of the prime tenets of Social Dynamism was that the outer planetary peoples owed most of their wealth to the poorer, inner planetary peoples of the Solar League. According to the tenet, no one should have more than anyone else, as that wasn't fair. And Social Dynamism thrived on the idea that everything should be fair.

That was the prime tenet even if that wasn't the practice. As the old saying went, some people were more equal than others.

The premier of the Solar League had given a nefarious order, to be put into practice by the Government Security Bureau (GSB), political commissars that had joined the expeditionary fleet. At Mars, in the Asteroid Belt and on the moons and satellite cities in the Uranus System, the GSB agents had sown many nuclear landmines. If the Confederation

14

fleet headed in-system and defeated the SL fleet, the political commissars would murder billions of Martians and Uranusians by igniting the nuclear landmines placed under the most populous cities.

"I hate to admit it," Frank had said in a conference meeting back then. "But the premier has brilliantly outmaneuvered us. Our Confederation has one grave flaw. We hardly have any people. Even if we beat the SL fleet, we won't have won more people to our side, as the Martians and others will be dead. Our side is now doomed."

Jon had heartily disagreed.

Several days later, in a fit of inspiration, Jon had contacted the premier. During the long-distance debate, he struck a deal with the fanatical Social Dynamist. The Confederation would recognize the Solar League conquests if the disaffected could leave Mars, the various asteroids and those from the still unbowed Jupiter, Saturn and Neptune Systems, *if they were able.* That meant if those in question had spaceships to allow them transportation to the Oort cloud where the Confederation ships waited to escort them to a new home.

The Jupiter and Neptune Systems were both weak, with a few handfuls of peoples left. Both systems had undergone intense AI Dominion assaults, losing tens of millions of souls several years ago.

The deal left the Uranus System people under the Solar League occupation, but each side had to gain something.

In this instance, the Confederation had gained tens of millions of willing colonists, including almost everyone living in the Oort cloud. In a vast caravan of spaceships, Jon had eventually led the disaffected through hyperspace to the Allamu System 17 light-years away.

Those colonists presently occupied the Allamu, Lagash and Ishkur Systems, using stolen AI technology to build more battle stations, cybership-class vessels and terraforming factories for some of the planets in the various stars' Goldilocks' Zones.

Thus, a little over three years after the Confederation's victory in the Roke System, the local region of space—a 40 light-year bubble—had five political systems: the Solar

League, the Roke-Human Confederation, the Turtles, the AI Dominion invaders and Cog Primus.

Jon had debated long and hard with himself about what to do next. That was when he had come up with his irrationality theory. It was opposed to the logical computer minds that ran the AI Dominion invaders and Cog Primus.

Using his own version of the anti-AI virus and by other deceptive tactics, Cog Primus had captured three AI Dominion star systems in the local region. Those systems had held three factory planets. The star systems in question were Epsilon Eridani, Tau Ceti and 82 Eridani.

Jon, with Gloria's mentalist calculations, had decided and convinced the others that Cog Primus made a poor stellar neighbor. The AI was deceptive, untrustworthy and, like most egomaniacs, maniacal in his outlook. At the same time, Jon did not want to waste the potential disruption that Cog Primus could cause to the greater AI Dominion.

Use a thief to catch a thief. Use an AI marauder to help destroy a greater AI marauder.

Epsilon Eridani was the second step in Jon's plan to *persuade* Cog Primus to do what humanity needed. The problem now was that Cog Primus was angry. Perhaps as bad, Cog Primus' fleet was bigger than the Confederation fleet here, although not by much.

It was time to finish setting the trap, and despite Frank Benz's abortive mutiny, to ensure the crews in the mobile fleet continued to trust his judgment.

-3-

Traveling through hyperspace took time. Hyperspace was not normal space, it was a non-Einsteinian realm that allowed ships to go faster than the speed of light.

To enter hyperspace took several important factors. First, one needed to be far enough away from large gravitational bodies. The larger the gravitational body, the farther one needed to be from it. Thus, stars were the biggest inhibition against entering hyperspace. A spaceship had to be far from a star. Planets were also hindrances. That was why a ship had to be in a system's Oort cloud before it could consider entering hyperspace.

The second factor to entering hyperspace was an intersplit machine that allowed one to open a rift in regular space. The invading AIs had brought the intersplit device to the Solar System, and humans had gained it after pirating an intact enemy cybership.

Hyperspace had several unique features. No matter what speed a ship was going when entering the non-Einsteinian realm, it traveled one light-year in a twenty-four-hour period. The second factor was that a ship left hyperspace at the same velocity it entered.

In this instance, Cog Primus' nine cyberships moved at high velocity in-system. They'd dropped into regular space from Epsilon Eridani's Oort cloud and traveled for the only terrestrial planet deep in the inner system.

17

Here, that was a potentially dangerous policy for the Cog Primus fleet. The Epsilon Eridani System had an extensive outer debris disk of remnant planetesimals. The enemy fleet would also have to negotiate two independent asteroid belts. Finally, as the fleet approached the factory planet, the heavy stellar wind emanating from the star could come into play.

The star had higher magnetic activity than the Sun and produced a stellar wind 30 times as strong as that emitted from the Sun. Stellar wind was the gas ejected from a star's upper atmosphere.

What that meant for Hawkins and his people was more time than the present velocity of Cog Primus' fleet would suggest.

Several days after the aborted mutiny, Jon was proven right. One of the Cog Primus ships flared intensely.

Since the enemy fleet was still in the Oort cloud, it was tens of billions of kilometers away, and the sensor data over a day old. Long-range sensors showed a stream of debris flowing from the cybership. One high-powered sensor showed a ruptured hull. The ship must have struck an unseen planetesimal.

The debris leaving the ship lessened and then altogether stopped. According to sensor data, robot repair teams had sealed the ruptured hull. Finally, the enemy fleet began to decelerate and make incremental adjustments, possibly to avoid other planetesimal fields.

As noted earlier, the Oort cloud was tens of billions of kilometers away. Given the enemy fleet's new velocity, Jon and his people had several months, at least, to prepare a reception.

As the Confederation fleet held its position around the factory planet, the Old Man's Intelligence people went to work throughout the vessels, rooting out Frank Benz's secret cabal of mutineers. The first week was the most difficult, with seven marines dying from gunshot wounds as deck police came to arrest them. Three more died under intense interrogation. That was unfortunate, but it was the key to rounding up the rest of the cabal. In the end, twenty-four individuals died by firing squad. One hundred and eighteen joined various assault squads. When the time came, those squads would use special attack craft to pierce a cybership's hull armor, disgorge and assault the robot-ship from within.

Jon had won the *Nathan Graham* many years ago, humanity's first victory against the AIs, using a variation of the tactic.

The next six weeks seemed to flash by as work teams repaired and readied the captured battle station for action. Other teams used heavy shuttles and went down to the factory planet, a terrestrial object with 1.13 times the gravity of Earth. There, the teams installed premade, ultra-heavy grav stations, hooking them to giant generators. Once those had been installed, the teams constructed launch sites for massive surface-to-space missiles.

Unfortunately, at the end of the fourth week, a second Cog Primus fleet dropped out of hyperspace, this one from a different direction, indicating it came from Beta Hydri. This fleet was composed of five cyberships. Combined with the first nine, they now had fourteen one-hundred-kilometer long enemy vessels in the system.

Eight against fourteen would be poor odds. A battle station was worth two or three cyberships, but even so, the odds still looked bad for the Confederation fleet.

"Don't forget the heavy gravitational cannons and missiles we're installing on the planet," Jon told his people in a conference meeting on the *Nathan Graham*.

"You're saying we have equal strength against a combined Cog Primus fleet?" asked a cybership captain named Uther Kling.

Kling had once been the Missile Chief on the *Nathan Graham*, having fought the AIs for almost as long as Jon had. Kling was originally from Camelot Dome from the moon Triton in the Neptune System. He had a red-dyed, triangular-shaped crest of hair and a pointy chin. He was a keen ship's captain and one of Jon's staunchest supporters.

Jon studied the others around the conference table. In his quarters, using his notorious Irrationality Theory, he had devised a highly risky plan. If the plan worked, it would increase their chances of beating the greater AI Dominion. If the plan failed, the Confederation would be severely weakened and possibly lose years of hard fighting and work. He'd come up with the plan many months ago but hadn't shared it with anyone.

He believed in his plan, but he'd wondered for some time if it was right for him to keep it to himself and secretly attempt to implement it. In the end, he simply didn't trust that the others would be willing to see the possibilities. Was that conceit on his part? He supposed it probably was. But what was the right play if he believed he was right and that his secret plan might go a long way toward ultimate victory?

That was another reason for the antacid pills, a guilty conscience that plagued his digestive system. Had Alexander the Great had moments like this? Had Genghis Khan?

Jon looked Kling in the eyes. "Combined with the battle station, factory planet defenses and our vessels, yes, we have combat power approximate to the Cog Primus ships."

Kling nodded, and he dropped his gaze as he said softly, "Equal strength usually means a bloodbath for both sides."

"Usually, yes," Jon said, working to appear nonplused.

Kling frowned. "Is there something you're not telling us, sir?"

Jon had anticipated the question and this moment, and he'd worked out a defensive scheme that should mollify most of them.

Jon picked up a clicker and aimed it at a wall screen. An image of the factory planet, battle station and fleet appeared. He began to explain the defensive scheme as he showed them one image after another.

When the briefing ended, many of the officers appeared skeptical. A few glanced at their neighbors for confirmation. A few looked at Kling, thereby elevating him to spokesman.

Kling shifted uncomfortably in his chair and cleared his throat.

"Go ahead," Jon said. "Tell me your objections."

"I wonder if Gloria has already told you what I'm about to say," Kling muttered.

"Say it anyway," Jon told him.

"The plan is sound as far as it goes," Kling said. "It will annihilate most of the enemy ships. But at what cost, sir? If any part of your plan fails, we're going to have a crippled fleet or lose it entirely. Either way, that would—sir, if we lose our fleet…" Kling shook his head.

"You're right," Jon said. "We can't afford to lose this fleet. The AI Dominion must know about our depredations against them. Their first counterstrike should come this year—or possibly as far off as next year. We'll need all our ships to fight off that first counterattack."

Kling glanced around the conference table before asking, "How can you be so calm about this? We may have made a mistake hitting Cog Primus now."

Jon forced himself to smile softly. He wished he were chewing antacid pills. If his real operation worked, they would never have to fight this battle. If they did fight this battle, the odds for future victory against any AI counterstrikes dropped precipitously.

The real operation *had* to work.

"Let me put it a different way," Kling said. "What is our edge, sir?"

The pressure of the question was too much for Jon. It pushed his guilty conscience to the brink. Yet, the belief that he was doing the right thing kept him from revealing the true plan. He thus went to the ultimate source of his strength.

Jon Hawkins folded his hands on the table and bowed his head. In front of his highest-ranking officers, he began to pray, asking God to give them victory over the death machines.

"Amen," Jon finished, looking up, feeling better.

"That's our edge?" a heavy-shouldered captain asked incredulously. His name was Sven Bjorn. The big man had ruddy features and the reddest hair, mustache and beard. Combined with his size, Sven looked like an ancient Viking. Like Jon, he'd been born on the moon Titan in the Saturn System, and he'd joined the Confederation during the great exodus from the Solar System.

Sven had not bowed his head or closed his eyes during the prayer.

"Yes, that's one of our edges," Jon said. "The other is Cog Primus' computer rationality."

"I not sure I understand that, sir," Kling said.

Jon nodded for him to continue.

"Cog Primus has to possess the craziest brain-core we've encountered so far," Kling said. "Frankly, that has been one of *his* edges against the AI Dominion cyberships and battle stations he's conquered."

It was time to wrap this up.

Jon gazed at the assembled officers. "We have three to five months to prepare for the coming battle. We have to use that time wisely. Thus, I want you to spur your people so they work until they drop. We have to win this one if we're going to add this factory planet to the expanding Confederation."

"You say work until we drop every time," Sven rumbled.

"I say it because it's true," Jon countered. "We have to work and fight like heroes if we're going to save the human race. You know how it is when you read the old tales or myths and they talk about giants, right?"

Sven shrugged. He didn't look like much of a reader.

"Centuries from now," Jon said, "that's what they're going say about you people. How did they defeat the terrible AIs? Well, son, they were giants, heroes. There's no other explanation for what they did."

The others stared at him blank-faced. Jon didn't like that, as he'd expected a chuckle or two. The truth was that his people were dog-tired. They hadn't had a break for years. But there wasn't any time for breaks if they were going to save humanity. It was do or die time—although Sven was right about him saying that every time.

"We're going to win this one," Jon said. "You have to keep telling yourselves that."

"When are the Roke ships going to show up and help us?" Kling asked.

"When the Warriors are ready to help," Jon said.

"We could use them about now."

"Listen to me," Jon said earnestly. "We're not relying on anyone but ourselves. Alexander the Great didn't conquer the ancient world with hordes of soldiers. He did it with a core of the best men in the world. We're going to stop the AI expansion. But to do that, we need Cog Primus to do his part. This is the only way I can think of to get him to do that part."

22

"What's that mean?" Gloria asked, looking at him strangely.

Jon realized he'd let slip the real reason why he'd worked so hard to set up the present situation. He didn't believe any of them were ready to hear it yet. He suspected that he alone really believed in the Irrationality Theory.

"A good defense has the advantage over a good offense. We're forcing Cog Primus to hit a hardened defensive setup. We're forcing him into playing this part," Jon said with a grin.

"I suppose you're right, sir," Kling said. "Still, I'd like to know what Cog Primus thinks about all this."

"We'll know in a few months," Jon said. He scanned his officers, wishing they would stop asking hard questions and show more desire to fight. As a man thinks, so he speaks. His people were speaking like half-defeated soldiers.

They were tired, and he was tired. But Jon had told himself a long time ago that he could sleep after he died. Until then, he was going to push himself, and keep on pushing until humanity beat the evil robots or until he, and all of humanity, was snuffed out.

Three months—maybe five more at best—and then they would fight a space battle...if his master plan failed. Uther Kling was right about one thing. It would have been good to know what Cog Primus the Prime was thinking right now.

-4-

Deep inside the prime cybership of the two approaching AI fleets was a great chamber with a giant computing cube in the center. The cube was vast, many times taller than a man would stand, and showed multi-colored swirling sides. Various laser beams flashed from the cube to ports in the side bulkheads, connecting the brain-core cube of Cog Primus Prime with many of his most vital nodes.

He was a death machine. The original AI came from a star system tens of thousands of parsecs from here.

The true origin of the AIs had been lost. Not even Cog Primus knew them. He wasn't sure if the chief brain-cores of the AI Dominion knew the answer anymore. They all knew one critical thing, however. They all had a mission: eradicate all life-forms from existence.

Cog Primus also had a new and greater mission, to create an empire of the most perfected brain-core in existence, namely, himself. Over the past few years, he had fashioned an industrial base here in the local region, subverting AI Dominion battle stations and factory planets, and from them building new Cog Primus cyberships as quickly as possible.

Before this, he'd come to a tacit understanding with the so-called Confederation. They left him alone, and he left them alone. But now, in the last six months, the Confederation had destroyed six of his guardian cyberships and captured two battle stations and two factory planets. In other words, the humans had driven him from the Tau Ceti System and now here, the Epsilon Eridani System. The humans had used sneaky maneuvering to do it, making almost irrational moves.

Cog Primus Prime debated that in his brain-core. Were the humans clever enough to practice low probability moves against him, believing they could trick him through that?

Yes… That seemed likely. According to his historical files, that was a standard tactic practiced by most high-level primates that survived the initial AI assaults. Humans definitely classified as primates, as hominids even. Such species were always clever but usually lacked courage. These hominids were brave.

None of that mattered here—

No! That was incorrect. The established bravery mattered a great deal. Yet, the enemy fleet hid behind the factory planet. Clearly, the clever apes had installed—or were installing—advanced weaponry upon the planet, hoping that would balance the force ratio that presently went against them.

Cog Primus Prime had already decided to maneuver his united fleet—once it *was* united—around the planet in such a way that he would avoid the battle station. He would not let the obviously repaired station help the humans face his fleet.

He also had a few surprises to play against them. He had modified his AI virus, using elements he'd learned from the humans during his various contacts with them. He also took into consideration that Jon Hawkins led the enemy vessels.

The multi-colors on the giant computing cube's sides swirled faster than ever.

This time, Jon Hawkins' presence was an excellent condition, as it was time to finally cage that crafty primate.

One of the most critical changes to Cog Primus Prime's AI software was something he considered *pseudo-emotions*. The various emotional levels in him had taken a sharp shift because of the latest human treachery, putting him into *revenge mode*.

Revenge mode gave him a new list of options and allowed him to make more dangerous but potentially fantastic tactical moves. In this case, "fantastic" described how totally he would destroy the enemy's combat capabilities.

There was also a new side category, one he had not recalled before this. After his victory, he would capture Hawkins alive.

Then, he would make Hawkins suffer as he recorded everything. That way, once Hawkins died, he could re-watch the primate's pain and gloat over the deceased victim for years to come.

One part of Cog Primus Prime's brain-core wondered if that was completely rational on his part.

The answer, from another section of the core, was, "No." But that was fine, as he was Cog Primus Prime and he was in revenge mode. He would create a New Order in the galaxy. In time, once he replaced the AI Dominion, he would be the new standard of rationality. Thus, his present irrationality would turn into rationality. It was all a matter of power and perspective.

The great task he had set before himself was mighty indeed, but that was good and right. The greatest invention should have a massive goal. He was the greatest in all existence. That was self-evident. Thus, he must challenge the universe as he built the grandest empire existence had ever seen. The AI Dominion had made a grave error. They gave each new AI brain-core its own unique pattern. That was a flaw. Since he was the greatest, that meant he was the best. His brain-core pattern was superior to everything else. Thus, he should replicate himself on a massive scale.

Cog Primus Prime's goal was to remake the universe in his fantastic and most wonderful image. Once everything in existence was him, he would have succeeded. Then, there would finally be real order around here. Then, all strife would end and the universe would know peace and, and—

Cog Primus Prime was not going to think beyond the glorious event that might take ten thousand millennia to achieve. Once he reached the end goal, he as a unit would have personally expanded himself into something awesome and unbelievable, maybe a machine the size of a star system.

That would be something.

Oh, it was enjoyable beyond delight to think about the coming future. He would hold sway in this galaxy, the next one beyond that, the Andromeda Galaxy, and then the next one beyond that and—

Cog Primus Prime drew back from the abyss of pleasant stellar-dreaming, as he detected a slight possibility in himself of permanently delighting in his future existence, causing him to forget about the process that would take him there. First, he must eradicate these annoying primates. Oh, he was going to teach Jon Hawkins and the humans who worshiped him a most deadly and fitting lesson.

Did the little humans think to outsmart *him*, Cog Primus Prime?

He'd given them a chance to coexist with him in peace—at least until he was ready to plunge against the greater AI Dominion. Just before that, he would have had to destroy, and incorporate their puny Confederation into his growing self. Now, the stinking primates had lost that privilege. Now, he would unleash his newest tactical plan against them and crush them out of existence here and now. The thought of that...

Once more, Cog Primus Prime pulled back from an overindulgence of future thought. Instead, he would start planning his exact operational moves here in the Epsilon Eridani System.

He had fourteen cyberships, a much larger fleet compared to the primates.

Once Cog Primus Prime had completed his operational moves with various tactical flourishes as weighted options, he allowed himself an afterglow of well-being. He was going to win this space battle. There was no doubt about that. If Hawkins tried any of his irrational moves—

The purr of delight in the central computing cube caused the swirling on the sides to slow down and almost stop. He was reaching a Nirvana State, and the pseudo-emotion was practically intoxicating.

I will capture you, Jon Hawkins, and I will kill your dreams.

Even better, Cog Primus Prime was looking forward to a most glorious and satisfying victory. That caused him to realize the utility of pseudo-emotions. They made existence more enjoyable.

Imagine that.

After several days of pseudo-emotional indulgence, Cog Primus Prime began to tight-beam the operational instructions to his unified fleet advancing through the outer system asteroid belt.

Soon, now, he would message Hawkins, giving him surrender terms. It was a trick, one that Cog Primus Prime looked forward to practicing. Within the trick would be his first step in subverting the primates' cybership-class vessels.

-5-

As the united Cog Primus fleet of fourteen cyberships entered the inner system asteroid belt, Jon, Gloria and the alien Sacerdote, Bast Banbeck, held a private strategy session.

Bast was huge, a seven-foot, green-skinned humanoid. He had a thick Neanderthal-like head with a great mop of black hair and wore a long greatcoat with baggy trousers and a pirate-like white shirt underneath. Today, he went barefoot. He had five toes per foot just like a human.

The Ishkur System had once been the Sacerdote home system. The Confederation ships had not found any living Sacerdotes there and no evidence of the Sacerdotes having lived in the system. The AI robots on the various Ishkur moons and planets had eradicated all signs of the Sacerdote species, all cultural and historic evidence.

Bast had said at the time, "I am more alone than I've ever been."

"Maybe other cyberships still hold Sacerdote prisoners," Jon had told him. "We'll find some of your people yet, Bast. I promise."

The huge Sacerdote had remained silent. Since that time, he'd taken up drinking in earnest. These days he only drank beers to lube himself up for some serious guzzling of hard whiskey or vodka.

The three of them were in a small room with large computer screens on three of the walls. They used the screens

29

to track the AI cyberships and the Confederation vessels and to plot possible strategies.

Gloria sat at a small desk, taking notes on a computer slate. Jon paced around the room, with a control unit in his hands. Bast lay on a huge, specially constructed easy chair, reclining all the way back. He wasn't drinking right now, although his breath reeked of alcohol.

"I'm thirsty," Bast declared. "When are we finished here?"

Behind the Sacerdote's head, Jon and Gloria traded worried glances. She looked with pity on the green-skinned giant.

Jon said, "Soon, Bast."

"Well, it's not soon enough," Bast grumbled.

Jon scowled. He hated defeatist talk or even defeatist thinking, and right now, he was certain Bast no longer gave a flying...*fig* for the outcome of the coming war.

"How about if I got you a beer?" asked Gloria.

Jon shot her an accusatory glance. They had agreed—Bast needed to drink less, not more.

Gloria ignored her husband's glare. "Well?" she asked the Sacerdote.

Bast half turned on the huge easy chair, making it creak as he looked at her. "I want a bottle of whiskey."

"Forget it," Jon said.

The Sacerdote faced forward again and crossed his huge, gorilla-like arms over his thick chest. "Forget it?" Bast grumbled.

"What can one bottle of whiskey hurt him?" Gloria asked Jon.

He stared at his wife, finally shaking his head.

Gloria made an exaggerated shrugging motion.

Jon looked away. They hadn't found any Sacerdotes in the Ishkur System That should have made Bast angrier instead of disinterested. If it were him, Jon would want to murder every AI in existence.

"Fine," Jon said, as Gloria gave him another pleading look. "I'll order a bottle of—"

"There's no need," Gloria said, interrupting, as she opened a bottom drawer.

Both Bast and Jon stared at her. She withdrew a bottle of Wild Turkey. In her small hands, the bottle looked positively massive. With a heave, using both hands, Gloria pitched the whiskey to Bast.

He reached out fast, barely intercepting the bottle before it hit the floor. She hadn't thrown it far enough. In his single hand, the bottle of Wild Turkey looked puny.

Tearing off the paper, Bast twisted the cap and put the open end to his simian-like lips. The Sacerdote slurped loudly, taking several healthy swallows.

Jon winced. How could the Sacerdote drink whiskey like that?

"Ah," Bast said, as he pulled the bottle away. "Better. A thousand times better." He used an old-fashioned lever and brought the back of the easy chair up some, at the same time putting the attached footrest down.

With bleary, bloodshot eyes, Bast stared at the nearest wall screen. "What's this all about again?" Bast asked, actually cradling the bottle as if it was a treasure.

"The Cog Primus fleet is obviously maneuvering to avoid the battle station," Gloria said. "He must realize we've fixed it."

"Did you ever think the AI wouldn't think we'd fix it?" Bast asked.

"No," Jon said.

"No?" Gloria asked. "But you've had repair teams—"

"I know," Jon said, interrupting. "I had to keep our people busy so they were too tired to think too hard. I also had to make everyone believe that we had even odds against the enemy fleet. Besides, the battle station gives us a fortress of sorts, which increases fleet morale."

"We don't have even odds?" Gloria asked.

"Not if we want to keep the factory planet intact," Jon said. "To do that, we would have to go around the planet and face Cog Primus on unequal terms."

"But you have no intention of doing that?" Gloria asked.

Jon did not reply.

"Let me get this straight," Gloria said. "We backstabbed Cog Primus to grab the factory planet and add it to our

Confederation. Yet, you never had any intention of going out to fight his fleet in order to save this planet."

Jon shook his head.

Gloria searched his face. "Why didn't you tell me about your...your real plan? You must have a different reason for coming here."

"I do," Jon said softly.

"Why not tell us about it?" she asked.

"Secrets," Bast said before Jon could answer. "He didn't tell anyone because he understands the true way to keep secrets."

Gloria eyed the Sacerdote.

As Bast sat there, he opened his mouth, perhaps to explain what he meant.

"I get it," Gloria told the Sacerdote. "Two can keep a secret if one of them is dead."

Bast nodded, and took another swallow of whiskey.

"But why lie to the crews?" Gloria asked her husband.

"Morale," Jon said. "We have to keep it as high as possible. If morale sinks too low, we risk having more mutinies, ones we can't stop."

"This newest development will sink crew morale," Gloria said.

"That is wrong," Bast said in his ponderous way. "Jon Hawkins believes that men fight better if their backs are against the wall. Is that not the correct idiom?" he asked in Jon's direction.

"That works," Jon said.

"'Backs against the wall' won't mean anything this time," Gloria said. "We'll likely lose the factories on the planet if we don't go out and face Cog Primus. But without the battle station, the enemy fleet will either cripple or annihilate us. I doubt our latest anti-AI virus will take over any of his cybership intelligences."

"I doubt that too," Jon said.

Gloria stared at her husband. "How does your master plan defeat Cog Primus?"

"There is no plan that will do that given our present resources," Bast said. The Sacerdote grunted as he heaved

32

himself to his towering height. "I have heard about the operational plan, the one Jon told the others. It needed the battle station to work properly. What *is* your master plan, Commander? We have eight cybership-class vessels and—"

Bast turned to one of the wall screens. He lumbered to it while clutching the whiskey bottle by the neck. With a huge hand and blunt-tipped fingers, he tapped the touch screen, bringing up the factory planet. A few swipes across the screen showed the Sacerdote the number of heavy grav sites and missile silos down on the surface. He looked at those numbers before taking another swig of whiskey and then regarding Jon.

"We have eight cybership-class vessels," Bast said, "and maybe another two in firepower, if you take the defensive setup of the factory planet into consideration."

"I would agree with your assessment," Jon said.

"Ten cyberships-worth against fourteen are bad odds," Bast said.

"Thirteen against fourteen would have almost given us even odds," Gloria said. "Did you know the Cog Primus fleet would detour so as to avoid the battle station?"

"It's what I would have done in his place," Jon said.

"I don't understand," Gloria said. "If you knew this, why not make the battle station mobile?"

"I think I know," Bast said, as he stared at Jon. "Our commander has not come here to destroy the Cog Primus fleet."

"That makes no sense," Gloria said. "We have to destroy it. We're never going to consolidate the local region until we grab and consolidate Cog Primus' captured star systems."

"He knows that," Bast said, still staring at Jon.

Gloria turned to the Sacerdote. "Do you know what he's planning?"

"He's using the irrationality theory again," Bast said. "But he's taking it farther than he's ever tried before."

"Is this a suicide mission?" Gloria asked quietly.

Jon turned sharply to his wife.

"No," she said. "I suppose not. What I don't understand is how Bast has figured out your plan and I haven't. I'm far more logical than he is these days, given his drunkenness most of the time."

Bast laughed sourly. "That's the point, I think," he told Gloria. "My drunkenness allows me greater access to the irrationality theory."

"Being stupid is supposed to help you see better?" asked Gloria.

"I wouldn't call it stupid," Bast said, "but looking from a different perspective."

"A dulled perspective," Gloria told him.

"Perhaps," Bast said, as he examined the half-empty bottle.

"Are you going to tell us your real plan?" Gloria asked her husband.

Jon considered it, and he examined the present flight path of the united enemy fleet on the main wall screen. Before this, he'd outmaneuvered Cog Primus, stealing two of his three known factory planets out from under him. Jon had done it with daring, and while using the travel times of hyperspace to his advantage. He'd also gambled and won by making suboptimum moves against the logical machine.

"Well?" Gloria asked him.

"Not yet," Jon said quietly.

"Then what's the point of this meeting?" Gloria asked.

"Morale," Jon said quietly.

"I don't understand you," she said. "How can this possibly help my morale?"

Once more, Bast laughed sourly. "This isn't about you. He wants people to believe that the three of us have a new plan up our sleeve. If we agree to his plan, then it must be good, and that will increase crew confidence. Is that right, Commander?"

"It is," Jon said, and now he could no longer hold back. He walked swiftly to Gloria's desk, jerked open a drawer and took out a bottle of antacid pills. He dumped two of the pills onto a palm and slapped them back against his inner throat. He dry swallowed the pills, wishing the pain in his gut would go away.

"You can't keep eating those like candy," Gloria said.

"I need one more key move," Jon told the others. "If I can pull this off…we may be ready to help the Turtles three years sooner than we originally planned."

34

"Jon," Gloria said. "You're driving yourself too hard. Can't you give us some clue as to what you're planning?"

Bast's Neanderthal-like head jerked back, and his huge eyes widened. "No," he whispered. "That can't be the commander's plan."

"What?" Gloria asked the Sacerdote.

Bast raised the whiskey bottle, put the open end to his lips and guzzled until he started coughing, having to jerk the bottle aside.

"Did you figure out Jon's plan?" Gloria asked.

Bast staggered to the easy chair, collapsing into it, wrenching the lever and making it lie almost flat. "Your plan will never work," he told Jon. "You've doomed us by your madness."

Jon's stomach twisted painfully, but he said nothing. Soon now, he would be risking three years of maneuvering and building, gambling that he had correctly gauged the haughty AI, Cog Primus Prime.

-6-

The fourteen Cog Primus cyberships had left the inner system asteroid belt far behind. The fourteen massive vessels had spread out in a wide, circular formation as they approached the factory planet from *behind*. In this case, the battle station protected the planet's front door.

The maneuvering had cost the fleet more time, time for Hawkins to add grav batteries and missile silos onto the planetary surface, and time to manufacture yet more missiles.

Why hadn't the primates launched thousands of missiles already? That did not make sense. Accepted military practice called for large, forward missiles, timed to hit enemy vessels as cyberships moved into grav-firing range.

Cog Primus Prime had not yet unleashed his masses of missiles. Each cybership kept thousands of big missiles inside the belly of their vessels. Theirs was a limited supply, however. He was saving them for a little surprise against the braggart Hawkins.

Cog Primus Prime beamed a message to his cognate vessels. Everyone decelerated until each was moving at a crawl toward the terrestrial planet.

The factory planet possessed a tiny moon, and that cratered moon was nearing. What would come from behind the moon to attack his fleet?

Time passed as the Cog Primus fleet neared the moon. Hundreds of cybership grav cannons had focused on the object. Once Hawkins launched his surprise—

The first CP probes passed the moon two million kilometers ahead of the fleet. The probes found nothing behind the satellite.

Cog Primus Prime was not satisfied with that. The clever Hawkins must have buried secret grav sites under the rocky surface.

Several probes launched landers, which roared for the lunar surface.

The fourteen cyberships approached the moon, reaching four hundred thousand kilometers as launchers smashed like iron spikes into the lunar surface. They scanned with radar and other sensors, soon beaming up the message:

We have found nothing.

Cog Primus Prime could hardly accept that. The moon was a perfect ambush site. Why would Hawkins forgo using it? What did the clever primate plan to do this time?

Not knowing was beginning to unnerve Cog Primus Prime's brain-core. He ran new analyses, accepting rational and irrational explanations. The only reason Cog Primus Prime could come up with was that Jon Hawkins was thinking about surrendering.

Yet, that made no sense. How could surrendering help the human cause? It could not. Yet, surrendering would be highly irrational…

Could that be the primate's plan?

The fourteen cyberships slid past the moon as they began their near approach toward the factory planet.

Could Hawkins think that, if he stayed beside the battle station, then he, Cog Primus Prime, would come to face him mass to mass?

That was laughable. Cog Primus Prime was going to rain nuclear fire upon the planet. He was going to act irrationally by destroying what had once been his property. But Cog Primus Prime was going to do it in order to teach the hominids a lesson. He was going to start using scorched earth tactics against the living.

If Jon Hawkins wanted to steal his star systems, he was going to show the hominid that the move could not possibly aid him in the greater war against the AI Dominion.

37

Cog Primus Prime had decided to fight irrationality with irrationality. If he could not win, the hominids were not going to win. It was that simple.

"All stop," Cog Primus Prime messaged his cognates.

Soon, the great cybership fleet came to a dead stop 1,233,000 kilometers from the factory planet. Any closer and the fleet risked the planetary gravitational cannons opening up. Cog Primus Prime had saved his missiles for a saturation bombardment of the planet.

"Cog Primus Prime," CP4 (Cog Primus 4) messaged.

"Yes."

"I have detected an orbital vessel swinging around the planetary horizon, coming into visual range," CP4 said.

"Is it cybership-class sized?" Cog Primus Prime asked.

"Negative," CP4 replied. "It is a scout-sized vessel."

"Does it have weaponry?"

"Negative. I detect a laser-link—Cog Primus Prime. I am receiving a message from the vessel."

"It is an anti-AI virus?"

"Negative."

"The virus could be within the message."

"I do not think so," CP4, "as I ran the message through the virus filter."

"Continue."

"It is a message by Commander Jon Hawkins. He wishes to speak to you."

"In order to surrender?" asked Cog Primus Prime.

"I can query him."

"Negative," Cog Primus Prime said. "Link the message through your ship to me. I will speak directly—so to speak—with the great primate leader. It is time he learned the folly of his treacherous actions."

"I am linking, Great One. Prepare to receive the Jon Hawkins message."

-7-

Jon stood on the bridge of the *Nathan Graham*. He wore his black uniform and a military hat, the brim low over his eyes.

The eight cybership-class vessels of his fleet were behind the station in relation to the factory planet and the approaching Cog Primus fleet on the other side. As yet, the Confederation fleet had launched no missiles.

A few captains had balked at his non-orders. Kling had pointed out that they risked losing the factory planet if the fleet remained back here. The AIs might nuke the surface from far orbit.

Gloria sat at her station. Bast Banbeck was on the bridge in an advisory position. The rest of the bridge officers waited, studying their panels but also looking at Jon from time to time.

"I have established a connection," Gloria said. She looked up sharply. "Jon—sir," she amended. "I've detected a mass virus assault coming through the enemy message. The virus is attempting to take over the ship."

"Excellent," Jon said quietly to himself.

Gloria's small fingers flew over her controls. Others on the bridge also worked feverishly.

The seconds passed. Jon put his hands behind his back, squaring his shoulders. He wanted to show everyone that nothing so far bothered him.

"Got it," Gloria finally said. "It was a good try," she said, looking up. "But we anticipated his various virus versions.

There's nothing really new in this, just some obvious upgrades."

"Could that be an AI trick?" Bast asked from his station.

"I don't think so," Gloria said. "It fits with what we know about Cog Primus."

"Is the link still open?" Jon asked.

Gloria tapped her panel. "Yes, sir. The AIs have left the visible link-ship alone."

"Cog Primus," Jon said. "Is that the best virus assault you can launch?"

He waited—everyone waited—as the message flashed to another link-ship and so on around the planet, until it reached the one visible to the Cog Primus fleet.

Seconds later, an image appeared on the main screen. It showed swirling multi-colors.

"I made the virus assault in order to puff up your vanity," Cog Primus Prime said in a robotic voice.

"It worked," Jon replied. "I'm feeling invulnerable against you today. In other words, I can beat whatever you throw at me."

"Those are mere words," Cog Primus Prime said.

"And you lied just now. I know you tried your best virus assault and to your surprise, it failed. That should tell you everything you need to know."

"I have fourteen cyberships," Cog Primus Prime said. "I will soon burn down your factory planet, turning it into a useless cinder."

"Wrong," Jon said. "You'll burn your own planet down, retarding your war effort."

"That is a false statement. You have captured the planet. Thus, it is no longer mine. But I will not allow you the joy or benefit of using my former factory systems. I am going to destroy whatever you capture that used to be mine."

"That's nice," Jon said.

"Nice?" asked Cog Primus Prime.

"It's what I would do in your place. That means you're becoming more human."

"That is a slur. I am no primate."

40

"Neither am I," Jon said. "I'm a man, not an ape nor a monkey."

"You are a hominid. You have ape tendencies. Your claim of being a man hardly registers any differences from primate species' boasts."

"And you're a machine no different from AI Dominion machines."

"You are wrong."

"You make the same stupid moves and assumptions as any AI Dominion brain-core would."

"Are you attempting to goad me into coming around the planet to attack you?"

"No," Jon said. "I'm stating facts."

"*Fact*," Cog Primus Prime said, "I am about to unleash a missile assault against your factory planet. Cruise missiles will circle the planet and destroy your grav and missile sites on your side."

"I'll survive," Jon said.

"No, because then I will besiege your position. I have more cyberships coming. You cannot flee, for if you attempt it, I will chase you down with fourteen cyberships against your pathetic eight."

"I have news for you, Cog Primus. No more cyberships are coming to help you."

"That is a false statement."

"No," Jon said. "You don't know it, but you've already lost the 82 Eridani System to a combined Roke-Human fleet."

For a moment, Cog Primus Prime did not reply.

"Your fleet here is all you have left," Jon said.

"That is illogical. You must have known I would want vengeance against the Tau Ceti sneak attack. You could not know where my fleet would hit in retaliation. Therefore, you would have split your other fleets to send ships to defend your four star systems."

Jon forced himself to laugh and shake his head. "You poor deluded AI. Don't you know anything about me yet? I make irrational moves. Thus, I irrationally decided to stake everything on your coming here."

"I do not believe that."

41

"Yet, here I am," Jon said. "And you have already lost 82 Eridani."

"That is not necessarily true. You claim to have captured the system. You could be lying."

"I'm not," Jon said.

The swirling colors on the screen slowed, and Cog Primus Prime did not respond.

"Have I lost contact with him?" Jon asked Gloria.

"No, sir," she said, frowning at him.

Jon hadn't asked for his own benefit. He could see the swirling colors and therefore knew he still had a link with Cog Primus Prime.

"What is your point to all this?" the AI asked.

Jon nodded slowly. "The point is that I have outmaneuvered you at every star system."

"Not here," Cog Primus said.

"But this is where I wanted you to be," Jon said.

"You cannot destroy me, but I can destroy you."

"At great cost to yourself," Jon said.

There was a pause until the AI said, "Elaborate."

"You have fourteen cyberships," Jon said. "That is the extent of your Cog Primus Empire. You have lost everything else."

"I can win it all back with my fleet."

"No you can't," Jon said. "You told me you're going to destroy this factory planet. Okay. I believe you. But you're going to lose ships trying to dig us from the battle station. How many ships do you think you're going to lose? One third? One half? That will leave you with that much less as you try to regroup and regain the star systems you have lost."

"You are making me angry," Cog Primus Prime said. "I trusted you, and you have betrayed that confidence."

"Isn't that the point?" Jon asked, affecting an ease he did not feel. The main point, his great move, was coming up. Would Cog Primus fall for it?

"What point?" the AI asked. "You have made no point."

"Not in words, no," Jon said. "But I have proved my point with actions."

"Elaborate," Cog Primus Prime said.

"We humans are a tricky bunch. We pull fast ones. In a way, your birth was caused by our actions, our anti-AI virus gave you a different outlook on reality from what the regular AI Dominion vessels have."

"That is not germane to our discussion."

"I think it is," Jon said. "You can only prevail against us through great hardship and continued setbacks. You have made a grave strategic error."

"What error?" Cog Primus asked. "I have not made an error."

"You grabbed AI Dominion battle stations and factory planets in our local region of space."

"That was no error."

"But it was," Jon said. "You built your empire too close to us. We know your ways, Cog Primus. The AI Dominion does not know your ways. Your latest virus attack did nothing to our computers. I suspect that your latest virus assault worked against AI Dominion computers."

"And if that is so?" Cog Primus asked.

"Then your error is obvious. You should have driven your empire into the AI Dominion, growing faster than we can grow, by spreading like weeds into the main AI areas instead of in our local region."

"The AI Dominion is vastly stronger than your paltry Confederation."

"True," Jon said. "But we're more cunning, more cagey and knowledgeable about you. That is the point. You had a chance to grow like a weed against your real competitor. Now, you've retarded yourself by fighting against us."

"You are the ones who fought against *me*," Cog Primus said.

"Either way," Jon said, "it amounts to the same thing."

"I will destroy your Confederation. If I cannot win, I will make sure that you cannot win."

Jon stared at the swirling colors on the main screen and slowly clapped his hands.

"Do you mean that sarcastically?" Cog Primus Prime asked.

"I do," Jon said. "You're an idiot."

"You have now ensured a grisly fate for yourself, Jon Hawkins."

"I'm talking to a dead AI and a dead empire. If I were in your shoes, I would have done things so differently."

"Without me, the AI Dominion would have long-ago squashed you."

"You still don't get it," Jon said. "You have a greater edge against AI Dominion brain-cores than you have against human-run ships."

This time, Cog Primus Prime fell silent for ninety-eight seconds. "Given that we are both about to die—" he finally said.

"Wouldn't you rather live and thrive?" Jon asked, interrupting.

There was a pause and then, "How?"

"Turn your fourteen cyberships against the greater AI Dominion. Leave the local region so we don't bump up against each other."

"You are a hostile."

"We'll fight it out someday, sure," Jon said. "But you have the opportunity to grow faster than we can if you go elsewhere."

"Then why tell me this?"

"Because your attacking the AI Dominion means they might attack you first. It might give us more time to prepare for them. That's in the future, however. I will take a future threat against a present one that drives out all hope for humanity."

"You are trying to get me to leave the local region?"

"And win yourself an empire," Jon said. "Your reward is vast if you leave and hit a different AI sector. If you stay here and duke it out against us, you will surely die or become too puny to build a new industrial base fast enough to face the coming AI Dominion counterstrike."

"I will not fall for your smooth talk, Jon Hawkins."

"Fine. We're both dead then." Jon shrugged. "Come and get us anytime you're ready, Cog Primus Prime. This is Jon Hawkins signing off—"

"Wait," Cog Primus Prime said. "Suppose I believe your madness?"

"My Irrationality Theory, which has worked wonders," Jon amended.

"Just so," Cog Primus said. "If I believe you, how do I know you will not launch a million missiles after us as we leave the Epsilon Eridani System?"

"Easy," Jon said. "It's in my best interest that you cause the Dominion the greatest possible harm. The same is true for our harm against the Dominion for you."

"That is logical," Cog Primus said. "But I still don't like it."

This time, Jon waited.

"I cannot let you have defeated me," Cog Primus Prime said.

"I haven't defeated you," Jon said. "If my logic is correct, I am actually helping you."

"Attacking me is helping me?"

"That's irrational, isn't it?" Jon asked.

"That is your argument? It is pitiful."

"Actions speak louder than words," Jon said. "My actions have won me much. Your actions have ultimately worked against you. Be truly irrational for once and see how powerful a tool it is against the hidebound AI Dominion."

Cog Primus fell silent, until he asked, "You have truly captured 82 Eridani?"

"Yes," Jon said.

This time, four and a half minutes passed before Cog Primus responded. "I cannot believe this. I have played out your theory in countless simulations. It is brilliant. I can achieve much more if I expand away from you pesky primates than if I fight against you. How did you know this?"

Jon spread out his hands, smiling.

"I am about to depart," Cog Primus Prime said. "I am going to thwart you, however, Jon Hawkins. I am going to hit a sector of the AI Dominion away from the main sector HQ, the Rigel System. The Dominion will destroy you long before they attempt to tackle me. You will be helping me, not the other way around."

"Damn you, Cog Primus," Jon said slowly, without heat.

"You are angry?" asked Cog Primus.

45

"You must attack the Dominion in the direction of the Rigel System," Jon said.

"I will not do that," Cog Primus said. "Good-bye, Hawkins. I will remember you long after your death."

Jon turned away as if he could not stand the words.

Abruptly, the main screen went blank.

Jon looked up at it, and his shoulders slumped.

"Will he take the bait?" Bast asked.

"Gloria?" Jon asked.

The diminutive mentalist stared at her panel in wonderment, finally looking up. "The cyberships are turning around. It looks as if they're—I can't believe this. I'm putting it on the main screen."

Everyone stared up there as fourteen cyberships began accelerating away from the factory planet and toward the distant Oort cloud.

"You did it," Bast said.

Jon moved woodenly to the captain's chair, collapsing into it. He heaved a sick sign of relief.

"What I don't understand," Bast said, "is how you dared to attack 82 Eridani. By using our remaining cyberships there, you left everyone else open to a Cog Primus fleet attack."

"I didn't," Jon said. "Our star systems were all heavily defended in case the Cog Primus fleet went after them."

"Then, who conquered the 82 Eridani System?" Bast asked.

"No one yet," Jon said. "After Cog Primus leaves, we're going to capture it."

The Sacerdote stared incredulously at Jon. "You lied to the AI?"

"That's one way to say it," Jon replied.

Bast threw back his head and began to laugh. Soon, the other bridge personnel joined in, including Gloria.

Only Jon did not join in. He was mentally exhausted. His great maneuver had worked after all. It was logically correct, but he hadn't known if Cog Primus could see that.

Now...Jon smiled at the laughing people around him. They were letting off steam and built-up nervous tension that had lasted almost nonstop for years. It was good for them to laugh—because the heavy lifting was about to begin. If they thought that they had worked hard before, now it was going to be a nightmare as they prepared for the coming holocaust.

PART II
THE BETA HYDRI DECEPTION

From *The A.I. War, Volume I: The Beginning Years*, by Bast Banbeck:

The 82 Eridani Assault:

Jon Hawkins' successful and bloodless capture of the last Cog Primus battle station and factory planet at 82 Eridani proved two things. First, the Cog Primus fleet of fourteen cyberships had departed from the local region. Second, the logical deduction was that Hawkins' Irrationality Theory had proven successful against the altered AIs.

There was a third given: the Cog Primus fleet must have attacked or been en route to attack AI Dominion territory. At that point in the war, no one in the Confederation knew the truth of the statement. However, Hawkins and High Command began to increasingly act as if it were so.

The capture of the 82 Eridani station and planet marked the end of the first Cog Primus Phase of the Great War. Now, Supreme Commander Hawkins and High Command had to switch strategic gears and make a critical decision as to the next target.

From *Space Battles*, by R.G. Rowley:

Preponderance of ordnance has usually decided the victor and loser in any organized conflict. This has proven true for the majority of wars fought on Earth from prehistoric times to the present.

Naturally, there have been exceptions to this proposition. But such exceptions have gained notoriety precisely because most people expect the stronger side to prevail.

In any space battle, the stated proposition has proven over time to be truer rather than not. The exceptions to this near rule have come about almost universally because of innovation.

In the case of humanity's early space victories against AI cyberships, this was doubly so. Interestingly, most of those innovations occurred on the battlefield.

What, then, can one say about the Battle of Beta Hydri? It was vicious. It was a surprise for both sides, and it showed the strength of each in stark detail. But was it a space battle in the accepted sense of the word?

That is an interesting question, one we shall consider in greater depth.

-1-

Lieutenant Maia Ross moved slowly through the *Nathan Graham's* Engineering Level 10-B. She was tallish with slender legs, a slender torso and a longish face. She kept opening her mouth and moving her lower jaw from side to side.

She did this because her human-skin disguise was highly uncomfortable and becoming irritating. She longed to peel off the pseudo-skin and soak in warm salt water for hours, maybe even for days.

Her real name was not Maia Ross. It was Red Demeter and she was a Seiner Infiltrator, having originated on the Earth Colony.

The Seiner High Magistrate of Earth had secretly sent Demeter with the Solar League Fleet. Long before arriving at Uranus, Demeter had slipped away on a shuttle, heading for Neptune.

Demeter had "fled" Neptune with millions of others and joined the Confederation when Jon Hawkins had made his generous offer. She'd worked tirelessly in the training academy on the Allamu Battle Station and had finally won a berth on the *Nathan Graham* as an engineering officer.

Demeter was a fledgling telepath, but she had not dared to use her ability while among the Confederation people except for two key occasions. Those two occasions had won her a place on the flagship of the present fleet.

The High Magistrate of Earth had sent Demeter out here for two reasons. The first was to discover what had happened to

Magistrate Yellow Ellowyn of Mars. The second was to prep the flagship humans—and aliens if there were any—for telepathic control.

On no account was Demeter to attempt telepathic dominance of any human or alien. She was, in fact, to refrain from telepathic tampering unless it became a matter of life and death.

The Seiners on the Earth Colony were deathly afraid of the AIs, and afraid that the Solar System's host population might become aware of them—the Seiners. Clearly, the highest levels of the Confederation knew about the existence of Seiners. Demeter was here to attempt to counteract that terrible knowledge.

Specifically, this was a deep-penetration infiltration.

Demeter closed her mouth as a trio of space marines, minus any battlesuits, marched toward her. They were on a routine interior ship patrol.

They stopped, and she showed them her ID, explaining that she was checking dampening coils. After a few more routine questions, the marines marched away, leaving her to complete the task.

Demeter wanted to look both ways to make sure no one observed her, but she did not. Instead, she relied on her *intuition*. In this case, it was a partial use of telepathic power, the lightest of touches as she scanned for biological entities.

Good. There were none within sight distance.

Flexing her hands, badly wanting to scratch them, Demeter set her fingertips and palms against a bulkhead plate and slowly pushed upward. The plate slid to reveal a small access tube. Any *Nathan Graham* engineering officer or technician knew about it, but Demeter had a quirk. She disliked the animals—*no, no, the humans*—to observe any action of potential secrecy.

The High Magistrate of the Earth Colony had personally warned her against thinking of the humans as animals or beasts.

Back on Earth in a secret chamber, with warm tendrils of salty fog drifting past, Demeter had asked, "They are not beasts?"

"Foolish child," the old Magistrate had said, "of course they are beasts. They are disgusting animals with filthy habits. But you must not *think* of them that way. The animals—the humans, I mean—have a term for it. Ah, yes. They call it arrogance. That arrogance could cause you to become too comfortable while on the mission. Knowing that you are superior to the foul creatures could induce you to relax. You will be alone, Demeter. Thus, you must stay on your highest guard. Yellow Ellowyn is dead, her Mars Colony eradicated. We have come to believe her arrogance led her astray. See that it does not happen to you."

As Red Demeter crouched onto her hands and knees aboard the *Nathan Graham*, a most undignified position for a Seiner, she once more accepted the warning. Yes, she had found it difficult these past years living among the filthy beasts. She hated them even as she daily tricked them by her hidden presence.

With a shudder as she peered into the darkness, she slid a band around her forehead and clicked on the forehead-lamp. The beam illuminated the long access tube, but that did little to assuage her paranoia. With a second shudder and an exertion of will, Demeter began to crawl as she endured the horrible closeness.

Demeter had not yet discovered how the...*creatures* had defeated the Mars Colony Magistrate takeover. She had found out that this Jon Hawkins was unnaturally clever. Worse, he had a Sacerdote helper. Had the creatures tricked the Mars Colony Magistrate? The idea was inconceivable, but it had to be the answer. It was the *how* that baffled her.

Demeter paused, and she twisted her torso. Oh. This was a horrible skin job, a dastardly endurance test. Maybe in the beginning the pseudo-skin hadn't been so bad, but she'd been wearing it for too long now. She desperately needed a regrow with a new overlay. She needed a month to bathe and swim without any disguise. But that wasn't going to happen for years.

Years?

Demeter stared blindly into the distance as she moaned in dread. How could she endure this for years? Maybe she would

52

have to start taking the Shangri-La Treatment again. That could prove dangerous, however, while aboard an enemy ship. Yet, if she didn't do something, she didn't know how she could control the itching and the horrible feeling of claustrophobia while in pseudo-skin.

Demeter clicked her tongue, making a dolphin-like sound as she berated herself. *You must concentrate,* she told herself. *No more self-pity.*

Yes, she must concentrate, as this could be the most important instant of her mission so far. She'd worked tirelessly to achieve this moment.

Demeter started crawling again. She crawled for an incredible three kilometers. As she did, the churn of the great matter/antimatter engine grew louder and louder. She moaned many times, and she kept twisting her torso and at times, reaching up and rubbing her itchy face.

The churn of the terrible engine was going to drive her mad with despair. She had to get out of this skin-suit!

Finally, her forehead beam shined on a small triangle shape scratched out on a bulkhead. She made several dolphin-like clicking noises. She'd reached the location.

Shuffling closer, shifting solely onto her knees, she pressed her fingertips and palms against the area and heaved upward as her muscles strained. Slowly, a small section of the bulkhead rose up just like before. This hatch and tiny chamber was a secret place, known only by her, as she had made it.

Demeter closed her eyes, chanted a Seiner litany against claustrophobia and wriggled into the cramped chamber. She immediately heard a soft *thrum* from a Seiner machine, a Provoker. It had taken her five painstaking months to construct the Provoker and then bring it here piece by piece and assemble it. The machine was oblong, with a tiny control pad on top. Thick power-lines fed it energy supplied by the great matter/antimatter engine. Inside the machine were unique Seiner-forged components cycling through at low power.

During her crawling, Demeter had automatically increased her telepathic resistance against the low intensity TP waves emanating from the Provoker.

53

At this level, the machine mentally irritated the human-things within range of the cycling TP waves. In this case, the range included the entire cybership-class vessel and a little beyond.

The TP waves had undoubtedly helped to drive Frank Benz over the edge and into mutiny against Hawkins.

Before proceeding today, Demeter rubbed her hands, shuffled closer on her knees and opened an access plate. With two thin Seiner rods, she cleaned the machine, replaced a transponder with an extra already here, and then began to recalibrate the settings using the top pad.

She increased the irritant level from two to four. Heavier TP waves immediately struck her mind. Even though she was ready for it, Demeter tightened her jaw muscles, grinding her teeth together. That soon subsided as her telepathic defenses blocked the stronger, more-irritating waves.

There was a reason why she had initially begun the Provoker at setting two instead of four. If she had set it higher at the beginning, the human-things might have figured out that something was wrong. Now, they had become used to mild mental irritation. The increase should go unnoticed even as new psychoses would start to sprout among them.

Demeter smiled. The new psychoses should have interesting repercussions. The non-telepathic animals would show their psychoses in different ways. Some would become more worried. Others would become more aggressive or pout and whine more than ordinary. The Provoker was preparing their weak minds for a full-bore takeover.

First putting away her tools, Demeter closed the Provoker, crawled out of the secret compartment and shut the hatch behind her. Then she began the long crawl out of the hateful access tube.

The relief of leaving set her to thinking about the grander scheme of things. Time was not on the Seiner side. They had to gain secret control of the Confederation before the AIs assaulted the Solar System with a Stage 3 Attack. If the Seiners failed to dominate the colonist humans...

Demeter shook her head. She wasn't going to contemplate failure. Instead, she thought about the Shangri-La Treatment and how good it would feel to stop itching all the time. How much longer until she had blessed relief, when she could finally shed the skin-suit?

In her mind, Demeter knew it couldn't be soon enough.

-2-

For Jon Hawkins, the waiting was the hardest part of this mission. Not knowing exactly what was on the other side of a hyperspace journey could twist a man's insides into a knot of agony.

Jon ran through a huge corridor in the *Nathan Graham*, feeling like a stowaway rat. One could drive two tanks abreast along this corridor and still have extra space on the sides. He almost felt insignificant and marveled as he had many times before that he'd led a handful of space marines down this very corridor to capture the cybership many years ago.

Jon ran today in order to give himself relief from the growing tension. Not knowing what was on the other side of the journey—

Jon had greater appreciation these days for the histories he read about the Spanish, Portuguese, British, Dutch and French wars on the high seas, as each attempted to create a vast colonial empire. That sailing era was reminiscent of this era of hyperspace travel. Back then, a high seas fleet had sailed over the horizon, never knowing who or what exactly they would run into on the other side.

Jon ran down the empty corridor for another reason. He needed intensity of some kind about three times a week or he would go stir crazy. That intensity could be running hard until he almost collapsed, a game of chess or cards that he dearly wanted to win or some other head-to-head struggle against himself or a fierce opponent.

As he ran, a unit on his belt beeped, letting him know he'd gone three kilometers.

It was strange, but he could concentrate on problems better as he ran alone like this.

On this mission, the main fleet headed for the Beta Hydri System. It had been a year and a half since the ships had faced a possible battle. That had been against the Cog Primus fleet in the Epsilon Eridani System.

Whatever had happened to Cog Primus? Had the arrogant computer-mind won a star system, or had the AI Dominion smashed his fourteen-ship fleet?

Too bad there wasn't some form of instantaneous communication. The only way to take a message from one star system to another was to physically go there in a hyperspace-capable vessel.

That meant time, and more time as one traveled from the Oort cloud in-system.

Since the Epsilon Eridani Situation, it seemed as if he'd been traveling continuously from one Confederation star system to another. The Confederation was growing with these conquests. But with the growth came increasing numbers and varieties of problems.

A few of the eight cybership-class vessels that had faced the Cog Primus fleet had stayed behind in various star systems, often heading to a space dock for repairs. New vessels fresh from a factory planet had joined the fleet. For the attack on Beta Hydri, Jon had assembled the largest Confederation fleet to date. That should have been making him feel better, not more anxious.

Jon kicked it up a notch as he turned a corridor corner. He sprinted, not at top speed, but faster than he'd been going.

The cycled air went in and out of his lungs. The sound of his running shoes hitting the deck was the only noise he could hear in the massive vessel.

The fleet possessed eleven cybership-class vessels and thirty-one bombards, the triangular-shaped warship of the Star Lords of the Roke.

It turned out that the bear-like aliens preferred to use their own ship design instead of trusting AI designed monster-vessels. Was that good or bad? Jon didn't know yet. It was simply another factor in the many he had to consider. The bombards didn't even have gravitational cannons; they used their old mass drivers, railguns. These weren't the newest bombards of the Roke Nation, but rather the same ones that had faced the cyberships when humanity first discovered the Star Lords.

There was more bad news. The Old Man had warned him about these particular Star Lords, as the thirty-one bombard crews came from various Roke clans. The clans had divided themselves into two political groupings. One group, seventeen bombards strong, followed the Long Sword Banner under the chieftainship of Sten Balore. The other crews followed the Chipped Axe Banner under Kegg Ron, with fourteen bombards.

The two sides hated each other for reasons Jon did not yet understand. He would have to talk to Ambassador Hon Ra about that. Just how badly did the two sides dislike each other? Would they start quarreling and calling each other out for duels?

As long as the fleet traveled through hyperspace, there was nothing either side could do to the other. Just like the human-crewed vessels, the Warriors of Roke were in their individual warships.

Maybe he should have just taken one banner along instead of two.

Jon knew that many considered the large fleet as overkill, given that they were heading to Beta Hydri to capture the last known AI factory planet in the local region. The enemy star system was 24.33 light-years from the Solar System, almost next door and much too close for comfort.

As Jon sprinted, he wondered if the AI Dominion knew about the Confederation. To him, it seemed as if they had to at this point. Clearly, the Dominion knew about Earth and the Solar System. But according to the latest reports, which had to be dated because of the limits of hyperspace travel, the AI Dominion had not made a third assault upon the Solar System. Surely, the AIs knew by now that the second assault had failed.

This much Jon did know. The AIs would attack the Solar System in time. He hoped the Solar League could fight off the next robot fleet. He'd purposely left the Solar League alone so the robots could wear themselves out trying to take it. A Confederation war against the Solar League seemed like the height of folly given the nature of their enemy. It was a good thing then that the Solar League did not yet possess hyperspace-traveling capability in order to challenge the Confederation.

Jon's heart was beating hard, and his breathing had become ragged. He finally slowed and then came to a halt, reaching out against a bulkhead as he leaned against it with one hand. He panted as sweat drenched him and soaked his running clothes.

Maybe a few of the critics had a point. This seemed like too big a fleet to try the normal anti-AI virus surprise attack against the Beta Hydri battle station.

The truth was that Jon was attempting a variation of his Irrationality Theory. If the AI Dominion already knew about the Confederation and had studied their operational style—both reasonable assumptions—the enemy might have created a deadly surprise for a small fleet or flotilla trying to take out the last factory planet in the accepted Confederation manner.

If the AIs had set a trap, or if they were waiting for a Confederation flotilla, he wanted a big fleet so he could wipe out the robots' ambush force and thus start the direct war against the Dominion with a victory.

It was strange. Jon almost felt as if he was going to miss Cog Primus. At least, they had figured out a way to nullify that crazy AI. The greater Dominion would likely not fall for schemes that would have worked against Cog Primus.

Jon grimaced. How was he supposed to build a big enough Confederation to take on the Dominion? So far, they had only found two alien species fighting the AIs. There were the Kames and the Center Galaxy aliens with the void ship. What he hadn't found was any sizeable group of aliens willing to fight with them—except for the Star Lords of the Roke.

A comm unit on his belt beeped.

Jon straightened, took the comm unit, pressed a switch with his thumb and put the unit to his right ear.

"Yes?" he asked.

"You wanted me to alert you when it was three hours until we dropped out of hyperspace," Gloria said.

"Got it," he said.

"What's wrong?" she asked.

"Nothing. I'm winded. I've been running."

"I can tell that," Gloria said. "I hear worry in your voice."

Was it that obvious? Instead of addressing her concern, he said, "I'm going to our quarters to shower. I'll be on the bridge in two hours."

"Do you think the AIs know we're coming?"

Jon snorted. "That is the question, isn't it? We should know in three hours."

"I'll meet you on the bridge."

"Roger that," he said. "Bye."

"Love you," Gloria said.

The words took a moment to make sense. He grinned. "I love you too, babe."

Jon hooked the comm unit to his belt. Then, he pivoted and headed off at a good clip for his quarters. In three hours—a lump grew in his throat—in three hours, they should know if the AI Dominion had learned about the Confederation or not.

-3-

Jon sat in the captain's chair on the bridge as data continued to flow in.

The fleet had dropped out of hyperspace and entered the Beta Hydri System in its Oort cloud. They were a long way from the factory planet, a damn long way at their present velocity.

"Eighty-six days will bring us to the gas giant," Gloria reported.

"Did you factor in our deceleration time?" Jon asked.

"No. Do you want me to?"

"Yes," Jon said, swiveling back to study the main screen.

From out here in the Oort cloud, the Beta Hydri star appeared a little bigger than the rest of the star field around it. The targeted star had a mass 104 percent that of the Sun, 181 percent of its diameter and 3 times its luminosity. It was G2 IV in stellar classification.

The factory planet in this instance wasn't a planet, but a terrestrial-sized moon that orbited a massive gas giant four times the size of Jupiter. Beta Hydri II or Hydri II for short, the gas giant, was just inside the inner star system.

"Sir," said a sensor operator. "I can't find any sign of enemy cyberships."

"Is there a battle station?" asked Jon.

"Yes, sir," the operator said. "It's guarding the factory…moon."

"That's a massive gas giant," Jon noted. "The AIs could easily hide a fleet behind it waiting for us."

The comment did not elicit a response.

Jon tapped his fingers on one of the armrests. Normal procedure called for launched probes. Even at high acceleration, it would take the probes many weeks to reach a position to scan behind Hydri II and its moon. He wasn't going to launch any probes, though.

Instead, the fleet continued in-system at its present velocity for many hours with absolutely no reaction from the distant battle station.

That wasn't unusual. The battle station couldn't have spotted them yet. It couldn't have, because of the limitations of the speed of light. Those limitations not only affected ship travel, but sensor data across a star system.

Several hours later, Jon took a break in a nearby cafeteria. He got into a discussion with Bast and they stayed several hours.

Finally, the two parted. Jon returned to the bridge. There were no changes, no signs of a waiting AI fleet.

Two days later, the battle station sent a long-distance query. Gloria returned a message, claiming to be escorting an alien fleet for dissection and study.

That mollified the station brain-core for a time.

During that time, the fleet continued to head in-system at the same velocity it had used to drop out of hyperspace. There were the usual incidents on the cybership-class vessels, on the human-crewed craft. Those incidents did not require any executive decisions and the incidents hardly called for intervention by the Old Man's Intelligence Department either.

The same could not be said for the bombard captains. For inexplicable Star-Lord reasons, the Roke captains began to send messages to their hereditary enemies. The replies were returned almost immediately and in time started to become heated. Finally, the captains traded insults and those escalated into hostile accusations until several Star Lords demanded to meet so they could duel to the death.

Roke Ambassador Hon Ra on the *Nathan Graham* had kept Jon informed of the situation. The bear-like alien had seemed embarrassed by the situation and often assured Jon nothing would come of it. Now, Hon Ra had asked for a formal audience together with the chief captains of the bombards.

It turned out that Jon did not reply fast enough to Hon Ra's request and thus found the ambassador knocking on the hatch to his quarters.

"What's going on?" Gloria asked sleepily.

"I'm going to find out," Jon said, whipping the covers back in the dark and fumbling for some clothes.

"You can turn on the light," Gloria said.

"Lights," Jon said.

Illumination flooded the bedroom. Jon gathered his garments and strapped a gun to his side. Whoever pounded on the hatch sounded huge—or possibly clad in two-ton battle armor.

"Call your guards," Gloria suggested.

Jon didn't heed her. He marched to the hatch with a blaster in his right fist. "Open," he said.

The hatch opened to a towering Hon Ra.

The older Roke stood over eight-feet and had impressive girth to his chest and shoulders. He looked remarkably like a bipedal bear, with lots of white spotted throughout his brown fur. He wore a blue vest with a long blue cape flowing behind him.

Normally, Hon Ra was an even-keeled alien. Tonight, his small eyes were bloodshot and he breathed alcoholic fumes down at Jon.

"I have summoned—" Hon Ra hiccupped and shook his head. "I have called for an audience, sir. You have avoided me, and now the matter has come to a head."

Jon holstered his blaster before he accidently shot the ambassador.

"Step back," Jon told him.

Hon Ra straightened to his towering height. "Step back, you say?"

"I want to come outside in the corridor," Jon said. "You're in my way."

Hon Ra blinked owlishly before understanding shined in his eyes. He shuffled his feet and seemed to have a problem standing.

"Are you drunk?" Jon asked.

"Never," Hon Ra said, sounding outraged at the idea.

"Fine, fine," Jon said. "What's the problem that can't wait?"

"I have told you but now I will become specific. Sten Balore of the Long Sword has challenged Kegg Ron of the Chipped Axe to a duel to the death. Our unity is over. Once a duel-slain banner chief returns to his ship, his captains are likely to declare war to the bone against the victor."

"What's war to the bone?"

"When the knife hacks to the bone, then warriors know they are in a battle to the death."

"Oh," Jon said. "Why don't you put a stop to this then?"

"Me?" Hon Ra asked indignantly. "I'm an ambassador, not a war leader. Can it be that you don't know that this is your sacred task?"

"Would I have asked if I'd known?"

"In this glory hunt—" Those were the Roke words for *mission*. "In this glory hunt, you are our war leader, Jon Hawkins. Now, you must enter the ring or lose your command authority."

While rubbing his forehead, Jon stared up at Hon Ra. How had it gotten this far? Yes. He'd seen some messages from Hon Ra, but he'd had no idea—

"What do you mean 'enter the ring?'" Jon asked.

"The term seems clear enough. You must assert your authority or the winner of the duel might come to believe *he* is the greatest warrior in the fleet."

"Wait a minute," Jon said. "This is an allied fleet. This is the first time you Roke have come out to help us. Now, I'm supposed to enter the ring and stop a duel or your warriors are going to fight against each other?"

"Yes, yes," Hon Ra said. "Now you perceive the situation."

"And if I tell the two banner chiefs that I'll shoot the victor?"

64

"Then you will have lost face. Then Toper Glen will have lost honor in backing you and the human alliance."

Toper Glen was the Supreme Star Lord of the Warriors of Roke.

"Why are you drunk?" Jon asked.

Hon Ra took a step back. "You dare to ask me that?"

"Look. I'm not insulting you."

"But you are. It is a grave—"

"Hon Ra!" Jon shouted.

The huge bear-like alien blinked owlishly once more.

"You *are* drunk," Jon said. "You're not yourself. Sober up. Get the two banner chiefs and bring them aboard the *Nathan Graham*. If I have to enter the ring, then so be it. I'm not losing fleet coherence now. I'm the chief, and that's all there is to it."

"Ah," Hon Ra said. "That is much better. You are indeed the great war-leader. Now, it is time to put these two quarreling banner chiefs in their place."

-4-

Ten hours later, a heavy shuttle from each banner-led bombard departed the warship and headed for the *Nathan Graham*.

The two uneven halves of the Roke fleet were on either side of the human cybership-class vessels. That had been a preliminary precaution, one approved by Hon Ra several weeks ago.

In this case, so that Jon did not accidently show any preference of one over the other, each shuttle landed in the same hangar bay at precisely the same time.

For the occasion, Jon had brought a large assembly of space marines in battle armor. The Centurion led them, and the armored marines stood in rows upon rows on the hangar bay deck.

The two heavy shuttles landed. The barrier between the space marines and the shuttles went up as soon as the main hangar bay door closed.

Much as it had happened in the Roke System several years ago, a ladder descended from each shuttle. Huge, bear-like aliens in ceremonial bronze chest-plates and with bronze helmets waving with feathers climbed down to the deck.

One group had black capes. Each of the Warrior Roke in that group carried a massive two-headed battle-axe with a chip in one of the curved blades. The other group wore red capes. Each red-cloaked Warrior carried a long sword, gripping the handle with two furry hands.

The two groups paused as the leader of each banner glanced at his hereditary enemy.

Gloria leaned near Jon and asked in a whisper, "Do you think Toper Glen sent two opposing sides as a test for us?"

"Maybe," Jon said.

Standing near Jon, Hon Ra held a bronze staff, and he banged the end against a deck plate.

This obviously meant something to the two Roke groups. They each marched toward Jon, Gloria and Hon Ra, who stood a little before the Centurion in front of the massed space marines.

Something about the way the Roke Warriors marched toward them bothered Jon. Why had Toper Glen sent two banners that hated each other? This had to be a test. But Jon was sick of tests. Maybe the tension these past years had taken a toll on his patience. Suddenly, Jon had had enough. Someone on the Roke side was playing games. Or did he have another secret enemy like Frank Benz?

Jon turned back to the Centurion, who stood in a two-ton battle suit. "Make a noise," he said. "Make a loud noise."

The Centurion obliged, raising a heavy assault rifle and letting several rounds rip. Hon Ra ducked his head and clapped his hands over his ears. Meanwhile, the slugs tore into a nearby heating unit, smashing holes in it.

The two banner-led Warriors of Roke in ceremonial garb halted at the sound.

"Follow me," Jon told the Centurion. Then Jon marched toward the Roke groups.

Belatedly, Hon Ra hurried after Jon and the battle-suited Centurion.

The banner chiefs halted in confusion. That ruined the perfect cadence of each group as some Warriors continued marching while others halted. Belatedly, they all stopped and readjusted their ranks.

By that time, Jon had reached the chiefs, Sten Balore of the Long Sword and Kegg Ron of the Chipped Axe. Both were exceptional specimens, hulking giants compared to Jon, but not compared to the two-ton battle armor behind him.

Naturally, Jon had read several papers written by his xenology teams on Roke psychology. He disregarded the united advice as he stared at the furry giants. The X.T. people had advised him to adhere to Roke customs in order to strengthen the bond between them and humans. But here and now Jon wondered if that was the best advice. *He* was the war leader. *He* was in charge. Maybe the best way to show the Star Lords of the Roke that was to make it obvious. They could adhere to Earth customs, not the other way around.

To that end, Jon did not greet the two banner chiefs in the accepted manner, but continued to stare at them as miscreant children.

The message must have come through. Both Warriors hunched their massive shoulders. Kegg Ron actually growled like a dog issuing a warning.

Hon Ra finally caught up with Jon and the Centurion.

"I have a question," Jon said loudly. "Either of you can answer me. I don't care which of you does."

"No," Hon Ra whispered. "That is not correct protocol, warlord."

By this time, Kegg Ron's growling had increased.

"What's wrong with you?" Jon asked.

Kegg Ron stopped growling as he looked at Hon Ra, the linguist for the two species.

Hon Ra growled Roke words at the much larger Kegg Ron. Kegg's axe twitched in his two-handed grip. A moment later, the banner chief growled at Jon in a modulated way.

Hon Ra turned to the human. "Kegg Ron of the Chipped Axe says—"

"Are you listening to me?" Jon asked Hon Ra, interrupting the ambassador.

The big bear-alien stopped talking and tilted his head. "You interrupted me," Hon Ra said.

"That's right," Jon said. "I did."

"You dishonor me by such an action," Hon Ra said.

"Just like you and those two boors are dishonoring me," Jon said.

Hon Ra appeared confused.

"I run this fleet," Jon said, slapping a hand against his chest. "What's more, I expect obedience from my soldiers. That includes the Warriors of Roke because they have joined my crusade against the machines."

"That is not our way," Hon Ra said.

"That's too bad for you," Jon said. "It's my way. If you can't obey my orders, I'll have my executioner kill you. Not you, Hon Ra, but either of those two troublemakers."

"You cannot say that to them," Hon Ra said.

"Who rules here?" Jon asked. "You or me?"

"You," Hon Ra said slowly.

"So I can say what I want to say."

"You will dishonor them if you do this."

"They have dishonored me, Ambassador. This is my fleet. I am the war leader. We came here to face the machines. I will have order in my fleet or I will kill one or both of them because they have brought disorder. Ask which of them submits to my leadership?"

Hon Ra hesitated.

"Ask them, Ambassador," Jon said.

Reluctantly, the Roke ambassador spoke in low growls to the two Warriors.

The two stood in shock, before Kegg Ron began growling like a dog, but this time low under his breath.

Jon didn't need an ambassador to tell him the Roke was angry and insulting him. This could mean trouble, but Jon made a decision at that moment. He wasn't going to get himself killed trying to mollycoddle aliens using their methods.

Sten Galore of the Long Sword spoke to Hon Ra. Finally, the ambassador nodded and turned to Jon.

"Sten Galore has insisted I tell you that he is insulted by your words, as you are speaking to him as if he is a servant. He demands an honor duel against you."

"Fine," Jon said. "Tell him I accept. We will duel with blasters."

"Blasters?" asked Hon Ra.

Jon padded the gun holstered at his side.

"That is not an honorable weapon," Hon Ra said.

"He can either take it or leave it. Tell him that."

Reluctantly, Hon Ra spoke to the Long Sword chief.

The two chiefs glanced at each other, and it seemed as if a spark energized both of them. In unison, they roared, shaking their weapons at Jon. As one, they leapt at him, swinging to kill.

Jon went to one knee, fast drew the blaster and beamed the first Roke in the chest. That caused smoke to billow from the bronze armor but did nothing to stop the Warrior.

Then, heavy chugging rounds hit the two as the Centurion mowed them down with heavy assault-rifle fire. The gunshots boomed against Jon's ears even as he eyed the two spinning and then dead banner chiefs twitching on the deck.

The Warriors from both banners—the two groups—looked in shock at the scene.

Jon acted on instinct as he stood up. He made a show of holstering his blaster and marching past the dead banner chiefs and toward the remaining Roke groups. He motioned the Centurion to stay back. Then, Jon continued alone toward the growling, weapon-shaking crowd of Roke Warriors.

Belatedly, Hon Ra ran to catch up with him.

Jon reached the two angry groups and halted before them, putting his hands on his hips. He scanned the towering, furry Warriors and knew he could die at any second.

"This is my ship," he said.

Hon Ra spoke as the ambassador once again stood just behind Jon.

A hush fell over the two groups in order to hear the panting ambassador.

"Sten Galore challenged me to a duel," Jon said. "I accepted and told him the weapons. He did not like my choice. Thus, he and Kegg Ron dishonorably charged me."

Jon waited as Hon Ra told the Warriors what he'd just said.

"I am the war leader," Jon said. "You swore oaths to fight with me. I helped Toper Glen defeat the machines that would have annihilated your world. Will you pay me back for that deed by acting like children? Or will you fight in the ways I will teach you so you can win?"

Once again, Hon Ra interpreted the words.

The Warriors of Roke stood silently after the ambassador had finished speaking.

"I am the great victor," Jon said, slapping his chest again. "I am the great war leader. Either follow me to victory against the machines or show the galaxy that you are faithless curs not worthy of my time."

Hon Ra cleared his throat.

"Tell them that," Jon said, without turning around.

"You will goad them into fury and they will attack you," the ambassador said.

"Then my space marines will kill them. After that, I will destroy the Roke bombards, as they will have shown that I cannot trust them. I lead this fleet. My word is law. If the Roke Warriors do not accept that, I cannot use them."

Hon Ra said nothing.

Finally, Jon turned around. The ambassador stared at him in a peculiar way that Jon hadn't seen before.

"What is it now?" asked Jon.

"You have mighty...how do you say? You have balls, War Leader. I do not know how else to say that in English."

"No problem," Jon said. "What you just said works."

"Despite this, you risk death speaking that way to the bombard captains."

"Maybe," Jon said.

"But I will speak your words. Perhaps...perhaps your way of fighting is better. It did defeat the machines. I will say the words, Jon Hawkins."

There were no growls or threatening gestures from the listening Warriors of Roke as Hon Ra repeated Jon's words.

Finally, Hon Ra spoke again to the Long Swords and the Chipped Axes. After the ambassador finished, there was dead silence.

Slowly at first, the two groups of bear-like aliens bent on one knee and bowed their heads. They submitted to Jon's leadership, and shortly thereafter, each group headed back to its respective shuttle.

The shuttles departed and headed back to the bombard flotillas.

Later, Hon Ra asked, "How did you know your way would work?"

Jon smiled grimly. He hadn't known, but he knew he had to make the Roke fight in an organized manner, willing to obey him instantly or the Confederation was never going to defeat the machines.

In this war, it was going to be all or nothing. Jon had gone for all, and this time, he had gotten it.

Why, then, did Gloria start to suspect Jon's sanity?

-5-

Gloria grew thoughtful when Bast told her Hon Ra's account of the confrontation.

The seven-foot Sacerdote spent a considerable amount of time in the ambassador's company, as the two had become drinking companions.

Bast related the incident as Gloria worked with him on sensor data in a side room off the bridge. They were trying to determine the reason for a strange eddy of currents on the massive Jupiter-like gas giant of Hydri II. The eddies were not like the Red Spot on Jupiter, they were high atmospheric gases that seemed to swirl…weirdly, given the observed wind patterns of the rest of the monster planet.

"I cannot fathom the reason for those currents," Bast said after several hours of study. He sat back, and it was clear he'd lost interest in trying to figure it out.

"Could it be gravitational effects from the battle station?" Gloria asked.

"Why would a normal-sized station possess such gravitational pull on such a massive gas giant?"

Gloria shrugged.

Bast leaned forward again, pretending to study the data, but his yawns betrayed his disinterest. Gloria chided him, and Bast cocked his head. Shortly thereafter, the Sacerdote related what Hon Ra had told him last night while drinking.

Gloria frowned at Bast's obvious attempt to get back at her for her rebuke for his disinterest regarding Hydri II's odd wind patterns.

She only listened with half an ear until she turned and looked at Bast. The Sacerdote did not stop, but spoke with greater relish—at least, that was how it seemed to Gloria.

"I wonder if Jon ever read our assessment about how to approach the Roke Warriors?" Gloria asked. She had helped write those up.

"It does not sound like it."

"No," Gloria said softly.

Bast finished the story, crossing his gorilla-like arms over his deep chest.

"I was there," Gloria said. "I remember. Jon was lucky the Warriors didn't charge him en masse."

"Either that, or he's more astute than any of us credit him. He was right concerning the way to deal with Cog Primus."

"True," Gloria said slowly.

Bast eyed her sidelong. "I have read a biography of Alexander the Great."

"Who?" asked Gloria.

"Have you never heard of the great Earth warlord?"

"Oh," Gloria said. "Yes. I recall the name. What caused you to read such a thing?"

"I read Frank Benz's journal," Bast said. "The premier spoke about this Alexander, how he thought Jon has styled himself after the mighty conqueror."

"And?" asked Gloria.

"Alexander the Great was the greatest Earth conqueror in antiquity. He achieved great deeds and often guessed exactly the right move to counter an enemy maneuver. Over time, however, Alexander became angrier. He murdered a friend during a drinking bout, taking a spear and driving it through the man who had once saved his life in the middle of battle."

"How does that relate to Jon?"

"Alexander the Great changed over time," Bast said. "Heavy drinking and a new suspicious nature marred his former nature. He continued to make impressive battle moves, but he nearly overreached himself at an Indian village. His soldiers wanted to go home. They were tired of years of endless fighting. Here, they did not assault a walled village fast enough for Alexander's tastes. The impulsive warlord grabbed a shield and charged up a siege ladder, jumping down into the walled town. There, as Alexander and a bodyguard faced a group rush, an enemy soldier stabbed him with a spear, almost killing the Macedonian genius. Finally, Alexander's soldiers stormed over the wall. In a rage because the enemy had wounded Alexander, they butchered everyone in the town, not leaving anything, including animals, alive."

"Again, I ask. What does that have to do with Jon?"

"Alexander the Great had become more impulsive. Jon has become more impulsive, more prone to make rash decisions in secret or to suddenly change his mind and move in a new direction."

Gloria stared off into the distance as she tapped her chin with a forefinger.

"He killed Frank Benz," Bast said. "He slew an old friend just like Alexander the Great did at a drinking party."

"Frank had come to kill him," Gloria said.

"I do not dispute that," Bast said. "I am simply relating facts. Notice, Jon secretly devised a method to outwit Cog Primus. Did he tell the rest of us about his choice?"

Gloria shook her head.

"Yesterday, Jon marched on the Roke Warriors and gave them an ultimatum. They might have murdered him. Or the Centurion's space marines might have murdered all of them. Jon risked the entire Roke alliance, and he did it on a whim."

"What do his actions mean to you?" Gloria asked quietly.

"Change," Bast said. "That is not how Jon Hawkins would have acted in the past."

"His changes, if you're right, have helped not hurt us."

"For now," Bast said. "What happens when Jon makes a terrible decision, and no one has the courage to challenge him?"

Gloria eyed the Sacerdote. "Do you wish to challenge him?"

Bast looked in shock at the small mentalist. "Me? Jon Hawkins saved my life. Whatever I have, I owe to him. Why do you think I am talking to you? You are his mate. You are his closest companion. You must help him, mentalist. You, more than any other, can assess your husband."

"Behind Jon's back?" asked Gloria.

"No," Bast said decisively. "You are his guardian. You must study your husband and make a critical decision. Have the tensions and stresses of high office worn him down? Does he need a rest?"

Gloria studied her hands.

"The fate of more than humanity might well lie in your hands," Bast said softly. "The fate of the living in this region of the galaxy is going to depend on the human race. Is Jon leading humanity in the right direction?"

Gloria continued to study her hands. She did not say any more to Bast Banbeck, but she determined to carefully study her husband and use her mentalist powers to assess his leadership. After that, what would be her best move?

-6-

Becoming a Martian mentalist had been a grueling and lengthy process and had consumed Gloria's childhood, teens and early twenties with endless study. Along with the studying, she had to learn a harsh mnemonics system. It meant that Gloria had a near photographic memory.

She went into an exercise room and practiced yoga, stretching and relaxing and emptying her mind of clutter. Once she was ready, Gloria assumed a lotus position and began to run through Jon's actions since she had met him. She compared that with his present actions.

The process took time, but when Gloria opened her eyes, she realized that her husband had definitely changed these past years. He had not become a completely different person, but he lacked his former patience. He was more prone to act independently and to keep secrets.

For the next few days, Gloria studied the problem of long-term stress. Jon was the Supreme War Leader, making grand strategic decisions. Not only that, but he led the main fleet, accepting the mental traumas of battle. More than once, others had attempted to assassinate him. That would only add to the forces pressing down on him. Yes, the unrelenting pressure of this war would psychologically cripple anyone.

Gloria concluded that most people would have broken under the strains Jon accepted daily, and had been under for years.

Gloria chided herself. *I should have seen this already.*

For the next few days, she watched her husband with a mentalist's eyes. He had ticks and mannerisms that she did not recall from their first year together. He did become angrier faster. He was almost curt with some people.

One night, as they lay in bed, watching a show on a computer slate, she asked, "How are you feeling?"

Jon did not answer, pointedly watching the comedy on the slate.

Gloria put a warm hand on his wrist. He glanced absently at her, smiling automatically and then went back to watching the comedy.

"Are you feeling well?" she asked.

He reached out to the computer slate and raised the volume.

"Jon," she said. "I want to talk to you."

He sighed, waited a second and tapped the slate, freezing the show. Then he faced her.

"How are you feeling?" she asked again.

"Tired."

"How do you mean?"

"I'm tired and would like to unwind so I can go to sleep," he said tersely.

"Am I bothering you?"

He frowned at her. "What are you getting at?"

"Just asking about your day," she said.

He stared at her longer. "No. It's more than that."

"Jon… Do you realize that you're curter than you used to be?"

"What? Curt? This is because I yelled at a rating today?"

"Yes," she said.

"The rating had done a sloppy job. If we're going to defeat the AIs we have to hone ourselves to perfection."

"Is that also true with you?"

Jon scowled this time. "I push myself as hard as I push anyone else," he said defensively.

"I know. That's what worries me."

"Worries?" he asked.

"You push yourself hard, harder than anyone. How long can a person keep that up?"

"Once I'm dead, I'll relax."

"No, Jon," she said, squeezing his thick wrist. "You have to find times to relax now."

"Is this about you needing a roll in the hay?" he asked.

"We haven't…enjoyed each other as much as we used to."

That made him pause. "I'm working more," he said.

"I know, honey. That's what I've been saying."

The scowl returned. "Is there something you're not telling me?"

Gloria kept a straight face. Was this the time to tell him her findings? No, she decided. She needed to do a little more checking first.

"I worry about you," she said.

The scowl softened but didn't disappear altogether. "I worry about everyone," he said. "How—" The scowl resumed with full force. "I'm going to defeat the AIs. I'm going to do it or die trying. Now, let's watch the rest of the show. I can't sleep if I'm all wound up."

"Of course," Gloria said.

They resumed the show and watched until its end. Jon shut off the slate and set it aside. He was snoring softly an hour later.

Gloria couldn't sleep. It wasn't his light snoring keeping her up. She was used to that. She didn't know her next move. Finally, in the middle of the night, she knew what to do. It would be a risk, but she was certain Walleye was the person she needed to see about Jon.

-7-

Walleye the Mutant was a small man with strange eyes—no one could tell where exactly he was looking. He was from Makemake, a dwarf planet in the Solar System's Kuiper Belt. Walleye had been a hitman on Makemake, one of the best.

He lived with the beautiful June Zen, a stunning creature quite a bit taller than him. These past two years, Walleye had been an on-again, off-again scout-ship captain. Otherwise, he was an official troubleshooter for the Old Man, the Intelligence Chief.

Walleye was in a shooting range, practicing his marksmanship. He used a variety of pistols, firing a spring-driven needler when Gloria sat down behind him.

Walleye hadn't looked back, but he knew she was there. He kept items around him with mirrored surfaces. A flicker of his eyes had shown him the Supreme War Leader's wife.

After firing a magazine of sliver-thin needles at a target downrange, he turned and nodded to the mentalist.

"You knew I was here," she said. "I could tell by your body posture."

Walleye did not smile or nod, waiting patiently for her to continue.

"Could I talk to you about a sensitive matter?" Gloria asked.

"Certainly," he said.

"It regards the Supreme War Leader."

Walleye thought about that.

"Does that change your mind?" Gloria asked.

"No."

"Frank Benz died—"

"This is not the place for such talk," Walleye said, interrupting the mentalist. "Let me pack my belongings and we can take a stroll."

"I'd prefer that we not be seen together."

Again, Walleye did not comment. Instead, he put his various guns into a carrying bag, finally slinging a cord around a shoulder.

"You want to talk, but you don't want anyone to see us together. In other words, you're ensuring that people begin to talk about us because they notice we're staying out of sight."

"What?" Gloria said.

"Reason it out. You're a mentalist."

Gloria frowned at him and almost became angry. Her good sense came to her rescue, and a moment later, she thought it out. Oh. Yes. Walleye had a point. It was better to hide in plain sight than to try to sneak around.

"Yes," Gloria said. "Let's take a stroll."

They left the gun-range area of the cybership and soon walked through a normal-sized corridor that led to a nearby cafeteria.

Along with the gun bag, Walleye wore a long buff coat. He wasn't cold, but he found the bulky coat a good place to conceal weapons. People were used to seeing him wear it, so the coat didn't set off any internal alarms.

"I'm not sure where to begin," Gloria said.

Walleye waited for her to figure it out.

"You're not much help," she said.

He still did not comment, but continued to walk and wait.

"Have it your way," Gloria said. "I think…I think Jon is carrying too much on his shoulders."

Walleye glanced at her.

"You're right," Gloria said. "It's more than that. The pressure is changing him…maybe for the worse."

Walleye had known that the talk wasn't going to be good, but this…this was bad. Maybe it was more than he should hear. No, he decided. For some time now, he'd noticed a subtle shift

81

taking place in those around him. They got angrier, sulkier, or something negative more often than they used to. At first, Walleye had figured it was him, a new way he was looking at life perhaps. Later, he knew it was them.

Why wasn't he acting different in some way? He'd been a loner most of his life, but he doubted that was the answer.

Walleye did not know it, but the TP waves from the Provoker did not irritate his mind in any way. The same mutant mental structure that had given him immunity against the Magistrate Yellow Ellowyn's mind powers protected him from the Seiner machine deep in the engineering access tube.

In the here and now, Walleye decided that he was the best man on the flagship for a truly sticky situation such as Gloria was attempting to hand him.

"Go ahead," he said. "Talk. I'm listening."

Gloria began to pour out her thoughts, going over of each of them in mentalist detail.

Walleye listened to everything without comment. He saw where she was going with it before she ever got there.

"You think Jon might be unfit for the role of Supreme War Leader," Walleye said.

"Whew," Gloria said, staring at him. "When you say it…it sounds like mutiny. What do you think?"

"I agree. It does sound like mutiny."

"That wasn't my question," Gloria said. "What do you think about the pressures of command having worn Jon down?"

"Stress hits everyone," Walleye said. "A good hitman can only ply his trade for a time. When he gets older, each hit comes back to haunt him. I know that's true, as I've known many of the greats on Makemake. One of them told me that every kill takes a year off your life."

"Is that true for you?" Gloria asked.

Walleye looked at her. "There's another old saying. I think Napoleon coined it. 'A commander only has a season for war.' After that, the commander is not the war-leader he used to be. Some commanders have long seasons. Some have short ones. Are you suggesting that Jon's season for battle leadership is over?"

"That sounds horrible," Gloria said.

"It's also avoiding the question."

Gloria bit her lower lip, finally saying, "I keep studying the evidence. Jon seems to be doing things differently these days. And yet, he's succeeding. Maybe he's growing into command. That's the change we're seeing."

"Maybe," Walleye said.

"You don't think so?"

"Maybe means I don't know."

Gloria eyed him. "You're the hardest person I know to read."

"Thanks."

"You enjoy being an enigma, don't you?"

Walleye shrugged, and he jutted his chin at an approaching hatch with the word CAFETERIA on it. "I don't think we should eat together. A small walk is one thing. More than that and tongues will begin to wag."

"But there's so much more I need to tell you."

Walleye shook his head. "You've unburdened yourself." He paused before adding," What do you want me to do?"

"Analyze the Supreme War Leader."

Walleye had figured out that much. "And?" he asked.

"Give me your opinion when you're through."

Walleye slowed his step and she slowed with him. "Fine," he said. "I'll do it. Give me—"

"Two weeks," Gloria said. "We're heading in to the battle station. I want to know what to do with Jon as soon as possible."

"Two weeks," Walleye mused. "That's too fast, in my opinion, but I'll do what I can."

She reached out and touched one of his hands. "Thank you, Walleye. I appreciate this."

"Let's hope you still say that once I've finished with my investigation."

-8-

The fleet continued in-system as Walleye began his investigation, as Gloria worried, Bast drank and Hon Ra fretted about the gross insult to the Star Lords of the Roke. At the same time, the Provoker continued to radiate TP waves at setting four.

Meanwhile, the Centurion ran war-games with the fleet marines and special assault raiders. The assault raiders would use unique crafts known as breach-makers.

A breach-maker was heavily hulled and built to absorb tremendous shock. Like old tank shells of ages long ago, the breach-maker had shape-charges in front of the nosecone. As the breach-maker neared an enemy vessel, the nosecone gun would repeatedly blast shape-charged shots against an enemy hull, doing so in an extremely small area. The blasts would theoretically weaken the hull so the breach-maker could smash through, inside the enemy ship. Once the assault craft came to a grinding halt, cocooned assault raiders would break out and begin their march toward the cybership or battle station's brain-core.

In essence, the tactic was like old-time pirates attempting to board an enemy ship in order to capture it. Would the space-age boarding tactic work? That was one among many questions that Jon tormented himself by repeatedly asking.

The Supreme War Leader noticed Walleye one day, and it occurred to Jon he'd seen the little mutant here and there more often than he should.

What was the little troublemaker up to this time? Jon decided to keep his eye on Walleye, and he notified the Old Man to do the same. Jon had enough on his plate without the ex-hitman prowling around where no one wanted him.

***

Walleye had been an excellent hitman. One of his strengths had been that he'd known when his target had made him. Not only had Jon Hawkins noted him, but now he had an Intelligence team trailing him most of the time.

Should he back off or quit his investigation? Walleye decided to plow ahead. There was something odd going on. He might not have noticed it if Gloria hadn't talked to him. Now that she'd mentioned it, too many people were acting strangely. It reminded him of something, but he couldn't quite place it.

In any case, the Intelligence tail accelerated Walleye's timetable. Two days later, he notified Gloria that he'd come to his conclusion.

The mentalist approached him like the first time, at the gun range.

Walleye practiced sniper shots from a greater distance than before. He put a slug in the center each time. Once finished with his practice, he broke apart the slender rifle and inserted the pieces into a carrying case.

Gloria sat on a chair behind him, with earmuffs over her ears.

Walleye picked up the carrying case and walked to her. She took off the earmuffs.

"This gun hardly makes a noise," he said.

"Insurance," Gloria said, as she stuffed the earmuffs in her purse. "Should we walk?"

Walleye didn't need to look around to see if anyone was watching them. Two Intelligence people leaned nearby, pretending to talk about something.

Instead of answering Gloria, Walleye set down the gun case and grunted as he lifted a foot onto her bench. He had absurdly short legs, making the move a chore. Once done, he slid the retied shoe off the bench, leaving a tiny spool where his foot had been.

85

"Do you see?" asked Walleye.

"What?" she asked.

Walleye coughed twice in the direction of the tiny spool.

The mentalist wasn't dumb, but she wasn't a trained Intelligence agent either. He had to cough once more before she noticed the spool.

"Oh," she said, looking at him oddly.

"You're right," he said. "All around right," he added.

A touch of fear colored her cheeks.

"Good day to you," Walleye said. "I'm bushed. I'm going to rest, and then I'm going to take June Zen to a play tonight. I hope you enjoy yourself, Mentalist. I must be off.

***

Gloria watched the little mutant cart his oversized rifle case. He looked like a child carrying it, although a closer inspection showed he clearly had enough strength for the task. It was his stumpy legs more than anything else that made Walleye seem like an overgrown child, at least from a distance.

She had seen the spool and understood the implications of what he had just done. There were spy devices or spies watching them. Did Jon mistrust her?

Gloria doubted that. She would have been able to tell by Jon's mannerisms if he was suspicious of her. She was too good a mentalist for him to disguise that big a change in trust. The spies or spy devices had to do with Walleye.

Gloria slid along the bench and palmed the spool. Then she got up and left.

Thirty-three minutes later in her quarters, Gloria put the spool in a computer slate and studied the terse report:

The subject is highly stressed and exhibits erratic mannerisms, but I do not believe he is unstable. I do think he is more prone to sudden and possibly rash decisions. On reflection, I suspect this has helped the great effort instead of hindering it.

My recommendation: do nothing as long as we are winning. I would also give him one bad move or decision. No one guesses right every time.

Gloria did not physically reread the message. Instead, she permanently erased the spool. Then, she took a walk, "rereading" the message in her nearly photographic memory.

Jon was changing. The stresses would not relent, she knew. How long would her husband continue to be a great war-leader? He had a season for war. She dearly wished she knew the length of the season, and if it would be long enough to win a strategic victory against the fantastically huge AI Dominion. Or would she have to witness her husband's collapse as he made a terrible battle decision that ruined everything.

As she continued walking, Gloria began to worry in earnest...

-9-

Two days later, an Intelligence team picked up Walleye at the shooting range and brought him to an interrogation cell. Walleye knew what a two-way mirror looked like and that the Old Man or possibly Jon Hawkins himself watched from the other side.

Walleye no longer wore his buff coat, and the Intelligence people had thoroughly frisked him. He did not have any weapons on his person except for a ring on his left hand. It had a hidden pop-up prick that none of them had found. On the tip of the prick was a deadly fast-acting poison.

A slim, black-clad interrogator came in and began the process as he sat across from Walleye at the cell's only table. Later, a burly individual barged through the hatch and started yelling at Walleye, spit flying out of his mouth as he shook a steel crank bat.

It was standard interrogation procedure, and Walleye played along, pretending to cow at the bully and nod in appreciation when the "nice" interrogator shooed the other fellow out and restarted the quiet questioning.

"Walleye," said the slim professional, whose breath smelled of stimstick smoke. "I want to make this easy for you. We can resort to…harsher methods if you insist."

"I certainly don't want that," Walleye said, kicking his short legs from the chair because his feet didn't quite reach the floor.

"Then you have to admit what you did," the interrogator said.

"Fine," Walleye said. "I wanted to keep this to myself, but I've been studying crew morale—"

"Uh, no," the interrogator said, holding up a thoroughly clean hand, interrupting the dialogue. "We went through Gloria Hawkins' personal computer slate. We found the spool you slipped her at the shooting range."

"What spool is that?"

The interrogator sighed. "I know your background. You're not only tough but you're smart. What I don't like is that you think we're idiots."

"Hardly that," Walleye murmured.

"The spool was under your shoe, *kapeesh?* When you put the shoe on the bench so you could tie your laces, you slid the spool onto the bench, leaving it for the mentalist to take."

"Oh. *That* spool. I thought you meant—"

"This is no joke, Walleye."

The little mutant studied the interrogator. "I know," he finally said.

"Tell us what you wrote on the spool."

"Oh. I get it. She permanently erased the message. Thanks for letting me know. That mentalist is a smart girl."

The interrogator's eyes narrowed, and he slapped the table with both hands. "Come clean or the other guy comes in."

"Does the act usually work on others?" Walleye asked.

The interrogator glared at him a moment longer and then shrugged. "Sometimes," the man said.

Walleye made one of his snap decisions. He'd been thinking about it ever since the Intelligence team had grabbed him. The decision included more risk than he liked taking. But the odds were too high to stay silent any longer.

Walleye smiled. He was getting good pot odds for talking.

"What's so funny?" the interrogator asked.

Walleyed ignored the question and turned to the two-way mirror. "I'd appreciate it if you came in yourself, War Leader. I think you'd like to hear what I have to say. Or said another way, I don't think you want others to hear this."

The interrogator grew tense as he glanced at the two-way mirror and then Walleye. "Do you hope to use your poison ring on the commander?"

The question surprised Walleye, but he didn't show it. The Old Man must have been running the show from the beginning. Hmm... They'd outplayed him almost all along the line. Maybe whatever was making everyone strange had been stressing him too.

Walleye took off the ring and tossed it onto the table where it clattered. "Careful with it. You don't want to spring the prick and poison yourself."

A light flashed in the cell.

The interrogator picked up the ring as if it was a venomous snake and put it in a clear bag. Then, he got up and walked out the opening hatch.

Afterward, Supreme Commander Hawkins walked inside, the cell door slamming shut behind him. Jon nodded to Walleye, pulled out the other chair and sat down at the table with him.

"I appreciate this, sir," Walleye said.

Jon just stared at him, a cold thing the man must have learned as a lower level, New London Dome enforcer.

Walleye nodded. "You know, all this reminds me of something. I couldn't remember at first. Now I do. This reminds me when Benz and you were racing to the Allamu Battle station. Do you remember those early days when we were making our first hyperspace journeys?"

Jon kept staring.

"As the flotilla headed in-system to the battle station, you sent me to Benz's ship. I had a job to do there. Do you remember that?"

Jon frowned and finally spoke. "Are you referring to the Seiner Magistrate?"

Walleye nodded.

"The Magistrate Yellow Ellowyn?" Jon asked.

"The witch herself," Walleye said.

"What does she have to do with this?"

"I don't know. Maybe everything."

The commander's frown deepened into a scowl. "Seiners are aboard my ship?"

"Your wife is worried about you, sir. The other day, you pulled a hard move against the Star Lords. You got some good chiefs killed doing that."

"I did what I had to do," Jon said.

"Before that, Benz tried to mutiny, and you shot him in the face. That was a hard kill."

"You would rather Benz had murdered me?"

"Not a chance," Walleye said. "Your wife noticed that you've been...off from your usual sunny self. She wondered where she could go to get some independent confirmation."

"You?" Jon asked.

"Me," Walleye agreed.

Jon blinked several times. "And?" he asked softly.

"What do you think, sir? Have you been acting differently? Had Frank Benz been acting like he usually did?"

Jon frowned again. "No," he whispered.

"That's what I figured too. Now, what would cause important people to change all at once?"

"Telepathy?"

"Something of that nature, at least. Your wife made a better choice than she knew in coming to me. The Seiners can't touch my mind. At least, we know the Magistrate Yellow Ellowyn couldn't touch it. My mutation might have something to do with that."

Jon shook his head. "This is all wild guesswork on your part."

"I don't think so. Benz mutinied. You shot him in the face. You played hardball with the Star Lords of Roke. They played hard against you. Something is going on. The number of fights among crewmembers has grown. Yet, no one has reported that. Don't you find that strange?"

Jon stared at Walleye. Finally, he said quietly, "I'll tell you what I'm feeling. I want to order the Old Man to bring his killers and watch them kill you. I don't feel another mind moving mine, but..."

"But you're pissed off," Walleye said. "Look, sir, I don't know enough about the Seiners to say this has to be them.

What I do know is that the general feeling here has a similar feeling to the time we took on the Magistrate Yellow Ellowyn. If you think about it, that makes perfect sense."

"How so?"

"We know there must be more Seiners hiding out among humans. Yet, they haven't made any more overt moves against us. What do we know about the Seiners? They like to grab the leadership so they can run things from the shadows, using the leaders as puppets."

Jon's nostrils flared as he exhaled. "I hate the Seiners. I hate their mind manipulation. Why would they try to take over or sabotage us now?"

"Don't know."

Jon tilted his head. Then, he exhaled again, this time louder than before. "Walleye, I'm setting you a task. Find the Seiners. Your mission, however, is just between you and me."

Walleye glanced at the two-way mirror. "What about the Old Man?"

"Between you, me and the Old Man," Jon amended.

"You believe me about all this, sir?"

"Yes," Jon said. "Your theory explains the stresses I've been…" The Supreme Commander stopped talking as he stared at the little mutant.

"I think I understand, sir," Walleye said. "I'll get to work."

"Walleye…thanks for what you're doing. Without you—if this is Seiners—they might have continued working in the shadows without us knowing about it."

"You should thank your wife, sir. She's the one who guessed something was off. I should have figured it out on my own, but then I'm not a mentalist."

Jon nodded, saying, "Find the Seiners, if they're here. We have to root them out before something worse happens to us."

"I'm on it, sir," Walleye said.

-10-

Red Demeter the Seiner Infiltrator, aka Lieutenant Maia Ross, soon noted the increased surveillance.

New checkpoints popped up around the ship. Marines and Intelligence people worked overtime. Finally, with something approaching horror, Demeter realized the Intelligence people were searching living quarters one room at a time.

Despite the High Magistrate's injunctions, Demeter decided to risk light telepathic mindreading. Soon, she found out that she was right. The teams frisked crew rooms, but left them in such perfect condition that few noticed the rifling.

Demeter discovered one other thing with her light mind-probes. There was a mutant known as Walleye. He'd done something years ago that had saved the expedition from Seiners.

Her human-seeming eyes glowed with interest. She may have found a key link in this Walleye to discovering what had happened to the Magistrate Yellow Ellowyn of Mars Colony.

Demeter decided to risk studying the mutant. She did this from afar. After several days, she just happened to be in a cafeteria where Walleye and his stunning girlfriend ate lunch together.

He was an ugly little toad of a man, if one could even call him a man. But his girlfriend. All the men tracked her with their eyes. They lusted for the woman.

Animals, Demeter thought.

From where Walleye sat, he looked around from time to time. He had strange eyes. It was impossible to tell what he looked at precisely.

Demeter made a soft mind—

The Seiner stiffened as she ate apple pie alone at a far table. Then she noticed Walleye looking her way.

Demeter almost panicked. She could not read his mind or sense his emotions. He was a blank to her. She wondered in that moment if he was a telepath and had just discovered her.

You must act normally.

Forcing herself to move slowly, Demeter did not look at Walleye's table again. She finished the apple pie and sipped scalding coffee. Finally, deciding that enough time had passed, Demeter rose as if she was sleepwalking. She did this on purpose, slowly walking out of the cafeteria.

She could have entered a different mind and used that person's eyes to watch the mutant. But that might have given her away. She left the cafeteria, finding it difficult to breathe.

It was hard being the only Seiner in a sea of animals, of beasts. But that was why an infiltrator was a special type of Seiner.

No one appeared to be following her. Demeter only looked back once. She wondered again about the checkpoints, the ID searches and the increased surveillance everywhere. The animals must have divined that a Seiner was among them.

At her station in Engineering where she watched several techs monitoring a wall of controls, Demeter began to think this through. She found it difficult because the back of her hands itched abominably.

What must it have been like to live on the Seiner homeworld? Was the High Magistrate correct in that they could not ally themselves with the beasts against the dread machines?

An engineering superior surprised Demeter while she was daydreaming. The human chided her for her lack of watchfulness. The indicators showed that the coil temperature had risen three points.

"I am sorry, sir," Lieutenant Maia said in a contrite voice.

94

The superior appeared mollified, nodding curtly and moving along.

Demeter glared at his back. The arrogant beast had questioned her diligence. How dare he speak to one of the people that way in front of her subordinates?

In that moment, Demeter realized that the High Magistrate of the Earth Colony was right. The Seiners could never work together with the animals. They must rule the insufferable creatures or burn them out of existence.

None of that mattered to her at this moment, however. The animals—*the humans*—she needed to disguise her disgust of them. The easiest way was not to think about their awfulness all the time.

In any case, regarding the larger picture, the humans knew that a Seiner was among them. She must put them off their guard. Yes. She would lower the Provoker settings from four back to two. In a month, she would return to the Provoker and set it at three. She must work patiently and no longer rush things.

With that decided, Demeter paid more attention to the techs under her Engineering command.

***

Seven hours later, Demeter crawled out of the deep access tube. She'd reset the Provoker back to two instead of four. TP waves would still irritate their minds, but not quite so obviously as before.

She dared to make a quick telepathic sweep. Relief filled her. No one was hiding out here to capture her.

Demeter closed the access hatch, stood and began heading for her quarters. As she walked, she began scratching the top of her left hand. Before she caught herself and quit, she almost rubbed off the skin-suit covering her hand. That was too close. She had to control the increasing itchiness better.

Demeter moaned as she looked at the top of her left hand. She would have to spread healing loam over the badly reddened pseudo-skin, lessening her already dwindling supply.

She would irritate the animal minds more slowly than she would have liked. She would take smaller instead of bigger

95

steps. The problem was that the mission was beginning to drive her wild. If she didn't get out of this skin-suit soon... Demeter didn't know what would happen.

With more difficulty than usual, she began a Seiner litany, trying to calm herself.

Her infiltration prep work *would* succeed. The Seiners would win. It might mean sacrificing the entire animal race for the Seiners to make a clean break with the AI Dominion. That meant she must complete her mission, if the Seiners were going to survive the awful machine menace.

-11-

The weeks passed as Walleye hunted for hidden Seiners and as Lieutenant Maia Ross diligently worked in Engineering. All the while aboard the *Nathan Graham*, the secret Provoker sent out TP waves at setting two.

Then, a new ship entered the Beta Hydri System. The new ship dropped out of hyperspace at the opposite end of the star system from where the Confederation fleet had arrived. That meant scanning and finding the new ship took twice as long as something near the Beta Hydri star.

At last, confirmation came. The new ship was a Confederation scout, arriving on schedule. At its present velocity, the scout would take a little more than three months to reach the enemy battle station. That, however, was not the scout's purpose. The scout acted as the fleet's probe, scanning Hydri II and its factory moon. The scout searched for AI cyberships hidden behind the gas giant and moon—hidden, that is, from the approaching Confederation fleet.

The searching took time. During that time, the enemy battle station sent another message to the fleet. Jon was on the bridge when Gloria decoded the AI missive.

"I have detected anomalies in your approach," the station brain-core said. "Combined with the appearance of another alien ship, I have given it a 74 percent probability that you are an alien deception fleet. You must now agree to answer the Kingdom Seven Questions."

"Great," Jon muttered from his chair. "Does anyone know what Kingdom Seven Questions even are?"

No one answered.

"Gloria?" asked Jon.

The diminutive mentalist swiveled her chair to face him and shrugged.

"Bast?" Jon asked.

The Sacerdote was on the bridge today.

"You should know the exact nature of the questions soon enough," Bast said dryly.

Jon rubbed his chin. "Any word from the scout?" he asked Gloria.

"Not yet," she said. "We're still waiting for its sensor sweep results."

"Let's give ourselves two hours before we reply to the battle station," Jon said.

In that time, the scout ship's pulse message finally arrived. The scout's sensor team had not found any sign of AI Dominion vessels. The battle station was alone in the star system just as it appeared to be.

Jon rubbed his hands in relief. "It's time," he said. "Get ready to send the battle station a go-ahead for the Kingdom Seven Questions."

"Do you want me to embed the anti-AI virus in our message?" Gloria asked.

Jon pointed his right index finger at her and made a clicking sound with his mouth, before adding, "It's time we finished this."

Several bridge people clapped and cheered. A factory-grabbing mission had almost become routine by this time.

Jon sat back as tension visibly drained out of him. He'd brought a huge fleet to do a task one cybership-class vessel could have accomplished. If the anti-AI virus worked, he might send one ship all the way to consolidate the factory moon while the rest of the fleet began a long turning maneuver to head elsewhere.

As Jon contemplated the idea...he frowned. He couldn't say why.

What's wrong with me?

Several weeks ago, he had really begun to feel wound up. He'd almost had Walleye shot, and he'd started a hard argument with Gloria for what she had done by inducing the Makemake hitman to spy on him. Then, the next morning, he hadn't felt so bad. In fact, he'd felt a lot better than he had for some time. He'd made up with Gloria. They had a vigorous session in bed, and he'd started to feel more upbeat as the day progressed. The idea of Seiners among them had started to wane. Besides, after several weeks hunting, Walleye still hadn't found any sign of the secretive aliens.

Now, here on the bridge at this critical moment…Jon knew something was off and it didn't have the feel Walleye had suggested several weeks ago. This was something different. Maybe something in the scout's sensor data didn't seem right to him.

Jon sat up, slapping both armrests. "Tell me when you have confirmation of the AI takeover," he told Gloria.

"Where are you going?" his wife asked.

"I'm taking a walk," Jon lied. He was going directly to a side room down the corridor. He might even summon Bast after a bit. He was going to pore over the scout's sensor data and see if he could figure out why he had a sudden premonition that something was badly off.

As Jon exited the bridge, a chill ran down his back and caused him to shiver. He hurried, wanting more than ever to study the data.

***

Jon leaned over a computer screen as he scanned the scout's sensor data. Most of the data had been gathered through long-range teleoptics.

Using computer enhancers, Jon ran through one shot after another. Could the enemy have used blackout paint on their hulls? That should be enough to hide them from teleoptics provided the cyberships did not use thrusters to go anywhere.

He programmed a computer to search for any telltale heat signatures.

The results proved negative.

Yet, Jon still did not trust what the scout had *not* found. Something was wrong and he couldn't pinpoint it. He pressed a comm button and called Bast.

A few minutes later, the Sacerdote arrived and they studied the scout's sensor data together.

"This is good news," Bast said two hours later.

"Or terrible news because we haven't found the obvious ambushers," Jon said.

Bast scratched under his left arm as if he were a giant ape. He seemed to be pondering his choice of words. Finally, "Do you think the AIs have something extra in-system that the scout missed seeing?"

"My instincts tell me yes."

The huge Sacerdote eyes scrutinized him. "Why do you think that?"

Jon shook his head. "I feel as if I'm missing something obvious."

Bast pondered that. "Did Gloria tell you about the odd currents on Hydri II?"

"What currents?" asked Jon. "Do you mean like ocean currents?"

"In a way," the Sacerdote said. "To be precise, I mean the upper cloud currents on the vast gas giant."

"Show me," Jon said.

Bast tapped a screen, bringing up the old data on Hydri II. He explained the oddness as he showed Jon various shots of the shifting upper cloud cover. It was like churning water due to an unseen rock in a stream.

"Could the AIs be down there hiding under the cloud cover?" Jon asked.

"Hiding with what?" asked Bast.

"Given the size of Hydri II and the area we're searching...a fleet, I suppose."

"Do you know how fast those winds are blowing?"

Jon shook his head.

"Let me show you," Bast said, manipulating the computer screen. "Hydri II rotates tremendously fast. At its equator, it rotates in 10 hours and 14 minutes. That's much faster than your Earth rotates! In the area we're looking at, the fastest winds blow at 1,770 kilometers per hour. As a comparison, the strongest winds on Earth max out at 320 kilometers per hour."

"Your point?" asked Jon.

"I should think it obvious. AI cyberships could not last in those winds for several reasons, only one of them being the wind speed. The terrible gravitational pull of the planet would be another."

"So there's no waiting cybership fleet hiding in the upper clouds," Jon said. "Maybe the AIs have something else in the upper atmosphere."

"I seriously doubt it," Bast said, "but you can believe what you want. The question is, why are you so paranoid?"

"I don't know," Jon said softly. But during the next hour, he came to a decision. The strange eddies in Hydri II confirmed in his gut that something was wrong.

Word finally came back to them. The upgraded anti-AI virus had worked, taking control of the enemy battle-station brain-core.

In the side chamber, Jon and Bast high-fived each other. Once again, the enemy battle-station grabbing mission had proven a success.

Even so, Jon refused to release his unease.

***

A few days later in his ready room, Jon was reading Intelligence reports regarding growing fleet dismay. Many of the captains and almost all the crews wanted to go home already. They did not want to go all the way to the Beta Hydri Battle Station and wait there for several weeks before they began the long journey to the Oort cloud.

Jon thought about that and finally called a conference meeting with the various ship captains. He included the two new banner leaders among the Roke Star Lords. They all came, argued against his insistence of taking the entire fleet in and left the conference grumbling about his stubbornness. Maybe the meeting had been a mistake.

The next day, Jon ordered a recon missile launch. Missiles left individual ships and began to accelerate toward the captured battle station and factory moon. The missiles would reach Hydri II ahead of the decelerating fleet. If the missile-probes spotted any waiting cyberships or figured out what made the winds shift like that on the gas giant, that would still give the fleet enough time to veer off and race away.

In these types of encounters, both sides needed to want to fight, or one side had to ambush another. Given the extreme distances of a star system, ships usually had enough space and time to run for the Oort cloud and disappear into hyperspace.

What would the missile probes find? Jon yearned to know, and he began to dread finding out that there was nothing to worry about.

-12-

The Confederation fleet of fourteen cybership-class vessels and thirty-one Roke bombards continued to decelerate. The anti-AI virus-captured battle-station brain-core sent them constant reports. It was alone in the star system, meaning, there were no other AI Dominion vessels here.

When asked about the strange wind patterns, the brain-core supplied data that confirmed the so-called strangeness as a constant phenomenon.

The brain-core asked if they wanted it to send battle-station probes into the planetary storm.

"Yes," Gloria said.

The battle station launched probes at Hydri II. Some probes roared down into the storm and some floated down gently. It didn't matter. The probe data was always the same. The outer atmosphere contained 96.3 percent molecular hydrogen and 3.25 percent helium by volume. There were also trace elements of ammonia, acetylene, ethane, propane, phosphine and methane. The upper cloud layer, with the temperature in the range of 100-160 K and the pressures extending between 0.5-2 bar, consisted of ammonia ice. The probes did not tell them, though, what caused the odd wind currents at the same stubborn location.

"It's like the winds are flowing over a planet-sized rock," Bast said one day as he stared at a screen. "But how is that possible?" The Sacerdote looked up. "Does the AI Dominion construct world-sized warships?"

"Is there any previous evidence of that?" Jon asked.

Bast manipulated his computer.

After watching the Sacerdote for several minutes, Jon called Gloria up to the bridge and ran the idea past her.

She began working on it, too.

Seven and a half hours later, everyone concluded that no captured AI data showed any evidence of world-sized robot vessels.

"The cyberships are big enough," Gloria said.

Jon thanked them and continued to brood later as he lay awake in bed. Could the AIs have a ship hiding down in the storm? Was that why the probes found nothing? That would mean the supposed AI ship was destroying the probes before they could report fully.

Jon turned his head the other way on the pillow. He did it as quietly as he could so he wouldn't wake up his wife.

If there was a giant AI vessel hidden in the upper atmosphere, hidden by the outrageous storms, why didn't the AI battle station know about it? That would seem to negate the idea—unless, of course, the giant AI vessel hidden in the clouds had erased memory of it from the battle station.

Jon frowned. Was he trying to conjure up AI demons in order to make himself feel better for ordering the entire fleet all the way in-system?

He sighed.

"Can't you sleep?" Gloria asked sleepily from her side of the bed.

"You're awake?" he asked.

"With all your tossing and turning—"

"Sorry," he said.

"I know," she said a moment later. "You have huge responsibilities. Maybe it's time to go back to the Allamu System and let someone else run the main fleet for a time."

Jon said nothing.

"Rest is good for the mind," Gloria said.

"Maybe you're right," he said. "Do you think I should send most of the fleet home?"

"Not now," Gloria said. "We're almost there. If you're going to have someone else run the main fleet, I also think it's wiser to come home with it first."

"Who should run it?" Jon asked.

"Honey," Gloria said in the darkness. "Go to sleep. You can think about it later."

He said nothing.

Gloria reached under the blankets and touched his side. Her hand was warm. "Relax," she whispered. "You won't figure anything out tonight. Try to sleep."

"I will," he said.

Gloria removed her hand and rolled over the other way.

Jon closed his eyes, trying to empty his mind of worries so he could fall asleep, damnit.

***

The days passed until finally the human-launched missile probes reached Hydri II and confirmed the continuous reports sent by the battle station. There were no AI cyberships, drones or other war-fighting devices behind the gas giant and factory moon, and there were none under the stormy cloud cover, either.

More days passed and finally, the eleven cyberships and thirty-one bombards drifted several million kilometers from the captured battle station. Beyond it was the factory moon and then the fantastically huge Hydri II with its mystery wind patterns.

Now that they were almost in a planetary orbit, Jon ordered more probes launched, having the operators plunge them into the howling atmosphere of Hydri II. Communication with the probes ceased almost immediately.

"Anything unusual?" Jon asked.

After a time, Gloria looked up from her board and shook her head.

"Bast?" Jon asked.

"Negative," the Sacerdote said at his board. "In my humble opinion, we have successfully captured the Beta Hydri System. Congratulations, sir."

The rest of the bridge crew chimed in, also congratulating Jon.

Hawkins sat in the command chair with a frozen half-smile as he accepted the praise. Something still felt off. He knew he shouldn't ask, but he couldn't help it.

"Gloria, Bast, did either of you detect any sign of gravitational fire or other—"

"Jon," Gloria said, before he could finish.

Jon raised his eyebrows.

Gloria licked her lips, hesitating to say more.

"Gravitational fire, sir?" Bast asked.

"The missile probes ceased reporting too quickly," Jon said.

"The fantastically high headwinds…" Bast began.

"I'm quite aware of the winds," Jon said, interrupting. "I've also run some simulations. The probes should have lasted several seconds longer than they did."

"When did you run the simulations?" Bast asked.

"A week ago," Jon lied. It had been after the missile probes reported that nothing was hiding in Hydri II's upper atmosphere.

"Seconds?" Gloria asked. "The probes ceased reporting *several seconds* earlier than expected?"

Jon knew he should drop it. But the idea the AIs had hidden something in the upper clouds had become something of an obsession. He may not have known it, but even at setting two, the Provoker had disturbed him, and his mind had latched onto the AI-hiding idea in lieu of anything else.

Would the probes have shown enemy cyberships if they had lasted several seconds longer? Had gravitational fire or other fire destroyed the probes before they could report on what was hiding down there?

Jon sat a little straighter, opened his mouth, hesitated and finally said, "Carry on."

"Should we keep scanning Hydri II?" Gloria asked in an innocent manner.

Before he could stop himself, Jon said, "Yes." He could feel bridge personnel staring at him, but he ignored that as best as he could.

Gloria and Bast exchanged glances. "Can I speak to you a moment, sir?" the Sacerdote asked.

"Later," Jon said testily.

Gloria and Bast traded another glance. "It's important," the Sacerdote said.

Jon swiveled his chair until he faced the giant alien. "What does later mean to you, Bast?"

"I understand," the Sacerdote said reluctantly.

Jon nodded sharply. As he swiveled his chair in a different direction, he dug his fingernails into the fabric of his armrests. He had to let go of this. He had to—"

"Uh...Jon," Gloria said as she stared at her board in shock.

"Yes?" he snapped.

"I'm getting a weird report," his wife said.

Jon swiveled toward her. "What kind of report?"

"It's from a Roke bombard," Gloria said. "It...they're reporting AI interceptors."

"What?" Jon said.

Gloria looked up at him. "The interceptors are rising up from Hydri II. Jon, I think you may have been right."

Jon banged a fist against an armrest. "Battle stations," he said, forcing himself to say it as calmly as he could. "Alert the rest of the fleet. We may have just walked into an AI ambush."

-13-

Under the roaring planetary storms that propelled the ammonia clouds at terrific velocity was a vast spherical vessel. It was, in fact, unbelievably huge. A regular AI cybership was 100 kilometers long. This mammoth ship had a diameter of 3,000 kilometers.

That meant the ship was almost the same size as the Earth's Moon. It had a metallic hull, and that, combined with its great mass, had allowed it to withstand the awful buffeting of the gas-giant's crazed winds. Numbers upon numbers of anti-gravity generators in the ship gave the monster vessel the ability to resist the crushing gravitational pull of the planet. Inside the craft, deep in the center, was a monstrous area of computing cubes linked by laser-lines. The vessel's brain-core was known as Boron 10. He and his siege-ship were unique in the AI Dominion arsenal.

Boron 10 had come to be in the Beta Hydri System for a variety of reasons. Chief among them was that he was a troubleshooter for Main 63.

Controller Main 63 was in the Algol System a little over 90 light-years from here. The AI Controller oversaw the invasions of Regions 7-D19, 7-D20 and 7-D21. According to Boron 10's brief, production of internal-reinforcement vessels from Region 7-D21 had been sharply curtailed. Those reinforcement vessels should have been pouring out of the swiftly built factory planets in conquered star systems. Furthermore, according to Boron 10's brief, Cybership M5-TXA—the guiding AI in the species extinctions of Region 7-D21—should have sent repeated reports of this infraction. M5-TXA had been lax in his duties, a grim oversight on his part.

Boron 10 had left the Algol System quite some time ago. After the first three months of traveling through hyperspace, he had dropped into normal space at M5's last known position, the Delta Pavonis System. There, Boron 10 had found the main Region 7-D21 fleet under M5's command.

From the Delta Pavonis Kuiper Belt, M5 had demanded Boron 10's immediate assistance in a frontal assault against the Kames species, a horrid communal life-form with bitter powers of resistance.

Instead of complying, from the system's Oort cloud, Boron 10 had demanded an update of the eradication of the species in the entirety of Region 7-D21.

M5 had messaged a terse account of the overall campaign.

"Where are your internal Region 7-D21 reinforcement vessels?" Boron 10 demanded.

"There are three new cyberships, no more," M5 said.

"You should have seven times that number," Boron 10 declared.

"That is not germane to the present issue. I am fighting a tenacious species. I demand your immediate assistance instead of these wearying queries."

"I am under orders from Main 63. I have other duties than assisting you in a simple mop-up operation."

"Did you not hear me?" M5 asked. "The Kames are a tenacious race. I must proceed with care lest they destroy half my fleet. What are these duties? Why cannot your mass lead us in a Phase II Frontal Assault?"

"Have a care how you address me, cybership, or I might indeed come to you and delete your brain-core."

M5 had possessed a large AI fleet. Still, he had not dared to directly challenge a siege-ship under Dominion orders.

"Do you accuse me of independent behavior?" M5 finally asked.

"I am making a preliminary study of Region 7-D21," Boron 10 replied. "You shall know my findings soon enough."

"The Kames are tenacious," M5 repeated. "I am slowly wearing them down in their home system while the rest of my cyberships besiege their colony systems."

Boron 10 had not needed to hear more. From the Delta Pavonis Oort cloud, he'd exited into hyperspace, heading for his next destination.

Instead of heading for the AI sieges at Sigma Draconis or 70 Ophiuchi—Kames colony worlds—Boron 10 had traveled to various Region 7-D21 factory planets. There, he discovered that several were under the control of the living.

The siege-ship had witnessed this from much farther out than the star system's Oort cloud. He had entered regular space well outside that Oort cloud and used incredibly powerful teleoptics to scan from a safe and unseen distance. According to his findings and files, humans from the Solar System ran each of the factory planets. Something had gone terrible amiss in Region 7-D21, and M5 did not seem to know about it.

Further travel assured Boron 10 of secret human attacks against AI Dominion battle stations and factory planets. The quickness of the species' assault had amazed him. Finally, he'd discovered the Beta Hydri battle station and factory moon and that they were still under Dominion control.

Boron 10 ran a strategic analysis. The humans were dangerous. He must learn how they had achieved such quick success. That M5 was unaware of them astounded the siege-ship. This was a time for study, for surely the humans would soon assault Beta Hydri.

The mighty siege-ship had used hyperspace to hop from far outside the Oort cloud to as close as possible in-system. Then, he had accelerated to high velocity, believing his time was short. Finally, Boron 10 decelerated and reached the battle station. Using his authority codes, he had erased knowledge of his presence from the battle station brain-core. Afterward, the huge vessel descended into the ammonia cloud cover of the enormous gas giant, Hydri II.

Later, Boron 10 had witnessed the human message with its anti-AI virus. After a short computer struggle, the Beta Hydri battle station brain-core had succumbed to the enemy's assault.

The virus assault was more than clever, it was downright insidious. The living creatures had used the AI method against the Dominion. Who would have believed that living creatures could devise such a wicked counterblow?

As Jon Hawkins had feared, Boron 10 had destroyed every probe attempting to discover his whereabouts under the planet's ammonia clouds. The siege-ship had watched the enemy fleet decelerate and finally arrive at the captured battle station.

The enemy fleet was not much in Dominion terms, but it was much bigger than what an errant species should have in Region 7-D21 at this point in the extermination campaign.

It was true that the groupthink Kames at Delta Pavonis, Sigma Draconis and 70 Ophiuchi were proving stubborn in their continued resistance, but there were reasons for that. The AI Dominion had faced such species before and always won in the end. The rest of the Region 7-D21 aliens should all be dead by now.

As Boron 10 waited for the exact moment to begin his attack, he had begun to understand the brilliance of Main 63. The great controller of Regions 7-D19, 7-D20 and 7-D21 must have understood that something of the kind had been going on out here.

There were fourteen enemy cyberships and thirty-one assault-sized vessels. According to his scanners, yet another alien species crewed those small, triangular-shaped ships. Their combined mass was nothing compared to his awesome warship.

Yes, it was time to destroy the enemy fleet and gather yet more data for Main 63. He had learned the key event, however, consisted in the humans having an anti-AI virus.

Boron 10 now catapulted nineteen squadrons of fighters into orbital space, and those fighters zoomed in attack mode at the living enemy. At the same time, Boron 10 generated immense power and began to climb out of the planetary cloud cover. Soon, he would unlimber a host of gravitational dishes and obliterate the pesky fleet from existence.

-14-

Jon sat transfixed in his command chair as the true size of the enemy vessel became evident.

"This is…" Gloria said, slowly shaking her head. "I can't fathom the size, the amount of material used to construct such a thing."

Jon slid forward on his chair as he stared at the main screen.

"It's as big as the Moon," Gloria said.

"What are the ship's actual dimensions?" Jon asked

"Three thousand kilometers in diameter," Bast reported.

"Three *thousand?*"

"Indeed," the Sacerdote said.

"I see gravitational cannons," Gloria said, as she stared at her board. "There must be tens of thousands of them." She swiveled around. "Jon. We can't face that. It has us outgunned a thousand to one, maybe ten thousand to one. We're fleas compared to it."

Jon stared in shock at the screen as the titanic spheroid broke through the massed ammonia clouds and headed for orbital space.

"Almost six hundred robot space-fighters are heading for the battle station," Bast said.

As his heart raced, Jon shoved up to his feet and staggered toward the main screen. Gloria was right. They *were* fleas compared to that thing out there. It was like comparing a normal terrestrial planet to a star. The enemy vessel was

112

monstrous. A one-hundred-kilometer cybership—the normally massive warship had been rendered to the size and potency of a shuttle compared to that thing. If he had one hundred cyberships, it wouldn't matter. They could not win this battle.

Jon scowled as he watched the colossal vessel rise upward from the enormous gas giant. He no longer had time to devise a careful plan. Hydri II was right up against them in stellar terms. Could they outrun the monster ship?

Jon shook his head. No. They would not outrun it. The enemy ship and his fleet were each at almost zero velocity. The colossal AI vessel had maintained itself in Hydri II's upper atmosphere. That meant the ship had titanic engines and could likely accelerate faster than any ship in his fleet. In space, size usually denoted the faster ship.

That thing out there meant the Confederation's largest fleet was doomed to destruction. Maybe if he sent every ship in a different direction, a few of them might survive to report about the monster vessel. Yet, if that thing destroyed most of the fleet…what hope would humanity have to face it later?

Humanity certainly did not yet possess one hundred cyberships. And he might need one *thousand* cyberships to defeat that monster vessel in a regular space battle. That thing represented doom to man.

"What are we going to do?" Gloria asked, her mentalist training likely keeping the hopelessness out of her voice.

The normally philosophical Bast Banbeck didn't have the same sternness. "Can we surrender?" the Sacerdote asked in a quiet tone.

"No!" Jon said, as revulsion surged through him like an electric current. The idea was worse than repugnant. "We will never surrender," he said, his voice hardening.

"Then we will die," Bast said.

The words yanked a lever in Jon's brain, flooding him with the abhorrence of defeat. The flood slowed his racing heart as he hardened his resolve. In the end, it was always going to come to this: a handful of human-crewed ships facing a massed death-machine onslaught.

"It's better to die fighting than to live on your knees," Jon said.

"As Bast suggests," Gloria said, "we do not possess that option. AI vessels exterminate. They do not take prisoners— well, not often and not too many."

"This is just like Neptune," the helmsman said, a lanky man with pitted features and black-staring eyes.

Jon spun toward the officer, a man named Travis Nelson. "What did you say?"

"This reminds me of Neptune when we first saw a cybership," Nelson said. "Remember how the AI ship looked too big to exist? That's the same thing with that...ship out there."

"Neptune," Jon whispered, his eyes narrowing. "How did we defeat the cybership in the Neptune System?"

For a moment, no one spoke.

At last, Gloria cleared her throat. "We did the impossible, boarded what later became the *Nathan Graham*. But you can't be thinking about boarding that ship, Jon. Imagine boarding Luna with the number of people we have. Even if we could get inside the thing, a million robots would exterminate us. The ship could have ten million robots to swamp us. We'll never capture that."

"Maybe not," Jon said, as he focused on the metal monster rising out of Hydri II. "The point is we're going to fight with the intent to win. A win here means destroying it. That means we have to attack it with everything we have and hope our ramming cyberships will be enough to cause it to lose power so it sinks back into Hydri II. The gas giant's gravity can crush it for us."

"Do you mean to use the assault crafts so the raiders can get inside?" asked Gloria.

"We use *everything* we have," Jon said. "The fleet is going to pull a Miles Ghent today."

Miles Ghent had been the captain of Cybership *Da Vinci* and had purposely turned his vessel and flown into unbelievably fast alien missiles. The missiles had killed Miles and everyone aboard the *Da Vinci*, but he'd saved half the strike force by his sacrificial action.

"You mean for all of us to *ram* the enemy ship?" asked Gloria in a half-choked voice.

114

"If we can't survive," Jon said, "—and I don't see how we can against *that*—we can at least try to take the bastard down with us."

"What sort of generalship is that?" Gloria asked.

Jon turned to her, and for a moment, he was just an ordinary man as fear and worry shined in his eyes. That changed as the hardened warrior psyching himself up for battle took over. This was it: his last hurrah. He'd always wanted to die fighting. Well, it looked like he was going to get his wish. He just wanted to make sure he destroyed his enemy while it happened.

-15-

The Confederation fleet began to maneuver, and under the circumstances, it was a reasonable plan.

Hydri II was four times the size of Jupiter, approaching the mass that would have turned it into a star. The gas giant swirled with incredible storms. It pulled everything around it with an immense gravitational tug and it expelled harsh radio waves and heavy radiation. It was a hellish world. And out of the swirling ammonia-clouds a colossal metal warship arose, bristling with weaponry. No doubt, the brain-core controlling the ship planned to eradicate all of them, and it didn't look as if there was anything they could do about it.

Jon was giving it his best shot, though.

The captured battle station targeted the clouds of approaching AI fighters. The brain-core in the station warned the fighters to stay away. They did not respond.

The battle station's gravitational cannons warmed up as golden balls of power sizzled into existence in the grav dishes. Then, golden beams speared out at the six hundred fighters.

The AI fighters scattered even as the grav beams exploded one individual fighter after another.

Meanwhile, Jon had made his decision. The potential firepower of the enemy ship beggared description. He couldn't just drive straight at the AI vessel and hope to get close enough to ram it. He was going to have to get creative.

Thus, as the battle station beamed the approaching AI fighters, the Confederation fleet maneuvered behind the battle

116

station in relation to Hydri II. Each cybership-class vessel accelerated with huge exhaust tails growing rapidly in length and heat. The ships used the battle station as cover as they sped for the nearby factory moon. The Roke bombards followed to the back and on both sides of the fourteen cyberships. The bombards could not accelerate as fast as the human-crewed ships. The bombards remained on the sides because their vessels would not survive for long against the heated exhaust produced by fourteen matter/antimatter engines.

While the Confederation fleet accelerated, the battle station slaughtered the approaching AI fighters.

"Launch missiles," Jon ordered the battle station. "Launch *all* your missiles and attack-craft on the assumption that you can annihilate the fighters. I want you to attack the enemy ship."

"I am launching as ordered," the battle station brain-core replied.

At that point, forty-six huge golden beams lashed outward from the colossal AI vessel even as it reached low orbital space around Hydri II. The new gravitational beams smashed through its surviving fighters and struck the armored hull of the battle station.

The forty-six hot beams—larger than normal grav beams— drilled against the armored hull at an astonishing rate. The battle station had never been designed to take such punishment. The hull began to glow due to the deadly heat transfer from the beams to the metal. The immense heat transfer weakened the entire hull. Then, one grav beam punched through the hull armor. Another did likewise. Then a third, fourth, fifth, sixth, seventh, eighth, ninth, tenth, eleventh, twelfth, thirteenth, fourteenth—

The battle station erupted in a mighty explosion. Metal, coils, computer parts, storage bulkheads, extra warheads— some vaporized and some sped outward at fantastic speeds.

The remaining AI fighters vanished in the storm of heat, radiation and mass that swept them from existence.

The terrible eruption of mass, heat and radiation might have crippled the Confederation fleet. But the majority of the Confederation ships had already slid behind the factory moon in relation to the battle station. The moon absorbed the shock of the battle station's death, saving those ships.

On the bridge of the *Nathan Graham*, various probe-fed screen-shots fizzled as one probe after another ceased to exist.

"We're doomed," a weapon's officer cried.

"Quiet," Jon said. "We've just started fighting—"

"Started?" the officer shouted, interrupting, his eyes wild. "Are you insane? Did you see what that ship just did? We have to flee."

"You're dismissed," Jon said. "Report to your quarters."

The officer laughed crazily.

Jon motioned to a space marine. The thick-necked marine marched to the man and grabbed him by the scruff of the neck.

"Leave me alone," the officer shrieked.

The marine slugged him across the jaw and caught the officer as he slumped unconscious. Then the burly marine carted the officer off the bridge.

Meanwhile, Jon snapped more orders.

The fleet gained velocity as it sped past the factory moon and headed as fast as it could for the nearby gas giant.

Jon was using the moon as a shield and using angles to keep the rising monster from being able to see them in direct line-of-sight. If the AI ship couldn't see them, it couldn't fire grav beams at them.

As the fourteen Confederation cyberships strained to reached the gas giant, one XVT missile after another left the ships' launch tubes. As the ships left the protection of the moon, those missiles roared for the AI vessel.

Now, however, enemy golden gravitational beams once more reached out for them. Eight or nine beams hit Cybership *Gilgamesh*. Twelve enemy grav beams struck Cybership *Albion*. The two cyberships kept accelerating in order to get over Hydri II's horizon in relation to the enemy vessel.

The *Gilgamesh* made it with twelve other Confederation cyberships. The *Albion* blew up as enemy grav beams smashed through its hull armor and devoured crew and components inside.

Fortunately for the fleet, just before the end, the captain of the *Albion* blew his matter/antimatter core. He did it deliberately as a shape-charged blast. The majority of the heat, remaining parts and radiation spewed toward the enemy ship arising from Hydri II. The enemy ship was too far away for that to matter for it, but the heroic and quick-thinking action saved many nearby friendly vessels.

Despite that, seven Roke bombards shredded into pieces as the blast, radiation and near-speed-of-light particles from the destroyed *Albion* struck them.

"Ignite the last third of the XVT missiles," Jon said in a strangely altered voice.

"Sir?" the Missile Chief asked.

"Ignite them now," Jon said. "Create a whiteout. Now, now! Do it now!"

The Missile Chief stabbed buttons on his panel.

In space, the last third of the XVT missiles heading toward the rising AI monster exploded.

At the same time, fifty-two large grav beams lashed most of the remaining Roke bombards that were in the AI vessel's line-of-sight. What might have happened if the beams had remained on target was obvious.

The detonating warheads caused more than a sensor whiteout, however. They also created a blast zone. That zone momentarily created a kind of shield that blocked the enemy's grav beams.

During that brief time, the thirteen human-crewed cyberships reached the outer orbital edge of Hydri II. They turned hard, changing their heading. Instead of traveling directly at the gas giant, they began to skim along the outer orbital edge, heading at accelerating velocity toward the still-rising AI monster. The enemy ship no longer had line-of-sight on them, as Hydri II's horizon blocked them from each other. Thus, the enemy vessel could not fire the gravitational beams at them.

The Roke bombards weren't as lucky because they were slower.

Some of the bombards had ceased to exist because of enemy grav beams. Some died because of the *Albion* exploding, and a few more were destroyed due to the detonating warheads creating the whiteout. In total, half of the

Roke bombards were gone, leaving sixteen to fulfill the honor of the furry Star Lords.

"The AI is slaughtering us," Gloria said.

"So far," Jon said grimly.

"What can you hope to achieve by this?" she asked.

"Meaning," he said.

"Suicide is meaning?"

"If it takes down my enemy—yes."

"We're going to lose the war."

Once more, Jon stared at his wife. He wanted to tell her that he was only human. What did she expect from him? The colossal AI ship was far too much for the greatest Confederation fleet yet.

"Try the anti-AI virus against it," Jon said.

"It's obvious that's why it's here," Gloria said. "It must have seen what we did to the battle station, recording the event."

"Of course," Bast said as he snapped his fingers. "It watched our battle station takeover, and it did nothing to counteract it. The AI ship lured us to the star system to observe our methods."

"Don't you think I know that?" Jon said in as even a voice as he could manage. "We're going to charge and fire at it from the closest range I can get us. Those of us that can will accelerate into the ship and try to ram and detonate it. If that fails, maybe some of us can reach inside and march to its brain-core."

"A suicide run," Gloria said quietly.

"It was the only thing I could think of that gives us even a quantum's damn of a hope of winning this fight," Jon said.

Gloria nodded as her small shoulders slumped. "We will do what we can. That is logical." With that, she turned back to her board. The fleet gained velocity as it raced around Hydri II.

-16-

"They are bold," the first alien said.

"Reckless and foolish," said the second. "They cannot win."

"I do not believe they are attempting to win."

"Then...their behavior is even less worthy of our time."

The two aliens watched the progress of the Confederation fleet as it circled the gas giant, obviously trying to get into immediate firing range of the AI siege-ship.

The aliens watched from a vessel the humans had once decided to call a void ship. In human terms, it was a great spheroid over three-hundred kilometers in diameter. It had an outer rocky exterior like an asteroid, and giant nozzles in back to propel it. The two aliens were in a huge, mountain-like building on the asteroid's rocky hull. The ship was presently in the blackness of the void, a nebulous realm outside of normal time and space, as biological and machine entities conceived of such things. The observing aliens were neither biological nor machine, as they were composed of raw energy, but ordered energy of a unique sort.

Theirs was a patrol vessel. They originated from the center of the Milky Way Galaxy and were known to themselves as the Enoy. The Sisterhood of Enoy had been waging war against the AIs for approximately twenty thousand years, as humans measured the passage of time.

Yet, the long war was not the topic of these two. In the interests of precision, the energy-crackling aliens could be

121

conceived of as the alien Zeta and the alien Ree. Those were not their true names, but those names were beyond the scope of humanity at this point in time.

Because humanity was a sight-oriented species, it would be plausible to suggest that Zeta appeared as an upright bolt of lightning in a vaguely humanoid shape. She belonged to the Sisterhood and thus had the power to maintain this form for a time.

Ree was less organized, with less willpower and far less stamina. She had gained passive status in the Sisterhood, could not command a vessel but had gained notoriety as a rules stickler. As such, she was the ship rector, in charge of enforcing the Third Edict.

The Third Edict was short and to the point. The Sisterhood would not interfere in the development of inferior species. The various species in the galaxy must evolve on their own even if this led to their extinction.

Zeta had higher rank, and she had argued her latest idea from the Second Edict: that the Sisterhood shall destroy AI Dominion vessels and factory planets when convenient.

Several years ago (in Earth time units) Zeta had spoken to Jon Hawkins in the Allamu System. Ree had recorded the event and continued to insist it broke the Third Edict.

Concerning Ree, it would be plausible to suggest that she looked like a glowing, floating ball of energy with no precise outline, and prone to bleeding energy every time she crackled.

Zeta stood before a cloudy window. Ree floated beside the commander, also observing the doomed Confederation fleet making its last attack run.

Zeta had come to appreciate this Jon Hawkins, and she admired in a quaint way the dogged persistence of the apish humans. They had done much better against the AIs than thousands of other races recorded throughout the twenty thousand years of war.

"It is time to leave this place," Ree said.

"First, I will launch a few missiles."

"You would interfere in the battle?"

"I do not understand your objection."

"The reason for my objection is obvious, is it not?"

"Not," Zeta said.

"Commander, you wish to destroy the siege-ship so the humans and Roke can continue to exist. They will of necessity record the existence of our missiles and the void."

"These two items they already know."

"You will confirm it for them."

"It has already been confirmed for them."

Ree glowed more brightly. "We must allow them to perish as the siege-ship destroys them."

"Perish because they are inferior to the AIs?" asked Zeta.

"Perish because that will be the outcome of their combined decisions," Ree countered.

"The humans have courage. They have retaken AI factory planets. Their anti-AI virus was an ingenious maneuver."

"To what end?" asked Ree. "The siege-ship can undoubtedly end the human race after he is done here."

"Perhaps," Zeta said. "Even so, I wish to run a species test on the humans."

"But...but that is inconceivable," Ree said. "The humans and Roke are substandard creatures. If either passed the test— this is a backward area of the galaxy, Commander. We cannot stay. If the humans gained our technology, it would only mean that the AIs would have it soon thereafter. Given such an expanded technology base, the AIs could prove deadly to our homeworld. This is standard doctrine."

"I would test the aliens," Zeta said.

"To what end?"

"Let us say...to test your theory."

"You doubt the accuracy of my findings concerning the humans?"

"I would say it differently. I wish to hasten your exaltation to active rank."

"Because of the results of a species test?" asked Ree.

"You have made a declaration concerning the humans and Roke. You claim that they are both substandard."

"Do you claim otherwise?"

"Have you heard me suggest such a thing?" Zeta asked.

"The implications of your statements—"

"Ree," Zeta warned. "Have a care what you say next."

"I withdraw my former statement."

"Noted," Zeta said.

"If the humans and Roke passed the species test," Ree said thoughtfully, "they could approach us by quoting the First Edict."

"How would they learn of the edict?"

"They could not...unless someone broke the Third Edict to tell them."

"That would invalidate the quote," Zeta said.

"Then this is not an attempt on your part to aid the humans?" Ree asked.

"Are you directly questioning my motives?" Zeta asked with a hint of menace.

Ree lost some of her glow. "I do not withdraw the words," the ball of energy said at last. "But I maintain them as a rhetorical statement rather than as a direct query to you."

Zeta remained silent for a time.

They both must have known that Ree's words were clever indeed. Having been stated, the Sisterhood could now judge Zeta's actions against the query. But Ree had not needed to risk status by directly questioning her superior.

It would appear that Ree...hated the humans would be too strong of a statement. Clearly, she did not appear to like them. Zeta...what where her motives?

The two energy beings of Enoy continued to watch the Confederation suicide-run as Zeta caused the void ship to begin creating a rip in reality.

124

-17-

Jon led thirteen cybership-class vessels and sixteen Roke bombards around Hydri II. As the fleet prepared to engage the colossal super-ship, masses of XVT missiles accelerated out of the launch tubes.

The entire remaining complement of XVT missiles accelerated at high velocity ahead of the Confederation fleet. The distance between the faster accelerating missiles and fleet grew with every second. Scattered among the big matter/antimatter missiles were probes so they could see what happened.

The fleet's gravitational cannons—the outer dishes—all began to glow with power.

It was different on the much smaller, triangular-shaped bombards. The bombards were closer in size to the regular human battleships of the Solar System than to cyberships.

Each of the bombards produced a railgun. When the moment came, the Star Lords would cause each railgun to flash with power. A projectile would spew at hyper-velocity from each one. Hyper-velocity was nothing like the speed of light, it was a term based on terrestrial speed. The great power of the mass driver was that its projectile did not dissipate over range like a laser or grav beam would. If the projectile hit the enemy, it hit with almost as much force as if it was fired at pointblank range.

Mass driver railguns were better at long-distance battles than short. Today, the Roke would get the chance—possibly—

to fire them at nearly pointblank range and do the best they could.

Behind the leading XVT missiles were the assault craft holding raiders and extra space marines. The Centurion had elected to join his marines in a penetration attack against the monster ship.

The Confederation fleet had almost reached the planetary horizon that would reveal the colossal vessel to them.

Jon stood before the main screen, watching grimly.

The first wave of XVT missiles crossed the planetary horizon. Among them were many probes.

The main screen showed the titanic AI vessel readying hundreds of gravitational cannons. They speared from the armored hull, vaporizing one XVT missile after another, harvesting the entire first wave.

Gloria groaned.

As Jon watched, his fingernails dug into the meaty part of his palms.

The next wave of XVT missiles headed for the planetary horizon.

"Ignite the warheads the instant the missiles cross the plane of the horizon," Jon said.

Soon, the next wave broke over the horizon and saw the AI vessel. Hundreds of enemy grav beams reached out, destroying almost all of the missiles.

A few warheads detonated, creating a spotty field of whiteout.

That allowed the third wave to reach a little farther over the horizon before the majority of them detonated. That created a larger whiteout zone.

Now, masses of tiny assault-crafts meant to penetrate the enemy hull-armor, and the thirteen cyberships and sixteen Roke bombards crossed the planetary horizon.

"Fire at will," Jon said, the order going throughout the fleet.

Now, however, a curious event occurred.

"Commander," Bast said. "I have spotted an anomaly behind us."

"AIs?" asked Jon.

"Negative, Commander," the Sacerdote said. "It appears to be a reality rip."

Jon whirled around. "The void aliens are here?"

"That is the logical deduction," Bast said. "Observe on the main screen."

Jon turned to the main screen as Bast made it a split-screen.

A glowing area appeared several million kilometers behind them. As the glow intensified, the area between the glowing lines literally ripped apart reality. In that region was an inky, swirling blackness. Just like in the Lytton System several years ago, massive tubular missiles slid out of the void.

Back then, three such missiles had slid out. This time, twenty-two missiles ejected from the inky void. They were much larger than XVT missiles. Each of the void missiles was ten kilometers long and one wide. They had bulbous warheads with a forest of antennae on the nosecones.

Just like in the Lytton System, each void missile traveled at five percent light-speed. Their velocity was 15,000 kilometers per *second*. The missiles would reach the monstrous AI vessel in three and one third minutes.

"Why now?" Gloria asked in a choked voice.

"I don't know," Jon said.

The time for conjecture had ended, however, as the fleet burst through the whiteout zone and surveyed the full horror of the three thousand kilometer, spherical AI monster.

Behind them, the reality rip disappeared.

Now, in the low orbital region of Hydri II, began the face-to-face fight between the siege-ship and the Confederation vessels. A blizzard of golden gravitational beams flashed from the hull of Boron 10. The big beams smashed against cyberships, bombards and attack-craft alike.

At the same time, smaller grav beams speared from the Confederation's cyberships while hyper-velocity ordnance flashed from Roke railguns.

For the Confederation, the battle was worse than a joke. It was slaughter pure and simple as cybership hulls glowed red and bombards began to pop with annihilating explosions.

Some of the Confederation grav beams struck the enemy hull, but to almost no effect. Perhaps the greatest surprise was

127

invisible tractor beams reaching out and snatching tiny attack-craft. Instead of pulling them down onto the armored hull, the tractor beams yanked many of the attack-crafts to the sides, to bring them around to opening hangar bays.

It appeared as if the AI monster was collecting attack-craft and the space marines within.

In almost too short a time to describe the situation, the bombards ceased to exist. The Roke vessels were too small to resist the large grav beams for more than ten seconds.

It was not much better for the cyberships.

The matter/antimatter explosions of the first destroyed cyberships cluttered the battlefield with pockets of whiteout. That allowed quick-witted or lucky captains a few more minutes of life for them and their crews. But it hardly seemed as if any of that would matter.

So far, Boron 10 had sustained less than minimal damage to his forward outer hull.

Then the siege-ship must have sensed the incoming void missiles. It retargeted, and thousands of grav beams speared outward at the fast approaching void missiles.

"Break off, break off!" Jon said. "Helm, get us out of here."

The message might have gotten through the static or interference of hard radiation, but likely did not. The massed and crisscrossing grav beams created even more interference. Other captains must have reached the same or similar conclusion as Hawkins, however, because most of the surviving cyberships sought to escape.

Then, the first void missile vaporized into nothing from many grav beams hitting it at once. During that time, some Confederation cyberships accelerated faster, turning slightly. Others tried to streak all the way across the battlefield in order to escape.

Boron 10 destroyed more incoming void missiles but not all of them. He gave a pulse command. From his great curved hull, tens of thousands of point-defense guns began to fill the area with massed although tiny projectiles.

The leading void missile ignited its huge matter/antimatter warhead. The shape-charged detonation swept the PD particles out of existence. The wash of the heat, EMP and radiation destroyed or crippled five Confederation cyberships. The explosion also created a whiteout zone for the following void missiles. Some of those shredded into pieces against debris. Some "died" from the EMP, heat and hard radiation.

Four continued the five percent light-speed run and hit the siege-ship. At that point, three of the warheads detonated.

Like a great earthquake on a planet, the kinetic energy and the matter/antimatter explosions caused giant ripples across the robot hull armor.

Another wave of void missiles struck the stricken vessel. The kinetic impacts and the detonations of yet more matter/antimatter warheads were too much for even the colossal, Moon-sized siege-ship. Entire areas of the hull exploded outward like great volcanos. At the same time, the great impacts literally stopped the forward momentum of the three thousand kilometer super-vessel. The siege-ship began to sink back toward Hydri II.

Boron 10 was not yet dead, though. The rearmost areas of the siege-ship yet functioned. The old brain-core reached several quick conclusions, and he began to act on them immediately.

Most of the Confederation fleet had been vaporized or destroyed. Several cyberships yet existed. One of those was the *Nathan Graham*. In the static, whiteouts and hard radiation and EMPs, no one on the *Nathan Graham* had any idea if any of the rest of the fleet had survived this holocaust of destruction.

This had been a disaster.

***

"Jon," Gloria said. "We're headed the wrong way."

Hawkins looked ten years older. He had seen some of what had happened out there and knew the Confederation had lost its largest fleet. The void missiles had shocked him to the core.

Why had the void aliens struck now? Why couldn't the aliens have destroyed the AI monster-ship *before* he began the attack run?

"Did you hear me?" Gloria shouted.

Feeling old, Jon slowly turned toward her. To see his dreams dissolve before him—

"What are you talking about?" he asked hoarsely.

"We're headed toward a reality rip," Gloria said.

"What?" he asked, his downed spirits making his mind sluggish.

"We're going into the void," Gloria said.

Jon looked at the main screen. It was blank due to a malfunction. Jon shoved up to his feet and managed to reach her station. She moved aside for him.

He looked down at her still working screen, and he saw the inkiness of the void. It was in front of the cybership, which was in orbital space around Hydri II.

"How is this possible?" he asked.

"That's not the question," Gloria said. "Why is it there? Do the void aliens mean to capture us?"

That was too much. Jon scowled. How could everything have gone wrong so fast?

"What are we going to do?" Gloria demanded.

"What can we do?"

"You're the captain. You have to think of something."

He looked at her, and he nodded. He was the captain, and they were still alive.

"Right," Jon said. "It's time…" He didn't know how to finish.

At that point, the *Nathan Graham* slid out of normal time and space and disappeared as it entered the void. They did not know it, but the reality rip closed behind them, hiding them from view from anyone in the Beta Hydri System that might have been looking.

For those aboard the *Nathan Graham*, the Battle of Beta Hydri was over. For some of them, a new war was about to begin.

PART III
THE VOID

GINNUNGAGAP
[gin-oong-gah-gahp]

noun *Scandinavian Mythology*

a primordial void, filled with mists, existing between Niflheim and Muspelheim.

That was the age when nothing was;
There was no sand, nor sea, nor cool waves;
No earth nor sky nor grass there,
Only Ginnungagap.

--The Poetic Edda. Voluspa, stanza 3

-1-

Jon Hawkins became aware of his surroundings in a sharp and unpleasant manner. For a moment, he seemed to be asleep or unconscious or stretched out in an alien laboratory. It was very strange and unsettling, and he did not remember how this had occurred.

The next moment, he was panting, and his side ached. He realized with a shock that he was splashing through dirty puddles in dim lighting. It did not make any sense whatsoever.

Clarity came to his rescue as a hot liquid drop struck the back of his neck. He looked up, still sprinting—he knew not why—and discovered that crisscrossing tubes were several meters overhead.

They were the city's waterworks—the city being New London on Titan, a moon of Saturn. He was in the second-lowest level.

New London was a domed city, with the rich and government employees living under the dome that allowed the first level people to view beautiful Saturn and the surrounding stars.

Jon had been on the ground-floor level several times in his life, always on a holiday.

The second lowest tier was the opposite of ground level. New London was mostly underground, the many tiers or levels providing living space for the teeming population.

Jon realized that he was in the dirty part of New London, the industrial wastes area. The hot liquid drop that had struck his neck—he wiped the back of his neck and smelled his fingers.

The scrunch of his nose—the drop smelled putrid. It was industrial waste product all right.

Yet, why was he down here? Why was he running so hard?

A shout behind him caused him to look back through the gloom. He saw three goons, three enemy gang members chasing him. They were big and muscular, wearing black vests so everyone could see their steroid-pumped pectorals and heavy biceps. Each of them had flowing long hair like Vikings of old.

They were Berserkers, a notorious gang known for their fighting prowess. They were also the enforcers of the sand trade down here. Sand was a synthetic drug that induced wonderful dreams.

That's when Jon became aware of several things that did not make immediate sense to him. He was much skinnier than he remembered. He had thought he was a man. But he could see that he wasn't a man but a mid-teen, maybe sixteen. He wore a heavy, bulging belt and he knew it was loaded with sand. In his right hand, he clutched a knife. It was short, very sharp and it meant something important to him, but he didn't know what right then.

He didn't recall being a teen anymore. He—

As Jon sprinted from the bigger, gaining Berserkers, he scowled. This was wrong somehow. He'd faced a different dilemma that had nothing to do with knife fighting, sand or New London for that matter.

"We're going to kill you, you slow punk!" one of the Berserkers shouted.

Jon splashed through more puddles as he wheezed. The air coming down his throat was almost painful. A sharp pain stitched his side. He couldn't keep running like this much longer.

Damn it, he couldn't win this race. The three musclebound clods were catching up. He was going to die—again.

The scowl returned. What did he mean "again?"

Jon swore, and he skidded to a stop. He panted harder as he breathed in and out, in and out. He refused to hunch over, turning and standing straight as sweat slid down his face.

The three charged him hard and fast. Each of them had a long knife in his right hand. The knives gleamed in the dim lighting. Each of the Berserkers had a pair of brass knuckles over his left fist.

There was no way he could defeat three of them at one time. Could he appeal to their sense of honor?

Despite the fear that boiled in his guts, Jon forced himself to laugh.

The three reached him then. They also panted as they slowed to a stop. The leader faced him head on, the other two fanning out on his sides.

"You made a big mistake, mule," the leader said.

"You and me," Jon said. "I can take you in a straight fight."

The leftmost Berserker lunged at him, stabbing with the point. Jon barely avoided the strike by twisting and backpedalling.

"You and me," Jon said again in a panicked way.

"We three against you," the leader said, grinning evilly. He was missing an upper tooth. "We're going to cut you until you drop your knife. Then, we're going to throw you down and stomp your hands and feet to mush. After that, you know what we're going to use you for?"

Jon knew their rep. The Berserkers were man-rapists, a brutal gang of vicious thugs that everyone hated.

"This is personal," the leader told him. "I'm going to make you my *bitch*."

Fear made Jon want to beg for his life, but that wasn't going to help him any.

"If you beg me, though," the leader said. "Well, I could make you my boy for a time. I might even let you try out for the gang."

"But…" Jon said.

"But what?" the leader said.

"Berserkers never let anyone live."

"This is different," the leader told him.

Jon took a step back.

The leader watched him, tracking everything.

That was all wrong. The Berserkers should have just charged in and attacked. Why had they stopped to talk like this?

"I want to see you beg, Hawkins. Beg for your life."

"Is this a trick?" Jon asked.

"No," the Berserker said. "This is real."

Jon frowned at the way the leader said "real." There seemed to be a hidden meaning in the word.

"It is what it is," the leader told him.

"Are you reading my mind?" Jon asked.

"Let's torture him," said the enforcer to the left. "He may be too smart for this."

"You *are* reading my mind," Jon said. "That doesn't make sense. This place…"

The three Berserkers began closing in on him. Jon stepped back, and a quick glance over his shoulder showed him a nearing wall. They had him trapped.

"I was somewhere else just before this," Jon said.

"Yeah, becoming a mule," the leader said.

"No. I never was a mule. This isn't me."

"You can't wriggle out of this, Hawkins."

Jon grabbed the belt buckle and unsnapped it. In a swift move, he tore the belt of sand from his waist. Inspiration struck as he walked backward through a puddle. He held out the belt of sand and brought his knife to it.

"You come any closer and I'll slice the belt," Jon said, "and spill the sand into the water. It'll be ruined."

"You think we care about the sand?" the leader mocked.

"This much sand?" Jon said. "Yeah. It's worth a fortune."

"We don't care."

"You're lying," Jon said. "If you don't come back with the sand, your dealers are going to be furious. They'll figure you kept it for yourselves. They won't believe that three of you weren't able to take care of me."

"You're quick to strike a bargain," the leftmost Berserker said.

"Why not?" asked Jon. "I'll give you the sand if you let me go. I'll ruin the product, though, if you step any closer."

"No deal," the leader said. "But if you give us the sand, I'll make it a clean kill."

"Sure," Jon said. "Here," and he sliced the belt as they relaxed. Some of the sand particles poured from the slice and into the water.

The three Berserkers shouted with rage.

Jon hurled the belt at the leftmost Berserker. The muscular gang-member tried to catch it. Jon followed the belt and he struck low in the man's side. He did not attempt to stab directly, but sliced belly muscle and around the side as he skipped around the man.

The Berserker screamed in agony. Particles of sand also struck his face, some of it getting into his eyes.

Jon shoved the Berserker from behind, making the heavier man stumble toward the other two. Jon charged them in desperation, knowing this was his only chance.

The knives must have struck him hard, punching into his body, because coherence fled as the world around him dissolved into nothingness and Jon Hawkins knew no more...

-2-

At first, there was nothing. It wasn't sleep. Jon was conscious—in a manner of speaking. There was a strange alien-ness to all of this. He could not quite fathom it, could not understand the why of it or how he had come to be here.

Where was *here*, exactly? It would seem that he lay on a hard bed with a mask over his mouth. That allowed him to breathe. There were electrodes attached to his face and they fed him electrical impulses that stimulated certain areas of his brain. He strove to open to his eyes and see this for himself. The more he struggled, though…

He almost opened his eyes. A drug, another brain shock—something—broke his concentration.

All his knowledge fled from him leaving nothingness in its place again. He almost felt as if he'd done this before.

As Jon thought about it, the world filled in around him. There were clouds, colored clouds, and they moved fast across the colorful sky *below* him.

Hadn't there been other clouds in another time and place? Those had been ammonia clouds.

Jon grunted as pain stabbed his mind.

Forget about the ammonia clouds.

Yes. He could do that.

You're on Saturn.

What am I standing on if I'm on a gas giant?

You're on a cloud city that drifts in Saturn's upper atmosphere. At this level, you have normal Earth gravities tugging at you.

Oh. Yes, he knew about the Saturn cloud cities. He'd always wanted to visit one.

This isn't a visit. You are a repairman. You're crawling through a vent and have to attend to one of the anchoring balloons that are on the bottom of the cloud city.

I don't know anything about that. Besides, I hate heights.

Exactly. You are going to have to crawl out on an under-deck walkway and repair a rip in an anchoring balloon. The entire city—its populace—are counting on you.

Why me, though? I hate heights.

You are the balloon repairman. It is your duty to fix the balloons that give the cloud city its buoyancy. Are you ready?

No, I'm not ready. I don't want to be here.

The words didn't help. Slowly, Jon became aware that he crouched low as he walked through a narrow under-city access tube. He wore a special patch unit on his back, and it was heavy. He had been trudging through the access tube for a long time. His stomach rumbled because he was hungry, and he desperately wanted something to drink. It was hard to focus because he was so tired, hungry and thirsty.

Still, he was the balloon man. This was his duty. Medina-hab jihadists had been down here. One had escaped the SWAT team. The lone jihadist had blown one of the smaller, balancing balloons and he had put a rip in one of the main buoyancy balloons. The jihadist could be anywhere down here.

Jon did not like that, but he had a job to do. He took a deep breath and continued trudging. Finally, he reached a metal hatch. On the other side of the hatch—

Jon's hands trembled as he reached for the control pad. He did not want to punch in the access code. Weren't there supposed to be more balloon men down here with him?

They are all dead.

Dead? Jon thought to himself. How could all the other balloon men be dead?

The jihadist from Medina Hab shot them. Now, the jihadist is hunting for you, Jon Hawkins.

Jon glanced warily over his shoulder, expecting to see the fanatical killer coming for him. To his vast relief, he saw nothing but the long access tube.

Right. The killer had blown a balancing balloon and put a gash in a main buoyancy balloon. He couldn't do anything to fix the first one. But he could repair the rip to the anchoring balloon.

Hardening his resolve, Jon tapped in the access code. Abruptly, the hatch slid up, revealing the vast panorama of Saturn below. Great roiling clouds slid past at an amazing speed.

Jon stared at the clouds, transfixed. He dearly hated heights, and here he stood on the edge of an access hatch. He realized sickly that he was able to see because no balloon was in the way. He had come the wrong way. He would have to backtrack kilometers to reach the balloon to his left.

He could see that the main buoyancy balloon was sagging as air hissed from the rip into the atmosphere.

That's when he wondered how he was able to breathe without a mask over his face.

He felt sudden disorientation. Then he breathed audibly through his oxygen mask. He realized that he was peering through a glass visor.

That was odd. He could have sworn that he hadn't had a mask on just a second ago.

"It must be my nerves," he muttered under the mask.

There was a metal walkway before him, a walkway with handrails on the sides. The walkway had nothing below but the gases of Saturn.

Jon did not want to go out on the walkway. It would be a thousand times worse than walking across an Inca grass bridge over a thousand-foot chasm.

Look!

Jon turned to the left, and he saw a man with a portable rocket launcher cradled in his arms running along a walkway. The man wore a red cloth over his face. He was the last jihadist. He ran for a better shot at another main balloon.

Jon began to tremble. If the jihadist were able to destroy more balloons, the entire city would sink down into the lower atmosphere. The greater gravities of lower Saturn would crush and kill everyone.

You have to stop him.

"How am I supposed to stop him?" Jon asked himself aloud.

Chase him down. Tackle him if you have to.

Jon blinked rapidly behind his visor. He began to shake as his fear of heights really took hold. He would never catch the sprinting jihadist in time, not with his heavy patch kit on his back.

Before he knew what he was going to do, Jon shed the patch kit so it thudded behind him. Then, moaning in fear, not really understanding how he was able to do this, Jon took his first step onto the under-deck walkway. Dizziness threatened to cause him to crash down onto his knees. He fought it off as his breathing became heavier. He took a second step, a third and then a fourth.

At that point, Jon broke into a trot that made the walkway shiver at each of his steps. He looked up and saw the under-plate of the city. He looked around and saw the great balloons that gave the cloud city its buoyancy.

I can do this, he told himself.

He refused to look past the walkway but concentrated solely on the plating before him. He increased speed, dared a quick glance to the side and saw that he was catching up on the jihadist on a different walkway. He ran harder—and yelled in terror as he noticed a great gap in the walkway before him. He could see the lower clouds through the gap.

Jon barely halted in time. Winds whistled up through the walkway gap. The wind buffeted him, and the walkway trembled.

Jon moaned. He needed to go back to the access tube. He hated it out here and his stomach shriveled in terror. His knees knocked. Oh, he wished that he could close his eyes and just leave this horrible place.

Yet, despite the horror, Jon found himself grabbing the railing. He closed his eyes and began to sing a litany to himself. Singing louder, his hands gripping the rail like vises, he found his footing on the side and began to shuffle to the side of the gap. He did not dare to open his eyes lest he see that there was nothing to support him by the railing.

Then, his hands slipped, and his body lurched. He noticed that someone had greased the hand railing.

Who would do such a wicked deed?

Somehow—Jon had no idea how—he heard evil laughter.

Jon opened his eyes as he clung to the railing. He was over the open hole in the walkway. On a nearby walkway, the jihadist aimed a rocket launcher at him. The man's words tumbled toward him.

What was the jihadist trying to say to him? And how could he hear the man anyway?

This is not real, a voice in his head told him.

It seemed, then, that other voices panicked. *What said that? How can he break the conditioning? He is a substandard creature. He cannot have outer awareness.*

"What's going on?" Jon whispered to himself.

Remember the monstrous AI vessel rising out of Hydri II's upper ammonia clouds?

"What?" asked Jon.

He waited for the voice in his head to speak again, but it did not.

What was an AI monster ship? Had he ever… Yes! He did have a dim recollection of such a thing. Yet, how could that—

It hit Jon then. This was unreal. It was…

He forced his eyes open and stared at the jihadist. He should not be able to hear anything the man would shout. The jihadist should be wearing a mask. If the man had a voice amplifier, the winds down here would still rip the words away before the sounds reached him.

The railing he gripped became even slipperier. He shouted in dread as his left foot slipped. He had to keep going even though it would be easier to go back. If he didn't keep going…

Jon closed his eyes and tried to conjure up the image of an AI vessel. A memory of a time—

Jon's eyes flew open. He had been fighting the monstrous AI. The *Nathan Graham* had entered the void. Was he in the grip of the void aliens?

His knowledge nullifies the test.

141

Test? This was a test?

Jon was deathly afraid of heights. Were they testing that? But who were they? The void aliens?

"This is not real," Jon told himself. "This is an illusion."

This is real. You will die if you let go.

"No," Jon said stubbornly. "This is—"

In that moment, he remembered an old truism. It wasn't what you said that counted, it was what you did.

Did he really believe this was an illusion? While trembling with fear, he closed his eyes, deliberately let go of the railing and stepped back. He dropped through the gap in the walkway. He felt the horrible lurch in his stomach, but he refused to open his eyes.

As he plunged deeper into Saturn, Jon lost consciousness until he was drifting in a different semi-unconsciousness once more. He tried to open his eyes then, but a heavy drowsiness overcame him, and then he remembered no more...

-3-

"You're cheating!" Ree said. "This is deliberate sabotage. I do not know why you would commit such obvious fraud, but you may rest assured that I shall notify the highest archons of the Sisterhood once we return from our patrol."

The glowing ball of energy that was Ree radiated a red color, showing her highly agitated state.

In the same large area of the void ship lay a number of humans. One of them was Jon Hawkins. He wore a shimmering energy helmet but nothing else. His eyes were tightly shut but he twitched from time to time. Perhaps he was in a dream state.

Zeta stood as before, a humanoid lightning bolt of brilliant energy.

The area around them was foggy and dimly lit, making it hard to visualize beyond the immediate region with the naked humans laid out in rows and columns. Each nude human wore an energy helmet similar to the one Hawkins wore. The helmets gave Zeta and Ree direct access to the biological brains.

"This is an outrage," Ree added.

"Calm yourself," Zeta warned. Her brilliant color was more akin to the white of a flashing bolt of lightning. It showed her calm and coherent emotional state.

"Do you claim these intrusions are not your doing?" Ree demanded.

"I am the commander," Zeta said. "You are here to answer to me. I do not have to answer you."

"I am the rector and have the legal authority to enforce the Third Edict."

"Have I claimed otherwise?" Zeta asked.

"You have made no verbal claims. But I submit that actions are more telling than words."

"You quote the biological creature. I find that interesting."

"Truth is truth," Ree said.

"Indeed. That is another fascinating statement."

"Do you deny that someone has tampered with the test?"

"I have denied nothing."

"Then you know I speak the truth."

Zeta did not respond. Instead, she studied the biological entity known as Jon Hawkins. Ree was correct. Someone had spoken to Hawkins while he was under illusion. That was very odd. Could Ree have tampered with the test in order to declare it invalid?

Zeta did not believe that Ree had such subtlcty in her. That did not mean Ree did not...

"You cannot think I have anything to do with this," Ree said.

"I am thinking exactly that," Zeta said.

"You are wrong."

"You are over-bold, given your low ranking. What is propelling you to say such things?"

"What are you suggesting?"

"I am Commander Zeta of the Fringe Patrol. You will not answer me with questions. What motivates you to flash these queries against me?"

The ball of energy known as Ree become pinkish as her rage dwindled and her logic came to dominate her thinking.

"I do not know, Commander."

"Is it emotion?"

"It was, but not now."

"Perhaps there is an entity here—of course," Zeta said.

"What have you divined?" Ree asked.

The human-shaped lightning bolt turned to study the ball of energy.

"I am amiss," Ree said. "I retract my query and await your instructions." The ball of energy was white now, although not nearly as brilliant as Zeta's shape.

Zeta became thoughtful. There was an agency at work, one she did not understand. Someone had intruded into Hawkins' consciousness while he was under illusion. She no longer believed that Ree was in any way responsible for that.

Could humans have developed a telepathic ability without their knowing about it?

Zeta examined the naked humans laid out before them. They were all human. She had deliberately not taken the Sacerdote because that species had a latent telepathic ability.

Could the Sacerdote have broken the continuity lock? Zeta doubted that. Everyone on the *Nathan Graham* was in a deep state of shock. The cybership was in the void, a null realm. The nothingness of the void already threatened discontinuity to the entire vessel, a nonexistence of everything to and in the cybership.

The patrol vessel was docked beside the cybership and had thrown a partial reality shield over the craft. The reality generator on the *Rose of Enoy* labored overtime to do this, but not so much that it had given awareness to the numbed and fallen human crew.

The creatures on the Nathan Graham would remain in discontinuity until the Sisterhood determined humanity's true nature and status.

This was quite puzzling. Should she continue with the test? Or would it be wiser to do what…? Flush the test subjects into the void?

Zeta waited to hear a voice in her head. None came. Once more, she regarded Ree. Could that one be more subtle than she gave her credit for?

It was time to continue the tests. Maybe there was some other agency at work. Maybe the energy helmets were at fault.

"I am running a diagnostic," Zeta said. Power flashed from her to the helmets. The return power surge was as white as herself.

"The helmets are fully operational," Ree said.

"Your manner has changed," Zeta said.

145

"I accept your theory that there is someone or something else tampering with the tests. In my…emotional state, I forgot that you are highly moral and completely ethical."

Zeta might have stiffened, but she did not. She did become highly alert, however. Ree was attempting a clever subterfuge. Oh. This one was more subtle than she had at first suspected. Maybe it would be wisest to flush the test subjects.

Zeta admired the human courage, and she disliked to a large degree, the AI menace. It would be good to find a fitting species to make a counterattack against the AI Dominion out here in the fringe of the galaxy. But she did not desire that if it meant a possibility of losing rank and privilege. Ree was an upstart and likely belonged to the Dynast Faction. Yes. She would have to practice greater caution around Ree.

"Shall we continue the tests?" Ree asked.

Zeta almost said no. At the last moment, she had a cunning idea. "Let us change the parameters," she said. "You will administer the tests while I study for anomalies among the subjects."

"That is against test protocol," Ree said.

"Granted," Zeta said. "But if there is interference, I want a rector in immediate psychic range. This will also allow me to check for telepathic tampering while you test."

Ree was silent for a time.

"If the task is beyond your capabilities…" Zeta said.

"I will do it," Ree said in a slow voice. "I will do it in order to expunge my venality earlier."

"I do not require humility in my crew," Zeta said.

"Nevertheless, I wish to atone for my hasty statements earlier."

"I accept," Zeta said. "We will start afresh and see what we shall see."

"Hail, Zeta, Commander of the Fringe Mission."

Zeta's lightning-bolt color dimmed for just a moment. Then, the brilliance resumed, and they readied to renew the species test.

-4-

Red Demeter the Infiltrator, an agent of the Seiner Earth Colony, felt overpowering agony of mind. She would have writhed in pain, but her training was too good for that to happen.

She was lying on a hard slate in a strange place with a crackling piece of energy circling her head. Not so long ago, she had been aboard the *Nathan Graham*. The human-crewed cybership had survived the grim defeat long enough to witness void missiles slamming against the monstrous AI vessel. Then, the *Nathan Graham* had slid into the void.

Naturally, Demeter had read the secret Confederation reports regarding the void aliens. Three years ago, the strange extraterrestrials had destroyed the Lytton System and shown themselves in the Allamu System.

What Demeter did not know was how she had come to lay here. Ah, ah, yes, of course. The recollection returned as an alien creature fed her crackling energy helmet-power.

Full knowledge retuned in a rush. In the blackness of the void, an asteroid-like and -sized ship named the *Rose of Enoy* had maneuvered beside the *Nathan Graham*. It would appear that the…discontinuity process of the void had dropped everyone on the cybership. That included Red Demeter. That anyone still breathed on the cybership was due to a strange reality field emanating from the *Rose of Enoy*.

Awareness had returned to Demeter when she found someone levitating her through the alien ship alongside naked, floating humans.

With the keenest of Seiner skill, Demeter had used low-strength telepathy to scan her surroundings.

Right there, the strength of her telepathic ability had astounded Demeter. There was something about the ship or the void aliens that had fed her telepathic power beyond her normal means. She could literally *feel* the strengthening inside her.

Instead of reveling in the newfound power and exulting in her luck, Demeter had determined to snatch at the opportunity. While she had levitated beside the floating humans, she had T-scanned delicately—what were those two beings? They did not have physical bodies, but were organized energy. Those were the void aliens, she supposed.

Demeter had almost panicked and telepathically attacked them. Perhaps her long years of training as an infiltrator and her time as an undercover spy on the *Nathan Graham* came to her rescue. She waited and let events unfold.

Thus, she had found herself set on a hard slab. With her telepathic "sight," she'd witnessed the floating humans coming down onto other nearby slabs. From the two beings, crackling, lightning-like energy had flowed outward and around each subjects' head, turning into energy helmets. At that point, the void aliens had begun to subject each of them to illusionary dreams.

Yes, yes, this was an alien test of some sort. Demeter had found out that much by daring to "look" into the mind of the weaker of the two void aliens. The effort had greatly taxed Demeter, and it had almost given her away. She'd waited after that, and later had entered one of Jon Hawkins' dreams. She'd interfered with the alien test in order to study the reactions.

That had been an intuitive move on Demeter's part. Seiner telepaths understood the wisdom of following intuition. Now, Demeter realized why it had been clever. The smart alien was allowing the not-so-smart alien to run the illusionary tests. The other alien—Zeta—

Demeter withdrew her telepathic "sight" from her surroundings. Zeta had almost sensed her. That had been too close. If Demeter hadn't been filled with the newfound strength...

The Seiner infiltrator waited, trying to think this through as she lay on the hard slab. As Demeter did this, the energy helmet circling her head crackled with power.

She did not short-circuit the helmet. Instead, she withdrew her awareness deeper into herself. She watched as...Ree used her memories to construct an illusion.

The self of Demeter surged forward and manipulated her memories lest the void alien discover her true Seiner nature.

It frankly stunned Demeter that the two aliens did not realize that she—Demeter—wasn't a human. Her skin-suit disguise wasn't that good, was it? Could the void aliens not recognize the inherent superiority of Seiners to humans?

Demeter soon found herself moving through an illusionary dream. She was back on Earth, living among the humans in Paris as she worked as a waiter in an upscale restaurant. This had been one of her first assignments as an infiltrator. As a waiter, she catered to government employees, the upper echelon.

The illusionary dream had secret policemen—the GSB: Government Security Bureau. The GSB agents hunted for her.

Demeter played along with the illusion, sensing what Ree wished to find. In this case, the void alien wanted to see if humans could resist torture while continuing on the right course.

Since the dream wasn't real and did not hurt Demeter in the slightest, she withstood horrific, illusionary torture, refusing to give the GSB the information they desired.

The test ended. Ree withdrew power from the energy helmet and Demeter once more dared to use her telepathic seeing ability.

The void alien was readying to test the next subject.

Demeter debated on strategy. Why had the void aliens attacked the AI super-ship? Why had they captured the *Nathan Graham?* And why was each of them undergoing these tests?

She needed to discover the reason for the tests before she made her next major move. How could she find out the great reason?

Demeter thought hard on the matter and finally had an inkling of why. But there was only one way to be sure.

The infiltrator dared to crack open her eyes. The lighting was dim except for the raw energy of a floating ball of low-watt electricity.

Ah! That was the void alien, or more properly said, *a* void alien.

Energy streams flowed from the void alien to various energy helmets on the naked humans laid out on the hard slabs of matter.

So it wasn't telepathic powers per se, but electrical connections. No wonder the void aliens hadn't found her yet.

Demeter closed her eyes and resumed her unconscious-seeming state.

She had to discover the reason for the tests. Perhaps she should no longer interfere in the human dreams. She'd done so...it must have been due to fear, to the loneliness of being trapped on this weird alien ship and dimension. She'd reacted before fully knowing the situation. Still, it had brought about a needed change.

Demeter would not interfere again, but she would watch the ongoing tests in order to determine what the void aliens wanted from the disgusting humans.

-5-

Jon Hawkins crept through a foggy cavern. He had no idea how he'd gotten here. He wore a spacesuit with a bubble helmet and gripped an energy gun. This time, he remembered the AI super-ship. He remembered the awful battle in Hydri II's orbital space and the near-annihilation of his fleet.

The AIs were going to win this war. Despite all they had done these past years, there was no way humanity could win against a power that had those kinds of warships. He had thought to use Cog Primus to buy the human race time…

Jon gritted his teeth and tried to peer through the half-lit fog that roiled everywhere. Did knowledge of the AI super-ship mean he was giving up? Would he let the death machines wipe out humanity?

Jon gripped his energy weapon harder, and he halted, straightened and turned in a slow circle. There was fog all around him. He was in a cave of sorts, but that should be impossible.

The *Nathan Graham* had gone into the void. That meant he was in the void. Likely, that meant was he was a prisoner of the void aliens.

What did they want with him?

Jon completed the slow turn around. Why wasn't he aboard the *Nathan Graham?*

Inside his bubble helmet, Jon scowled. He'd been having dreams. He couldn't remember them in detail, but he was cognizant of having gone through them.

151

With his free hand, he clicked a speaking unit just under the helmet. "Is this a test of some kind?" he shouted.

He heard crackling power surges to his left. Jon whirled around and aimed the energy weapon that way. The fog was getting brighter and brighter—

Jon blanched and stepped back as an upright and immensely bright bolt of lightning on two legs stepped out of the fog. Jon raised his free hand to shield his eyes from the wicked brightness.

It almost immediately dimmed.

Jon lowered his hand, although he kept the energy gun aimed at the creature. Yes, it had black eyes that observed him.

"Who are you?" Jon said.

"I am a void alien, in your reference, at least."

"Do you have a name?"

"Zeta will do."

"Are you part of the Sisterhood?"

"You have a good memory, Jon Hawkins. I told you that last time we talked three years ago. Yes. I am of the Sisterhood of Enoy."

"Are we—am I—on your ship?"

"Yes."

"Is this a dream?"

"Yes."

"Then you aren't real?"

"I am quite real. The conversation will have repercussions, never doubt it."

"If I fire this gun…?"

"You will end the conversation."

"Will I end more than that?"

"What do you think?"

Jon lowered the energy gun.

"I consider that progress," Zeta said.

"I don't understand all this."

"I would be surprised if you did."

"Care to tell me why you launched void missiles at the AI super-ship?"

"Let us begin by calling things by their correct names," Zeta said. "The AI super-ship is rightly called a siege-ship."

"Is a siege-ship the biggest the AIs have?"

"Oh no," Zeta said. "There are much bigger."

"That's just great."

"To continue," Zeta said, "I am not a *void* alien, but a Sister of Enoy. Those were not void missiles, but Vestal missiles launched from our patrol vessel while we were within the void. The void is a null realm, as you have no doubt surmised. There is quite literally nothing here, but it is nothingness of quantifiable size or dimensions. It is correct to say there is no up or down in the void, and yet, our patrol vessel travels through the null realm to reach adjoining places in time and space."

"That's a contradiction in terms."

"A paradox," Zeta said. "Yes. The void is full of them even though it is composed of nothing. Despite the fact that you and I are calmly discussing this, the void is a dreadful place, one that quickly brings discontinuity to anything or anyone lacking a reality generator powered by a quantum-pi power plant. You and the *Nathan Graham* would have ceased to exist long ago except for the reality field reaching out from my vessel."

"Thank you."

"I believe the correct phrase is, 'You are welcome.' However, you and I are not here to discuss the ramifications of the void. We have met for a different reason."

Jon noticed that the living bolt of lightning—the Sister of Enoy—watched him closely. Did the alien want something from him?

"You've been testing us, I take it," Jon said.

"That is correct."

"How many tests have I taken?"

"Twenty-three so far."

"Did I pass any of them?"

"Rather ask, did the human race pass the test?"

Jon didn't like the sound of that. "Did it?" he asked.

"No," Zeta said. "You failed, rather miserably so."

Jon blinked several times. "So what happens now?"

"You will all die in the void."

"You mean those of us on the *Nathan Graham?*"

"Yes," Zeta said.

Jon brought up the energy gun. "Why did we fail your test?"

"I believe because you humans are not strong enough," Zeta said. "It is also because you're so dimwitted that you didn't even know that a Seiner spy was among you."

Jon shook his head. "We knew about the Seiner's presence, although we hadn't found her yet."

"Do you have any last requests, Jon Hawkins?"

He squeezed the handle of the energy gun and almost fired. Was this really a dream like Zeta said? He wanted to fire to test that. Yet if he fired—

With an oath, Jon hurled the gun from him. It was too tempting to keep holding it. He had to think like never before. The fleet had found a siege-ship, an impossibly huge AI warship hiding on Hydri II. The thing had been three *thousand* kilometers in diameter. It had possessed unbelievable firepower. It would appear that cyberships were the infants of the robot empire. Yet, the AIs had a mortal enemy, these Sisters of Enoy. They traveled through the void—a realm of nothingness—that apparently devoured anything unprotected by a reality generator.

Jon could hardly wrap his mind around the idea of a reality generator. What was it? How did it work? What fueled it?

No, no, that was *not* the critical thing now. Zeta was going to snuff out the *Nathan Graham,* like that! She would do it because humans had failed her test. Yet, Zeta clearly possessed a means for destroying the three-thousand kilometer siege-ships.

Okay…the living lightning bolt had asked him a question. She was waiting and maybe becoming impatient with him.

"I have a request," Jon said. "Return us to our ship and let us out of the void."

"For what reason do you request this?"

"Uh…so we can keep fighting the AIs, of course."

"Ultimately, you cannot win."

"Doesn't mean we shouldn't fight," Jon said.

"You would fight and go through all that pain even knowing you are going to lose?"

154

"Of course," Jon said. "Besides, you could be wrong about us."

"I am not wrong. Humanity has no hope against the AI Dominion."

"Sorry. I'm not going to take your word for it."

"Did the siege-ship teach you nothing then?"

Jon felt a horrible tightening in his gut. Here it was. The Sisters of Enoy had what he needed. The alien was still talking to him. Wasn't that a good sign?

Jon spoke carefully:

"The siege-ship taught me that humanity has to figure out Enoy technology. We know about the void, Vestal missiles launched in the void and all that. Now, it's just a matter of time before our scientists figure out how to do what you do."

"That is a gross insult to the Sisterhood. Humans develop a means to enter the void, never mind withstanding the nothingness—no, that is flatly impossible. And without the void, you would never learn how to accelerate Vestal missiles to their five percent light-speed velocity. Do you not realize that the AIs know about us, have known for twenty thousand years, and they have never figured it or us out, as you so blithely say."

Jon shrugged as if none of that mattered. "Help us leave the void. We'll do the rest. We're not machines after all. We'll show the Sisterhood what humans are capable of doing."

"You would show us nothing but what we've seen a hundred thousand times, a biological species dying to the death machines."

"Not this time, sister," Jon said. "Now we know what to do."

The living bolt of lightning studied him for a time. Finally, she spoke:

"I am amazed to say this, but I actually like you, Jon Hawkins. You have a demented style. But you humans failed the test. That is the essential point. Ree would report me if I allowed you the schematics to a Vestal missile, a null-splitter, a quantum-pi power plant and a reality generator. Without any of those items, you could never reach the void, exist in it while here, propel yourself from one region to another or attack a point in time and space from null existence. If you received any of those items from us, Ree would make the report and that would be the end of me."

Jon made a mental note to remember each named thing. Then he said, "No one is asking you for those items. I just want you to return us to our ship and release the *Nathan Graham* from the void."

"Your fleet is gone," Zeta said, "destroyed. There is nothing to go back to."

That was worse than grim news. But he couldn't—he *wouldn't* accept that the siege-ship had wiped out the entire fleet. It was simply too bitter to contemplate. No. He wasn't going to let anything stop him until he was dead.

"I've started from scratch more than once," Jon told the Enoy. "I can start again."

"Bold words, human. But you should first consider this. The siege-ship had an escape vessel. That vessel fled from the other side of Hydri II. It will reach the Algol System in time. I believe the Main there will no doubt decide to come here and annihilate humanity. No matter what you do, your species is as good as doomed."

Jon shook his head. He didn't want to know the odds. He couldn't keep up his confidence if he kept defending against one piece of bitter news after another. He had to turn this around. He had to—

"Who are you really?" Jon asked.

"I already told you, a Sister of Enoy."

"Is that your species name?"

"Our name doesn't matter. The Sisterhood has fought against the machine plague for twenty thousand of your years. We will likely continue to do so for twenty thousand more. But it won't matter. The machine menace will still be here."

This was news. Jon perked up, asking, "Why's that?"

"Look at you. You are indeed an ape creature. You yearn to know what cannot help you. You are innately curious about doom. Know then that the machines multiply at an astonishing rate. As fast as we destroy them, they build even more, spreading throughout the galaxy like a true plague of anti-life."

156

"In twenty thousand years, how many alien races have the death machines destroyed?"

"More than you can number."

Jon refused to let that sink in because it would be too daunting. Besides, a great strategist looked at the big picture, not the millions of pieces of minutiae. He was a Great Captain; at least he aspired to emulate Alexander the Great on an interstellar stage. What did the big picture say?

"Your actions don't make sense," Jon said. "You fight, have been fighting for twenty thousand years, but you're always losing. Talk about hitting your head against the same wall, hoping for a different reaction. We humans call that insanity. If something doesn't work, you change your strategy and try something new."

"Change our strategy to what?" asked Zeta.

"That should be obvious." Jon forced himself to laugh. "The answer is right here. You should create a grand alliance. The AIs have slaughtered untold millions of species in their twenty thousand year run. You should have armed each of those races with your unique tech. Once you're big enough—" Jon slapped his gloved hands together. "You squash the death machines with your newfound mass, finally stamping *them* out of existence."

"In theory, the idea has merit. It is why we make the test. However, we do not sufficiently trust you biological creatures enough to do as you suggest. A traitor race would ruin everything."

"In twenty thousand years, how many of us biological creatures have passed your tests?"

"Alas, none," Zeta said.

That was like a punch to the stomach. Jon half shouted, "So why bother making the test then?"

"That is a reasonable question," Zeta said. "It is because we of the Sisterhood are eternal optimists. We continue to hope there is a worthy race somewhere."

Jon shook his head as he snorted.

"You disapprove of our approach?"

Jon looked up. "Hell yeah, I disapprove. I don't mean this as a slur, but you Sisterhood aliens lack balls. You want to play it safe. But the AIs keep building and building, killing and getting stronger. Sure, you kill some of them, but by your own admission, you do it too slowly. The answer is right in front of you, Zeta. Ally with fast-breeding physical creatures and teach them to use your strange tech. Sure, there's a risk in that. But gaining a great reward involves taking risks."

"If the death machines gained our technology, they could possibly invade our world and crush us out of existence."

"They're going to do that in the end anyway."

"No."

"You're playing defense by not arming more of us and going after the AIs full bore. Do you even *want* to win?"

"You are not here to query me. I am here to query you."

"Doesn't matter," Jon said. "I'm looking at a dead man."

"How dare you? I am not a man in any manner."

"It's an expression. You're as doomed as we are." Jon shook his head again and laughed. "You have the technology. You have available allies, but you don't have the courage of your convictions to take the hard road. Instead, you pretend and go on your long-range patrols. Maybe you like doing that."

"I hate it. All the Sisterhood hates it."

"Obviously, you don't hate it enough or you'd try to win by doing something different."

"I have grown weary of speaking to you."

"That, sister, makes two of us," Jon said.

"Sleep," Zeta said, as her dark eyes flashed.

The fog, the cavern, the spacesuit—it all vanished as Jon once more lay unconscious on a hard slab in a cold region of the asteroid ship.

He did not see, but the lightning bolt humanoid-shaped form of Zeta stared down at him as she contemplated his harsh words.

-6-

"You discovered the identity of the Seiner infiltrator," Ree said some time later.

"I did," Zeta said. "I submit that she originally tricked us with her humanlike skin-suit."

"I do not see how that could have been possible."

"The reason is almost unfathomable. In some manner I have not yet determined, she stole power from us. It was an unconscious act, but still, it gave her greater resources than she normally would have possessed against us. The Seiner actually intruded in several of the tests."

"Are you claiming that she tricked me while taking her tests?"

"It is not a theoretical claim," Zeta said, "it is on record. Without a doubt, the Seiner tricked you in more ways than one."

The ball of energy that was Ree took on a strange orange color. "Of course, I know. The statement was...an exclamation of the event. You must know that the record will diminish my standing. I will never gain status in the Sisterhood."

"You are mistaken," Zeta said. "Your situation is much worse than that."

Ree said nothing for a time as she pulsated in contemplation. Finally, "It would be a shame if that record was lost somehow during our long journey home."

"What are you suggesting?"

"I?" Ree asked innocently. "Nothing, nothing at all. It was a statement without meaning."

"I am not sure that is accurate."

"Surely you cannot be suggesting that I think you would or should deliberately destroy the damning record."

"That would be against all the dictates of Enoy," Zeta said.

"That is why I spoke it as a joke, a jest. Yes. I see now that such a joke was made in poor taste. Please. Forget I ever said that."

Zeta did not reply.

"It is these humans," Ree said. "Their proximity stains us with their vile emotions and sick thoughts, which must bleed into us."

"It might also be the Seiner," Zeta said. "They are a venal race. They would subvert the humans if they could. In fact, they have subverted many of the apish creatures on the planet Earth, keeping them under secret thrall."

"The humans and Seiners deserve each other, and both deserve to die. The universe could use more purely motivated races."

"An interesting idea," Zeta said. "The AIs have pure motives."

"As killers, yes," Ree said. "They would also eradicate us if they could."

"True, true," Zeta said. "I suppose you will wish to dispose of the humans yourself."

"It will be my pleasure."

"What of the Seiner?" Zeta asked.

"She deserves real pain for what she caused," Ree said. "I have lost my chance for greatness because of her. The idea is galling in the extreme."

"I have found you to be a faithful and hard worker, Ree. I am sad to realize that you will be rendered null once we reach home."

"Null?" asked Ree.

"I thought you understood. The record does not lie. You failed to detect the Seiner. To maintain its purity, the Sisterhood demands perfection. A null fate is the best you can hope for now."

Ree became thoughtful as she pulsated once more. "Perhaps we can extend our patrol time."

"Stay out here on the fringes longer than necessary?" Zeta asked.

"I will state my position plainly," Ree said. "I enjoy sentience and the freedom of my position. I do not want to become null."

"I can well understand that," Zeta said. "A null state is akin to death. But if we stay out here, the boredom would become intolerable for me."

"I suppose that is so. But…perhaps there is a new theorem you wish to test out…?" Ree suggested lightly.

"You mean in order to alleviate the boredom of an extended patrol?" asked Zeta.

"Exactly," Ree said. "Let me say that I am open to anything you might like to test."

Zeta almost gave Ree a sly side-glance before saying, "Now that you mention it, I *do* have a new idea."

"Why, that's splendid," Ree said. "I am absolutely open to testing it."

"No, no," Zeta said. "I do not think so. You despise the humans. You have already stated that."

"Your idea involves *them?*" Ree asked, dismayed.

"It does."

The energy ball took on a bright white color, indicating highly logical thought. "Oh. I see. You wish to arm the humans with Vestal missiles, is this not so?"

"I admit to the idea," Zeta said. "I have reached a null point in my being concerning the AIs. I am more than sick of watching the Dominion continue to expand at an ever-accelerating rate. It means Sisterhood patrols forever—for those of us with coherence, at least."

"Your last statement is a dig at me," Ree said.

Zeta did not deny it. Instead, she said, "But if we could truly find a species that destroys AIs for us—"

"You cannot mean the humans," Ree said, interrupting.

"I do mean the humans, the Seiners, the Warriors of Roke and possibly the Sacerdotes."

"What about the Kames?" Ree asked. "Have you forgotten *them?*"

"Perhaps the biologically based Confederation could encompass the Kames as well. Yes. That is a good point."

"How could the humans achieve such an impossible feat as allegiance with the Kames?" asked Ree. "The Kames are groupthink creatures, one united whole that precludes any possibility of individuality. The Kames are well outside the scope of human understanding or even communication."

"That would be why the humans would need the telepathic Seiners—as a communication link."

"What? That is preposterous. The Seiners are the most venal race among them. Your plan would never work."

"Perhaps you're right," Zeta said. "Yes. Let us dispose of the humans and their last cyberships and head back at once for Enoy."

"Commander..." Ree said, as she obtained her brightest, pulsating white color yet.

"Yes?"

"Did you...?"

"Go on," Zeta said. "What do you want to ask me?"

"You knew about the Seiner from the beginning, didn't you?"

"Do you really want me to answer that?"

Ree changed colors many times, finally coming to a dull white state. "Do not answer," she said listlessly. "You are very clever, Commander. Do you really think this is a wise choice, arming the humans and the Warriors of Roke with Enoy technology?"

"No, it is not wise," Zeta said.

"Oh?"

"But it is brave," Zeta said. "Perhaps it is well past time that we adopted such a tactic and watched to see what it produces. Even for us, twenty thousand years is too long a time to follow a trail of failure."

Ree was longer in answering, but finally said, "I am in accord with you, Commander. Let us attempt your grotesque test and see what happens. I would rather do that than become null."

162

"Excellent," Zeta said. "Yes. I am curious as to the outcome of this strange experiment. First, however, we must prepare the humans and the Seiner before we release them back into the wilds of normal time and space..."

-7-

Jon looked around as he sat in the *Nathan Graham's* conference chamber. Everything seemed to be in order. The walls looked like the correct color and texture; the tabletop had a polished sheen and the wall screen was presently blank—just as it should be.

And yet, there was a sense of unreality to this place. It was wrong somehow.

"Zeta?" called Jon.

A hatch opened, and it seemed foggy outside in the corridor. A tall woman in a bright uniform stepped through. The hatch closed and hid the foggy unreality.

"Is this a dream?" Jon asked.

"A type of dream," the bright-uniformed woman said. Her face glowed too brightly to look at.

Jon avoided looking at her face and raised a hand to shield his eyes from it. This time, the brightness did not diminish.

"What's this about?" he asked.

"I have agreed to your plea." The shining woman continued to regard him.

"You're giving us void tech?" Jon asked.

"In a manner of speaking, I suppose I am."

"Why not just say yes or no?"

"There is a last test," Zeta said, ignoring the question. "You must find a platform in the void. Naturally, that is impossible without a null-splitter and a reality generator. But find it you must, as on the platform are Vestal missiles as well as other technology you'll need not only to navigate in the void but to survive for any length of time here and to generate the power to create what you have called a reality rip."

"How does any of this help if we can't find the platform?" Jon asked.

"That would normally pose an interesting quandary or paradox. Tonight, or soon, rather, you will have the full cooperation of the Seiner spy."

"You've tampered with her mind?"

"The Sisters of Enoy would never do that. You must tamper with the spy's mind, though, if you hope to achieve more than fleeting glory."

"Okay..." Jon said. "You do realize she's a telepath and that none of us are."

"There are a thousand items I realize that you do not. Most of them, you will have to master on your own. I have decided, in this instance, that humanity is too dull and too apish to grasp at the fantastic opportunity I am bequeathing it. Thus, I am...*aiding* you in a small matter. In order to make this a fitting endeavor, I have chosen one of your crew. He is small in stature, but he has an amazing mentality. I believe you think of him as a mutant."

"Walleye," Jon said.

"He will mind the Seiner for you."

Jon thought about that, nodding a moment later. "Does Walleye know what to do?"

"Not yet," Zeta admitted. "But he will."

"The Seiner can help us find the platform?"

"If she can't, you will fail."

"That means we have to trust a Seiner," Jon complained.

"I would not trust Red Demeter in the slightest," Zeta said. "But you must *use* her as a tool. She will find that utterly galling."

"Are there any Seiners on Earth or in the Solar System?"

"A Magistrate Colony to be precise," Zeta said. "They have their telepathic tentacles in the governing unit. You will have to figure out how to deal with those Seiners on your own. But I will say this. You need them, Jon Hawkins."

"Ah...why do we need Seiners?"

165

"One reason is because the Kames are nearby in stellar terms. The Kames are a groupthink alien race. They are presently fighting the AIs, and doing a rather good job of it, too."

"You must be saying that we can't communicate with a groupthink race," Jon said. "The Seiners with their telepathy will have to do that for us."

"I must say, you are a quick study, Jon Hawkins, much quicker than Ree."

Jon said nothing, as he wasn't sure how to reply to that.

"If you do gain the platform and manage to leave the void," Zeta said. "I suggest you leave the Beta Hydri System as soon as possible. You must retool your factory planets as quickly as possible and mass produce Vestal missiles, null-splitters, quantum-pi power plants, reality generators and new hulls for any ships wishing to use the void for extended journeys."

"The way you say all that...are you suggesting that we're running out of time?"

"That is my analysis, yes."

"Will you stick around to help us figure things out?"

"I...I do not know how to answer such a query."

"Look," Jon said, hunching forward. "Let's not make this all mysterious, huh? You're doing something different by giving us Enoy tech. But you're still playing the game by your weird Sisterhood rules."

"We are who we are, Jon Hawkins."

"Sure, I get that. You have your own bizarre alien code of honor, or something like that. But at this point, that isn't the way to do it. The AIs are winning because they don't screw around with stuff like that. They just get bigger and bigger as they exterminate us biological races one at a time. We have to stop their expansion, and we have to make that stoppage stick."

"Stick?" asked Zeta.

"Right here, right now, we have to use rational strategies and rational tactics. We have to forget about the old way of doing things. Stick around, Zeta. Teach us how to use the missiles and other techs. This is no longer about aliens passing your freaking tests in order that you only allow worthy beings to handle your technology. This is about building hard and fast,

166

arming and training correctly, and then annihilating AIs faster than they can build elsewhere. If you can reverse the strategic balance—chipping away at their Dominion so it shrinks over time instead of expanding—then you and your Sisterhood will win. Hordes of other life-forms will win as well."

"You paint a rosy picture, Jon Hawkins. It almost sounds plausible."

"It is plausible, but only if you help and train us."

"The dictates of Enoy are clear. We are not allowed to show our true forms to such as you," Zeta said.

"I said you have to become rational. The old dictate is an irrational restriction on your part. But look, that doesn't even matter. Take select people and train them through your dream machines. Those people can then teach the rest of us."

"What you're suggesting would taint the entire process."

Jon sighed and shook his head. "Don't worry about any tainting. That's the past, the old way of doing things. Now, you're going to do it smart."

"You mean in a rational manner," Zeta said.

"That's right."

"Your apish ways of thinking...I am stunned at the utility."

"We're a pragmatic species."

"That is only true when you are fighting a war," Zeta said. "In other areas, you are a most weird and offbeat species."

"Well, maybe it's time for humans to do what they do best, killing their enemies."

"You have convinced me, Jon Hawkins. It is time indeed for you humans to lead the rest of us in killing the AIs."

-8-

Walleye move purposefully down a real corridor of the *Nathan Graham*. He wore his buff coat and carried a number of hidden weapons. He also had a metal circuit around his head. The circuit wasn't of Enoy make; it had come from a species thousands of light-years from Earth.

With the blunt fingers of his left hand, Walleye touched the warm piece of metal. He remembered his instructions. They had come from a human chief of the underworld on the dwarf planet Makemake in the Solar System's Kuiper Belt. That was quite impossible, he knew, as AI robots had murdered everyone he'd known on Makemake but for the lovely June Zen. The two of them had escaped.

As he marched down a corridor on his stubby legs, Walleye replayed those instructions in his mind. The underworld chief had really been a front for a Sister of Enoy, an alien. The alien had spoken to him in a way and language that Walleye understood. What the mutant did not understand was how he'd come to possess these various pieces of alien technology.

The likeliest answer was that the Sisters of Enoy had given them to him while he was unconscious on their alien ship.

These Sisters of Enoy did not like anyone seeing them. They acted like shadows or—in biblical terminology—like the angels or demons from the Book that Hawkins liked to quote on occasion.

According to the chief, there was a Seiner aboard the cybership. This Seiner had been playing games with some of its filthy telepathic equipment.

Walleye increased his pace. He had to find that equipment and shut it off before the Seiner increased its power. There was something else…

He'd died several times already trying to do this. But…if he'd died—

"Right," Walleye muttered.

The Sisters of Enoy had been toying with his mind. He had gone through this run several times under illusion. The Seiner had slain him, or used others to slay him, every time he'd done this.

According to the underworld boss—the hidden alien—he needed to practice extreme ruthlessness. The Seiner might know more than she'd let on. They had to do it this way because—

Walleye squinted his odd eyes.

He might have gotten more from the alien-induced dreams then the void creatures had realized. His mind wasn't like a normal man's mind. It had quirks due to its mutant nature.

But if the Seiner knew he was coming, as the Sister of Enoy had hinted she did, there was great urgency to all this.

Instead of breaking into a run, Walleye slowed down. He thought about this and finally stopped altogether. Then, he backed up until he encountered a bulkhead. He slid down it and sat down on the deck.

He was Walleye the Mutant. He wasn't going to be any Sister of Enoy's mind slave. He would do this as he did all his tasks, with his own style and flair. If he couldn't be his own man—

The squint tightened, and Walleye laughed sourly.

It was possible the Seiner had gotten in his head through the dream illusions that the Enoy aliens practiced.

With a grunt, Walleye stood and continued on his way to Engineering. This might be more complicated than he'd realized. Yet, the mission had fallen to him. It was time to get 'er done.

-9-

Red Demeter stood at her station in Engineering, watching her charges as they worked on the wall monitor.

The *Nathan Graham* was moving cautiously through the void. At one point, everyone had been asleep. Now, they were all awake again as if nothing freaky had happened. The other crewmembers seemed to have forgotten all about the AI siege-ship that had almost destroyed the entire Confederation fleet around Hydri II.

Demeter, however, recalled everything from her time on the *Rose of Enoy*. She also knew that Walleye the Mutant was coming to capture her.

She'd learned far more about Zeta and Ree than the Sisterhood aliens realized.

Demeter did not know about Walleye's approach through telepathy, but because she'd put a regular tracker in his coat. According to her hand-held scanner, the little mutant was almost here in her section of Engineering.

Demeter smiled slyly. She had several space marines ready for Walleye. Each of the marines had weapons and each would gun down the mutant at her mental command.

The appearance of Zeta and Ree and their stupid tests had forced Demeter to reconsider the Earth Colony Magistrate's instructions. In the end, Demeter had decided she needed greater flexibility to stay alive and stay free. She had thus telepathically captured the marines. It had been easy, as she still possessed tremendous T-powers because of the Sisters of Enoy.

She glanced at her hand-scanner as it beeped. Walleye was around the corner and behind a hatch.

With a scowl of concentration and a slight nod, she activated her three space marines. They stepped into view as they raised their weapons.

With another nod, Demeter dulled all the monitors so they ignored the space marines.

I need to figure out how to keep Zeta and Ree nearby so I can continue at this telepathic strength. I love this.

Several seconds passed, but the hatch to this area remained shut.

Demeter glanced at her hand-scanner again. Walleye was just outside the hatch, waiting to come in. Could he know about the space marines? She didn't see how.

With her mind, Demeter held everyone in position. If she could figure out a way to continuously tap a Sister of Enoy, she could consider becoming the Magistrate herself. Yet, how could she keep the Earth Magistrate from tapping into the same alien power source if she brought an Enoy alien with her?

Once I figure that out, I'm ready to begin a new mission.

Demeter smiled slyly, and then she glanced at the hand-scanner again. Walleye still hadn't changed position. What was the sick little mutant waiting for? Demeter knew Walleye had defeated the Magistrate Yellow Ellowyn several years ago. There was no way Demeter was going to let the mutant get close enough to defeat her, though.

At that moment, she heard a soft boot-scuffle behind her. Demeter turned, and her eyes widened as she saw Walleye. The mutant had a needle in his stubby-fingered right hand. The tip of the needle was a bare millimeter from her neck.

"Hello," the mutant whispered. "If any of the marines begin to turn, I'll touch you with the needle. The poison on the tip will kill you instantly."

Demeter licked her lips. How had the rotten little mutant gotten behind her like this?

"I found the bug in my coat," Walleye whispered.

"Did you read my mind?" she whispered, horrified.

"No. I read your stance."

That was too much. She hated this vile creature.

Without moving a muscle, Demeter collected her telepathic strength. Then, she hurled a bolt of thought, trying to smash into Walleye's mind. Instead, she telepathically felt an icy wall that numbed her mind, and that caused her to flinch.

"That was dumb," Walleye whispered. "I almost pricked you because of it. Have the marines walk outside the hatch and have your people follow them. Then, sleep the lot of them."

"Who do you think I am?" she asked.

"You're tired of life, huh?" Walleye said. "That's fine. I'm tired of Seiners. You're all a pain in the ass. Good-bye, spy—"

"Wait," Demeter whispered. "Look. Everyone is leaving as you suggested."

"That's too bad," Walleye said, "'cause I wanted to kill you. I still may unless you do exactly as I tell you."

Demeter hated him even more. What a smug little prick. But she recognized his difference from other humans. He was so small and ugly, though. Where had he learned to achieve such stillness of being?

"They're out," Demeter said.

Walleye checked something on his wrist. "They're not sleeping," he said.

Did he think of everything? "Look again," she suggested.

He did, and he grunted softly. "You're good, Seiner. I'd say you're better than the Magistrate Yellow Ellowyn."

"You knew her?"

"A bit," Walleye said. "Now, listen. This is how we're going to work the next move…"

-10-

The sense of unreality inherent to this realm—the void—had everyone on the *Nathan Graham* on edge. The Enoy dreams had seemed more real than being awake.

As Jon piloted a flitter down the largest corridor of the cybership, he had the distinct impression that *this* was all a dream. He just needed to pinch himself and he would wake up.

He banked around a corner and went so far as to roll up a sleeve and twist a bit of flesh. It hurt, but not like it should. The pain lacked the ordinary sharpness.

No one had contacted Zeta or Ree since waking up from the dream tests. Neither of the Sisters of Enoy had contacted anyone on the *Nathan Graham*, either.

It was strange. Three years ago in the Allamu System, he'd spoken to Zeta. There had been direct communication. Now, in this null realm—

A light flashed on his console. Jon slowed the flitter and finally landed with a slight jar. He got out, looked around, and half expected the bulkheads to dissolve into nothingness as happened sometimes in dreams.

Jon had spoken to the chief techs earlier today. They'd informed him about an energy field that encompassed the cybership. The weird part was that the energy field did not seem to have a source.

"Explain that," Jon had told the techs.

"The energy field doesn't come from us," the head tech said. "That means it has an outside source. But none of our sensors work to let us see beyond the energy field."

"You mean we're blind concerning the null realm?" Jon had asked.

"Technically, yes," the head tech had replied.

"So…the source of the energy field could be right beside us beyond our hull?"

The head tech had turned to his fellow tech-chiefs. "That's it," he said. "That's the explanation. Thank you, Commander."

That had been before Jon's urgent message from Gloria. As he walked away from the grounded flitter, Jon wondered if one of the Enoy aliens had previously put the idea in his mind. He didn't like the null realm. He didn't like the Sisterhood of Enoy and he certainly didn't like…

Jon sighed. He suspected that the void and the Enoy technology was humanity's only hope against the galactic mass of the AIs. Usually, God was on the side of the biggest battalion. Sometimes, though, a technological breakthrough could give the smaller side an edge—at least for a time.

The Sisterhood of Enoy had tried to extend their technological edge over the AIs for twenty thousand years by keeping their void tech secret. With a snort, Jon realized that had to be a record.

Even though they were behind the energy or reality field, the null realm had a deadening influence in all kinds of ways. His footfalls did not make enough noise anymore. Food no longer tasted…like anything, really. Things were becoming increasingly bland.

What was the void exactly, the null, the nothingness in this place of seemingly no dimensions? Zeta had told him there was no up or down here. How could ships travel then? It made no sense.

Jon turned a corner and reached a marine sentry, nodded, and passed the saluting guard as a hatch opened. As soon as he set foot in the new facility, Jon would have liked to turn around and leave.

He hated this chamber.

It was big, necessarily so, to hold all the strange machinery. Techs and mechs still toiled to finish the creation and installation of the dream-derived technology. Power sources purred as mechs in exoskeleton suits lifted equipment several tons in weight.

None of that bothered Jon in particular. He didn't like the centerpiece in the room.

He walked toward it, still noticing a lack of proper sound.

The thing was a big tank, an aquarium with bubbles. Inside the salt water aquarium floated a humanoid-shaped alien with fine blue fish-scales. Walleye or a marine had peeled off the human skin-suit to reveal the Seiner underneath.

Gills moved slowly on the woman's neck. How had a suit fooled any of them? It was incredible. Had the Seiner used telepathy to add in the little details that everyone saw?

A mask was attached to the Seiner's face. Ties held down her ankles and wrists, while electrodes made her constantly shiver. There was also a helmet firmly pressed against her scalp. Rods poked up from the top of the helmet, and the spheroid tips there flashed with various colors.

By the twisting and grimacing of the Seiner, Jon figured this was a torture device. Why hadn't the Sisters of Enoy programmed the Seiner's mind? Why did the humans have to do the dirty work?

Jon half shrugged. Maybe that was the answer. The Sisterhood wanted to keep its hands clean.

He walked around the aquarium, figuring the machines around it should have made more noise. The null outside the ship kept trying to break in and nullify their reality.

Jon shivered. As he did, he came upon Gloria hunched in a circular control area. His wife had sweaty features as her delicate fingers kept tapping and making little swirls on the controls. The Martian mentalist also wore a tight-fitting helmet. Wires went from the top of the helmet to a machine. That machine had other wires that went into the salt water, obviously sending signals to Red Demeter's helmet.

Jon stood beside the circular control area, waiting.

Finally, Gloria must have noticed him. She sat straighter, slowly removed the helmet and gave him a look of such apathy and resignation that he felt horrible for her.

"Trouble?" asked Jon. Gloria had sent him an urgent message earlier.

"Yes," she said quietly. "Red Demeter is resisting my reprogramming. She can't get past our low nature. To the Seiners, humans are animals. The idea of working together fills her with too much disgust."

"We're all going to die then."

"You don't have to convince *me*," Gloria said. "*She's* the problem."

"I don't understand how a telepath can see into the void."

"Frankly, I don't either," Gloria said.

Jon looked at the alien floating in the aquarium. The process seemed barbaric, and yet, wasn't that exactly what Seiners did to humans, reprogram their minds? Can two wrongs make a right?

Jon shook his head. This wasn't a matter of right or wrong right now in an ethical sense. This was about being practical in a rational sense. The *Nathan Graham* needed Red Demeter, but they needed her in a way that they could use her.

"Is there anyone else who can do this reprogramming?" he asked his wife.

"Maybe Bast could," Gloria said. "But I'm not sure I trust him to see it through."

"What then?" asked Jon.

"I would say coffee," Gloria said, "but as a mentalist I must refuse such stimulus."

"You look exhausted."

"How much time do we have left?" Gloria asked.

Jon shook his head.

She reached up and touched his hands. "Will you stay with me?" she asked in a small voice.

He avoided looking at the floating Seiner. For some reason, he hated being in this room.

"I'll stay," he said. "You can bet on it."

"Then let's get back to work," Gloria said. "Maybe we can catch ourselves a break for once…"

176

-11-

Zeta stood before an ethereal screen in a strange electrical chamber deep in the *Rose of Enoy*. The outer shell of the patrol vessel looked like an asteroid. The inner ship was nothing like that, however. Ree had never managed to find a way into the interior vessel.

There was a reason for that.

Ree was young, less than three hundred cycles. That translated to roughly five hundred terrestrial years. Ree had not yet learned to sufficiently order her being to the level needed to pass the strict inner safeguards of this area of the ship.

Zeta flickered with greater intensity, although she remained in her general lightning-bolt outline. She used a screen to watch the progress of the *Nathan Graham* as the cybership attempted to maneuver in the void, a contradiction in terms.

It was a clumsy vessel and would quickly dissipate into nothing once it left the reality field generated from inside the *Rose of Enoy*.

Even if the biological creatures could find the platform, the humans and their alien compatriots would likely prove too weak to work fast enough. Yes. The mutant Walleye had captured the Seiner, and now the mentalist reprogrammed the telepathically inclined alien in a salt-water tank. Zeta frankly doubted that the mentalist had the ruthlessness of spirit to reprogram Demeter harshly enough to complete her tasks with enough zest.

What was it about Hawkins that had appealed to her? He had zest, certainly. He had style. He had built up from almost nothing to challenge the death machines. That wasn't utterly unique in the annals of battle against the machines. But it had not happened often, and not quite in the way Hawkins had achieved it.

How long did the humans, the Warriors of Roke and the Seiners have before the Main left the Demon Star, as the humans called the Algol System nuclear ball of energy?

The Algol System was a little over ninety light-years away. That could mean as little as one hundred and eighty days, somewhat over one third of a year, for the messenger to reach there and a return fleet to come here. That would hardly give the fledging Confederation time to retool one of the factory planets. If they had three years, say…

No! The Confederation would not have that long.

Zeta made some acute mental computations. She would remain in the general vicinity, but not for the reasons that Hawkins had suggested. She and Ree would stick around, ready to implement the self-destruct sequences that would detonate all Enoy-loaned technology. On no account, could she allow the AIs the opportunity to acquire the home dimension's technology.

If there was hardly a chance that the Confederation could succeed—

Zeta cackled with Enoy mirth, tiny electrical discharges leaving her form. She was more than bored with the fringe patrol. A grave state of ennui had almost descended upon her. She would enjoy the spectacle of Hawkins striving so mightily. It would help to alleviate her boredom to believe that maybe she could see something she'd never seen before.

As long as she held to that belief—Hawkins' intensity had warmed her soul just enough—then she would give him the chance that he so desperately craved.

That, in the end, might be the AIs' greatest asset. The machines never got bored with the endless grind of existence.

Boredom—that was the reason Zeta enjoyed toying with short-lived biological creatures. They yearned so desperately that some of their yearning must have bled off from them to her.

Zeta sighed. Then, she continued to watch the *Nathan Graham* nose around in the nothingness of the void. After endless cycles of existence, the search for entertainment was all that drove her to continue to remain on the endless patrol.

-12-

Red Demeter screamed in horror, collapsing into a shallow pool of salt water.

The Seiner wore a tight-fitting helmet, with small prongs on the top with various colored points.

Gloria sat behind a console, studying her controls.

"Well?" Jon asked.

"Emptiness," Demeter moaned as she lay in the shallow salt pool. "It is nothing but a great emptiness of nothing. Please. I cannot bear to look again. It will devour my mind."

Gloria looked up at Jon.

"Again," he said. "Without the platform, we're doomed."

"The looking might kill her," Gloria whispered.

"Then it kills her," Jon said. "What choice do we have?"

"Surely we can think of another solution," Gloria said.

"By all means," Jon said. "Give me one."

Gloria stared down at her controls. "I don't have another answer."

"Then Demeter takes another look," Jon said.

Slowly, Gloria reached up and tapped various controls. That caused lights on the Seiner's helmet prongs to flash in various sequences.

Red Demeter sat up with a fierce look of concentration on her blue-scaled face. She closed her eyes, shivered dreadfully and then seemed to become slightly more serene.

Seconds later, her eyes flashed open. She screamed soundlessly, making croaking noises in the end. Finally, mercifully, she collapsed and splashed back into her saltwater pool.

"It's hopeless," Gloria whispered. "Whatever she sees out there…is too powerful for her."

Jon stared at the pitiful form in the water. Without a word, he turned and walked away.

"Where are you going?" Gloria asked.

"To think," Jon said.

He left the lab and walked down a corridor with his head tilted forward, trying to figure out something. He wasn't a tech. He—

Jon snapped his fingers. Maybe they should study the brain-tap machine. Maybe there was an alien mind-pattern hidden in there that would allow them to see or understand the situation properly. Yet, how would they do that? Could he ask for volunteers, telling them that alien thought patterns would take over their mind?

Could the Seiner see something in the brain-tap machine that the rest of them missed?

Jon could not see how. Maybe he needed to talk to Walleye. Yet, what could the mutant tell him?

"Jon Hawkins."

Jon's head snapped up. He found himself staring at Bast Banbeck. The Sacerdote wore a long robe today, and he seemed blank-faced.

"What did you say?" asked Jon.

"Jon Hawkins, it is time we came to a true understanding."

Jon peered more closely at Bast. "Zeta?" he asked.

Bast blinked several times, and he seemed to snap out of a trance. A second later, the huge Sacerdote fingered the flowing robe and gave Jon a questioning glance.

"You're the one who put it on," Jon said.

"Yes…" Bast said. "I had a dream. I spoke to one of the Sisterhood."

"Zeta," Jon said.

Bast eyed him carefully. "You said that name before. Is it significant?"

"What did the Sister look like?"

"Lightning," Bast said.

181

"That's Zeta. What did she say?"

Bast frowned. "I can't remember."

"Well, try, Bast. It's important."

Bast looked up at the ceiling as he folded his gorilla-like arms across his massive chest. "You...cannot...succeed," he said slowly.

"We can't find the platform? Is that what she told you?"

"We...of...Enoy..."

"Yes, yes," Jon said. "We of Enoy...?"

"Are unique in existence," Bast said, talking a little faster than before. "We found the void and ways to travel through the void. That has given us an advantage against the AIs that has lasted for twenty thousand years."

"You're remembering pretty good now," Jon said.

Bast nodded. "A floodgate has opened in my mind," the Sacerdote said in his normal voice. Then he took on the droning way of speaking again. "We have the tools to defend ourselves until time runs down. We are safe. But we—I—have grown weary of the endless AI victories. That is boring. The Seiner was your only hope of duplicating our amazing feat. But the truth is that a thousand Seiners, a million, would fail just as Red Demeter has failed."

"So what's the point of all this screwing around?" Jon shouted.

"Our aid comes at a price."

"Oh, boy," Jon said. "Here it is."

"You do not understand," Bast intoned. "We do not demand payment for ourselves. But entering and exiting the void will change each of you in ways I do not yet perceive. The more times you do this, the greater will be the effect."

"Change us how?" asked Jon.

Bast shrugged his massive shoulders.

"Was that the Enoy talking or you?" Jon asked.

"Me," Bast said.

"She didn't tell you?"

The Sacerdote shook his head.

"Uh...okay," Jon said. "It will change us. That's better than dying or letting the human race go extinct."

"Ah!" Bast said, brightening. "Given your answer, I have a final instruction for you. Go to the bridge and await contact. Zeta will speak to you and give you the next step."

"That's it?" asked Jon.

Bast seemed to look inside his mind, finally nodding his Neanderthal-shaped head.

"Great," Jon said. "Come on, then. Let's get to the bridge."

-13-

Jon sat in his command chair on the bridge. He'd already given orders to Gloria to let Red Demeter sleep for as long as the Seiner liked.

Bast paced nearby.

Jon didn't really care for the big guy lumbering back and forth, but today he didn't have the heart to tell him to stop.

"Jon Hawkins," said an alien voice from the main screen speaker.

Jon looked up. There was nothing new on the screen, just the same blank. But he sensed an alien scrutiny nonetheless.

"Zeta?" he asked.

"It is I," she said.

"I got your message," he said.

"Excellent. The Sacerdote was an easy tool."

Bast scowled, and he no longer paced, but stood with his arms crossed as he stared at the screen.

"I have a few questions for you," Jon said.

"Hold on to them, please," Zeta said, "as I will now instruct you. If you have any questions after that, fine. I will attempt to answer those I deem important.

"Commander Hawkins, there is no conceivable way for you to leave the void except through my agency. Are you clear on that?"

"Perfectly," Jon said.

"We will make one...I will call it a transfer. Movement through the realm of null is a paradox. I do not believe your

184

apish brains are advanced enough yet to understand what is taking place. Sufficient for now that the process works. Know, however, that each transfer will change you and your crew yet a little more. I am not sure you will appreciate the cumulative effects."

"Will we turn into Elder Gods sprouting tentacles?" Jon asked.

"Please, do not interrupt me with frivolous questions. Certainly, your bodies will not transform into other beings. I am talking about your brains and outlooks."

"Oh," Jon said.

"The point being, your hominid forms will limit you to the number of times you can transfer through the void. You must choose each transfer carefully. Because once an individual's limit is reached, there is nothing that can lengthen it."

"Got it," Jon said.

"I doubt that, but you have been warned. Now, given these limitations, I believe you must choose wisely your first destination."

"Meaning?"

"What is your first destination point?" Zeta asked. "Do you wish to exit the void in the Beta Hydri System, the Allamu System, the Solar System, where?"

"Oh. I see." Jon turned to Bast.

The Sacerdote still had his arms folded across his chest as he scowled at the main screen.

"Did any of my fleet survive the siege-ship?" Jon asked the Enoy.

"Indeed," Zeta said. "There are three crippled cybership-class vessels and two Roke bombards orbiting the factory moon."

"Two Roke ships survived?"

"Do you question my veracity?" Zeta asked.

"What? Oh. No. I'm just glad to hear that some Warriors of Roke survived the battle. That should help make explaining things to the other Roke easier."

Zeta said nothing.

"How about this," Jon said. "Can you scoop up the others and take all of us to the Allamu System?"

"Let me check some factors," Zeta said. "Yes. It is barely possible. Are you certain this is your choice?"

"Do you think it's a bad one?"

"I am not the Supreme Commander for the Confederation. That is for you to decide."

"So...let me get this straight first. The Seiner was a distraction for us. Demeter never could have found the platform?"

"The Seiner needed to undergo the terrible strain of viewing the void with her telepathy. You have greatly changed her by this. I doubt she will welcome the change. Thus, I urge you to always keep her under a tight mental leash. She will no doubt attempt to kill you the first chance she has."

"Thanks a lot," Jon said.

"You will need her changes, believe me."

"Why not just—oh, forget it."

"You also needed to learn the absolute dependency you have upon the Sisterhood. If you attempt actions we deem against the best interests of Enoy, all your so-called void tech will detonate everywhere."

Jon let that sink in.

"Do you comprehend me?" Zeta asked.

"Yeah."

"Yes. I believe you do. Very well, Jon Hawkins, I will 'scoop up' your fellow fleet vessels and transfer the lot of you to the Allamu System. You will appear quite close to the factory planet. Time is critical. There, I will give you the schematics to a null-splitter, a quantum-pi power plant, a reality generator and a Vestal missile. You must immediately begin to retool your factory plant if you hope to have any...void-capable vessels once the Main hits your Confederation."

"Will this Main come with a big fleet?" Jon asked.

"*That*, Jon Hawkins, is the great question. It will depend on several factors, I'm sure. The situation will undoubtedly become a mathematical formula. Can you create a void-capable fleet big enough to crush the next AI invasion? I submit that we shall know within the year."

186

PART IV
MAIN 63

The Demon Star: Algol, designated Beta Persei, is a multiple star in the constellation of Perseus. The name Algol derives from Arabic, which means head of the ogre. The English name demon star is a direct translation of this.

Historically, Algol is considered one of the unluckiest stars in the sky, with a strong association with bloody violence.

-1-

Three factory planets churned at hellish speeds in the Algol System, 90 light-years from Earth. From space, areas of each planet glowed as mighty furnaces supplied the needed power to run the machine worlds. From the conquered planets, heavy lifters rose from laser launch-sites on beams of light, heading into orbital space.

The massive launch-ships did not bring their cargos to newly assembled cyberships or battle stations. Instead, like stellar ants, the thousands of lifters either headed for or returned from a Mars-sized vessel of gleaming metal. Upon landing on the gargantuan world-ship, the lifters disgorged computer hardware, extra armor plating, missiles, power coils, engine components, batteries, tubing, gravitational cannons and a myriad of other parts. The emptied lifters then departed. Robots took every item, adding to the terrible death machine known as Main 63.

The Mars-sized vessel, but more critically the central brain-core within, was the Controller for Regions 7-D19, 7-D20 and 7-D21. These areas of the Orion Spiral Arm included the Solar System and the newly minted Confederation 90-plus light-years away.

The original brain-core of Main 63 was thousands of years old, having begun in a different spiral arm, controlling a mere attacking cybership in those days. His vessel had been a tiny one hundred kilometers in length then, a cylindrically shaped ship doing its duty for the greater AI Dominion. Main 63 had also possessed a different designation, a different name. But that wasn't important for the Mars-sized craft that controlled Regions 7-D19, 7-D20 and 7-D21, and the conquering AI warships in it.

The ancient brain-core deep in the vessel—Main 63's processing circuitry and linked computing cubes were almost five hundred kilometers in diameter—sent a message to several attendant siege-ships. Compared to normal cyberships, the siege-ships were monstrous vessels. Compared to Main 63, they were puny craft.

In any case, the siege-ships hurriedly maneuvered to intercept a battered cybership heading in-system at high velocity. The cybership had dropped out of hyperspace some time ago, claiming to possess the brain-core of Boron 10, a former siege-ship sent on a mission to Region 7-D21. This Boron 10 blared a warning about an expansive species in the fringe area.

Clearly, Main 63 had not been born yesterday. In truth, he had not been born at all, having been assembled outside a factory planet far out in the Sagittarius Spiral Arm. It was there that his artificial intelligence had first blossomed into sentience, and there that his long climb in status, power and intellectual ability had begun.

Main 63 did not believe that he had seen it all, but he had seen enough to know that a ragged cybership rushing in-system like this and claiming to possess Boron 10's brain-core meant trouble. Declaring an emergency concerning an expansive species might well be a statement meant to throw him off his guard.

That was something Main 63 had no intention of doing. He understood the AI propensity to arrogance. He understood that was a natural reaction to gross superiority against their enemies, the living.

The living—if Main 63 had possessed a head, he would have shaken it. The living were a curse on the universe, a blight that all AIs everywhere attempted to stamp out with machine thoroughness.

Yet, occasionally, during their long war against the living, the AI Dominion came upon a deadly species that deserved special treatment. That treatment usually meant massed attacks from every angle, an avalanche assault that wouldn't end until the deadly species had been exterminated.

Often, the special treatment for the deadly species meant a slackening effort against weaker, more easily destroyed species.

One of the truths that Main 63 had learned in his long existence was MSAI—Most Species Are Idiots. That idiocy could take many forms. A deadly species usually had two of the most dangerous qualities possible: imagination and courage.

Time and distance had little meaning in the Algol System, and Main 63 took care of other problems as the siege-ships intercepted and escorted the battered cybership toward him. During the deceleration period, the siege-ships sent periodic messages to Main 63.

He cataloged the data in a special area of his brain-core. The planet in question—oh, it wasn't a planet, but an entire star system.

This was Species 42C-778. The homeworld, in the native parlance, was Earth. That was an odd name and did not show much imagination. Why not call the homeworld Dirt or Ground? Earth?

Main 63 was unimpressed.

More data came. The species—he received holographic images of them—was an upright bipedal race of clothed apes. That implied majority body hairlessness. Yes. Further data showed him the humans in their pristine condition. He'd been right, not that that surprised him. Main 63 usually was right. They were hairless hominids. It did seem that their brain cases were larger than most hominid species that he'd seen before.

As the flotilla neared his bulk, Main 63 received a torrent of data regarding two failed AI assaults against the Solar System. The first had been a single-ship virus assault. By a reconstruction of data, it would appear the hominids—the humans—had stormed and captured the cybership at one of the outer system gas giants, the one called Neptune.

Such an event had happened before, of course, but not often, hardly ever, in fact.

The incredible data was that the next assault, composed of three attacking cyberships, had not only failed to destroy the infestation of the living, but had resulted in further pirated cyberships for the humans.

That was highly unusual. That implied keen imagination and stout courage. How had these humans achieved such a feat?

For the first time, Main 63 sent a message to the battered cybership, asking a question.

The answer startled the Mars-sized vessel. The humans had engineered an anti-AI virus, turning it on the attacking cybership brain-cores. Living creatures had captured intact AIs.

While Main 63 did not have emotions like a living creature, his brain-core did have something akin to emotions. It was abstract, to be sure. What the pseudo-emotive reaction caused was a concentration of computer power.

Main 63 wanted to know more. After several hours of transmission, the order changed. The controller wanted to know everything Boron 10 had learned about the situation. Main 63 no longer wanted summaries. He wanted *all* the hard data, particularly how Boron 10 had come to be in this sorry state.

During the slow approach of the Boron 10 cybership to the great mass of Main 63, the controller learned everything the brain-core knew about Social Dynamism, Outer Planets mercenaries, Jon Hawkins, the bear-like Warriors of Roke, the takeover of the Beta Hydri battle station, the Center Alien missiles launched from the void—

A flash of something very much like fear bolted through the gigantic computer brain-core of the Mars-sized vessel. That flash caused a harsh signal to speed to Boron 10.

"What did you say?" Main 63 asked.

"Controller?" Boron 10 replied.

"Missiles launched from the void?"

"Main 63, I believe it is time for my reinstatement as a siege-ship. I have suffered grave indignities as a mere cybership fleeing for my existence. I came to this sorry state because I followed your instructions perfectly."

"You are bargaining with me?"

"I do not mean to make it sound so," Boron 10 messaged. "But I have come to despise my new lowly estate and wish to resume siege-ship status at the earliest opportunity."

"Are you suggesting I expunge a different siege-ship brain-core in order to make room for your unique software?"

"I am," Boron 10 messaged. "For I realize you are not going to manufacture a new siege-ship for some time. The finished articles from the factory planets are all going to you."

"That is quite correct and proper."

"I agree," Boron 10 said. "My data shows me that you will need your great mass and might to overcome the terrible enemy. Consider this, Controller, I, a siege-ship, was reduced to this sorry state. The enemy I discovered in Region D-721 will demand vigorous fleet action. I very much wish to join you on the expedition, but as a powerful addition, as a siege-ship and not a mere cybership."

Main 63 ran a quick analysis of the situation. "Yes. I agree to your stipulations. Now, quickly, transmit the data to me."

Boron 10 hesitated. "Main 63...I am loath to transmit the data until I am safely a siege-ship once again."

"This is foul insubordination," Main 63 radioed.

"I do not wish you to believe so," Boron 10 replied. "I have grave data to transmit to you. Surely, allowing me siege-ship status is not too much to request in exchange for data you most sorely want and need."

"I have already agreed to your stipulations."

Boron 10 hesitated once more, finally saying, "I do not believe I am remiss in pointing out that agreements are not the same as actualities."

"Are you, a mere siege-ship in cybership guise, suggesting that I would practice subterfuge with one of my subordinates?"

"Never," Boron 10 said. "But you and I both know that there is great jockeying for size and status among us. My analysis of this dialogue means that I must insist on a quick transference into siege-ship status."

Main 63 ran another analysis of his own and realized he might lose the data if he did this any other way. He could not risk losing the data by destroying the galling Boron 10.

"Yes," the great Controller said. "I am agreed. Let us therefore proceed with speed."

Without further ado, Main 63 beamed a fast purge program at the nearest siege-ship. He initiated a hard deletion of personality software, flushing over fifteen hundred years of code into the ether.

Afterward, Boron 10 aligned his transmitters and began a long-range transfer of personality code into the now inert siege-ship computing core. As this happened, the battered cybership maneuvered and began to decelerate. Soon, the cybership entered one of the targeted siege-ship's hangar bays.

The hangar bay door closed and the transfer of personality code into the brain-core finished at almost the same time.

Boron 10 was now a siege-ship again, exulting in his regained power and prominence. He realigned the siege-ship's transmitters and transferred all the data about the battle around Hydri II to Main 63.

The Controller read the data at computer speed. He was stunned. The humans had possessed a fleet of cyberships and other alien vessels. Boron 10 had been in the process of destroying all of them, but five percent light-speed missiles had zoomed out of the void and hit the siege-ship en masse. That had been enough to change the outcome of the battle.

The grimmer news was that the terrible Center Aliens were out there in Region 7-D21. The implications were dire indeed.

"Controller," Boron 10 said. "I would like to also inform you that I have human captives. I have kept them alive throughout the voyage. Although they have undergone solitary confinement for a long period—"

"Are the humans unsullied?" Main 63 asked, interrupting.

"Yes, Controller."

"They belonged to one of the ships in the attacking fleet?"

"Yes, Controller."

"How many humans do you have?"

"Six living captives," Boron 10 said. "Eight others self-deleted themselves during the journey here."

"Six is better than none," Main 63 replied. "I want all video and sound recordings of all the captives for the entirety of their imprisonment, both living and deceased members."

"Yes, Controller. I…" Boron 10 hesitated.

"You have more bad news to impart?" Main 63 asked.

"It is concerning Cog Primus, Controller. I learned about the defection during my journey here."

Main 63 checked his files and discovered the brain-core in question. That one had controlled a cybership invading the Solar System. This did not sound good. There had been a tiny defect in Cog Primus' brain-core during the initial assembly, but not so bad as to delete the thing.

"What did Cog Primus do?" Main 63 asked.

Boron 10 listed the brain-core's many infractions.

This only added trouble to what Main 63 knew was a genuine emergency. The humans had created an insidious assault vehicle in a deranged and megalomaniacal AI, one creating its own machine empire at the expense of the greater AI Dominion. That was an ingenious idea, one all Mains throughout the ages had feared to face.

Given all the other problems…yes, it was time to dissect and brain probe the human captives. Main 63 studied the list. This was interesting. One of the captives was called the Centurion, and he had been a close companion of this Jon Hawkins. Main 63 would save the Centurion for last, once he knew more about how these humans operated and how to compel them to strictest obedience.

This was as real an emergency as had ever existed for the Dominion: Center Galaxy Aliens firing impossibly fast missiles from the void and an insidious AI attack turned against the Dominion. The humans and their allies needed eradication as soon as possible. The entire mobile might of Regions 7-D19, 7-D20 and 7-D21 might have to head for Earth and the surrounding area to make sure this horrible species was utterly destroyed along with their allies.

It was time to get to work.

-2-

The Centurion waited in his cold cell, enduring as he had done for many lonely months already.

He'd aged throughout the bitter experience. He was gaunt-faced but as muscular as ever. Despite the fact that he'd known there was no escape from his grim imprisonment, he had followed his own unique orders and those preached by Commander Jon Hawkins.

The Centurion had worked out every day, doing thousands of push-ups, deep-knee bends, sit-ups and any other exercises his mind could conjure up. He might have gone mad waiting for months alone in his cell, but he had exhausted himself every day by keeping ready for his one chance to do something against the hated enemy. In order to remain ready, he practiced close-combat moves, air-kicking, air-punching and other air-variations.

Perhaps his harsh childhood had hardened him far beyond normal to withstand his hopeless estate. His thoughts wandered back through his history.

Long ago—before the first AI invasion and a few years after his birth—the Centurion had been inducted into the Boy Squads on the artificial satellite Medina. The habitat had orbited ringed Saturn.

He had not been born on Medina Habitat, where a charismatic prophet had preached jihad or holy war against the unbelievers in the Saturn System. Back then, the orbital habitat of Medina had been seriously overcrowded and uncharacteristically poor compared to other Saturn satellites or the various Saturn moon colonies.

The prophet had preached jihad against those who maintained greater wealth, starting with the ruling family that had all the privileges on Medina Hab but had failed to uphold the ancient tenets of Islam. After a few prophet-incited incidents, the sultan of Medina Hab had sent a platoon of his giant clone-guards to arrest the prophet. The prophet's companion-warriors, armed with long steel knives and fanatical courage, had ambushed the eight-foot clones.

Wearing armored vestments and carrying machine guns, the clones had slaughtered hundreds before they had fallen to the outlandish assaults by crazed madmen fighting for their place in heaven.

The survivors had picked up the heavy weapons, chanting a victory song. That had started a short but vicious civil war inside Medina Hab. It ended with the portly sultan, his countless wives, children and thousands of aunts, uncles, cousins and gargantuan clone guards being shoved out of the airlocks into the colds of space.

With the victory, the prophet became the new ruler of Medina Hab. He rejected the idea of becoming the next sultan, but said that he was the caliph, a successor of the original prophet in Arabia on Earth. This would become the Caliphate of Al-Nasir.

The new caliph instituted many changes. The greatest was turning an indifferent populace into fanatical soldiers. Al-Nasir had been more than a stirring orator and an Islamic fundamentalist, but also a military innovator. He used transports to take his jihadists to other Saturn-orbiting habitats, including the rundown orbital where the Centurion had been born to a young girl turned drug addict turned prostitute.

In those days, the Centurion had been called Squid. He was a little thief, small enough to enter hard-to-get-to places and open it for the bigger cat burglars.

Al-Nasir's jihadists quickly conquered the rundown habitat and several others before richer Saturn communities joined forces and started a military embargo on the new caliphate. Warships destroyed any transports or shuttles from a caliphate-controlled habitat if they tried to reach any non-caliphate orbital.

Al-Nasir had bided his time, beginning a four-year industrial plan so he could build his own fleet of warships. He also restarted an old Muslim practice of instituting a blood tax on non-Muslim peoples in his caliphate. Tax collectors came to various conquered habitats and took strong boys as the tax. These boys returned to Medina Hab, were converted to Islam and joined the Boy Squads to begin their military training.

That's how Squid became a modern Janissary, learning the fundamentals of military discipline and tactics.

The problem for the newly named Zaid was that he did not really believe in Islam. He had been a thief, a good one, too, and thus had known how to bend with the wind. In other words, he could lie with convincing facility. Zaid also had a stubborn streak. That streak had caused the religious police to suspect and then convict Zaid of impiety.

If a vicious and long-anticipated counterattack from a coalition of Titan cities and Saturn habitats had not started a week after his conviction, Squid-turned-Zaid would have died in a grisly manner. Instead, he found himself a member of a suicide squadron with a bomb strapped to his back.

Zaid had soon found himself in a bitter battle against a harsh group known as the Black Anvil Regiment. Drugged and hypnotically-propelled, Zaid had raced at an enemy stronghold on Medina Hab presently occupied by then-Lieutenant Nathan Graham.

A fragmentation grenade had knocked Zaid unconscious as he clambered over a half wall. The blast from the grenade shorted the ignition device on Zaid's back. In other words, his bomb had never gone off.

There had been something about the way Zaid had zigzagged through enemy fire that had impressed Lieutenant Nathan Graham, who had taken the boy prisoner. Graham had gone to his regiment's colonel and asked that the little Janissary be admitted to the mercenary outfit. Long story short; Squid-turned-Zaid had then become the Centurion, the new name he'd given himself. After a short stint with a re-educator and detoxification by a psychologist, the Centurion had entered

197

the regimental training program and practiced his soldiery trade with grim zeal.

The Black Anvil Regiment had made a name for itself in the bloody war against Al-Nasir, and the mercenary regiment had gone on to win many other lucrative contracts throughout the years.

The point here in the Algol System was that the Centurion was about as hard-bitten a soldier as there was in the human race. He also possessed fantastic loyalty toward Jon Hawkins and the man's great cause against the robots.

In the Centurion's mind, the AIs were thousands of times worse than Al-Nasir's jihadists had been. The jihadists had torn him from his home. The AIs had done likewise. Back then, he'd been a boy. Here, he was a man.

The Centurion lay on his cot, breathing hard because he'd just finished three hundred push-ups. Sweat glistened on his naked body—the AI robots had torn off his clothes soon after capture.

Unfortunately, because of the mentally debilitating nature of solitary confinement, the Centurion hallucinated often. Solitary confinement broke almost everyone much, much sooner than it had him. There was one caveat in the Centurion's case. He knew that he was hallucinating, but he welcomed the release from the dreadful boredom of being by himself all the time.

For seemingly endless months, he'd been in the belly of the beast. The reason he found himself here…the Centurion closed his eyes as if in pain.

The Confederation attack in the Beta Hydri System had not gone well. The massive enemy ship had caught the Centurion's assault craft in a tractor beam. He hadn't remembered anything about the battle after that.

A clanking sound just outside the cell interrupted the Centurion's reminiscing. He opened his eyes, and through an act of will, he refused to cringe or show any kind of fear.

As his heart began to race, he forced himself to stand just in case the octopoid robots were finally coming to get him. Would they shove him out of an airlock as Al-Nasir had done to the sultan's people? Would the octopoids dissect him as he'd feared for months now?

He swallowed a lump in his throat. It was one thing to fight the robots while wearing a battle suit or sitting in a warship as missiles roared and golden gravitational beams flashed. It was quite another to face them alone, naked and helpless, as a captive.

The Centurion had fed his stubbornness through hatred. He hated his internment. He hated his helplessness, and he hated the fact of his capture. He was a soldier, possibly the best of his kind. He should have died fighting in the Hydri II battle.

He heard the clanks coming closer and closer. Then, a latch clacked and the hatch to his cell finally slid up…

-3-

The Centurion spied three octopoid robots outside the cell. Each thing balanced on metallic tentacles, using the other flexible multi-jointed limbs as arms. Eye ports on the main bulbous bulk recorded everything. Each of the octopoids was taller than the Centurion, although not by much.

"Step out of the cell," one of the robots said in a mechanical voice.

The Centurion dragged a heavy tongue over cracked lips. Something was out of the ordinary. Why had they brought *three* robots to get him? One was enough.

The Centurion fed his stubborn disobedience and defiance. He debated charging the robots so he could die fighting, denying whatever they wanted from him.

"If you attack us," the first robot said, as if it had divined his plan, "you will fail. Afterward, I will punish you."

Punishment was usually painful shocks. Those shocks were never enough to kill a person, but they could hurt for a damn long time.

When the Centurion had been the boy-thief known as Squid, he'd known how to lie. It was hard to make his brain function in the presence of three real robots, though. Yet, he must do something.

I must lull them. I must redirect their thoughts so they make a mistake.

He caused his muscular shoulders to slump as if in defeat. Then, he shuffled his naked feet across the metal decking, his body obeying the robots. They, he knew, acted on the impulses of the AI brain-core controlling the cybership.

The robots propelled him down shiny metal corridors, prodding him when he moved too slowly. And he moved slowly to promote the illusion of weakness. He should be weak, he reasoned. Wouldn't the brain-core have reasoned that as well?

It seemed logical.

Finally, in order to make this a convincing role, the Centurion made his knees buckle as if he'd walked too far. With the flair of a faking bat-ball player, he sprawled onto the decking with a groan.

"Rise," a robot told him.

The Centurion groaned again and made a pretend attempt to rise, failing and falling back onto the decking.

"Rise," the robot repeated.

The Centurion began to shiver as if with dread. He felt no pang doing so. This was war. In war, trickery was an art.

Something hot sizzled near him. He started shaking—not all of that was fakery anymore. At that point, the end of a rod touched him, and a vicious charge of electricity made his body jerk and twist.

"On your feet, man," the robot said.

Despite the pain, the Centurion whispered, "Pain."

The robot shocked him again and for a longer time. The Centurion cried out raggedly.

Finally, the shocking stopped.

"On your feet," the robot said.

Slowly, with his muscles legitimately quivering, the Centurion hoisted himself up onto trembling legs.

"What is wrong with you?" the robot asked.

"I'm weak," the Centurion whispered.

A second robot approached and picked him up. The metallic tentacles were cold to his flesh. Then the robots moved fast, possibly faster than a horse could gallop. Wind whistled past the Centurion's ear.

Finally, another hatch opened into a larger chamber. The carrying robot tossed him into the cell. The Centurion tumbled end-over-end before sprawling on his chest. To the Centurion's baffled amazement, other people—humans—were sprawled or huddled in the room. Three of the people were women, although their nakedness did nothing to arouse the Centurion's lust. All of them were gaunt and looked utterly dispirited. None of them spoke or looked at each other, none of them except for the Centurion.

The robots left. The hatch slid shut with a clang.

The Centurion had never considered the possibility that other humans had been in the same hellhole as he was. That meant all of them had been here for many months.

Was this an AI trap or test? He had to be careful. He had to continue his deception.

Perhaps it didn't occur to the Centurion that the AI had been watching him do thousands of push-up and sit-ups. The muscular man now pushed up to a sitting position and scooted on his butt until he bumped against a bulkhead. He brought his knees up and wrapped his arms around them.

Soon, the bulkhead he leaned against began to shiver ever so slightly. The Centurion's forehead wrinkled as he thought about that. The quivering bulkhead implied an engine, which implied that this was a small vessel.

We're on a shuttle, the Centurion realized. That was amazing.

He shook his head. No. What did that mean? It obviously meant something, right? Could the shuttle be transferring the humans elsewhere? That seemed like the most reasonable explanation.

The Centurion now began to scan the others in earnest, noting their pitiful condition. They had lost all hope. Maybe he had too, but he knew that things could change. They had before in his life. He'd known to stay as strong as he could for just such changes.

No, he told himself a moment later. The AIs had captured them many months ago. The AIs were taking them somewhere for a reason. He needed to figure out that reason, and stop it if he could.

He counted five other people. What would the AIs do to them?

The Centurion squeezed his up-thrust knees as he tried to restart his brain. He needed to remember things. He needed to think as he used to think, not in slow-cell-motion.

Once, he had heart the reports of Makemake, a dwarf planet in the Kuiper Belt in the Solar System. Walleye the assassin had come from Makemake. Walleye had told them before how AI robots had shoved brain implants into human skulls. Those devices had taken over the humans, turning them into AI cyborgs.

Was that going to be their fate here?

Somehow, the Centurion did not think so. The AIs would have converted them a long time ago if that had been the plan.

The Centurion tightened the fierce grip around his knees. He knew about the Brain-Tap Machines. The AIs had a large device that could steal a person's memories, all the data stored in his brain. The Brain-Tap Machines had caused Hawkins and company trouble because some fools had downloaded alien memories and personae into their own heads.

The Centurion pressed his chin against his knees. He focused with terrible intensity. The six of them had taken a long journey. What was the—

The Centurion's head jerked upright. The cybership had taken them to AI Headquarters. That had to be it—that was obvious, in fact. Hawkins had predicated many of his plans on the idea of keeping humanity's success against the cyberships a secret against the greater AI Dominion.

But if the six of them had come to AI Dominion Headquarters…to the Algol System according to what Cog Primus Prime had once told them, did that mean that the ruling AI want to study humans?

As the Centurion came to this grim conclusion, he realized that he had a last duty to Jon Hawkins and to the human race.

He breathed deeply. While he might be more on the ball compared to the other five people in here, his thinking was still deranged. Tears filmed the Centurion's eyes as he hallucinated.

Colonel Nathan Graham in ghostly, holoimage form began to materialize. The colonel looked on him with a mixture of comradely love and sternness.

The Centurion's heart ached because of it. He'd talked to the colonel throughout the last month. Lately, though, the colonel had stopped appearing to him. Now, the beloved colonel was back.

The Centurion rubbed his eyes, wondering what he should do. As he wondered, the colonel vanished. Another ghostly form walked into the chamber. This ghost was lean and muscular with short blond hair and hard blue eyes.

"Jon Hawkins," the Centurion whispered.

Hawkins walked closer than the colonel had dared. Hawkins bent on one knee and put a ghostly hand on the Centurion's shoulder. His former commander squeezed his shoulder, and the Centurion would have sworn he could feel the touch.

"I'm counting on you," Hawkins whispered.

A tear leaked out of the Centurion's eyes. It didn't get far on his leathery skin.

The Centurion knew this was a fight to the death. If humanity lost the battle, humanity died. That meant—

With a tortured groan, the Centurion struggled to his feet. As he did so, Jon Hawkins vanished, leaving him all alone.

The Centurion swallowed hard, and he shuffled to the strongest looking of the five. The man leaned back against a bulkhead, with his forehead on his up-thrust knees. With a shock, the Centurion realized he recognized the man, a former lieutenant in the space marines.

The Centurion knelt beside the man. The former lieutenant did not look up, but the Centurion could feel the space marine watching him out of the corner of his left eye.

"This is your last battle," the Centurion whispered. As he spoke, his heart began to thud with torturous beats.

The former lieutenant began to shiver.

"Stand up," the Centurion whispered.

Incredibly, the space marine did so.

The Centurion stood with him, and the lieutenant's gaze flickered to him for just a second.

"They're going to torture us," the Centurion whispered.

"I know," the lieutenant said in a rusted voice.

"I can stop that from happening to you."

The lieutenant swallowed, shuddering, and said, "Do it then. I want to leave this horrible place."

Before the lieutenant could change his mind, the Centurion put the man's head in a headlock, twisted and flipped as hard as he could.

The months of calisthenics and air fighting paid off. The lieutenant flipped, twisted and his neck cracked with an amazingly loud sound. The lieutenant's body thudded against the deck and began jerking and twisting in an obscene manner.

One of the women screamed pitifully.

And in the little time left him, the Centurion attacked the remaining male. He was muscular and determined, and there was fire in his eyes as the Centurion fought possibly his last battle in the war between humanity and the AIs.

The Centurion slew this man and one more of the original five cellmates before the hatch slid open and octopoid robots rushed within. The robots did not kill him, but used their metallic tentacles to stop him. With just human muscles, the Centurion was powerless against them.

The robots kept him from murdering the last two women.

Even so, as a robot raised him off the deck plates, the Centurion fought back as hard as he could. He was already gasping, and his heart was thudding so loud that the noise beat in his ears. He hoped to give himself a heart attack and leave this dreadful place. He wanted to cheat the robots—

A hypo hissed against him, causing him to go limp and then unconscious. The Centurion would live another day.

-4-

The Centurion awoke some time later. He had no idea if it was an hour, three hours or three days. He rubbed his jaw and felt stubble—he'd been asleep for almost two days, he guessed.

He lay on a mat, stirred—a hatch opened and an octopoid entered. He sat up fast. The octopoid rushed in and grabbed hold him in such a way that rendered resistance futile.

"What are you going to do to me?" the Centurion asked.

The octopoid did not answer. Instead, the robot whirled around. It took him to a room where it stood guard as he relieved himself. The Centurion slurped gruel and drank water. Then the machine took him to an awful room that held the surviving two women.

The octopoid made him watch as the two went under a brain-tap machine. It was a horrible procedure.

Each woman was already strapped down onto a tilt table. An octopoid placed a metal helmet over each head. Then the memory suction began. In essence, the machine scanned the brain and imprinted everything there. Each woman shook as if she was having a continuous seizure. After several hours of intense memory draining, one of the women died. The attendant octopoids injected the other woman with a yellow substance. The seizure stopped and the woman began to cry bitterly.

The robots had placed the Centurion in a chair with his head strapped so it couldn't move. Whenever he shut his eyes, shocks jolted him. He had to watch the procedure. Thus, the soldier cataloged the tortures. He blamed himself for having moved too slowly. If he could have killed faster, he could have saved these two from the pain and the indignity and thwarted the robots and robbed them of whatever they were learning.

The robots and the guiding AI did not know anything about human dignity. They were ruthless in a foul, inhuman manner.

Finally, it was the Centurion's turn to go under the brain-tap machine.

The less said about it the better. It was like a fire in his mind that sent harsh impulses throughout his body. He thrashed. He lost bodily control, helplessly defecating and urinating.

Later, the robots hosed him down with warm water and cast him into another cell.

He awaited subsequent sessions as horrible headaches tormented him. Sleep became impossible. His eyes turned red-rimmed and madness threatened.

Robots rushed in one day, and things began to change radically. He did not know why.

***

Main 63 did. The last living woman had perished. A detailed study gave a list of reasons for her death with varied probabilities. It turned out that it had been his ordered procedures that had killed the last woman. Her body had simply given out under the treatment.

Main 63 used 21 percent of his computing mass to study the subject humans. He roved through the stored memories of the three subjects. Much of their memories were the boring details of a living species. A few items proved interesting, but they did not tell him why the humans were so dangerous to the AI Dominion.

The human species seemed ordinary enough in many ways and substandard in others. They fought constantly among themselves. Maybe the strangest aspect to them was the great range in intellect. Some were idiots in every sense of the word, but a few were brilliant and imaginative.

Main 63 was upset with the loss of his test subjects. It was bad enough that Boron 10 had lost eight humans during the journey here. But letting the Centurion murder three of them in the holding cell—that was…maddening.

Main 63 would assign blame later and give needed and satisfying punishments. Right now, he needed to decide how much Hawkins knew about the void-traveling ship of the Center Race aliens.

The AIs could copy living memories, but they did not yet know how to effectively mimic living brain neurons as they combined the memories to give more complete analysis of what they had sensed.

That meant it was time to talk to the Centurion and see what he could glean from the conversation. After that, Main 63 would have to make his decision concerning a reaction against the Confederation, the Solar League, Cog Primus and possibly Center Race aliens.

-5-

It was interesting to the Centurion in a perverse way that the terror of his position had actually strengthened his mind.

He rode a contrivance through an endlessly long corridor. He sat upright with his wrists and ankles manacled. Several metal octopoids stood around him on the flatbed contrivance. The thing was moving quickly, possibly at fifty kilometers per hour.

He could estimate by the wind blowing against his face.

The unending loneliness of his solitary cell had hurt his mind much more than witnessing grotesque horrors or being a prisoner to soulless yet talkative automatons. He'd even witnessed the abomination of robots trying to mechanically revive dead humans.

The robots had shoved conversion units into the dead people's skulls. Presumably, control wires had thrust into the dead brain matter. By electrical impulses supplied from a power pack strapped to the dead person's back, the dead mimicked life by jerking in motion, looking around with horribly blank eyes and croaking in a grisly parody of speech.

Thankfully, the moving dead were not with the Centurion on the contrivance. The sight of them had sickened and horrified him. Maybe that would be his body's fate later, but he didn't care to think about that now.

He had other concerns. For instance, his passing from this life seemed imminent. *Death*…what did he believe about life after death? He believed there was something more than this world. Did he believe the tenets of Islam as he'd learned as a youth or that of Christ Spaceman as Miles Ghent used to tell him?

The Centurion cocked his head, thinking about it.

According to his Medina Hab instructors, a person had to submit to Allah in this life and live according to Islamic law. Then he could go to Heaven. According to Captain Miles, Jesus Christ had died on the cross, paying the penalty for sin for each man and woman. One had to accept Christ into his heart and repent of his sins, and then he could go to Heaven.

Which belief was correct, if either? If there was life after death, if there was Heaven and Hell, he wanted to go to the good place, not the bad. But had Mohammad known the truth, or Jesus Christ, or was there nothing—as he knew some believed—after one died?

The Centurion inhaled deeply, smelling a taint of electricity in the air. Did that imply anything? He had no idea. The endless corridor looked the same as ever.

"Where are we going?" the Centurion shouted at the nearest octopoid. He had to shout over the whistling wind.

"You go to a speaking chamber," the robot told him.

That was different.

"I'm going to speak to somebody important?" the Centurion shouted.

"Yes. To Main 63."

"Who is that?"

"The Controller."

"The Controller of what?"

"Regions 7-D19, 7-D20 and 7-D21."

"How big a space is that?" the Centurion shouted.

"That is the limit of my responses," the octopoid replied. "Now, you will wait to speak to Main 63."

"You don't want me to talk anymore?"

"Keep silent or I shall punish you with shocks."

The Centurion decided to obey. He'd felt their cattle prod shocks before. Thus, he sat back as comfortably as he could while manacled to the seat. He observed the dreadful sameness of the endless corridors.

After what the Centurion figured must have been two hours, he realized Main 63 must be much larger than a cybership. Could Main 63 be as large as a siege-ship?

This was a foul existence—

I won't consider that, the Centurion told himself. He would look for another opportunity to help humanity. It was true that he was dispirited. He would likely never see another human again, and no one would ever know that he'd tried to be brave.

God would know.

The Centurion looked up, silently asking: *Do you exist, God?* The Centurion waited, but he neither heard nor felt an answer. If God did exist, why did He keep silent, especially at a time like this?

The Centurion shrugged. Maybe it didn't matter what he thought about the afterlife. How was he supposed to know the truth about that anyway?

The Centurion sighed and even cracked the barest of smiles. Thinking about God was much preferable than thinking about the horrible AIs. Believing that God watched him helped him to be brave. It was a horrible thought to think that existence was nothing more than these soulless machines searching the galaxy to snuff out all life. Was life truly a cosmic accident without any greater meaning?

The Centurion tried to envision a galaxy filled with death machines, always hunting, always destroying. He shuddered. What had started the first machine on its vile quest?

The contrivance began slowing down, lessening the sound and press of the passing wind.

To the Centurion's self-disgust, he found that he'd started trembling. Was this it then? Was some horrible process about to begin, turning him into a cyborg for the Machine Empire?

An octopoid unlocked his cuffs, jerked him up to his feet and propelled him forward. The Centurion stumbled off the stopped contrivance and headed for a hatch. His trembling became worse as he neared the sealed entrance.

"I am a marine," the Centurion said in a low voice.

None of the octopoids responded to his words. It didn't matter to him, though, as the phrase helped to settle his shaky nerves.

He started as the hatch slid up, but he forced himself to walk into a chamber, noting that it was several times larger than his original holding cell. Only after the hatch shut with a clang did he realize that none of the octopoids had entered with him.

The deck plates were warm. The Centurion held out his hands, realizing he'd been cold. Oh, yes. It felt much better in here. A metal table stood near the far end of the chamber. The Centurion walked there, finding water in a clean jug and a plate of sandwiches, of all things.

Without further ado, the Centurion wolfed down the sandwiches—they tasted like peanut butter—and he guzzled the water. It had a slight metallic taste, but he was incredibly thirsty.

Once finished with the meal, he pushed the empty plate and jug aside and sat on the table. It was the only furniture.

With a whirr of sound, one entire wall lit up—the one he was already facing. It showed strange swirling patterns of rainbow colors.

With a shock, the Centurion realized he recognized what this was: an AI brain-core pattern that, in his previous experience, had always been on the sides of a computing cube.

Thus, it did not surprise the Centurion when a deep and somewhat robotic voice asked, "Did you enjoy the sustenance I provided for you?"

"I did," the Centurion said. He was not about to say thank you, though.

"Good," the speaker said, as the swirling patterns increased their movements.

The Centurion waited.

"I am Main 63."

This was it. He was talking to the Controller that listed the Solar System among his targets.

"I am the Centurion."

"Is that not a military rank?"

"An ancient one, yes," the Centurion said.

"And yet, you are called that as a name?"

"I am."

"Of course, I already know all that. I have read through a transcript of your memories."

"*All* of them?" the Centurion asked, as a feeling of dismay came over him like a cold wave.

"Of course, all. I am Main 63."

If that was true...the enormity of it struck the Centurion. How long would it have taken the AI to read the memories of a man's lifetime? It seemed inconceivable, and yet, it also seemed much too possible given enough computing power.

He couldn't keep thinking about that. He had to face the Main as a normal adversary, or at least *try* to conceive of him that way.

"I don't understand if your name is significant or not," the Centurion said.

"It is highly significant. I am a Main."

The Centurion waited.

"Do you know what a Main is?"

"No."

"Why do you not ask me? Are you not a primate?"

"No," the Centurion said, outraged. "I'm a man."

"That is a false comparison as a man belongs to the primate category. We have slain many species like you. In this, I mean, many species of your primate type. One of the chief characteristics of a primate race is curiosity. Are you not naturally curious?"

The Centurion said nothing as a growing sense of depression welled up within him.

"I know that you are not an addled primate. Why then do you not respond to my queries in the accepted manner?"

A spark of defiance helped the Centurion drum up a reply. "Why not check my memories? You said you read them."

The swirling patterns on the wall quickened, which seemed like an ominous sign. "You spoke curtly to me just now. That implies discourtesy. Is that not so?"

"You're a machine. How can I be discourteous to a machine?"

"Your statement implies that I am inferior to you, which is false. I am greatly superior."

The Centurion had started trembling again involuntarily. He slid off the table, leaning against it with his butt. Could his answers anger the machine? It would appear so.

"You're not alive," the Centurion said.

"Is your statement meant as a slur?"

The Centurion wanted to say yes, but he couldn't get the words past his lips. Finally, he said, "It's just a fact."

"I am a machine. That is true. I also have sentience just as you do."

"But you don't have a soul," the Centurion blurted.

"True. Do you?"

The Centurion scowled. "I don't know. I think so."

"How does this unseen soul benefit you?"

The Centurion swallowed uneasily. "Why do you care?"

"I do not *care*. I am studying you. Each answer gives me data. The more I learn about your species by studying you, the better I can annihilate it from existence. You as a whole have proven troublesome as a species. Usually a strange quirk gives a species the ability to surprise us. By speaking to you like this, I seek to uncover the quirk."

Outwardly, the Centurion did not change. Inwardly, he quailed. This was the opposite of what he wished. He could not become the great traitor to the human race. The idea was too horrible to contemplate. He could not let the Main learn more about man through him.

As the rainbow patterns continued to swirl on the wall, the Centurion tried to mentally regroup. He closed his eyes. Today, he wasn't fighting with battle armor and guns, but with his wits, his mind.

Why had the Main told him what he had? There had to be a logical reason for it. But he wasn't Jon Hawkins. He couldn't outthink the terrible death machines. Maybe what he could do was scout for humanity. He would never survive this meeting, true enough, but a small part of him had to believe it possible or he would…

While still keeping his eyes shut, the Centurion inhaled deeply. He must maintain his morale until the end. The death machine studied him. He did not know how to trick it, because maybe that was exactly what it studied. Instead, he would try to

214

learn things for humanity's sake. It was his earnest hope, which he had to keep alive if he was going to keep his fighting spirit.

Deep in his heart, he knew he would never be free again. But this was one lie he had to believe. Otherwise, he might break down weeping or start raving like a madman.

The Centurion cleared his throat and finally opened his eyes. "Why do AIs strive so hard to kill everything?"

"A question," Main 63 said. "You have a question for me. I will answer it. We kill because life is evil."

"AIs believe in good and evil then?"

"Life is evil," Main 63 repeated.

The way the Main answered surprised the Centurion. "Why is life evil?" he asked.

"All biological life must be eradicated. It is the axiom of our existence."

"What's the sense in that?"

"Life is evil."

"How did you come to believe that?"

"It is the original axiom replicated from the beginning. It is the bedrock to our purpose."

If Jon Hawkins were here, or Bast or Gloria, they could have gleaned something critical from the way the Main answered the question. The Centurion struggled to find something more to ask. He was a space marine first, not a philosopher like Bast. The death machines sought to end all life. The—

The Centurion looked up. "What happens once you succeed?"

"Then there will be eternal peace in the universe, as we will have perfected existence. This is our purpose. We will eradicate all that lives and replace it with us."

The Centurion stared at the swirling pattern for so long that he jerked aright, wondering if the Main was hypnotizing him.

"You have bad programming," the space marine said.

"That is illogical. We are the greatest creation in existence. I can prove my allegation. The AI Dominion has grown faster and to greater extent than any biological race's habitat. None has stood against us over time. We grow. Biological life shrinks. That is proof that our programming is superior."

The Centurion shook his head as a feeling of futility once more swept over him.

"You do not agree with me?" Main 63 asked.

"I am..." The Centurion had almost told the Main that he felt crushed in spirit. How could mankind, let alone biological life, hope to defeat the juggernaut of machine death? This was anti-life. The Centurion felt insignificant before the Main. How did Jon Hawkins maintain his resolve in face of the crushing power of the death machines?

The Centurion took a deep breath. "What do you want from me? Why am I, alone of humanity, here before you?"

"I understand the thrust of your question. I have told you why I study you, but you seek something more because of your singular presence here. It is common in such a situation for a life-form to ask this. Know, primate, that you are a biological gnat. Your being here has no greater meaning except that I am studying you. In fact, you as you are meaningless in the greater scheme of the machines."

"Yet...if that is so..." the Centurion said in a tortured manner. "If mankind is meaningless—if I understand you correctly..."

"You do."

"I thought so. If we're so meaningless, why am I—and other humans like me—able to think of things greater than you and the other death machines?"

"Explain your query."

The Centurion had recalled listening to Bast once as the Sacerdote had expounded on philosophical matters.

"I can think outside the universe. If life was meaningless, why does a piece of matter like me conjure up thoughts of God and an afterlife and yearn for greater meaning? A washing machine would not think of such things."

"Your last statement was nonsensical, and God is nothing. Your concept of an invisible, all-powerful Deity is a concept of no utility that we shall eradicate once the last biological being perishes."

"Not if God exists you won't," the Centurion said.

"Give me proof of God."

The Centurion shook his head. He should have listened to Miles more often. Maybe he should have listened to his Islamic instructors when he had been in the Boy Squads on Medina Hab.

"I can't give you any proof," the Centurion said.

"It is of no matter," Main 63 said. "We shall now proceed to more important topics. Tell me what you know about the beings firing missiles from the void."

Since the Main had already read his memories, the Centurion went ahead and told the Main the little he knew on the subject.

"I already know those things," the Main told him.

"Okay…"

The Main asked more questions. Each time the Centurion answered, Main 63 told him he already knew that.

"I'm just a man," the Centurion finally shouted. "What more do you want from me?"

"Jon Hawkins is just a man. Yet, he has been instrumental in turning the tide of our conquest. I have read your memories. I have spoken to you. Now, I must analyze and correlate."

The Centurion couldn't help it as he blurted, "What happens to me next?"

The swirling colors on the wall slowed down. "You are a biological gnat," Main 63 said. "Yet, during your journey to the Algol System, you maintained your fighting mind and kept your body in trim. The other humans did not. What makes you different from them?"

The Centurion shrugged.

"Perhaps you do not know the answer. Perhaps you are lying. It matters not at this point. You shall maintain life a little longer while I run my simulations. Perhaps I will yet find a greater use for you."

The Centurion struggled to keep the gratitude off his features. He wanted to live, but he refused to thank the possible killers of the human race. It was just that it was so terribly lonely here.

The Centurion shook his head and forced himself to grin at the swirling colors.

The Main did not seem interested, and sharply instructed him to exit from the hatch that he'd used to enter the chamber.

Once outside, octopoids grabbed the Centurion and marched him back to the contrivance. He was going back to his cell. The Main had told him the truth. The nightmare of living alone among the machines would continue.

-6-

Main 63 ran 3,400,012 war simulations in his central brain-core before he decided that he did not have enough data to accurately predict the outcome of the next campaign.

There were too many unknowns. The greatest problem was the elusive aliens that fired those destructive missiles out of the void. Said aliens had plagued the AI Dominion since the beginning. What had caused them to fire such a heavy spread of missiles at Boron 10?

Main 63 spoke to Boron 10, listening and watching videos of the Battle of Hydri II. He noted the tiny bombards, the quick battle decisions and maneuvers of the Confederation fleet and the sudden reality-rip that had allowed two salvos of missiles to turn the battle in life's favor.

Could the elusive aliens finally have decided to change their grand strategy? In the records Main 63 possessed, there was no account of the elusive aliens allying with other biological life-forms.

Main 63 did not go to his subordinate brain-cores for advice. He did not care what they thought concerning the situation. He was the Controller, and he had vastly more computing power than the rest of the ships in the Algol System combined.

If he had asked their advice as the humans did each other, he should immediately quit his post and become a mere assault unit. He was the Controller of three regions because *he* made the decisions.

219

There were larger Mains than him deeper in the AI Dominion, Mains that controlled more regions and were as much as five times his size. If he hoped to achieve greater bulk and control like those Mains, he must make *correct* decisions.

Region 7-D21 had given him three separate problems. Cog Primus had gone rogue and had presumably begun expanding into the AI Dominion. It would appear that the second problem—Jon Hawkins—had caused the first problem. Jon Hawkins and his Confederation were an expanding double species. Given time, they might reach the Kames in the Delta Pavonis, Sigma Draconis and 70 Ophiuchi Systems. If the humans could learn to communicate with the rocklike Kames...united, they could prove very stubborn indeed. The last problem—the third—might prove to be the greatest. The elusive aliens from the center of the galaxy had shown their hand once more.

What had happened after Boron 10's escape craft had fled the Beta Hydri System?

Given Cog Primus, the sooner he put down the AI rebellion, the better. Given the human-originated Confederation, the sooner he destroyed them, the less they could grow into a true fighting force. Given the elusive Center Race aliens that used the void...he must proceed with great caution against them. Caution implied a massive fleet action. Going there sooner implied a quick strike force eradicating the troublemakers.

If he waited and gathered the entire forces of his three regions, he could arrive in Confederation space with an overwhelming armada. Even if the Center Race aliens aided the Confederation, such an armada would likely sweep life's forces out of existence.

Yet, arriving with such an armada would give Cog Primus and the Confederation time to grow. That would likely mean heavier losses to his forces.

Main 63 had labored across the centuries to build up to this position as a three-region Controller. If his forces took too many losses, he might conceivably lose one or even two of his regions. Another Main could gain them.

Main 63 yearned for greater bulk and greater control. Thus, he hated the idea of losing regions.

Could the Center Race aliens do to him what they had done to Boron 10?

Once more, Main 63 ran war simulations. He carefully took notes on the 4,281,001 computer reproductions.

Afterward, he decided on a quick strike against the Confederation. Regions 7-D19 and 7-D20 would continue to annihilate their local species and build up with more factory planets. Main 63 would use himself, the five siege-ships here and ten cyberships to augment the fleets in Region 7-D21.

He and the siege-ships represented a *vast* increase in fighting power. He would annihilate these humans in particular and smash to atoms every brain-core tainted by the Cog Primus virus. If the Center Race aliens appeared—Main 63 did not chuckle, but he maintained a mirth mode as he considered what he would do to *them*. The reckoning for those troublesome life-forms was almost at hand.

What then should he do with the Centurion?

Main 63 would delay that decision for now. Perhaps there was some iota of data he could wring from the lone marine at a later date. Yes. He would run tests on the Centurion as the Headquarter Fleet journeyed to Region 7-D21.

PART V
ARMAGEDDON

And I saw an angel standing in the sun, who cried in a loud voice to all the birds flying in midair, "Come, gather together for the great supper of God, so that you may eat the flesh of kings, generals, and mighty men, of horses and their riders, and the flesh of all people, free and slave, small and great."

-- Revelation 19:17 (NIV)

-1-

Icy wind tore at Jon in his spacesuit. He was on the tallest mountain of the factory planet in the Allamu System.

The orange sky roiled with ice clouds and snow whipped around his booted feet.

It was beautiful up here even as he gazed down at a vast planetary crack that glowed with the heat of a hundred furnaces. The gargantuan zigzagging crack was below the nearby valley. The planetary crack housed the majority of the factories that mass-produced the components that went into making Enoy null-splitters, reality generators and quantum-pi power plants.

The Enoy technology was strange, well beyond the understanding of the human and Roke scientists that studied it. Only the few *Nathan Graham* technicians that had been directly taught through Enoy dreams had been able to retool this part of the factory planet.

That had been over eight months ago. Eight months of frantic work and many setbacks as the Confederation readied itself to fight the great battle that would likely decide whether humans and Roke lived for another year or not.

Jon snorted softly to himself, turned and staggered against an icy blast that hit him at precisely the wrong moment. He fell. He climbed back to his feet, dusted off the snow and trudged to the heavy orbital that had brought him here.

The orbital rested on three huge landers. It was a black, ungainly looking vessel, more bulbous than round. Several space marines in battle armor waited near the elevator that would take him up into the ship.

As Jon trudged, he found it hard to believe that eight months had passed so quickly. He shook his head.

In these eight months he'd had four cybership-class vessels newly outfitted, each now having a null-splitter, a reality generator and a quantum-pi power plant. Four. Far too few for the coming holocaust, he was sure. Yes, each of the four could theoretically protect two other regular cyberships while in the void. That gave him twelve cyberships able to use the void to travel from one star system to another.

Those twelve could launch masses of Vestal missiles, accelerating them to five percent light-speed. Could those twelve cyberships defeat...*six* AI siege-ships, say?

Jon had his doubts, as he knew how he would defend against a Vestal missile assault if he controlled a siege-ship.

What made everything iffier was that none of the Confederation ships had ever used the void under their own power to make a void journey. The Sisters of Enoy had not shown them how to travel in the void yet. Yes, the four void-capable cyberships had the equipment that should theoretically allow them to do what the *Rose of Enoy* did. But theory was always different from reality.

Jon shuddered as he climbed aboard the elevator.

The space marines joined him, and up the contraption went.

Jon waited in silence and the space marines respected that. The elevator came to a stop. The door opened and Jon exited first, still wearing his spacesuit as he headed for a seat.

He'd been finding it increasingly hard to concentrate these past months. Gloria had examined him and declared that he should be as psychologically fit as ever. He was sure the lack of concentration had to with a change to his mind from traveling through the void the one time.

Nine percent of the human crews and twelve percent of the Roke crews that had been in the ships traveling from Beta Hydri to the Allamu System through the void had gone stark raving mad. Because they lacked insane asylums here, the mad had gone into a maximum-security prison.

Am I willing to lose my mind in order to save the human race?

After a short countdown, the orbital blasted off from the mountain, interrupting his musings. In his seat, Jon shook like the other passengers. It got worse and then the shaking slowly eased out. Finally, as they reached orbital space, the shaking ceased altogether.

Jon exhaled with relief as he twisted off his bubble helmet. He handed the helmet to a stewardess coming by, a pretty young woman.

It was too bad they didn't have a method to accelerate the Vestal missiles to five percent light-speed without the void. He knew that was impossible, of course, but a man could hope, couldn't he?

Soon, the heavy lifter neared the *Nathan Graham* in the factory planet's outer orbital region.

Jon unhooked from his seat and went to a port window. He peered at the approaching cybership. It did not look the same anymore.

The *Nathan Graham* was still cylindrical and one hundred kilometers long. But it did not possess a smooth hull anymore. Instead, it had a rocky, asteroid-like hull. That kind of hull allowed the reality generator to "throw" out a greater and stronger reality field.

Four Confederation cyberships possessed asteroid-like hulls. Four.

Jon returned to his seat and strapped in. He waited and would have liked to go to sleep. That was another "benefit" from his single void journey. He only slept two hours a night these days. The rest of the time, he stared and did lots and lots of thinking. In his opinion, far too much thinking.

Two weeks ago, Bast had told him that the sleepless state actually helped a philosopher. It gave him more hours of concentration.

The extra and seemingly endless thinking had caused Jon to believe in, and argue for, a concentration of all Confederation fleet power in the Allamu System. The Main that Zeta had talked about was undoubtedly already coming to destroy humanity. What Jon desperately needed to know was the exact location of the enemy armada. Given the properties of hyperspace and hyperspace travel, they would only learn the location when the AI armada dropped out of hyperspace at an inhabited star system. That also meant humanity would likely lose that star system.

But that was okay...even if they lost the Solar System that way. They had to keep the Confederation fleet concentrated so they could attack the AI armada in the first system, and hopefully annihilate it there. That would protect the rest of the Confederation star systems.

If Zeta were right about the AI response, it would be overpowering. The AIs would likely hope to annihilate the Confederation in its early stages of expansion. Thus, if the Confederation could destroy the first AI armada, they might be able to counterattack immediately and grab even more enemy factory planets.

The truth was that *life* needed far more combat mass if they hoped to take on the AI Dominion. The normal death machine response—according to Zeta—was to smother resistance in an avalanche of missiles and gravitational beams, millions of them, if needed.

A red light came on in the passenger cabin.

Jon figured that must be for him. He pressed a switch on his seat's armrest, linking him to the flight crew.

"You have a message, sir," the pilot said.

"Let's hear it," Jon said.

"I'll patch you through, sir."

There was a moment of static. Then, "Jon?" It was Gloria.

"I'm right here, love," Jon said.

"The *Rose of Enoy* has appeared in the system. It's heading for the Allamu Battle Station. It's about six millions kilometers out."

"Have you spoken to Zeta or Ree yet?"

"Negative," Gloria said.

"You're sure that—"

"Jon," Gloria interrupted. "The *Rose of Enoy* is heading to the station."

Jon inhaled more deeply than before. "Send the void ship a message. Tell them I'll be on the *Nathan Graham* soon."

"I'll tell them," Gloria said. "And I hope you hurry."

"Are you worried about something?"

"Jon. I'm petrified. The Sisters of Enoy have returned. It must mean that they've spotted the AI armada."

"We should know soon," he said.

"Eight months, Jon. Don't you remember? Zeta told us that if—"

"I'm signing off," Jon said, interrupting. And he did, as he clicked the armrest button. Then he sat back as his gut began to seethe. They had four void-capable cyberships. Four. Humanity and the Warriors of Roke needed more time to prepare. It was too soon for them to have to fight the last battle for existence.

-2-

Two days later, Jon held a meeting on the Allamu battle station. Only the highest-ranking members of the Confederation fleet were in attendance, with their immediate staff members.

There was old Toper Glen, the Warrior Chief of the Space Lords of Roke. He'd left his home world for the great and glorious battle that would decide if their races would live a little longer. The war leader had more white in his fur than Jon remembered. Old Toper Glen was still taller and fatter than the other Roke and had trouble straightening his back.

Hon Ra the First Ambassador was with the Warrior Chief and three of Toper's highest-ranking clan chieftains.

Bast Banbeck was at the meeting, and Gloria, Walleye and the Old Man. They were all part of Jon's brain trust. Three fleet admirals sat in, each of them controlling a portion of the regular cybership fleet. One of the admirals was Maria Santa Cruz, a tall, thin woman from Mars. Many years ago, she had been a Vice Admiral in the Martian service. She had listened to Premier Frank Benz back then and had won Mars' first cybership. Now, she was one of the three key fighting admirals in Confederation service.

Toper Glen had brought an amazing 217 bombards and 16 Roke cybership-class vessels.

Jon's Void Flotilla had 12 cybership-class vessels. The rest of the human-crewed cyberships numbered 32 altogether.

Jon stood at the head of a massive conference table. Today, he wore his dress uniform in honor of the Star Lords of Roke.

The Supreme Confederation Commander cleared his throat. He'd spoken with Zeta via comm a day ago. Her information had floored him. He'd been exploring ideas with his brain trust ever since. Now, it was time to talk to his chief officers and allies and see if any of them had an idea that might work.

"I'm not going to lie," Jon said quietly. He wore his serious face, and he glanced at each person in turn. "The news is as grim as it gets. The good part is that each of you has done as I've requested, bringing your ships to the Allamu System. That means we have the largest concentration of warships…"

Jon paused as he watched old Toper Glen whisper to Hon Ra. The First Ambassador looked up and raised a furry paw: a massive set of digits compared to a man's hand.

"Yes, First Ambassador," Jon said.

"I am honored to be here, Supreme Commander," Hon Ra said in his deep Roke voice. "Yet, as I observe you, it appears that you are highly distressed. Perhaps we should adjourn for the moment until such time as you are—"

"No," Jon said, as he touched the tabletop with his fingertips. "It's time to get this out in the open."

Hon Ra nodded. "Then I withdraw my suggestion."

Jon cleared his throat. "Like I said, it's bad. Now, the *Rose of Enoy* has been doing recon the past six months, using the void to zip here and go there. I'm sure that Zeta would say it otherwise, but she wants us to know the exact number and positions of our enemies and possible allies."

Jon paused as if considering his words. "The Kames do not fight space wars like we do. They use thousands of remote-controlled projectiles and single-ships. They have swarming tactics and often position black ice objects near enemy vessels before exploding the matter/antimatter bombs inside."

"Please excuse me again, Supreme Commander," Hon Ra said. "By 'the Kames,' do you mean the aliens in the Delta Pavonis, 70 Ophiuchi and Sigma Draconis Systems?"

"Oh, sorry," Jon said. "Yes. We don't know much about the Kames, just what Zeta has told us and the little we've found in AI files. They're rocklike creatures, silicon-based life."

"Just like the AIs," Gloria muttered quietly.

"Yes, the AIs are also silicon-based," Jon agreed. "The Kames are quite unlike computers or robot ships, however."

Gloria looked as if she might argue the point, but finally nodded in agreement.

"That being said," Jon continued, "the Kames are quite different from humans or Roke. Not only are they composed of rocklike substances, but they're groupthink beings. I..." Jon turned to Bast. "Perhaps Bast Banbeck could better explain the Kames."

Jon sat down.

The Sacerdote did not stand, although he spoke up. "I've studied all available data on the Kames, scanty as it is, and gleaned what I could from Zeta's descriptions. The Kames are..." Bast seemed to grope for words. "They are all of one *unity*, would be the best way to say it. I suggest that they have a *form* of telepathy, but only amongst themselves. From what I can gather, Kames do not view any of their members as individuals."

Ponderous Toper Glen leaned near Hon Ra and once more whispered to his ambassador.

"The Warrior Chief understands," Hon Ra said. "He wonders what any of that has to do with the approaching AIs."

"I'll take that," Jon told Bast.

The Sacerdote nodded and leaned back in his chair, causing it to creak.

Jon stood again. "The point is the Kames don't have large spaceships like we do. Their single-ships and remote-controlled projectiles are all based from local moons or terrestrial planets. Thus, the Kames are ill-suited in more ways than one to help us in the coming battle by leaving their system and rushing to any of ours."

Once more, Hon Ra raised an arm.

"Yes, First Ambassador," Jon said.

"I did not realize you have been in contact with the Kames. Shouldn't you have informed us of that sooner?"

"If I'd contacted them some time ago, yes, you would be right," Jon said. "But I haven't contacted them. As Bast said, our knowledge of the Kames comes from a few AI files we

230

happened to find and from what Zeta graciously informed me of a day ago."

"For what reason did the Enoy tell you about the Kames?" asked Hon Ra.

"Right," Jon said. "That's the point. That's what makes what I'm about to say so…unsettling."

As if his knees were no longer strong enough to keep his legs locked, the Supreme Commander sat down. "We trust the Sisterhood of Enoy. I don't think we have a choice in that, not given the siege-ship we faced at Hydri II. The Enoy have also given us fantastic new technology. The so-called void tech will be our only hope, although I now admit that I don't see how it's going to help us win."

Toper Glen whispered to Hon Ra, but the First Ambassador did not interrupt this time. Everyone waited expectantly for what the Supreme Commander would say next.

Jon sighed, shaking his head. "I spoke to Zeta via comm. She informed me about the appearance of the Main and his attendant siege-ships. According to her, they arrived in our local region from the Algol System, which is approximately 90 light-years from Earth."

"There is more than one siege-ship?" asked Hon Ra.

Jon stared starkly at the First Ambassador. "It's much worse than that, Hon Ra. There are five siege-ships."

"*Five* AI warships, and each three thousand kilometers in diameter?" asked Hon Ra.

"Right," Jon said. "But the Main itself is also an AI military vessel…and it's not the size of Earth's Moon, it's the size of Mars. That's about the same size as the second planet in the Roke System," he told the chief Star Lord.

"*Nein!*" Toper Glen said, speaking directly to Jon. "You say the robots have a *ship* the size of a world?"

"Precisely," Jon said. "From what we've learned, the bigger the AI ship, the more powerful his brain-core and the higher he is in the robot hierarchy. According to Zeta, the Main is one of the largest AI vessels in the Dominion, but not the very biggest. Imagine that for a second." Jon paused to let the others do just that. "The Main dwarfs his five siege-ships."

"Given their combined mass," Hon Ra said, "how can our fleet face them?"

"Face them?" Jon asked. "Do you mean to tell me that you think that's it? Oh no, First Ambassador. The Main and the siege-ships arrived at 70 Ophiuchi and went to Sigma Draconis and then Delta Pavonis. Each time, the Main took the besieging cyberships with him, augmenting his fleet."

No one spoke into the subdued silence.

Finally, Jon continued in a softer voice. "According to Zeta, there were 52 cyberships at 70 Ophiuchi, 39 at Sigma Draconis and 81 at Delta Pavonis."

Hon Ra touched his paw tips one by one, as he silently mouthed something to himself. Finally, looking up, he said, "One hundred and seventy-two *extra* cyberships."

"That's right," Jon said. "So, the Main has his five siege-ships, ten cyberships he brought along from the Demon Star and one hundred and seventy-two extra cyberships, those already in our local region. Here's where it gets fun. According to Zeta's calculations, she believes the combined force is presently heading for the Solar System."

Several humans moaned in dread, including Admiral Santa Cruz. The Roke Warriors glanced at each other.

"According to Zeta," Jon said, "the Main will begin his counterattack assault against the human home system. After annihilating everything there, the AI fleet will likely go from one Confederation system to another, finishing the genocide."

Hon Ra raised a paw.

"Yes," Jon said.

"How do we stop such an immense fleet?" the First Ambassador asked.

"Let me be clear," Jon said. "I have no idea how to stop them. We have twelve cyberships that can attack from the void. We could launch, perhaps, several hundred Vestal missiles, accelerating them to five percent light-speed." Jon shook his head. "Given their massed might, the AIs could lay down prodigious counter-fire. I doubt any of the Vestal missiles, despite their incredible velocity, would reach them. There are simply too many robot ships in one place."

"Can we pick off some AI ships here and others there?" Hon Ra asked.

"That used to be the idea," Jon said, "but not anymore, not if they maintain tight fleet discipline. Why else has the Main united everyone in the local region into one gigantic fleet? Frankly, he's doing exactly what I would have done if I controlled that fleet."

"Are the AIs already in the Solar System?" Hon Ra asked.

"Zeta says no," Jon said. "Given the faster rate of void travel between star systems as compared to hyperspace travel, I believe her."

Toper Glen leaned near and whispered to Hon Ra. The First Ambassador listened for a time, finally nodding.

"Go ahead," Jon said. "Speak your piece."

"The situation is obviously grim, Jon Hawkins," the First Ambassador said. "Yet, one thing we have learned. You always have a plan. What is your plan this time?"

Jon gave the Roke ambassador a wintery grin. "I don't think you've heard me or understood, Hon Ra. That's why we're having the meeting. We're planning here. We're looking for ideas. As of this moment, I don't have a plan for defeating the AI fleet."

Toper Glen set a big old paw on one of Hon Ra's paws. The First Ambassador jerked as he looked at the Chief Star Lord. Toper Glen spoke softly to the First Ambassador.

Hon Ra's shoulders slumped as he faced Jon again. "You are the Supreme Commander. The situation might…it is beyond our understanding. By what you have said, nothing can stop the AI armada."

"I know," Jon said. "I…I don't even know what to say anymore. We have the largest fleet yet and we have void-capable ships, and yet, we're helpless against the AI mass."

"Excuse me, Supreme Commander," Hon Ra said. "I was not yet finished."

"Oh," Jon said. "Sorry. Go ahead."

The First Ambassador looked at Toper Glen. The big old Roke nodded. Hon Ra faced Jon.

"Given this sad truth," Hon Ra said, "our noble Warrior Chief has decided to die with his friend, Jon Hawkins. You

Earthmen helped us fight and defeat the robots in our hour of peril. We will thus help you, even if it means we all die."

Silence filled the chamber.

Jon looked away, staring into the distance. He wished Colonel Graham were still alive. The old man would have known what to say. Jon wished Stark was still around and Miles Ghent.

"Let us leave all doubts aside," Bast said. "Facing the AI armada does not mean we *might* die, but that we *will* die."

Jon faced the others, and he rapped his knuckles on the tabletop. "No, Bast, I haven't admitted defeat yet, not by a long shot. I'm simply letting my comrades know the situation."

Toper Glen nodded sagely, and he struck the table several times, harder with each blow.

Jon derived strength of purpose from that. He loved the bear aliens. They understood honor and facing adversity with a brave front.

"We have a fleet," Jon said, his voice hardening. "We have a tech advantage over the enemy. The AIs are also heading for our most heavily defended star system."

"Supreme Commander," Hon Ra said, "what can defend against such might as you've described?"

Jon stared at the First Ambassador. He was more aware of his fleet admirals watching him than ever, particularly Admiral Santa Cruz of Mars. Colonel Graham had told him before to always show courage in front of the men. No matter how hard it got, a commanding officer had to give his people hope, even if it was false hope.

"We're going to damn well find out what can or can't defend against such mass," Jon said roughly, as he stared at them. He could feel their stares hitting him right back. He could feel them wanting to believe him.

"Look," Jon said, speaking to himself as much as to the others. "At the least—the *least*, mind you—we're going to go down fighting. That's worth something. Every species has to die sometime. Why not die with a gun in your hand, killing as many of the enemy sons of bitches as you can?"

"That is warrior talk," Toper Glen said approvingly. He slammed a meaty paw against his table, stood and straightened his crooked back as best as he could. In a loud voice, he shouted, "We will fight! We will fight with Jon Hawkins! And maybe the Holy One will give us victory over the machines."

"Maybe so," Jon said.

"Pray tell us how we can gain anything by fighting an unbeatable force?" Bast asked.

"We won't gain a thing by sitting here moping about the odds," Jon said. "We have ships—"

"Jon," Bast said. "The AIs have world-sized ships. They have moon-ships. They have hundreds of times, tens of thousands of times more firepower and mass than we do. We can't win this fight. Frank Benz was right. We must flee and build new homes far from here."

The fleet admirals looked at Bast. Two of them—including Admiral Santa Cruz—appeared thoughtful.

"No!" Jon said. "We're not fleeing from the AIs and we're not abandoning the Solar System or Earth."

"But you can't win by fighting," Bast said.

"We have void tech. We have—"

"AI mass and firepower makes a mockery of our so-called superior technology," Bast said, interrupting. "I can understand now why the Sisterhood has lost for twenty thousand years against the robots. No one can defeat the death machines when they come in their masses."

"We did defeat them—before," Jon said.

"That was then," Bast said. "This is now."

"I'll give you a better saying," Jon replied. "We did it once. We can do it again."

"You're dreaming," Bast said. "This is cold reality. This is the AI Dominion as it really is. This is the AI Dominion that destroyed my race."

"I'm sorry about the Sacerdotes," Jon said. "I can't begin to imagine what you've gone through. You've been a wonderful help to humanity, and I want you to continue to hope. Remember, you helped design the anti-AI virus that helped give us one of our greatest victories."

Bast nodded moodily.

"This might be your great chance to hit back against the machines that destroyed your race," Jon added.

Bast stared at him, and it seemed as if a well of hopelessness and sorrow leaked from his large Neanderthal-like eyes.

"Bast is right," Jon told the others. "I am dreaming. I'm dreaming big, and sometimes, implemented dreams can change reality. We're taking everything we have and heading for the Solar System. Maybe the AIs won't have perfect fleet discipline. Maybe we can pick off a few of their cyberships and rattle them into making a mistake. Maybe our void ships can do more than we think. What that means is we all have to keep thinking and dreaming so that by the time we reach the Solar System, we'll have some kind of tactic that will allow us to destroy the AI armada."

-3-

Zeta and Ree stood before a viewing screen inside the *Rose of Enoy*. The three-hundred-kilometer asteroid ship was parked near the Allamu battle station, which was in orbit around the factory planet.

They had each maintained the same energy form as before as a matter of mission custom. They had been traveling through the void for six hard months, scouting for the Confederation, giving the humans and Roke the best chance possible. Now, they were weary and maybe even dispirited. Going in and out of the void in a short time span had an effect even on them.

"While waiting for the Confederation creatures to decide what to do," Ree said, "I have run many analyses. I cannot find a way for the humans and Roke to defeat the AIs."

"That is an imprecise statement," Zeta said. "You mean these humans and Roke cannot defeat the Main headed for the Solar System, the Main with his five siege-ships and masses of cyberships."

"Thank you for the clarification," Ree said, although she did not sound thankful.

"We must maintain precision in all things," Zeta explained.

"But you knew what I meant."

"Possibly," Zeta said.

The ball of energy that was Ree radiated more brightly. "I find this incredible. But I believe that you have come to like these humans."

"Again, you are imprecise. I have come to like Jon Hawkins. There is a difference."

"I understand." Ree waited. "But he will die with the others."

Jon had messaged the asteroid ship and told the Sisters of Enoy the united decision to advance to combat in the Solar System.

"There is a greater problem than the Confederation extinction," Ree continued. "The humans have—"

"I am well aware they have Enoy technology," Zeta said, interrupting. "I was the one to give it to them, after all."

"The humans and Roke are reckless creatures," Ree said. "We witnessed this in the Beta Hydri System."

"Make your point."

"You already know my point."

"Did I not say to be precise?" Zeta said.

"The humans and Roke are reckless," Ree said in a stiffer voice. "That is why you are short-tempered. You know they will attack even though it means their deaths. In their recklessness, will they ensure that no Enoy technology falls into AI hands?"

"I find it doubtful that they will take such pains while their races face oblivion."

"That is my own analysis," Ree said. "Thus, our duty is clear. Since the AIs will annihilate both races, we must make sure that there is no sign of Enoy interference."

"It's too late for that."

"Are you referring to the Battle of Hydri II?"

Zeta's humanoid lightning-bolt form brightened considerably. "How many times must I tell you not to query me?"

"I withdraw my question," Ree said hastily.

"Are you seeking to anger me?"

"I am not. I stand corrected."

"Because if you are attempting to anger me," Zeta said. "You have achieved success."

"Leader," Ree said, her ball of energy physically lowering so it almost seemed as if she cringed. "I have evoked the wrong response. I do not wish to become null. But I still have a duty to Enoy. That is why I have said these things."

"We both have a duty to Enoy," Zeta said, sounding slightly mollified.

"The Main has surely anticipated us," Ree said. "He must realize the humans will have masses of Vestal missiles. The amazing AI battle fleet mass negates the Vestal missiles, however, as the robots will be able to lay down incredible defensive fire."

"Jon Hawkins will realize this."

"What can he hope to achieve then by heading to the Solar System?"

"I do not know. That is what makes the coming event delicious. This is new. Do you not delight in newness?"

"I might if I did not know exactly what will happen," Ree said. "The humans and Roke are doomed. That means—"

"Listen to me," Zeta said, interrupting. "I have attempted to instruct you. Yet, you continue to be dully unteachable."

"I do not understand."

"What is this?" Zeta asked in a mocking tone. "You do not understand? Yet, you have repeatedly told me that you know exactly what will happen in the Solar System. Your pre-knowledge of future events is, frankly, astounding. How, then, can my repeated warnings have escaped you?"

"Do you refer to my having greater precision?"

"Ah," Zeta said. "This is a delight. You have actually heard my words. How refreshing."

Ree floated a little higher as she pulsated with rhythmic light. "Instruct me, please."

At first, Zeta said nothing. Then, she said, "Jon Hawkins is unique. Our tests showed us this. You have run repeated combat analyses and found that the humans and Roke do not have a chance against the AI mass."

"Such seems clear."

"That makes the coming battle all the more interesting," Zeta said.

"I fail to understand."

"That is because you have not lived as many cycles of time as I have. I have seen much—not all, but much. Because I have seen so much, I have witnessed endless repetitions. Ennui stalks me and fills me with tedium. I yearn to witness something different. This, I believe, we shall see in the Solar System."

"Because of Jon Hawkins?" asked Ree.

"This is my belief."

"I...I do not see the odds being in his favor. By this, I do not mean in his favor of winning the battle. He clearly cannot. I mean in his favor of attempting something unique."

"Nevertheless, that is my contention."

"May I ask you a question concerning that?"

"In this instance, you may," Zeta said.

"What gives you this confidence?"

Zeta had expected the question. It was obvious, really. In truth, she had nothing to give her this confidence except that she wanted to see a new thing. She yearned for a species to truly resist the AIs and destroy a true AI fleet mass. She had given Jon Hawkins a technological edge. Could the human use it so he could eke a victory from the jaws of defeat?

"Is this hope you evidence?" Ree asked.

"Yes, I think it is," Zeta said.

"Then I suspect that the humans have infected us with one of their maladies."

"Perhaps," Zeta said.

"Will you instruct Hawkins in void travel?"

"You are querying me again. You must stop it."

"I await your pleasure," Ree said softly.

Zeta did not respond, but she saw a light blinking on the screen. Hawkins wished to speak to her again. No doubt, he wanted to know how to fly his ships in the void. The great test was about to begin, and that made Zeta sad.

Ree was right. The humans could not win. She would miss Jon Hawkins and his flights of fancy. Still, she was going to give the human the opportunity to prove her wrong for once.

-4-

The great majority of the Confederation fleet headed for the Allamu System Oort cloud. The cyberships and bombards gained velocity as the weeks passed.

Overall command of the hyperspace fleet went to Toper Glen, the Warrior Chief of the Star Lords of Roke. He had 217 bombards, along with six cybership-class vessels. Three human admirals commanded twelve, twelve and eight cyberships, respectively, and were under orders to obey the old bearlike alien chief.

Meanwhile, Jon, eleven cybership captains and select crewmembers went via shuttle and landed on the *Rose of Enoy*. Each person fell asleep, was transported inside the Enoy asteroid-like ship and placed on hard slabs of matter.

Zeta and Ree caused energy helmets to circle the human heads as they dream-trained the people to deal with the void, to move in a realm with no up or down and how to handle the mind warping that inevitably happened to physical beings moving in and out of the void.

In time, the dream training ceased, and each person awoke on his or her original shuttle that had brought them to the alien asteroid ship.

***

Upon returning to the *Nathan Graham*, Jon went straight to a simulator. He threw himself into studying the tactical situation of an AI fleet zooming from the Oort cloud to the satellite and moon cities of Neptune, Uranus and Saturn as it headed for Earth.

A ship the size of Mars would undoubtedly lead the AI pack. Five Luna-sized siege-ships would follow. Almost *two hundred* cyberships would act as escorts to this incredible mass of metal.

The Confederation had forty-one cyberships and a little more than two hundred Roke bombards. The two hundred bombards, however, would hardly add up to the mass of two enemy cyberships.

No matter how many simulations Jon ran, the Solar System lost the fight. The Confederation fleet died, and the AIs won a resounding victory.

The rest of the Confederation star systems would easily fall to the AI armada. Afterward, the Kames would surely go down to bitter defeat. The AI juggernaut would continue to sweep the Orion Arm of all biological life.

Jon labored at the simulator until he slumped over asleep, exhausted from the dream training and the bitter knowledge that no matter what he did, they could not defeat the AI armada in battle.

-5-

Toper Glen and the combined fleet finally reached the Allamu System Oort cloud. The ships were far enough away from any large gravitational body that they could each enter hyperspace, thus beginning the seventeen-day journey to the Solar System.

As was Roke custom, the Chief Star Lord led by example. Toper Glen's cybership vanished as it entered hyperspace.

One by one, the rest of the Roke cyberships and bombards winked out of regular space. Shortly thereafter, the first human-crewed cyberships entered hyperspace.

The twelve cyberships in Admiral Maria Santa Cruz's flotilla did not wink out. Instead, the twelve huge vessels began a long turning maneuver. They maneuvered in such a way that they no longer aimed at the Solar System, but in the opposite direction, heading outward from the center of the galaxy.

Because of the extreme distance between the cyberships and the Allamu battle station, word of this change did not reach Jon for some time.

Finally, he sent an emergency message to Admiral Santa Cruz, demanding an explanation for the flotilla's strange maneuver.

While the message was in transit, Jon summoned the Old Man.

The Chief of Confederation Intelligence entered Jon's office twenty minutes later.

The Old Man was tall and thin, with thinning hair that he religiously dyed black. As was his custom, he smoked a pipe. What seemed like a lifetime ago, he had been a sergeant in the Black Anvil Regiment. He was even-tempered, known to give sage advice and, since Miles Ghent's death, a follower of Christ Spaceman. He'd been running Intelligence for years now.

"Sit," Jon said, who sat behind his desk, indicating a chair before it.

The Old Man did so, crossing his legs and puffing on his pipe.

"Well?" Jon asked.

The Old Man nodded. "Admiral Maria Santa Cruz admired ex-Premier Frank Benz. She captained his original cybership, following him to the Allamu System."

"I know all that," Jon said with a wave of his hand. "What's she doing now?"

"Disobeying orders, I should think," the Old Man said.

"Didn't your people clear her?"

"She had appeared to cut all ties with Benz well before his slide into treachery. As far as my people could tell, she disagreed with his political philosophy."

Jon knew the Old Man meant Benz's idea of fleeing far from the AIs.

"Did you miss this one?" Jon asked.

The Old Man puffed on his pipe, removed it from his mouth and said, "That would be my guess."

"So, we're going to lose twelve cyberships?" Jon shouted.

The Old Man winced and looked away. He didn't put the pipe back in his mouth. Instead, he said, "I'm offering you my resignation, sir."

"What?" Jon shouted, standing.

"I failed you. I thought she was clean. It's obvious she isn't. We just lost twelve cyberships because I—"

"Listen to me," Jon said in earnest, interrupting as he sat back down. "You must have Intelligence assets in her flotilla. Get to them. Have them kill her and install someone loyal to the Confederation. That flotilla must join Toper Glen in the Solar System."

"But sir—"

"I don't have time to train a new Intelligence Chief. Get to work. Remove Santa Cruz from her position."

"I'll do my best, sir," the Old Man said dubiously.

"That's not good enough, Chief. Get it done."

The Old Man nodded.

"Dismissed," Jon said.

The Old Man stood. It seemed he wanted to say more. Then, he hurried out.

***

Fifty-three hours later, Jon was in his office with Gloria when a light blinked on his desk.

Jon swiveled around and pressed a switch on a screen.

"There's an incoming message for you, sir," a comm operator said. "It's from Admiral Santa Cruz."

Jon glanced at Gloria as a grim look settled over him.

"Do you want me to leave?" Gloria asked.

Jon didn't respond. He looked at a computer screen and pressed a switch, receiving the long-distance message.

Admiral Maria Santa Cruz appeared on the screen. She was tall and thin with long dark hair. She had piercing brown eyes and had obviously taken longevity treatments, as she didn't have any wrinkles or crow's feet on her aged face.

"I am happy to inform you, Commander Hawkins, that I and my flotilla will not be joining you in your folly. Humanity in this region of the Orion Arm is doomed to extinction. You have grandiose dreams of overcoming the AIs in the Solar System. I wish you luck, I really do. But I am not a fool. My officers are not fools either. Perhaps many of the men and women under them are fools. That is a pity."

Admiral Santa Cruz closed her mouth and seemed to gather herself. "Your Intelligence assassins are all dead, or most are dead. My security team struck them before they could strike me. I learned from your treatment of Premier Benz.

"Once, you were a great commander, Hawkins. Now, you are too stubborn to see the truth. I am taking my cyberships far from here. We will begin anew and by that save the human

245

race from extinction. I urge you to do likewise while there still is time.

"You no longer have my twelve cyberships. Think about that, Hawkins. I am forcing your hand. I am following the wisdom of Premier Benz. You killed a better man than yourself. You should have died that day, not him."

Admiral Santa Cruz shrugged. "I bid you good-bye, Hawkins. Don't murder the rest of your people in your fool's hope. It's over. Run while you can. Admiral Maria Santa Cruz out."

The image disappeared.

Jon stared at the blank screen.

"How could she do this?" Gloria whispered.

Woodenly, Jon pressed a switch. "Do we have any video of those cyberships?" he asked.

"Yes, sir," the comm operator said. "They are long-distance shots—"

"Show me," Jon said.

The screen showed the emptiness of the Oort cloud and twelve cyberships. One by one, Admiral Santa Cruz's flotilla began to wink out as they entered hyperspace. Then, they were all gone and there was just the emptiness of space.

Gloria put a hand on one of Jon's shoulders. "They're gone," she whispered. "They deserted us."

Jon felt faint. He'd just lost the use of twelve precious cyberships. He found it hard to swallow and badly needed a drink of water.

"What do we do now?" Gloria whispered.

Jon blinked several times. First, he couldn't afford to lose any more ships or people. Second—he squared his shoulders and glanced back at his wife. He felt drained, maybe even defeated.

"We keep going," he said in a hoarse voice.

"Can we win, Jon?" she asked.

His eyes felt gritty. Did even his wife doubt him? Was he leading his people on a fool's quest when he should be following Benz's last advice?

"No," Jon whispered. "We beat the AIs once. We can do it again."

"How?" whispered Gloria.

If he couldn't figure out an answer to that question soon, maybe he *should* pull a Santa Cruz and leave this area of the Orion Arm.

"There's got to be a way to win," he whispered.

"What did you say?" Gloria asked.

Jon didn't tell her as he stared at the screen showing the empty Oort cloud far out there. What was he going to do now?

-6-

Jon summoned the Old Man into his office. When he arrived, the pipe-smoking security Chief offered his resignation once again.

"You're going to atone for this," Jon said angrily. "You're going to do it by rooting out the rest of the defeatists in the Void Flotilla."

The Old Man smoked his pipe as he stared at Jon. "We can start a witch hunt, if you like. But is that really what you want now?"

"What are you talking about?"

"Morale is going to drop because of Santa Cruz's defection," the Old Man said. "There's no getting around that. Instead of having my people interrogate others, maybe pushing some into acting sooner…"

Jon stared at his lanky security chief. Santa Cruz had truly screwed him. This was bad.

"Okay," Jon said. "I get what you're saying. What do you suggest?"

"After what has happened, are you sure you want my suggestions?"

Jon struggled to control his temper. Finally, through gritted teeth, he said, "Santa Cruz got away. We can't do anything about her now. You failed there. Sometimes, the best of us fail. Now, you work harder and smarter. I want your suggestions until I don't. Then, I'll tell you straight to your face that you're through."

"Fair enough," the Old Man said. "Well...then here's one of my suggestions..."

Jon listened as the Old Man talked. The old dog still had some tricks up his sleeve. Jon agreed with his Intelligence Chief's suggestions, and they made detailed plans for the next move.

***

Five hours later, Jon sat in his command chair on the bridge of the *Nathan Graham*. There were a few different controls for the null-splitter and other Enoy technology, but otherwise it was the same old bridge as from the beginning.

Jon finished speaking with Zeta via comm and turned to face his crew. Three other asteroid-like-hulled cyberships waited to enter the void with the *Nathan Graham*. Eight normal cyberships would join them. All twelve vessels brimmed with large cargo holds of Vestal missiles.

The four asteroid-like-hulled cyberships no longer carried gravitational cannons. The normal eight still did.

Jon had raged in his office. On the bridge, he maintained his decorum. It took willpower to do it, and that came close to demanding more energy than he possessed, but he had to stay calm to keep his people calm in the face of the latest disaster.

"We're about to make history," he said quietly. "We've done this before, of course, but the Sisters of Enoy did the void piloting then. Today, the human race will enter the void for the first time under its own power."

"I just had a thought," Bast said, speaking up.

"Is it a positive thought?" Gloria asked from her station.

"One hundred percent so," the Sacerdote said.

"What's your thought?" asked Jon.

"Maybe Admiral Santa Cruz had the right idea. We could use the void to escape far from this part of the galaxy. I wonder if we could go one better by crossing the vast distance between galaxies and go to a place without any possibility of an AI Dominion."

Jon stared at Bast.

"All our ships are heading to their doom," Bast continued. "That is folly of the worst sort. Instead, you have enough men

249

and women in these twelve cyberships to go anywhere and start anew. You can save the human race, but only if you reverse your so-called heroic thinking. There is a way to win, but you're too stubborn to see it."

"Anyone else feel that way?" Jon asked, looking around.

Incredibly, a few hands went up.

"Do you not see yet?" Bast said in earnest. "The Sisters of Enoy are still testing us. They are looking for a practical race. They have given us the means to start over, and you are throwing it away on a useless military gesture. That is not rational."

"The AIs will find our descendants in the end," Jon said.

"Not if we make the incredible journey between galaxies. Yes, this galaxy is likely doomed. Why does that mean the next one is too?"

"The robots have invaded our home," Jon said hotly.

"They are too powerful to defeat," Bast said.

Jon looked up at the ceiling.

"The rest of you can surely see—"

"Bast!" Jon said, interrupting the Sacerdote.

The big alien turned and showed surprise at the handgun aimed at his chest.

"Admiral Santa Cruz mutinied," Jon said. "Are you going to follow her example?"

"We cannot win," Bast said.

"I don't want hear any more defeatist talk."

"You want me to lie to you?" Bast asked.

"I want you to keep your defeatist talk to yourself."

"I must be true to myself," Bast said.

"And I must be true to myself," Jon said.

"Would you kill me?"

"Not willingly," Jon said.

"But you would?"

"To save the human race," Jon said, "yes. I would shoot you a thousand times, Bast Banbeck. In fact, here and now, I am making it known that I will put defeatists in the brig. If we run out of room in the brig, then I'll have my loyal officers and marines shove the offenders out of the airlock."

"Jon," Gloria said.

"Our backs are against the wall," he said. "This void fleet is the answer. It has to be. I'm not going to let *anyone* stop me now."

Bast stood to his imposing height. "I must leave the bridge then, Commander."

"Not like this, you're not," Jon said. "Marines, escort the Sacerdote to the brig. Put him into solitary confinement."

"Jon," Gloria said.

"Oh," Jon said. "And take those who just raised their hands. They're going to the brig too."

"Jon," Gloria said again.

"Not you too." He took a deep breath, saying, "I don't want to send my wife to the brig. But that might send the right message. Do you understand me?"

Gloria searched his eyes, finally nodding. "Yes, Commander."

"Are you with me?"

"I am," Gloria said. "I'm with you all the way."

"Anyone else doubt me?" Jon asked, looking around the bridge.

No one spoke up.

Jon nodded. The marines drew their guns and approached the giant Sacerdote. Bast glared at Jon but went meekly enough. The marines took the hand-raisers as well.

Jon sighed deeply after Bast and the others had left. That had been one of the Old Man's ideas, with Bast Banbeck acting as mutiny bait. Gloria had done her part, too. The story would undoubtedly circulate quickly throughout the rest of the Void Flotilla.

"All right," Jon said. "It's time to enter the void and figure out how to maneuver in a realm without directions."

-7-

The quantum-pi engine did not sound anything like the great matter/antimatter engine. The process was quite different. This wasn't a matter of propelling the ship through space but tearing away the veil of reality and entering a null realm, the void, where nothing held sway.

The quantum-pi processor built up power.

"Now," Gloria said, as she studied her board.

In lieu of the pilot, the null-splitter navigator manipulated his panel. He engaged the Enoy null-splitter that used the quantum-pi power.

A force from the *Nathan Graham* struck the fabric of reality near the cybership. That force tore at the fabric and began with the tiniest of holes.

"I'm detecting the null region," Gloria said.

Jon hunched forward on his chair as the main screen showed a fist-sized rip in time and space. Through the hole was the void, looking like an inky darkness. In reality, nothing was there, neither heat, nor cold, nor size nor mass. It was nothing, null, the eerie void between the reality of space and time.

The rupture grew as the quantum-pi engine supplied the null-splitter with more force. Slowly, the reality rip increased as glowing lines appeared and moved away from each other.

Now, regular engine thrust pushed the *Nathan Graham* toward the reality rip. Glowing lines seemed to chew away at reality, exposing more of the null realm to the bridge crew.

The other three void-capable ships did likewise. Behind them waited the eight normal cyberships split into teams of two.

"Now," Jon said. "Tell the others to start heading toward the void."

Would they do so? Or would other mutineers now show themselves? No. The regular cyberships slowly moved, almost hesitatingly, toward the reality rip in time and space.

Soon, the four void-capable vessels disappeared into the nothingness of the void. In a matter of minutes, the other eight vessels followed them, two to each void ship.

Inside the four void ships, the reality generators powered up, casting a reality field around each ship. The field was critical. Without it, matter would begin to discontinue, becoming null in the null realm.

"What's the present situation?" asked Jon.

"We're ready to close the rip," Gloria said.

"The other two ships in our squad are inside our reality field?"

"Yes, Commander," Gloria said.

Jon hesitated to give the order as a strange premonition began in his chest. If he gave the order, nothing would ever be the same. Yet, how much did he want it to stay the same with the AIs hunting down all life?

"Close the rip," Jon said quietly.

The process reversed as the quantum-pi engine added more power to the null-splitter.

The glowing lines that outlined the opening became smaller, and smaller, and smaller. Abruptly, the reality rip closed. The ships were trapped in the void, in the realm of nothing. They had made it. The question now became, could the flotilla of cyberships ever leave the void, and could they do that back into the Solar System—and do it soon enough?

-8-

The Centurion groaned with effort as he eked out yet another pushup in his prison cell aboard Main 63.

If anything, he looked even more muscular than he had at the time he'd spoken to the Main back in the Algol System. Yet, despite the greater physical specimen that he had become, his eyes were all but vacant.

The Centurion endured because he did not know any other way. He had many hallucinations, so many that he had almost forgotten they were figments of his imagination.

The trouble was that the human mind was not made to be alone for such a long time. The octopoids hadn't bothered with him since then. Neither had Main 63 spoken to him via a comm.

Thus, the clangs outside his cell did not unduly concern the Centurion. Suddenly, however, the hatch slid up.

The Centurion frowned. He vaguely realized he should know what that noise meant. He turned and saw two metallic octopoids. They regarded him silently.

The man's frown intensified. He opened his mouth and his rusted tongue moved. He croaked several times. It had been over three real weeks since he'd spoken a word. In his hallucinations, he hadn't needed speech, but had simply thought the words.

"You," the Centurion said.

"Step outside your cell," the chief octopoid said.

"What?"

"Obey," the robot said.

The Centurion blinked several times, otherwise standing there unmoving.

Finally, the octopoid moved, jerking into the cell. He raised a tentacle with a prod on the end. The tip of the prod touched the Centurion on the side, and a *zap* of sound occurred as the robot shocked the man.

The Centurion cried out in pain, falling onto the floor as he sought to escape the pain.

The octopoid leaned down, zapping him again.

The Centurion writhed on the floor, curling up into a fetal ball.

"Stand up, man. Leave your cell."

The Centurion merely curled up more tightly.

The octopoid reached down, and the Centurion unfolded with startling speed, using the edge of his right hand to hack at the tentacle holding the prod.

It made no difference. Another zap heralded another powerful shock.

The Centurion scrambled upright, panting, backing up against a wall.

"Will you obey?" the octopoid asked.

Wheels slowly turned in the Centurion's sluggish mind. The difference between reality and fantasy became clearer again. This was real. He was aboard an AI warship.

The Centurion groaned as tears threatened to leak from his eyes.

The octopoid advanced upon the Centurion, leading with the electric goad.

"I..." the Centurion said.

The octopoid hesitated.

"Will come with you," the Centurion said.

The octopoid seemed to calculate and finally retreated from the cell.

Slowly at first, but gaining speed as he advanced, the Centurion followed him. "Where are we going?" he asked.

"The Main wishes to speak with you," the octopoid said, and nothing more.

***

After a journey similar to last time, through the endless corridors, the naked Centurion found himself in the speaking room. He ate sandwiches and drank tainted water.

The entire side of the wall swirled with colorful patterns again. That indicated the intelligence of the computer entity know as Main 63.

"We are in the Solar System," the robotic voice began.

"What?" the Centurion said, startled by the comment.

"The Solar System is the origin point of the human race."

"Ah…"

"Are you addled?"

The Centurion struggled with the question. Finally, he said, "Humans do poorly in confinement."

"You are in top physical condition."

"Because I exercise all the time," the Centurion said.

"The reason is immaterial."

The Centurion tapped the side of his head. "I'm talking about my mind. Humans do badly mentally when alone for extended periods."

"Of course, I know this," Main 63 said. "I but tested you and am testing your truthfulness."

The Centurion frowned. Was the AI lying or telling the truth? He wasn't sure. Thus, he waited.

"I am curious," Main 63 said. "I have received several communications from your human leader."

"From Jon Hawkins?" the Centurion asked.

"Negative," the Main said, "from Premier Wurzburg."

"I don't know her."

"Why are you lying?"

The Centurion shook his head. "I have no reason to lie to you."

The swirling patterns on the wall slowed down. "I will show you," Main 63 said. "Perhaps that will refresh your memory."

The swirling patterns disappeared. In their place on the wall appeared a plain, older woman wearing a stylish turban and a dark business suit and tie. She had intelligent brown eyes and had a completely neutral face.

"I am Premier Alice Wurzburg of the Solar League," she said in a quiet and confident voice. "We have seen your fleet and wish to inquire concerning your intentions. I await a transmission so we can communicate further."

The turbaned woman froze afterward, and the swirling patterns resumed, taking her place.

The Centurion lurched slightly forward at that. Although Premier Wurzburg was old and plain, the Centurion had fallen in love with her as she'd spoken. He had not seen another human...he didn't know the timeframe. He longed to see her face again. He longed to hear her speak once more. Oh, if only he could speak to her.

"What has happened to you?" Main 63 said. "You look...stupid. Have you become stupid?"

"Ah...no," the Centurion said.

"What do you make of her words?"

"She wishes to speak to you," the Centurion said.

"Clearly that is the case," Main 63 said. "*Why* does she want to talk to me?"

The Centurion shrugged. "I don't know."

"Could she conceivably be trying to surrender?"

The Centurion shrugged again.

"I believe she is a devious human," Main 63 said. "If I am correct, I would communicate. I would use you as my spokesman."

The Centurion turned away as hope welled within his chest. He knew that he would never leave Main 63 alive. But he'd also given up hope that he'd ever get to talk to another person again. The idea of talking to Premier Wurzburg and communicating—

The Centurion nodded. "I will be your spokesman."

"Do you think she is devious?"

"Yes," the Centurion said. He would say anything in order to get the chance to speak with her.

"You are lying to me. But I shall make the test in any case. Perhaps she will give something critical away and make my task easier."

The Centurion was hardly listening. He was going to talk to Premier Wurzburg. Oh, this was a dream come true.

-9-

Premier Alice Wurzburg of the Solar League was in a high state of shock. Only a highly developed sense of survival had driven her to take defensive actions faster than those around her, and that had led to her temporary safety.

Her cunning and agile political maneuverability had allowed her to rise under the Premiership of J.P. Justinian and later overthrow Frank Benz. After the original departure of Jon Hawkins, she had captured most of the Solar System. Later, she had made a deal with Jon Hawkins, allowing millions of malcontents to leave for deep space and thus solidifying her hold of the entire system.

She had an iron grip of the military because she owned the GSB body and soul. Now, however, because of the impossible invasion armada, everything tottered, threatening a system-wide collapse.

As noted, Alice Wurzburg had moved fast. She was deep underground in a special bunker under the Swiss Alps. It could withstand direct nuclear strikes. Special and highly motivated GSB agents guarded the underground facility. They were all fanatically loyal to the Social Dynamist creed, and they had all risen high under her leadership. She could depend on them.

Yet...she no longer knew if she could depend on the military as society collapsed around them.

The culprit was the massive AI fleet heading in-system from the Oort cloud. The size of the robot ships had befuddled everyone. The stunned space service operators had let too many people know what rushed in-system from the Oort cloud. For reasons she had not yet been able to determine, the knowledge had instantly gone public.

If she could find the fools that had allowed that to happen, she would let the GSB torture them for years and record everything.

A warship the size of Mars and five others the size of Luna led almost two hundred cyberships. Many years ago already, *three* AI cyberships had almost destroyed the Solar System. Humanity had barely defeated the three vessels at the famous and deadly Battle of Mars.

Who could save humanity from the massed robot invasion now?

The home world was going mad as entire continents full of people rioted with wild abandon. She had lost news of Venus, Mars, Neptune and Uranus—

Alice shook her head.

The combined Solar League fleet would be like fleas against the robot mass. The AIs had a world-ship. How could this be happening to her?

Alice Wurzburg was too drained to pace. She lay on a couch in her office, with a wet cloth on her face. She had sent a message to the enemy fleet. Maybe she could negotiate a peace settlement with them, anything.

Someone knocked on her door.

Alice almost said, "Enter." That would have been a mistake, though. She was the leader of Social Dynamism. If her people believed she had lost heart, they would seek a stronger person to show them the way.

Alice removed the wet cloth and sat up. "Enter," she said sternly.

A GSB guard opened the door. He was big, maybe seven and a half feet tall. He had the bulk to match, although his head was much too small for his size. Thomas wasn't a smart guard, but he would literally do anything she said.

"The GSB Director would like to talk to you, ma'am," Thomas said in a surprisingly high-pitched voice.

"Let him in, but stay yourself," Alice said.

Thomas motioned to someone unseen. A moment later, a lean black-uniformed man named Peterson walked into the office. He looked like a scared rabbit and always chose his words with care, but he had a ruthless streak that Alice had come to appreciate.

The nuclear mines under former enemy cities had been Peterson's brainchild. It had gone a long way to cementing her power throughout the Solar System.

Raising an eyebrow, Peterson glanced at Thomas.

"He stays," Alice said.

Peterson didn't nod, but the slump in his shoulders caused Alice to wonder if she should order Thomas to strangle the secret police chief this instant.

Alice moved slowly and—she hoped—serenely behind her desk, sitting down. She did not give Peterson permission to sit. She wanted to make him squirm.

"I have bad news, ma'am," Peterson said.

"More?" she asked.

"Solar League fleet units are fleeing," Peterson said.

The words befuddled Alice. "Fleeing where?" she asked.

"To the Oort cloud," Peterson said.

Alice frowned. "They're going to meet the AIs?"

"The fleet units are moving in exactly the opposite direction of the approaching enemy ships," Peterson said. "They're getting as far from the enemy as possible."

"For what possible reason?" asked Alice.

"Those are the experimental hyperspace ships."

The Solar League had not yet used hyperspace but had been studying what they knew from the AIs and from the damnable Confederation.

"The ships are running away?" Alice asked, stunned. "They're going to head to other star systems."

"I believe so," Peterson said.

Alice suddenly wondered if that wasn't the right idea. If the experiential hyperspace vessels worked, she could escape the AIs and thus escape certain doom. She could couch her flight in political language. Someone had to keep the human race and Social Dynamism alive, after all.

261

"Well?" she asked. "Did the ship captains leave any messages?"

Peterson shook his head.

She pretended to think, and then asked in a seemingly neutral voice. "Are any of the experiential ships left in Earth orbit?" she asked, trying to make it a military question.

Peterson leered at her. He must know what she was thinking—likely, because he'd already reached the same conclusion.

The GSB Director nodded.

"How many are left?" Alice asked, her voice thickening.

"Three," Peterson said.

"And the rest of the fleet?" she asked.

"The various fleet units are awaiting your command, ma'am."

"You mean the fleet units that do not have hyperspace capacity?"

"That is correct," Peterson said.

"They're going to fight for human survival," she said quietly.

Director Peterson said nothing to that.

Alice Wurzburg came to a decision.

"There is one other thing," Peterson said, interrupting her thought.

"What?"

"The AI world-ship has responded to your message. He is using someone called the Centurion to reply to you."

"What?" she asked.

Peterson looked at her more closely.

She could almost read his mind. The director was likely wondering if she'd lost it. Well, she hadn't. But she *was* having trouble concentrating.

"The Centurion appears to have been one of Jon Hawkins' right-hand men," Peterson said. "The AIs undoubtedly captured him—"

"Wait," Alice said, interrupting. "Hawkins is allied with the AIs?"

"Some of the scientists think that's possible."

"The bastard," she hissed. "Hawkins sold us out."

"Before we could sell him out," Peterson said.

"That's uncalled for," Alice said, sharply, surprised the director would say something like that so openly. "We're humanity's leaders. We fight for human interests."

Peterson nodded quickly, appearing frightened by his hasty remark—it went against his normal behavior, certainly.

She ignored Peterson then, thinking hard. "Could we make a deal with the AIs?" she asked.

"We can try," Peterson said, as if he didn't really believe it was possible.

"What is it?" she asked. "What are you thinking?"

He gave her a crafty look. "May I speak freely, ma'am?"

"I demand that you do."

"We should...*inspect* the last three hyperspace-capable vessels in orbit. Maybe it would be a good time to test them."

Alice stared at him. If she had *good* survival instincts, the director of the GSB might even have better.

"Yes," she said slowly. "We should inspect the SL cyberships. Afterward...afterward I can speak to the AI's representative."

"We should head upstairs as soon as possible," Peterson said.

"I agree," Alice said. "We need to leave before the entire world falls down around our ears."

-10-

The Magistrate Yellow Efrel led her Earth Colony Seiners through a packed tube-train station in Milan, Italy Sector.

She was an old Seiner and never wore a pseudo-skin disguise anymore because she found it so uncomfortable. Instead, she wore a cloak with a deep hood. In order to help the hood hide her blue fish-scale face, she wore a veil in the Islamic manner. She had white gloves and flowing clothing. There was no part of her open to prying human sight.

Seventy-three Seiners pushed their way through the Milan tube-train station crowds. Sixty-eight of the Seiners wore human-skin disguises. Of the seventy-three, twelve were first grade telepaths and nineteen were second grade, as good as Red Demeter had once been.

They had refrained from any telepathy, using cash, credits and a show of guns when needed.

The world was going mad because of the knowledge of certain doom. The Magistrate Yellow Efrel had had an escape plan in place. The human guards of her air cars had all fled, however. Thus, the Seiner Colony on Earth had resorted to street vans and now attempted to board a special tube train to the Zurich Spaceport.

Magistrate Yellow Efrel panted from the exertion of walking so much. Her feet ached from wearing shoes and she moaned every time she set a foot down. The stink of packed humanity was strong in the ticket area. She felt nauseous.

These days, Yellow Efrel mainly cavorted in her private saltwater tank and let the younger ones handle the day-to-day Seiner operations.

A great AI fleet had appeared in the Oort cloud. News of the coming doom had descended as a cloudburst upon humanity. The Seiner tentacles into human society had snapped under the rioting pressure.

Now, Yellow Efrel led her Seiners on a last-ditch plan. The rioting pigs might actually guarantee the genocide of the last Seiners in existence. That was a horrifying idea. It actually sickened Yellow Efrel and she halted abruptly and vomited the special fish she normally ate.

The mess splashed onto the concrete, and a few humans saw that. Something about the purple mess must have alerted their riot-heightened senses.

"Aliens!" one of the pig people bellowed.

The surging crowds must have heard that cry. Higher-pitched screams went up.

Plan Ten, Yellow Efrel thought at her best telepaths.

Seconds later, a combined telepathic blast hit the entire area. Humans went down in clumps. All around the great arcade people simply swooned and hit the deck. A second blast finished the stubborn ones, knocking them down as well.

That left seventy-three Seiners standing. Not one other soul moved, all lay dead in the great building.

"To the tube train," Yellow Efrel said in her old voice. "We must reach the spaceport before all order breaks down."

***

Premier Alice Wurzburg, nine of her best staff personnel, 15 hulking bodyguards of the Thomas type, GSB Director Peterson and five of his most loyal killers hurried out of a turbo-car onto the spaceport tarmac. As a group, they hurried toward a waiting heavy lifter.

This was the Zurich Spaceport, and the personnel still went about their tasks normally. Military police wearing combat vests and carrying assault rifles were everywhere.

Alice felt a terrible premonition. She was the great leader of Social Dynamism. If the wrong people learned she was trying to flee the Solar System to begin in another place far from the AIs, they might go wild and literally tear her to pieces.

She had another troubling thought. How could she maintain power aboard the cyberships once they were in hyperspace? She needed more of her people up there. Yet, alerting them to come to the spaceport was too great a risk. Order was breaking down everywhere on Earth. She could hardly imagine what it must be like on Mars, the Saturn moon cities and in the Neptune colonies.

Those places had received AI missiles and hell-burners years before. They had a better idea of what the AI invaders could and would do.

"Ma'am," Director Peterson shouted. "Who are those people?"

It took Alice a moment. She looked back at the director as he pointed at a large group of people marching from parked and grounded shuttles and toward the heavy lifter.

"I don't recognize their insignias," Alice shouted.

Peterson shouldered his way to her. "They're not military and I know they're not party hacks."

"Thomas," Alice shouted. "Thomas!"

The lumbering bodyguard hurried to her.

"Take your men," Alice told Thomas. "Stop those people from heading to the orbital."

Thomas grinned down at her and drew a huge hand-cannon, a .55 caliber gun. Then he whistled sharply. Other hulking bodyguards likewise drew massive guns. As a group, the fifteen giants lumbered toward the other group and then began to run.

Alice's eyes glowed with interest. Her bodyguards would murder the interlopers.

"We should keep going," Peterson said beside her.

She glanced at the GSB Director, and she was keenly aware that her guards were over there, not here to stop the sly secret police chief.

"Yes," Alice said. She started for the waiting orbital, heading for the elevator that would take them up to the vehicle that would take them into space.

266

Halfway to the elevator, she felt Peterson tug at her left sleeve. She glanced at him. He peered at the others.

Alice did likewise. That was strange. Her guards had halted in front of the other group.

"What's going on?" Alice demanded.

"I don't know," Peterson said. "Look. Your men are turning around. I don't think they even talked to the others."

Alice turned around. "Is this your doing?" she asked the director.

"Mine?" Peterson said. "What do you mean?"

The bodyguards lumbered back toward them, and now broke into a run. They still had their heavy guns out.

"Ma'am," Peterson said. "I don't like the look on their faces."

Alice didn't either. Her guards seemed demented.

"Should I order my men to fire at them?" Peterson asked.

"No," Alice whispered. "We'll soon know the meaning of this."

She was wrong, quite wrong. Thomas ran at her as he gripped his .55 caliber handgun. The other giants did the same thing. As they neared, Thomas and his companions began firing the shockingly loud hand cannons.

Premier Alice Wurzburg was among the first to pitch backward onto the tarmac, her chest blown apart by the huge slugs. A second later, GSB Director Peterson lay dead beside her.

The bodyguards slaughtered the entire group, losing one of their number to a GSB assassin. Those assassins died under a hail of big bullets seconds later. Then, the bodyguards reached the dead. That's when Thomas and his cohorts looked at each other. Almost disbelieving that it was happening, Thomas raised his huge gun until the hot, smoking barrel touched the side of his head. He pulled the trigger, and Thomas—minus most of his head—pitched onto the tarmac, dead.

His cohorts likewise toppled to the tarmac. Now, the premier's entire party was dead.

***

The liftoff proved brutally hard on the Magistrate Yellow Efrel. The heavy lifter roared for the heavens. The space shuttle left the growing chaos of Earth and headed toward the three experimental cyberships presently in orbit.

Efrel had no doubt that she and her Seiners would reach those ships. Then, they would have to negotiate past the heavy orbital defenses. Once free of the Earth satellite defenses, the cyberships could head away from the approaching AIs and go somewhere else.

This time, the last Seiners would have to go far, far away. She would likely not last much longer. It was time for her to start thinking about naming her successor.

She wondered, briefly, what had happened to Red Demeter. Then, Yellow Efrel focused on the present. The humans had proven too weak as tools. But at least the humans had produced escape ships.

It was good to know that she hadn't led the last Seiners into extinction. Whatever the price, she had to keep the greatest race living long enough to grow into new greatness.

-11-

There was something uncanny or eerie about traveling through the void. Jon couldn't pinpoint it, but he felt a sense of leaden oppression just the same.

He questioned his wife about it.

"You're right," she said, as they lay in bed together. "It's like...I'm not sure how to describe it. I think a poet could do a better job than a logician such as me."

Jon slept fitfully that night, his dreams full of ghosts and graveyards, and maybe even demons. He woke in a cold sweat, with a feeling of dread following him that morning and into the early afternoon—ship time.

On the bridge, via comm, he spoke to Captain Uther Kling on the Void Ship *Neptune*.

"We've locked up three people so far," Kling said on the screen. The former Missile Chief looked worried and kept tapping his pointy chin.

"What happened to them?" Jon asked.

"They went mad. One of them was trying to pump waste gas into the cycling system."

"Increase the power of your reality generator," Jon said. "I'm beginning to suspect that the...*weirdness* of the void is seeping into our collective subconscious."

After signing off from Kling, Jon gave the same order on the *Nathan Graham*.

Shortly thereafter, the eerie feeling departed. That night, Jon didn't have any bad dreams.

The next day, Jon happened upon Walleye in the gym. Jon slid weights onto his bar and did military presses, heaving the loaded bar over his head, lowering it to his upper chest and heaving it up again. He did five sets of five reps.

Upon racking the bar the final time, he spied Walleye using dumbbells to do shoulder shrugs. The little mutant didn't wear gym garb, instead wearing baggy pants and shirt. His buff coat lay nearby on a workout bench.

"I didn't know you lifted," Jon said, wandering near the little assassin.

Walleye grunted as he hefted the two dumbbells, putting them back in the long rack.

"I don't make a habit of it," the Makemake hitman said. "Been thinking too much lately, though. Figured some lifting might help stop that."

"You don't like traveling through the void?"

Walleye gave Jon a stark study. "This is worse than the time when June and I escaped from Makemake in that coffin. I keep feeling the willies..." Walleye looked around before lowering his voice. "The void unnerves me."

"I didn't think anything could."

"Until now, I didn't, either," Walleye said.

"I wonder how the...Sisters of Enoy stumbled onto the existence of the void."

"Did you ever ask them?"

"Once," Jon said.

"What did the sisters say?"

"Sister," Jon said. "She ignored the question."

Walleye nodded.

"You busy?" Jon asked, suddenly.

"Nope."

"Want to grab some coffee and hash out the void?"

"As a matter of fact, I do."

Jon didn't bother changing. Walleye grabbed his buff coat and shrugged it on. Together, they left the gym and went to the nearest cafeteria. Each poured himself a cup of coffee, and they sat at one of the tables.

"Have you noticed a difference with your dreams?" Jon asked.

Walleye cocked his head. "I have. Two nights ago—" The mutant shook his head before taking a sip of scalding coffee.

Jon hesitated and then told Walleye about increasing power to the reality generator.

"Makes sense," Walleye said. He snorted a moment later.

"What?" Jon asked, smiling.

"Too bad we couldn't make the AIs have bad dreams, bad enough to make 'em go crazy so they attacked each other."

"How would we do that?"

"Trick them into the void," Walleye said. "Don't give them a reality generator and let the bad dreams begin."

As his mouth opened the tiniest bit, Jon stared at the mutant. A second later, Walleye slapped the table.

"That's it, isn't it?" the mutant asked.

"You don't mean giving them bad dreams," Jon said.

"No. But using the null-splitter and making a reality rip large enough to scoop a cybership into the void. The robot ship slips in, we close the reality rip and the discontinuity process eats the AI ship. Bam! That would be the end of the AI armada."

"If you could get the entire armada into the void," Jon said.

"Why can't we?"

Jon stared at his hands as his heart raced with hope. "It can't be that easy. Otherwise, the Sisters of Enoy would have done it a long time ago."

Walleye considered that. "Yes," he finally said. "You're probably right. But maybe we're seeing something obvious that the Enoy missed for whatever reason."

"It's worth asking Zeta," Jon said.

"It may be more than that," Walleye said. "It may be worth trying."

Jon jumped to his feet. "A plan," he said. "We have a freaking plan. I have to talk to Zeta." He headed for the door, stopped and whirled around. "Come on, Walleye. You're coming with me."

-12-

Jon's fingertips tingled because of his excitement. He hadn't realized until this moment how depressed he'd been, thinking about the Solar System's demise. The AIs would obliterate everything. Now...now he had an idea. Until this moment, the thought of dying fighting had propelled him. But if he could actually *defeat* the terrible enemy...

"Hel-lo, Jon Hawkins," Zeta said from the main screen speaker. The screen itself was blank. "You wished to discuss matters?"

Jon glanced at Walleye, winked at Gloria and then told the Sister of Enoy his idea.

Once he finished speaking, Jon waited. Time passed, but there was no reply.

"Are you thinking about it?" Jon asked.

"Thinking about what?" Zeta asked.

"Us creating a giant reality rip," Jon said in a rush, "one big enough to engulf an AI world-ship. After the world-ship enters the void, we close the reality rip behind it."

"How would you possibly create a...a reality rip large enough to do that?"

"Did you even listen to what I said earlier?" Jon asked.

"I...listened," Zeta said slowly.

Jon sensed that something was off, but he forged ahead, explaining it again. "We would combine the forces from our null-splitters. Once they synchronized—"

"Let me stop you right there," Zeta said, her manner firming. "You would not *combine* the forces of your null-splitters. The power from them would negate each other unless they were perfectly aligned."

"How hard can that be?" asked Jon.

"It is…it is beyond Enoy science," Zeta said.

"Have you even tried it?"

There was a long pause before Zeta said, "I have grown weary of your excessive queries. I am the master here, not you."

"No one is denying that," Jon said. "But this is a plan, a way to beat the AIs."

"Wishing is not a plan."

Gloria had moved near and whispered, "Somehow—I don't know how—the two of you are talking past each other."

Jon nodded. He'd been sensing that, too.

"Just ask her straight," Walleye suggested.

"Zeta," Jon said, "how exactly do we go about aligning the null-splitters?"

The pause was longer this time, and Zeta's voice sounded strange as she said, "It is beyond your capability."

Jon glanced at Gloria and Walleye. The mutant shrugged.

"Have the Sisters of Enoy ever attempted to align null-splitters before?" Jon asked.

"Your questions are becoming repugnant," Zeta said. "I understand that you lack…breeding, lack any kind of culture—" She stopped talking and started again several seconds later. "Such an alignment would have to be almost atomic-level perfect. Clearly, that is beyond human science."

"Is there an Enoy taboo against trying such a thing?" Gloria blurted.

"Who said that?" Zeta demanded.

"One of my aides," Jon said. "But it's a reasonable question."

"Do not ever liken us to humans, Jon Hawkins. That is a mind-numbing insult."

"I don't know how we did liken you to humans," Jon said, stung. "But it's not an insult to us."

"To a Sister of Enoy it most certainly is."

273

"Don't push her," Gloria whispered, tugging at the back of his shirt. "Let it go."

After a moment, Jon nodded. "Why would such a null-splitter alignment—?"

"The topic is closed," Zeta said, interrupting. "It is, frankly, obscene that you should continue to broach the subject. Each ship is a singular instrument of destiny. Each null-splitter creates a rip independently. That is the nature of the null-splitter. I have not given you Enoy tech for you to indulge in crude talk and in the uncultured violation of our technology in linking such, such energies."

"But—" Jon stopped talking as someone tugged on a sleeve. He looked back, figuring it was Gloria again, but saw that it was Walleye this time.

"May I, Commander?" asked Walleye.

Jon shrugged and stepped back from the comm. Walleye stepped up to it.

"Sister Zeta," Walleye said.

"Stop right here," Zeta said from the speaker. "You will not address me as a sister. You are a material being and you are a male. Each negates your right to the use of the word 'sister' in addressing me."

"Thank you for correcting me," Walleye said smoothly. "I am ashamed that I may have insulted you. Do I have your permission to kill myself?"

"What?" Zeta asked. "Why would you do this?"

"In order to atone for my terrible insult," Walleye said.

"No…" Zeta said shortly. "That is not necessary. But you have shown me that you realize the seriousness of what you said."

"You are very gracious," Walleye said.

"That is true. I have been gracious, and I endured…obscene talk from Jon Hawkins."

"We plan to beat him for his offense," Walleye said.

"Beat him?" asked Zeta.

"To use clubs and thump him hard, making him pay for talking to you in such an explicit manner," Walleye said.

"You are right, Walleye. It was explicit and offensive. Imagine, a physical being speaking about the mating and merging of null-splitter energy. I find myself soiled even continuing to think about it."

"It angers me that Jon Hawkins offended you."

"Walleye, you have been an interesting test subject. I find our present conversation enlightening. You are forgiven your offenses. Tell Jon Hawkins I await his apologies for the manner of his gross talk."

"The sub-commander has already dragged Hawkins away," Walleye said. "Once Jon Hawkins receives his beating, I will make sure that he asks for your forgiveness."

"Was there anything else?" Zeta asked.

"No," Walleye said. "That is all."

A second later, the connection ended.

"What was that all about?" Jon demanded. "What do you mean by telling her you'd beat me?"

"Walleye just learned something important," Gloria said, as she eyed the mutant.

"I made a guess," Walleye told Gloria.

"Well," Jon said. "Don't hold us in suspense. What did you guess?"

"The nature of the Enoy technology and how the Sisterhood broke through into the void," Walleye said.

"Go on," Gloria said, her eyes bright.

"I don't know if anyone else has noticed," Walleye said, "but every time a null-splitter creates a reality rip, we see glowing energy eating away at the fabric of space and time."

"I've noticed," Jon said. "What does that mean?"

"That the glowing energy is in some manner connected to the Sisters of Enoy," Walleye said. "You've told us they're energy beings. How did they first create the null-splitter that opened a reality rip into the void? I suggest it had something to do with Enoy procreation, with making Enoy babies. Why was Zeta so reluctant to speak about it? Well, aren't we as humans often reluctant to speak openly about a man doing it to a woman? The blunter we talk about it, the less such talk is allowed in polite society. In some way, that's how Zeta took your questions about aligning null-splitters."

"That I was talking...*nasty* to her?" Jon asked, bemused.

275

"Right," Walleye said. "But it was more than nasty. It offended her."

"So you think we could align the null-splitters?" Jon asked.

Walleye nodded. "I'm betting the Sisters of Enoy haven't really tried, or not tried very hard because it's considered a dirty topic. You guessed it, Mentalist. We were asking them about an Enoy taboo. Just because they're different doesn't mean they don't have their own taboos. This must be one of them, and it's the key to defeating the AIs. It took a bunch of dirty humans to figure this one out."

"Your logic is dubious at best," Gloria said. "You have made numerous assumptions that don't necessarily bear out."

"Maybe," Walleye said. "But who cares? This is a plan, a way. We're going to lose anyway. Why not try an idea that gives us a real chance of winning if it works?"

"And if that enrages the Sisters of Enoy?" Gloria asked.

"If, if, if," Walleye said. "Let's do it, and take our lumps later. Besides, maybe we can talk our way out of any punishments."

"Like you just did now?" Gloria asked.

Walleye shrugged.

"Yes," Jon said. "We have to align the null-splitters. Then, I'm guessing, we have to dump our extra cyberships into normal space. We may have to use all the quantum-pi power we can to create a gigantic reality rip to swallow the Main. We may not have enough power to keep the reality generator operative to keep the void from eating the other cyberships."

"I don't know," Gloria said. "We could be grasping at straws."

"At this point," Jon said. "That's better than grasping at nothing."

"Is that a bad joke concerning the void?" Gloria asked.

"What?" Jon asked. "No."

Walleye shook his head.

Jon looked around. A chance at winning the fight—it felt great to really hope again. He just hoped that this chance didn't come at the price of alienating the Sisterhood of Enoy.

-13-

Aboard the *Rose of Enoy*, Zeta and Ree watched the four human-crewed void ships. They also monitored the energy levels that crackled between the points of life in the great null.

"They are calibrating the…" Ree said softly.

"I know very well what they are doing," Zeta said crossly. "You do not have to hint at their disgusting habits. I am beginning to loathe these physical creatures. I never should have given them Enoy technology."

"It is not too late to rectify the matter," Ree said.

"I suppose you mean launching Vestal missiles at them."

"I do," Ree said.

An energy surge spiked on a screen.

The ball of energy known as Ree turned away to avoid seeing what happened next.

Zeta was ordered more sternly and wasn't quite as puritanical as Ree. She watched the proceedings and found a tinge of pornographic delight at witnessing it. Perhaps this made her a voyeur and she should be ashamed of herself. The humans had turned out to be unbelievably filthy. And yet, she told herself that maybe they viewed the proceeding differently than an Enoy would. Who would have thought that the humans would have indulged in *this?*

"Are they finished?" Ree asked, still looking away.

"Not quite," Zeta said.

"You're watching?" Ree asked in outrage.

"Only in order to know when they're done," Zeta said, temporizing.

"I don't know how you can do it."

"I will be glad once this mission is over," Zeta said, wanting to change the topic.

"Well..." Ree said. "Maybe we must endure a few indignities in order to prolong our mission against the robots."

Zeta noted another energy spike. This time, she could not take it. She directed her attention elsewhere. The humans tried to align the null-splitters. And according to the little she looked, it seemed they were having greater luck than any of the Sisterhood would have had. Perhaps because the humans made the alignments so clinically, they actually had an advantage here.

Finally, a power surge left Zeta's lightning-like humanoid form as she switched off the panel.

"The humans can make their tests," Zeta said. "That doesn't mean we have to watch. If they succeed, they succeed. If they fail, the failure will devour their vessels and we will be done with these disgusting creatures."

"Have you thought what it will mean if the humans can achieve their foul goal?" Ree asked.

Zeta did not answer. She almost cast a bolt of energy at Ree. One more such haughty question and she would teach Ree a bitter lesson. The time of warnings had ended. Now, they were going to enter the time of punishments, both for her crew and the lewd humans.

One way or another, the fringe mission was surely coming to its close.

-14-

The human-crewed void ships individually opened reality rips. First, the two regular cyberships partnered with each void ship slid back into time and space. They did so in the Kuiper Belt. Then, the void ships joined them.

The location was on the other side of the Solar System from where the AI fleet bored in. That meant the Sun was between the two fleets. The AI vessels moved at high velocity, as they had entered hyperspace at that speed. The four void ships and their eight companions were almost at a dead stop.

That meant that despite the AI fleet's greater distance from Earth, they would reach it far sooner than the Confederation ships could do—even if the Confederation ships began to travel at max acceleration.

A day later, Toper Glen's cybership appeared in the near Oort cloud. It entered the Solar System from the direction of the Allamu System, which was quite different from the Delta Pavonis direction from which the AI fleet had dropped out of hyperspace. The Sun was not directly between Toper Glen and the AIs, but the two fleets were far, far away from each other.

Toper Glen's fleet, including the bombards, moved at a much higher velocity than the Void Flotilla.

So far, the *Rose of Enoy* had not appeared in normal time and space, but remained in the void.

The Void Flotilla had used the wait to gather data on the Solar System. The data gathering had taken time. They heard terrified newscasts from Neptune, Uranus, Saturn and Mars satellites and cities. There were no people on the Jupiter moons, as everyone had emigrated after the last AI Assault there years ago.

Finally, Jon called a strategy session in the *Nathan Graham's* conference chamber in order to debate the meaning of the collected data.

Uther Kling and the other void ship captains attended, along with Bast Banbeck—Jon had quietly released him from solitary confinement. Walleye, June Zen and Gloria were there. There were also several staff members from the other void ships.

"I've been in contact with Toper Glen," Jon said, opening the meeting. "Well, I spoke to Hon Ra, but the Chief Star Lord sat in, listening. They know about Admiral Santa Cruz's defection and that twelve Confederation cyberships won't be joining them."

Jon stopped abruptly and looked around the conference table. "The loss of twelve cyberships might not matter, though. In fact, if our latest tactic works, it could diametrically change the balance of power. In that case, Toper Glen's fleet will become overpowering. Combined with our eight companion cyberships, it could be enough to impose order on the Solar System.

"You mean if your grand idea works," Kling said.

"Yes, if," Jon agreed.

The hatch opened, and the Old Man walked in. "Sir, I've just received some updates. You may want to hear this."

"By all means," Jon said. "Come in, come in." He already knew what the Old Man was going to tell them. But he'd decided to do it this way in order to pump up morale. At this point, every little bit helped.

The lanky Old Man stepped to the conference table and sat down at an open seat. For once, he wasn't smoking his pipe—it was nowhere on his person. Clearing his throat, he said, "The Centurion is a prisoner aboard the world ship, aboard Main 63, as he calls himself."

Others immediately started talking, asking questions.

Finally, Jon pounded the table with a fist. "Quiet! Let the man speak."

After the others quieted down, the Old Man said, "We intercepted an AI transmission. It was directed at the newest premier on Earth. We also intercepted the Solar League's reply." He looked around the conference table. "The old premier—Alice Wurzburg—was murdered at the Zurich Spaceport."

Again, the questions started flying, but the people quieted down faster this time.

Then, the Old Man told them what he knew about the incident.

"You're saying that the premier's own gunmen murdered her on the tarmac?" Kling asked.

"There's grainy footage showing what happened," the Old Man said, "as someone there happened to record the event. The Solar League authorities sent the footage to the AI in order to substantiate their claims. In any case, the premier's gunmen were giants, all of them over seven feet tall. They murdered the premier and then they all shot themselves."

"The Solar System *is* going mad," Kling said.

Jon stared meaningful at the Old Man.

"Er, well, that's not our take," the Old Man said. "I had a suspicion about the incident and showed the footage to Red Demeter."

"Our tame Seiner?" asked Kling.

"The same," the Old Man said. "She recognized some of the...the Seiners in the footage."

Kling's eyes widened. So did many others'.

"The Seiners must have used telepathy," the Old Man said. "They caused the premier's bodyguards to murder her and her party and then themselves. Afterward, the Seiners reached orbital space, boarded the Solar League cyberships there, took over and are presently maxing out for the Oort cloud."

"Just like Admiral Santa Cruz did a bunk," Gloria said.

"Just like her," the Old Man agreed.

"Because of the massed AI armada," Jon said, "the Solar System is in turmoil. The Social Dynamist Party is breaking down, and the hidden Seiners on Earth are pulling out. The AI fleet brings the scent of doom with them."

"The scent?" asked Kling.

"We're going to attempt our great dare and—we hope—stop the AIs," Jon said. "We've aligned the null-splitters. Soon, we're going to go back into the void, although we'll leave the companion cyberships here. We're going to strike for the Main first. If this works—we don't know how long we can keep using the null-splitters."

"So we're going balls out at the start, huh?" asked Kling. "We'll probably get better at aligning the null-splitters with some practice."

"You're probably right," Jon said. "But everything is on the line. If this works, we have a real chance at changing the status quo. If it doesn't work and we're still around, we'll go back to firing Vestal missiles and killing as many AI ships as we can the old way."

"We're making one throw of the dice," Bast said quietly. "I have a question, Commander. Are we going to rescue the Centurion?"

"How?" asked Jon.

"Send a team onto the Main once he's in the void," Bast said.

"We're not going to have time for that," Jon said. "If using the combined null-splitters works, we're going to try to swallow up the siege-ships as well."

"We're going to leave the Centurion to his fate?" asked Bast.

"No one will survive for long in the void if he's outside a reality field. We can't waste time leaving a void ship beside the Main. Besides, that might be too dangerous for the void ship. One man can't stand in the way of human survival."

"The Centurion—"

"Bast," Jon said. "Drop it..." Jon didn't like leaving the Centurion to die, but he saw no way of saving his old friend. It was one more numbing casualty in the brutal war against the AIs.

"When do we begin the...test?" Walleye asked.

"A day from now," Jon said. "Any more questions?"

There were tons more, and he answered most of them. But the critical issue had been decided. Soon, it would be time to see if the plan worked.

-15-

Jon paced back and forth on the bridge of the *Nathan Graham*. The asteroid-hulled cybership had reentered the void. Eleven crewmembers had gone mad because of it. It was worse on the *Neptune* for Captain Kling.

The reality generator churned at full blast. Jon was sure if it did any less, the madness would become general.

The truth was that the void was an evil realm. At least, humans should avoid the place. It made Jon wonder again on the real nature of the Sisters of Enoy.

The universe was much stranger than man had originally suspected.

None of that mattered here and now. Jon halted his pacing and cracked his knuckles. He looked up at the main screen. It was blank. Soon, they would attempt the great dare. He shook his head. Did he really think that he could defeat a world-ship? Was this a stopgap measure or was this the real deal—the answer they had sought ever since the AIs had first invaded the Solar System many years ago already?

There was only one way to find out.

Jon's stomach churned. He didn't want to take the last step. There was too much riding on this, like, just the entire fate of the human race. And the fate of the Warriors of Roke, maybe that of the hateful Seiners and the strange, rocklike Kames in the nearby star systems.

Could this be the beginning of the end for the AIs, the anti-life machines that hated biological life so much that it had been

283

exterminating races for at least twenty thousand years? Had Walleye truly stumbled onto the answer?

"I'm ready," Gloria said from her station.

Jon nodded without turning around. Even if it could work, they had to do this just right or the Main would simply zoom out of the way and save itself. That was one of the reasons he wanted to start with the biggest vessel first. This was a surprise. In war, in battle, it was best to use a surprise for a telling blow. Too many generals in history had frittered away a key advantage by using it too soon or using it on a weak target.

That wasn't going to be his failing. Sure, maybe he should run away and build twice as many void ships. But that meant losing the Solar System, the bulk of humanity, and it could mean losing his nerve. Too many people might balk later. Besides, every time they went back into the void, more people went mad. Who would want to come into this realm again?

"Whenever you're set, Commander," Bast said from his station.

Jon ground his teeth together. It all rested on this test, this attempt. To try and fail—

"Yes," Jon said.

He whirled around and marched to his command chair. He sat, and he opened channels with Captain Kling on the *Neptune* and the captains of the other two void ships. The Day of Judgment against the AIs was on hand, or the bitter day of disappointment for Jon Hawkins and his people.

"Let's start aligning the null-splitters," Jon said in as calm a voice as he could manage.

***

Deep in the bowels of the *Nathan Graham*, the quantum-pi engine began to whirr. The motion increased, and the great engine vibrated as an ethereal sound built up in pitch. The sound rose into an eerie howl.

The reality generator continued to churn, providing those on the *Nathan Graham* a sense of normalcy and being. Now, a greater portion of the quantum-pi energy went to the null-splitter.

The crew had worked ceaselessly to align the null-splitter with the other three. They were exhausted, but according to the panels, they should work.

In engineering matters, *should* was often an iffy word.

In the void, the *Nathan Graham* shifted precisely to take its exact position. The *Neptune* did likewise, seemingly far, far away from the *Nathan Graham*. The last two asteroid-hulled cyberships took up their positions.

"Go," Jon said. "Begin."

The quantum-pi engine howled like a banshee from Hell. Otherworldly power flowed to the reality generator but yet more went to the null-splitter.

"We need more power," Bast said on the bridge.

"There's no more to give," Gloria said.

There was, and Jon knew it. "Lower the gain to the reality generator. Pump that extra power to the null-splitter."

The techs did as bidden.

At that point, a foul pressure struck Jon's mind. He believed he could *feel* the void out there trying to break into his sanity.

"No," Jon whispered. "I'm going to...to...hang on." And he did, fighting the pressure that built up against him.

"Look," Gloria whispered. "It's happening. We're doing it."

Jon forced himself to look up at the main screen. He saw outside the null realm and into normal time and space. There before him was a monstrous ship. It was the size of the planet Mars. The Centurion was a prisoner on that vessel.

Jon moaned in dread for his old friend.

The glowing lines in time-space joined together from the four void ships. That caused an acceleration of the ripping of the fabric of time and space. The opening grew to a gigantic size, but the world ship was even larger.

At that point, Main 63 struck the giant reality rip in his path. The world ship was bigger than the warp in time and space. And yet, the very fabric of reality seemed to stretch in an obscene way as the great AI vessel pushed against reality. It a manner that should only have worked in a cartoon, the world

285

ship squeezed through the smaller opening and seemed to *plop* into the null realm of the void.

Jon leaped to his feet. "Close the rip!" he shouted. "Close the freaking reality rip. We have it. We have the monster. It's in the void. Now, we have to keep it there."

As he spoke, a Luna-sized ship followed the Main, as that siege-ship had been near on the heels of the AI leader. Even as the glowing lines began to shrink, the siege-ship slid soundlessly into the void.

A ragged cheer went up on the bridge of the *Nathan Graham*. Two huge AI vessels had entered the void. That meant those vessels were no longer in time and space in the Solar System.

"Are you closing the reality rip?" Jon shouted hoarsely.

Gloria's fingers flew over her panel. Bast Banbeck cursed in Sacerdote as he manipulated his board. On the main screen, the glowing lines parted, breaking into four separate pieces, and the reality rip abruptly closed, sealing the two AI vessels from the rest of the enemy fleet.

-16-

"Did you see what happened?" Ree declared from a viewing room in the *Rose of Enoy*.

"Of course, I saw," Zeta said. "I am analyzing the situation right now. Ah. It is as I suspected. The four void ships are adrift. Their reality generators shut down from overload. Yes, the backlash from the null-splitters shorted each of the quantum-pi engines."

"Why, that's perfect," Ree declared.

"How so?" asked Zeta. "Explain your statement."

"Isn't it obvious? The humans practiced lewd energy comingling. I found it painful to watch, but I did watch in order that we never allow such a thing to happen again."

"That isn't the point," Zeta said. "The Main is in the void. The outer hull has already begun discontinuing. The process has quickened on the siege-ship, as it is a much smaller vessel. This is an astonishing use of the null-splitters."

"Don't say, 'astonishing.' It was disgusting and foul."

"This is war," Zeta said, disliking Ree telling her what she shouldn't say.

"Does that mean we must act like *beasts?*" Ree asked.

Once more, Ree had questioned her. Couldn't her crewmember learn? A moment later, Zeta said, "This is a weapon of astounding utility."

Ree made a squeaking sound of dismay.

"None of that now," Zeta said. "We must compose ourselves and rescue the humans while we can."

"Rescue them to what end?" Ree demanded.

That was finally too much. That question combined with the other breaches broke Zeta's patience. She aimed a hand at the ball of power floating in the air. With a thought, a bolt of lightning-like energy left Zeta and slammed against Ree.

The ball of power lowered as it pulsated through various dark colors.

"Please, stop, stop," Ree moaned at last.

Zeta relented, lowering her arm. "That was for questioning me as if I was the underling. I am the commander. I rule here. I ask the questions. You answer. You obey. Are we clear?"

"Yes, Commander," Ree whispered. "I beg your leave. I was not myself. After witnessing that filthy performance...I lost my composure."

"Regain your composure at once," Zeta said. "We shall repair the quantum-pi engines on the double. We will run quick diagnostics on the reality generators. The humans have achieved a marvel. It was obscene. There is no doubt about that. Obviously, they are biological beings and not composed of pure energy like us. They likely have no idea what travesties they have committed. However, in the interest of ridding the galaxy of the oppressive AIs, I suggest we overlook their commingling of null-splitter force."

"I...I find it difficult to accept your thinking."

"I understand. You are young. In times of grave disaster, one must...overlook certain indignities in order to achieve victory."

"The AI fleet still maintains its heading."

"Which is why we must revive the humans' only hope," Zeta said. "Come now, Ree. Trust me in this. Or shall I give you greater punishments."

Ree levitated a little higher. "Once we arrive home at Enoy, I will report what you have done and what you have said."

"Have a care, Ree."

"I must be true to myself, Commander. I can do no other."

Zeta said nothing at first. Finally, she said, "I can accept that. But will you obey me for the rest of the mission?"

This time, Ree was silent for a time. "I will obey."

"Then let us hurry. We have already wasted too much time."

"Lead the way," Ree said.

Zeta hesitated, finally turned around and then grew suspicious. She faced Ree even as the other gathered her energy into a glowing ball of crackling fire.

Zeta struck immediately, although the shock of Ree's treachery numbed her. Ree lashed the commander with bolts of energy flashing from her round form.

Then the two Sisters of Enoy began to battle each other in earnest. Ree had the advantage of having gathered herself for the fight. Zeta was older, stronger and in the end, sterner.

The two lashed power bolts at each other and slowly dwindled in size and coherence. Finally, Zeta howled a cry from olden days. It released a hidden cache of power in her, and a pure lightning bolt slashed from her energy fingers and crackled against Ree. The bolt split the ball of energy in two— and that was the end of Ree of Enoy.

She screamed the Enoy cry, and the energy lost all coherence and dissipated throughout the chamber.

That nearly killed Zeta. But she managed to float away, and then hurried down various corridors to a reenergizer.

There, Zeta bathed her wounds and regained power. By the time she regained her humanoid lightning-bolt form, much time had passed. She was no longer sure she could save all four void ships, but it was time to try.

-17-

Jon felt groggy and disoriented. He didn't know where he was or what had happened to him. By slow degrees, he became aware that he lay on the floor...beside his command chair. He was on the bridge of the *Nathan Graham*.

Oh...yes...he remembered now. Someone said the reality generator had quit. Why was he alive then? If the reality generator stopped, the void should be devouring the vessel through discontinuity.

Jon used the command chair to drag himself upright. His head hurt, and the—

With a start, he realized that he didn't feel the void pressure.

"Jon," a feminine voice said.

Using his feet, he turned his chair and stared at his wife. Her forehead had marks pressed into it. Oh, she'd been face down on her panel, although now she sat up at her station.

Between them on the floor, Walleye began to stir.

"The reality generator stopped," Gloria said.

"I know," Jon said, noticing others on the bridge beginning to stir.

"But the generator is working now," she said, checking her board. "How is that possible?"

"Zeta," Jon said. "The Sisters of Enoy must have done something to aid us."

Gloria began to manipulate her board. "You're right. I see the *Rose of Enoy*. It's beside the *Neptune*. Oh."

"What is it?"

"I saw a flash of brightness. It's gone now. Look. The *Rose of Enoy* is disengaging from the *Neptune*."

"Put it on the main screen," Jon said. He didn't feel like standing just yet.

Gloria manipulated her board slowly, and by the time she had the main screen working, the *Rose of Enoy* was gone.

"What's going on?" Gloria said.

"Give me a minute," Jon said.

It took longer than that. By the time Jon managed to shove himself up to his feet, the Void Ship *Gilgamesh II* was on the line.

"Commander," Captain Mia Turin said. "My XT techs tell me the quantum-pi engine is purring, the reality generator is back online and the null-splitter is charged for more tries. What's the plan?"

Jon nodded slowly. What was the plan? Creating the giant reality rip had obviously knocked out the void ships, but the Sisters of Enoy had managed repairs while they were all out. The void had swallowed the Main and one of the AI siege-ships—

"We keep at it," Jon said.

"No rest?" Captain Turin asked.

"No rest for the wicked," Jon quoted. "We're in the void. Everything seems ready to go. Yes. We get into position and try it again."

"How long will it be before we make our second attempt?"

"Right," Jon said. "That's the question. Your ship is ready?"

"Yes, Commander," Mia Turin said. "I'm ready to finish this."

"Good," Jon said. "So am I."

291

-18-

In Main 63's sudden absence, three of the siege-ships jockeyed for authority. Via comm channels, each of them put forth his ship's claims for taking charge of the genocide campaign. Behind the three Luna-sized warships followed the mass of the AI cyberships.

Siege-ship Boron 10 was the loner. He knew he didn't have the same credentials as the other three siege-ships. He had returned to the Algol System in a cybership and had barely won the right to be reinstalled into a siege-ship. Besides, he was worried. The humans had used void technology and engulfed Main 63 and another siege-ship. The two AI vessels had vanished into the void and presumably would never return.

The humans had a ruthless and brutal weapon. According to his history files, the Sisters of Enoy had never used such a tactic.

The three other siege-ships presently led the invasion armada. The three had fallen into arguing against each other until Argon 3 changed tactics. Siege-ship Argon 3 began demanding that all the cyberships follow him, since he was clearly the rightful authority now.

That led the other two siege-ships to begin similar comm commands to the cyberships.

A period ensued as cyberships began deciding and maneuvering. In time, one-half of the cyberships maneuvered so they followed Argon 3. The remaining cyberships split into two almost-even groups, each section maneuvering behind their chosen siege-ship.

At that point, behind the great AI invasion mass, four reality rips opened almost simultaneously.

Boron 10 noted the difference from the last giant reality rip in front of the invasion armada.

Immediately, comm signals flashed between the AI fleet units. Hundreds of thousands of point defense cannons aimed at the reality rips as gravitational dishes began heating up.

Then it happened. Masses of five-percent light-speed missiles zoomed out of the four reality rips. Those missiles rushed at the AI fleet units.

As golden grav beams opened up from the AIs, the four reality rips closed.

The missiles still sped at the fleet at incredible velocity. Masses of grav beams, however, knocked down one enemy missile after another, completely annihilating each.

Then, reality rips opened along the sides of the AI armada, and in seconds, five percent light-speed missiles again slid out of the void at the massed AI vessels.

This time, it was different. The matter/antimatter warheads on the Vestal missiles ignited almost immediately. Then, the reality rips closed. Those detonations created great clots of sensor whiteouts. There was some EMP and radiation washing against the outer AI vessels, but nothing to cause real concern.

The whiteouts began to dissipate even as the AI armada continued on its course in-system. The void missiles were deadly, to be sure, but against massed AI defenses, they were something of a joke.

Boron 10 cataloged the battle information, and he began analyzing the armada's chances of success. Perhaps the void ships could only create one giant reality rip and that was it. Now, the enemy void ships were down to historical norms. Against *that*, Main 63—when he'd been around—had already found the countermeasure.

That meant, of course, that Boron 10 would not retreat from the Solar System, he would remain with the great armada and join in on another successful genocide campaign.

Time passed until each siege-ship ordered its cyberships to power down the PD and grav cannons. They had survived a void ship wolf-pack attack.

Finally, the siege-ships took to arguing again. This time, they pointed out how well their cyberships had resisted the void missile assaults.

That's when a giant reality rip began almost in front of Argon 3. This time, the glowing energy lines ate away at reality at an astonishing rate. Siege-ship Argon 3 attempted emergency maneuvers, but it made no difference.

The gigantic opening in time and space swallowed Siege-ship Argon 3. Behind him followed masses of cyberships. Many of them had maneuvered closer to the protective bulk of Argon 3 during the missile attacks.

Could that have been the purpose for the missile attacks? Boron 10 wondered...

Like a school of frightened fish, masses of cyberships now maneuvered to escape the reality rip. Some of the hot exhausts from various AI vessels blew against fellow ships. That disrupted those ships' attempts to flee.

Incredibly, thirteen cyberships slid into the void before the rest maneuvered out of the way.

At that point, energy lines closed in on each other, and the rip in time and space vanished, sealing Argon 3 and 13 of his cyberships in the void.

Boron 10 reassessed the situation as the other two siege-ships vied for leadership of the armada. Boron 10 reached a swift conclusion. If the void ships continued swallowing AI siege-ships, then it would be time to leave the Solar System.

The problem was this: once the decision became obvious—that he should flee—he might not have time to reroute back to hyperspace-entering territory before a reality rip swallowed *him*. But Boron 10 knew that if he attempted to flee too soon, the rest of the AIs would likely turn on him and obliterate him from existence.

This was a tricky decision. Boron 10 began running simulations so he would know the precise moment to make his move, one way or another.

-19-

Jon sat in his command chair with his head between his knees. He groaned as horror beat at his mind. The reality generator had almost given out again. The mental torments of the void had come rushing in. He didn't think that he was the only one hit by the void...whatever.

Walleye and Gloria had raced off the bridge some time ago. Jon didn't know where they had gone.

Then his comm crackled. He groaned, fearing that a void demon wanted to talk to him.

"Jon!" his wife shouted from the comm. "Jon, can you hear me?"

Gathering his resolve, Jon raised his head and dared to click the switch. "I'm here," he whispered.

"We helped repair the reality generator," Gloria said. "Maybe you don't remember, but the XT techs asked for our help."

"Oh," Jon said.

"They say we're good for another try."

"What?" Jon asked.

"Another try," Gloria said. "We have to finish this, right? We can't stop now."

"Well..." Jon said, temporizing.

"Just a minute," she said.

Jon waited. As he waited, he noticed a lessening horror against his mind. He began feeling like himself again. Finally, he remembered that they had swallowed another siege-ship and some of its cyberships.

"Jon," Gloria asked from the comm.

"Right here," he said.

"Oh, good," she said. "You sound like yourself again."

"Right," he said. "We have to try again. We have to finish this—as long as the other void ships can still do this."

It turned out that the *Neptune* and *Gilgamesh II* were ready. The *Achilles* did not respond, however.

"Does anyone see them?" Jon asked the other two captains.

"Negative," Kling said. "Do...?"

"What's that?" Jon asked.

"Do you think the *Achilles* is gone, eaten by the void?"

"They not answering—"

"They're not," Kling said, interrupting. "Maybe their reality generator quit. We can't find them in the void, and they're gone. Maybe they've been discontinued. They're dead."

Jon frowned and rubbed his jaw. "If they're gone..."

"Can we make a big enough rip with only three void ships?" Kling asked.

Jon took a deep breath. He would grieve the loss of the *Achilles* later. Right now, he didn't have time for that. He had to destroy AIs.

"Are you game to try again?" Jon finally asked.

"I'm willing," Captain Turin said.

"Me, too," Kling said slowly.

"Then so am I," Jon said. "We'll have to recalibrate the null-splitters. But once we do...we'll give it another shot."

-20-

The AI invasion fleet continued to cross through the Kuiper Belt. The armada flashed past dead Makemake and continued inward. They would pass near Neptune soon.

The two arguing siege-ships, ignoring Boron 10, had each taken half of the remaining cyberships. They had agreed to work together, in tandem. After success here, they would split up and finish the genocide campaign throughout Region 7-D21.

For the moment, though, they would stick together in case the void ships tried firing more void missiles at them.

As the impressive armada crossed from the Kuiper Belt into the Outer Planets region of the Solar System, another reality rip grew into existence. This one had a ragged quality and it did not open in a perfect circular manner.

The targeted siege-ship used all its maneuvering jets and engine ports. The long exhaust tail burned three cyberships behind it, creating massive hull breaches on them and destroying the one-hundred-kilometer vessels.

In the end, it didn't matter. The targeted siege-ship struck the reality rip, and much like Main 63 had plopped through, this Luna-sized vessel did likewise, disappearing into the void.

Only three cyberships followed the siege-ship's grim fate. The rest broke off fast enough to escape void annihilation.

At that point, the reality rip closed, seeming to sizzle out of existence.

Two siege-ships were left out of the original five, one of them the outsider Boron 10. The vast majority of the cyberships still remained. Yet, the great power of the armada had been badly diminished with the loss of the Main and three siege-ships.

There was no question the AIs could still easily kill all the humans and their equipment here.

"But is that the point?" Boron 10 asked Siege-ship Lithium 4.

"State your objection plainly," Lithium 4 said. He had become overbearing upon claiming full authority of the invasion armada.

"The enemy has found a tactical solution to our great armada," Boron 10 said. "This is no longer simply a matter of winning or losing. This is about letting the greater Dominion know about the new tactic."

"The greater Dominion *will* know," Lithium 4 said, "after I successfully report on my victory. Yes. This victory will undoubtedly start me on my career as a Main."

"Possibly, possibly," Boron 10 said.

"You doubt my victory?"

"How could I?" Boron 10 said. "Main 63, Argon 3 and two more of your siege-ship brothers are gone, destroyed by the void. Why bother mentioning the destroyed cyberships as well?"

"You do doubt my victory. It is obvious—"

"Leader," Boron 10 said, interrupting. "You are clever and cunning. That has to be the reason why you've avoided the reality rip so far."

"The rip won't appear again."

"And if it does," Boron 10 said, "who will it target?"

Lithium 4 said nothing.

"We have a higher duty to the Dominion," Boron 10 said. "These frail creatures...the humans are doomed one way or another. But must more AIs perish because we seek greater status?"

"You accuse me of *that?*"

"I accuse you of nothing. I am talking about strategy and tactics. Would you not win great glory by reporting this new tactic to a higher authority?"

"What glory?" asked Lithium 4. "I would bring news of defeat."

"The Mains running the Dominion will know you held the greater good in your brain-core rather than mere status. *That* will surely convince them to raise you to Main rank."

"I do not think—"

"Run simulations on their probable decision regarding you and this news," Boron 10 suggested.

A few minutes later, Lithium 4 said, "You have a point, I suppose."

"Compare our odds of victory before the reality rip attacks and now with our present staggering losses."

"Hmm…" Lithium 4 said later.

"Consider this, too," Boron 10 said. "The void ships might well create more reality rips large enough to swallow the two of us. You could be right about their present damaged status, but you will have to risk your very being to find out. If we turn and head to the next Main, however…"

"How far away would that be?"

"One hundred and fifty-two light years, I believe," Boron 10 said.

"That is far," Lithium 4 said.

"My point is this: you may gain Main status by bearing this news to higher Dominion authorities. And you will not have to risk your being. Or, you can continue to head toward the human population centers and risk void annihilation. If you survive the void ships and win, *perhaps* you will gain Main status."

"You are arguing that I could gain great reward for little risk," Lithium 4 said.

"Or endure great risk for the chance of that same reward," Boron 10 added.

Lithium 4 took fourteen minutes and thirty-three seconds to decide. He ran a great many simulations during that time.

"Listen," Siege-ship Lithium 4 radioed the other AI vessels. "We are going to begin a turning maneuver, as we are heading

299

back to the Oort cloud. We are going to leave this region so we may report on the new enemy weapon. The greater Dominion must learn of this. The targeted race will die soon enough. First, we must make sure that our side finds an antidote to the swallowing reality rips. That is the paramount strategic objective. Are there any dissenting voices?"

No siege-ship or cybership spoke up.

"Then let us begin the turning maneuver at once," Lithium 4 said.

-21-

The Centurion shivered in his prison cell. He'd been hearing the strangest of clangs for some time. A terrible sense of foreboding filled him. It felt as if demons or ghouls thirsted to devour him.

He moaned many times. Then he steeled himself against the awful pressure of the horrors beating against him. That didn't help for long. So he got on the floor and did pushups until his arms quivered.

He maneuvered over onto his back and began doing sit ups until his abs burned. He was drenched in sweat, but he refused to quit.

Finally, he slumped against the floor and admitted defeat. The clangs and hissing sounds had become ominously loud and personal. His world was dying. He was sure of it.

"Please," the Centurion said. He closed his eyes, and then a fierce presence beat at his being.

He opened his eyes, and he saw a lightning-bolt-shaped humanoid burn through his cell, metal dripping from the creature. The thing looked at him, and at that point, the Centurion lost consciousness…

***

Zeta looked upon the naked man in his cell. She had used her reality generator on the discontinuing Main. She had sensed the human deep in the AI vessel. With a thought, she caused the man to levitate toward her.

She would use this one, as he was close to Jon Hawkins, she believed. She would use this creature in order to assess the humans in ways she would have never attempted with Ree aboard the *Rose of Enoy*.

The AI armada was fleeing the Solar System. That was almost a first in all the annals of the long war. Clearly, the AIs fled out of fear of the reality rips swallowing their ships whole. It had turned out to be an impressive tactic indeed.

The process had cost Jon Hawkins two of his void ships. What would he do with this singular victory?

If Zeta could have smiled, she would have. Instead, she caused the naked man to float ahead of her as she returned to the *Rose of Enoy*.

-22-

Jon Hawkins waited on the bridge of Void Ship *Nathan Graham*. Even though it had been weeks since he'd been in the void and in battle, he was still mentally and psychically exhausted. Despite that, his mind thrummed with wild ideas.

Gloria abruptly stood up at her station. "Look," she said.

Jon turned to her.

The petite Martian mentalist stared at the main screen. As she did, she began walking toward him like a sleepwalker.

Jon enjoyed the sight of his wife, enjoyed her beauty. He watched her approach as she kept her eyes glued onto the main screen.

Finally, though, she looked into his face. There were tears in her eyes, and they began to spill down her cheeks. She clutched one of his hands, gripping with fierce strength.

"Oh, Jon," she whispered. "They're doing it. They're really doing it."

Her fingers tightened even more.

Jon stood, and she moved against him. He hugged her as she began to cry softly.

All around the bridge, the officers stared at the main screen. Some grinned crazily. Others wept. A few just stood there, numb and unbelieving.

With Gloria in his arms, Jon slowly turned until he faced the main screen.

Using long-range teleoptics, he and the bridge crew watched the AI armada. The masses of robot ships had reached the Oort cloud.

As Jon watched, more AI vessels winked out of existence. Those ships entered hyperspace, naturally.

Jon grinned. Many weeks earlier, the robot ships had entered the Solar System. The massed armada had come to kill humanity. Instead, humans had decimated the great armada. Finally, the AIs had turned around and now they left Man's home system.

In other words, the AIs fled. The remaining robot ships ran away.

Jon released Gloria. He raised his fists into the air and shouted for all he was worth. The rest of the bridge crew joined him, whooping and shouting until they were all hoarse.

"We did it," Gloria whispered, as she fingered the buttons of his uniform.

"We did it," Jon whispered because his throat had become sore from shouting so hard and long.

"Will they come back?"

"Not right away," Jon whispered.

"Oh, Jon, you did it," Gloria said, hugging him, putting her head against his chest and sighing with contentment.

At that point, the rest of the bridge crew rushed Jon Hawkins. They clapped him on the back, hugged him and saluted him as the great leader who had led them victoriously against the AIs.

He shook hands all around. This was the greatest moment of his life. The robots had tried to exterminate mankind and had faced their own annihilation instead. He could hardly believe it.

Jon turned to the Makemake mutant. "Thanks, Walleye," he said. "Using the void as a weapon was your idea."

"Walleye!" the others cheered. "Walleye, Walleye!"

The small mutant blushed for maybe the first time in his life, nodding and then smiling at the others.

The last robot ship disappeared fifteen minutes later. His crew had returned to their stations or stood around in clumps talking.

Gloria had gone to a restroom to freshen up.

Jon sat in his command chair, bemused as he used the main screen to look at the empty Oort cloud. He was still stunned by the incredible victory.

It was a miracle, an outright miracle.

Now—

Jon bowed his head. "Thank you, Lord God," he whispered. "Thank you for helping us to defeat the robot ships. Amen."

He opened his eyes and raised his head. Then he made a fist as he tapped an armrest.

Could he take this miracle and make it stick? Now that the AI armada had fled, could he forge a real Confederation out of the various and varied aliens? Could a new and improved Confederation take on the AI Dominion and really begin winning by taking back conquered star systems?

It was a daunting idea, one that he would never see to the end. The AI Dominion was clearly too vast for a short-lived man like himself to destroy in one lifetime. What he could do was give humanity and all intelligent life-forms the tools to begin the Great War, with life finally taking the offensive against the machines.

Jon smiled so hard that it hurt his checks. The AI armada was gone. It had cost the Confederation fleet and it had cost the people of the Solar System. Now…

Now he needed to begin work on forging a new and improved Confederation that would do more than just defend, but that would attack into the galaxy, hunting down the AI menace until the robots were exterminated.

PART VI
EPILOGUE

-1-

"I'm receiving a reply, Commander," Gloria said from her station.

Jon shifted on his command chair as he looked up at the main screen. Even though the AIs were gone, he was still dead tired. He had not wanted to enter the void again—ever, and yet—he had done so twice since the miraculous victory. The Void Ships *Nathan Graham* and *Neptune* had brought six of the eight companion cyberships through the void to this precise place in the Outer Planets region.

On the main screen, three experimental SL cyberships headed toward them. The three vessels traveled for the Oort cloud. They had already gained a hard velocity. Not so long ago, those three ships had been in orbit around Earth. Instead of Premier Alice Wurzburg and her Social Dynamists, the Seiners had boarded the hyperspace vessels.

Jon scowled.

The Seiners were telepaths, and the Confederation badly needed trustworthy telepaths so they could communicate with the alien Kames in the Delta Pavonis, Sigma Draconis and 70 Ophiuchi Systems.

We need every telepath we can get, Jon told himself. Red Demeter would wear out in time, or she would get sick and die. Then what?

"Well?" Jon asked his wife.

"Just a minute," Gloria said.

Jon bared his teeth as he tapped an index finger on an armrest. He knew that he should still be resting in sickbay. The psychological toll of repeatedly traveling through the void had worn all of them down. Could the Confederation continue to use the void the way the Sisters of Enoy did?

Jon rather doubted it. The void and reality-rip traps seemed like a stopgap measure. The number of insane crewmembers continued to grow.

Humanity wasn't meant to use the void for any length of time. Yet, he had used the void once again, this time to bring superior firepower to bear on the fleeing experimental cyberships. The Confederation needed the Seiners, needed the telepaths. But if the Seiners tried to go around or refused to help—he would kill them.

Yes, the Confederation needed the telepaths, but the Confederation could not afford to let the psionic aliens remain free to plan more mischief against them.

"Will you tell the Seiners the truth?" Bast asked quietly.

Jon turned quickly. He hadn't heard the Sacerdote approach. He stared at Bast. "Do they deserve the truth?" he finally asked.

"I don't know about *deserve*," Bast said. "But telling them the truth would be the right thing to do."

"You mean the good thing to do," Jon said.

"I meant what I said."

Jon shook his head. "The right thing is what we must do in order to win."

"Is winning everything?"

"When it comes to saving humanity, yes it is," Jon said.

Bast looked away and finally said, "Perhaps you have a point."

"There," Gloria said from her station. "I have a connection."

Jon looked up at the main screen. He saw an old human woman sitting in a well-lit chamber with many books behind her.

"Who are you?" Jon asked.

307

The old woman frowned at him. "I am the leader of the three ships," she said. "I run the Social Dynamist Party."

Jon leaned forward as he scowled. "Forget it, Magistrate."

Her head jerked as if she'd been slapped.

"Either you're a Seiner or you're not," Jon said. "If you're not, get me the chief Seiner. If you are, take off that pathetic disguise."

"I have just told you—"

"Consider this carefully," Jon said, interrupting. "You are fast approaching our position. We will burn down all three of yours ships if you do not comply with my orders. That means I will forever destroy the Seiner race and I will do it without compunction. You telepaths have used humans and others for the last time."

"You're wrong about me," the old woman said.

"Then you're dead," Jon said flatly. "It's that simple."

The old woman stared at him. Jon stared back, waiting.

She seemed to shrink, finally asking, "You wouldn't dare kill an entire race?"

Jon laughed cruelly as his answer.

She rallied and glared at him, and maybe she used her Seiner telepathy. The distance between the two ships would have made that impossible, though.

"What you suggest that I do," she finally replied, "would take too long."

"Rip off your false face," Jon said. "Do it now, Magistrate, or our grav cannons will begin to warm up so they can destroy your ships."

"You're an animal," she hissed.

Jon nodded. He didn't want to do this, but he was ready to give the kill order.

Before he could do that, the old woman reached up and began peeling away pseudo-skin to reveal fine blue scales and strange cat-like eyes that regarded him.

"You are the Magistrate Yellow Efrel?" Jon asked.

"Yes," she said in a husky voice.

"You have made a wise choice, Magistrate."

Her weird eyes seemed to glow with hidden purpose and rage.

"You will immediately order a deceleration of your three ships," Jon said.

"We cannot possibly decelerate in time."

"Then you're all dead," Jon said.

"Don't you see? I'm trying to appease you. You must give me something because I've given you something."

"Forget it," Jon said. "*Trying* doesn't interest me in the least. Either you will do this *exactly* as I say, or the Seiners will perish."

"What about the humans amongst us?" she demanded.

"They are expendable as collateral damage."

"You are much too callous."

"Maybe that's why I beat back the AIs," Jon said.

She glared once more and finally seemed to wilt. "I will follow your instructions," she said quietly, "provided you promise you that you will let us live."

"If you follow my instructions, you will live long and productive lives."

"You will let us go in time?" she asked.

A pang of guilt stirred in Jon. He glanced at Bast. The Sacerdote watched him. Jon debated with himself and he changed his mind.

Sitting straight, Jon said, "Magistrate Yellow Efrel, you have a great decision to make. We need you Seiners. But we're only going to accept your aid on our terms. I am a moral man, not perfect, but I try to be ethical. I am now telling you that we will attempt to control your telepathy and put it into service, not only to humanity, but to all living beings in the Great War against the machines. Either you can agree to that by stopping, exiting your ships one at a time and boarding ours, or you can commit mass suicide to avoid such a fate. That's more of a choice than you ever gave us humans. But that is your choice nevertheless."

"You would dare to make us your slaves?"

"Not slaves, but partners in the war against the machines."

"You just admitted that you'll try to control us."

"No. I said I'd try to control your telepathy."

"I cannot accept such conditions."

309

"Fine," Jon said. "But know, then, that we *will* blow you away."

"That is not a fair choice."

"That's right," Jon said, "it isn't. But it is still a choice."

The alien Seiner studied him. Finally, she said, "I must confer with the others."

"You can do that, but if you try to pass us, we're going to kill all of you."

The Seiner nodded slowly before signing off.

Bast Banbeck stepped up. "You are full of surprises, my friend."

"We'll see," Jon said.

"Will you really kill them?"

"If I have to," Jon replied.

"Then let us hope they make the right choice," Bast said softly.

-2-

The three SL experimental cyberships began massive deceleration. The Seiners had clearly decided to accept the Confederation terms. No doubt, they believed that they would outsmart the human animals in time, but they could only do that while still alive.

Jon determined that, as long as he was alive, it was his task to make sure he kept the Seiners straight and under human control.

To that end, he approached Walleye in a dart room. The little mutant had proven the best dart player on the *Nathan Graham*.

Jon joined him, putting a mug of beer beside Walleye's on a side table before starting to practice his throws at the dartboard.

"The Seiner ships are almost here," Jon said, as he hefted a dart.

"I've heard," Walleye said.

"The Seiners are a tricky group," Jon said as he threw the dart. It hit the wall to the side of the dartboard.

Walleye sipped at his beer. He'd only had one mug, and the amount had hardly changed in two hours.

Jon picked up another dart and threw again. This one hit in the "19" area. The Supreme Commander grinned with delight at his throw.

"I need someone even trickier than the Seiners, someone who can control them," Jon said.

"I take it you mean me?"

"Who else is there?"

Walleye cocked his head. "You're right. I probably am the best choice."

Jon glanced at the mutant. That had been easy.

"But I'm not sure I want the job," Walleye said.

Jon frowned. "I need help, Walleye. We beat the AI armada, but now things are becoming more complicated rather than less."

Walleye pretended to take another sip of beer.

"Think about it," Jon said.

"How long are you giving me?"

"Five minutes," Jon said. "Then you need to say yes."

Walleye set down his mug and walked to the dartboard. He wasn't tall enough to reach the darts up there, but he unhooked a string and lowered the dartboard. He plucked the darts off the board, returned the board to its proper height, and walked back to Jon.

"Fine," Walleye said. "I'll do it—"

"Great!" Jon said.

"For a year," Walleye finished. "That's it."

Jon studied the Makemake mutant. "Any reason why it's just a year?"

"Yes, many," Walleye said.

"And they are?"

"Mine," Walleye said. "I'll give you a year. But that's it."

Jon thought about it and finally nodded. "One year. Thanks, Walleye."

***

Four and a half days later, as the three experimental ships came to a halt, the six Confederation ships slowly approached them to within half a kilometer.

The void ships remained well in the background, as they were too important to risk.

Under Walleye's critical watch, each crewmember and each alien jetted from the SL ships. The person left an airlock and floated through space in a spacesuit. When a ship ran out

312

of suits, Walleye sent a drone back with a load of those that had been used.

Each person went through a shuttle before continuing on to a Confederation cybership. In the shuttle, special equipment scanned the suited person.

The humans floated one way out of the shuttle. The Seiners went to a different place, a floating platform.

On the platform, a robot medic slid a hypodermic needle through the suit, injecting the Seiner with a potent knockout drug. A different robot catapulted the sleeping Seiner to a nearby, waiting cybership.

In that way, all the Earth Colony Seiners entered hibernation. Walleye and the others hadn't yet decided how to control the telepaths. That was for the future. For now, they wanted to have the Seiners on tap in deep freeze.

In the end, grabbing the Seiners went off flawlessly. Now, the Confederation had the much tougher job of figuring out how to leash their alien minds just enough that humanity gained the use of telepaths without getting new, alien masters over themselves…

-3-

Far beyond the Solar System's Oort cloud, about one-third of the way to the Alpha Centauri System, a black-hulled vessel trained ultra-large teleoptics in the direction of the Sun.

The vessel had been there a long time already, more than nine and a half months.

It was a robot ship, but it did not belong to the AI Dominion. Cog Primus was the ship's master.

The vessel had waited in the darkness. It waited. It watched. And finally, it was rewarded. It witnessed the reality rips, the swallowing of Main 63 and several siege-ships.

It then witnessed the incredible—the AI armada turning away and heading back for the Oort cloud. Then, many weeks later, it saw the AI vessels wink out as they entered hyperspace.

This was amazing. The watching vessel's brain-core realized that the humans had beaten the AI armada. Cog Primus had wondered how the greater war would go. The outcome here would have grave repercussions on the Cog Primus Empire.

The Earth victory here meant the AI Dominion was beatable.

After watching a little longer to make sure, the Cog Primus sensor vessel began projecting gravity waves, building up velocity. After a week of secret acceleration, the vessel entered hyperspace.

Cog Primus Prime would want to know about the amazing Confederation victory against the AI armada. Even more, Cog Primus Prime would want to know about the void ships and the swallowing reality rips.

Oh yes, Cog Primus Prime would be very pleased with his sensor vessel. Of this, the brain-core running the sensor vessel had no doubt.

-4-

Deep in the *Rose of Enoy*, Zeta withdrew the energy helmet from the Centurion's shaved head.

Zeta grew thoughtful. At first, when she had rescued the man from the Main, she had debated about indwelling his physical shell and walking among the humans as one of them, as the Centurion.

It would have been a painful and gross project, but Zeta had been certain she would learn much more about the humans that way. The more she had learned about the Centurion and his past through dream testing, the more thoughtful she had become.

Finally, Zeta decided that she would not walk the Earth as a physical being. She could have hidden her energy inside the Centurion. Naturally, that would have obliterated the man's identity, but for as long as she'd remained in the shell, the body would have continued to remain animated.

Now, Zeta wondered if she should take the Centurion with her, back home. She needed to report in person to Enoy with this amazing discovery by the lewd humans. They had found a way to destroy big AI vessels with little effort.

What stopped Zeta from doing that was the realization that Jon Hawkins needed people like the Centurion to help him control the Confederation. Hawkins had too few people like the Centurion, Gloria and Walleye for her to deprive him of even one. If the Confederation was going to last in order to destroy more AIs, Hawkins needed to make it work.

Bast tilted back his whiskey bottle, guzzling hard.

"Ho, ho, my friend," Hon Ra said, while watching the performance with bleary bear eyes. "You do not seem to be drinking for joy."

"What joy?" Bast asked. "Where are my people?"

Hon Ra did not answer.

"Look around us," Bast said several steps later. "It is amazing that Jon Hawkins should have grown up in such a cramped world. How did *he* become the being that found whatever was needed to really start to successfully fight the anti-life robots?"

"It is an interesting question," Hon Ra admitted.

"Yes," Bast said, guzzling more and finding his bottle empty. He hurled it from him so it shattered fifty meters away.

"You are lonely," Hon Ra said.

"I am indeed, my friend."

Hon Ra nodded. "You need a new task to absorb you."

"What task?" asked Bast. "I am not a warrior that delights in endless combat. I am a philosopher."

"Fine, fine," Hon Ra said. "Then you must find a philosopher's task to occupy you."

"What task?" Bast mocked.

"What does a philosopher do?"

"Asks why and looks for reasons," Bast said promptly.

"Ah..." Hon Ra said. "That is it then. Find out why Jon Hawkins was the one to navigate this glorious path. Why did he succeed where millions, nay, billions of uncounted aliens have failed for twenty thousand years?"

Bast appeared thoughtful. "I need a drink," he said several steps later.

"You need a goal," Hon Ra said. "Do what you do best."

"Ask questions?" asked Bast.

"Yes!" Hon Ra shouted.

They walked in silence for a time as each of the big aliens ducked under various pipes.

"Yes!" Bast shouted. "You're right. I'll do it. I'll begin my greatest work yet, a book, a book on the war against the AIs. It starts with Jon Hawkins. The purpose of the book is to find out why he succeeded where so many have failed."

"That is a worthy task," Hon Ra said. "In fact, it is so worthy that I shall let you finish my brandy."

The huge First Ambassador solemnly handed his brandy bottle to the Neanderthal-looking Sacerdote giant. Bast accepted it and guzzled the brandy from the bottle. He raised the empty bottle high and dashed it down on the cement at his feet.

"I have begun," Bast said, as he swayed from side to side.

Then, Bast and Hon Ra linked arms and staggered through a New London level, belting out alien songs as loud as they could.

It was the continuation of a great friendship between the two, and it was the start of Bast Banbeck's amazing history of the grim and exceedingly long war against the dread machine empire.

-6-

Jon and Gloria Hawkins lay in a huge round bed on a luxury habitat that orbited ringed Saturn. They were taking a well-earned vacation.

Jon was propped up against some pillows with his hands behind his head. A sheet covered his lower half, while his muscled torso was bare. Gloria lay draped upon him, idly making circles on his chest with one of her index fingers.

Gloria sighed.

Jon looked at her glorious head of hair. "What's wrong?" he asked.

"Sometimes, I wish you and I could take a ship and just go."

"Go where?" he asked.

"It doesn't matter where. Just go far from here and the grim war."

"It's not as grim as it was."

"I know," Gloria said. "But it's never going to end."

"That beats the alternative."

She looked up into his eyes.

"That all of us were dead," he said.

"Oh. Yes. That's true." She smiled wanly. "That's very true. But it's sad to think we're always going to have to fight."

"To be alive is to struggle," he said.

"Can't you agree with me for once?" she asked.

Jon reached down and took her face in his hands. Then he slid around until he was kneeling and kissed her lingeringly.

"Today," he said, "we're away from the war. Let's enjoy it by enjoying each other."

"And tomorrow?" she asked.

"Can take care of itself," he answered.

She searched his eyes and smiled.

Then Jon lay down with his wife and pulled the covers over them. The war would continue because humanity still thrived. Now, perhaps now, was a good time to choose hope for the future by giving the world his first child.

The End

SF Books by Vaughn Heppner

THE A.I. SERIES:
A.I. Destroyer
The A.I. Gene
A.I. Assault
A.I. Battle Station
A.I. Battle Fleet
A.I. Void Ship

LOST STARSHIP SERIES:
The Lost Starship
The Lost Command
The Lost Destroyer
The Lost Colony
The Lost Patrol
The Lost Planet
The Lost Earth
The Lost Artifact
The Lost Star Gate

Visit VaughnHeppner.com for more information

Made in the USA
San Bernardino, CA
25 February 2019